THE BERINFELL PROPHECIES
BOOK TWO

Venom

and

Song

Other Books by . . .

Wayne Thomas Batson and Christopher Hopper

The Berinfell Prophecies

Curse of the Spider King

* * *

Wayne Thomas Batson

The Door Within Trilogy

The Door Within
The Rise of the Wyrm Lord
The Final Storm

Pirate Adventures

Isle of Swords
Isle of Fire

* * *

Christopher Hopper

The White Lion Chronicles (series)

Rise of the Dibor
The Lion Vrie

THE BERINFELL PROPHECIES
BOOK TWO

Venom
and
Song

By Wayne Thomas Batson
and Christopher Hopper

THOMAS NELSON
Since 1798

NASHVILLE   DALLAS   MEXICO CITY   RIO DE JANEIRO

To the One who lifts the chin of the downcast,
picks up the downtrodden, repairs the broken,
and finds the lost, we bow our knee and offer
this novel as a sword in your armory.

Published in Nashville, Tennessee, by Thomas Nelson. Thomas Nelson is a registered trademark of Thomas Nelson, Inc.

Thomas Nelson, Inc., titles may be purchased in bulk for educational, business, fund-raising, or sales promotional use. For information, please e-mail SpecialMarkets@ThomasNelson.com.

Page design by Mandi Cofer.

Library of Congress Cataloging-in-Publication Data

Batson, Wayne Thomas, 1968--
 Venom and song / by Wayne Thomas Batson and Christopher Hopper.
  p. cm. — (The Berinfell prophecies ; bk. 2)
 Summary: Trapped in Allyra by the evil Spider King, seven young Elf lords raised on Earth must learn to control their new-found powers, follow mysterious clues left by the Old Ones, and learn to work together to find the Keystone that might save the Elves and their allies.
 ISBN 978-1-4003-1506-2 (hardcover)
 [1. Fantasy. 2. Christian life—Fiction.] I. Hopper, Christopher,
 1979– II. Title.
 PZ7.B3238Ve 2010
 [Fic]—dc22
 2010004264

Mfr: Worldcolor / Fairfield, PA / May 2010—PPO# 106779

Contents

Principal Cast

Allyran Elves: All Elves who live in Allyra.

Ethon Beleron: First Raptor Ward of the Old Ones; of the Nightwing tribe, distant cousin to Jett.

Alwynn Belkirith: High Cleric of the Tribes of Berinfell.

Berylinian Elves: A rare race of Elves noted for their bluish skin.

Asp Bloodthorne: A Drefid commander and messenger for the Spider King.

Tommy Bowman: Curly-haired seventh grader from Seabrook, Maryland. Known in Allyra as Elven Lord Felheart (Fell-heart), son of Lord Velaril and Tarin Silvertree.

Autumn Briarman: Petite, blond seventh grader who lives outside Depauville in upstate New York. Known in Allyra as Elven Lord Miarra (Me-air-uh), daughter of Lord Galadhost and Salura Swiftstorm.

Johnny Briarman: Burly seventh-grade student who lives outside Depauville in upstate New York. Known in Allyra as Elven Lord Albriand (Al-bree-and), son of Elroth and Lord Tisa Ashheart.

Annelle "Nelly" Brookeheart: Assigned as Johnny and Autumn's Sentinel.

Flet Marshall Brynn: Second-highest-ranking Elf military officer.

Mr. Charlie: Dreadnaught protector of Tommy Bowman, thought dead after the battle at Dalhousie Castle. Known in Allyra as Merrick Evershield, but prefers Charlie. Often uses a deep Southern accent.

Children of the Light: The ancient name of Allyran Elves.

Cragons: The monstrous black trees of Vesper Crag.

Dreadnaughts: Elite warrior Elves who practice Vexbane, a profoundly effective form of combat. Elite Dreadnaughts are assigned to protect the Seven Lords.

Drefids: The Spider King's ghoulish assassins. Drefids have four deadly claws that extend from the knuckles of each hand.

Elves: One of the ancient races of Allyra. Elves are known for their books of prophecy and their woodcraft.

Anna Rosario Delarosa Espinosa: The Simonson family's housekeeper, and assigned as Kat's Dreadnaught.

Miss Finney: Lochgilphead school's reading teacher and part-time librarian, and assigned as Jimmy's Sentinel.

Sarron Froth: The Drefid assassin who helped the Elves.

Eldera "Elle" Galdarro: The mysterious librarian at Thurgood Marshall Middle School, and assigned as Tommy's Sentinel. Known in Allyra as Goldarrow.

Gnomes: Experts in maps, they wander far and wide, and have a longtime feud with the Elves.

Jett Green: Seventh grader in Greenville, North Carolina. Rides motocross bikes and plays football. Known in Allyra as Elven Lord Hamandar (Ham-and-ur), son of Lord Vex and Jasmira Nightwing.

James "Jimmy" Lewis Gresham: Redheaded seventh grader who lives in Ardfern, Scotland. Lived in an orphanage until he was adopted at six years old. Known in Allyra as Elven Lord Thorwin (Thor-win), son of Lord Xanthis and Dreia Valorbrand.

Guardmaster Olin Grimwarden: Commander of the military forces of the Elves and their allies.

Gwar: One of the ancient races of Allyra. Gwar are known for their brutish strength and their affinity for spiders.

Lyrian Elves: A very strong race of Elves. They are dark skinned and have violet-colored eyes.

Regis McAuliffe: Gresham family friend who works at a local pub, is assigned as Jimmy's Dreadnaught.

Migmar: Barrister King of the Gnomes.

Mobius: The Spider King's most decorated Drefid assassin, killed in the battle of Dalhousie Castle.

Edward Rengfellow: Sentinel posing as the curator of Dalhousie Castle outside of Edinburgh, Scotland.

Sentinels: Very wise, very traditional Elves who are rumored to still follow the "Old Ways." Elite Sentinels are assigned to protect the Seven Lords.

Kat Simonson: Known for her constantly changing hairstyles and alternative music. Known in Allyra as Elven Lord Alreenia (Al-reen-ee-yuh), daughter of Beleg and Lord Kendie Hiddenblade.

Mr. James Spero: English teacher at Jett's school in Greenville, North Carolina. He is assigned to protect Jett.

The Spider King: The ruler of all Gwar, who harbors an ancient grudge against the Elves. Lives in Vesper Crag.

Sir Travin: Clever warrior for the Elves.

Mr. Charles Wallace: Kat's American history teacher who is assigned to protect her.

Warspiders: Spiders that are so large they can be ridden like horses. Red Warspiders have lethal venom.

Wisps: Enemies of old. Vapor-beings, shape shifters. Thought extinct. Only Holy Words and a weapon can kill one.

Kiri Lee Yuen: Child prodigy cellist and violinist from Paris, France, whose adopted parents were killed by Wisps. Known in Allyra as Elven Lord Lothriel (Loth-ree-ell), daughter of Charad and Lord Simona Oakenflower.

Manaelkin Zoar: Chief of the Elven High Council.

Principal Locations

ALLYRA

The world where the Elves, Gwar, and Spider King reside.

Locations on Allyra include:

Berinfell
The capital of the Elves, who once resided
across the many continents of Allyra

Moon Hollow
The heavily forested home of the Gnomes in northern Allyra

Nightwish Caverns
A vast network of caverns beneath the Thousand-League Forest,
used as an emergency home by the Elves of Berinfell

Terradym Fortress
Engineered and built by the Gnomes, this fortress
holds a relic of great importance to the Elves

Vesper Crag
Volcanic home of the Spider King and his minions

Whitehall Castle
Ancient training facility for the Elves,
far to the northwest of Berinfell

THIS SYMBOL ❈ INDICATES

BONUS CONTENT

FOR A LIMITED TIME

ON THE UNDERGROUND AT

WWW.HEEDTHEPROPHECIES.COM.

The Dark Veil

FROM A rocky perch high on the Dark Veil in Allyra, a pair of narrow green eyes tracked the two lines of creatures racing ever closer. The eyes blinked with deliberate interest, pupils dilating to better ascertain what manner of prey drew near. The first group was far smaller than the second, and they stumbled along slowly. Wounded, perhaps. A shrill screech rang out, and a moment later the eyes were joined by another pair, and another, until the whole ridge of the mountain was aglow with bobbing eyes that flickered hungrily in the murky twilight. . . . There would be no better time. The creature launched itself off the ledge and emitted a shrill screech. It spread its wings and was joined by a cloud of its own kind. The creatures began to spiral down, soundless on the still air. 🌀

Guardmaster Olin Grimwarden stopped and passed back the order. "Hold." Elf-to-Elf, the command traveled until the entire line came to a halt. Grimwarden, Elle Goldarrow, Flet Marshall Brynn, Regis, Nelly, Miss Finney, Mr. Spero, Anna, and Mr. Wallace silently formed a perimeter around the seven young lords. Edward, from Dalhousie Castle, kept a close watch out behind, covering their retreat.

Tommy felt a tap on his shoulder and jumped.

"Sorry, lad," said Brynn. Tommy couldn't see her, just a phantom outline. She held something out. "Take these," she said. "Grimwarden commands that you put them in your ears."

Tommy felt something drop into his hand. There were two objects, both small and very spongy. "Earplugs . . . why?" he asked.

"It is litigen," she said. "It grows on stumps and dead trees. But earplug is a good name." Then Brynn was gone.

Grows on dead trees? thought Tommy. *Great. And I have to stick it in my ears?*

Tommy heard Sentinel Goldarrow's voice, "Grimwarden, you sly fox . . . at last I understand."

At least someone understands something, Tommy thought.

Mr. Wallace strained to see back through the Veil, but his eyes couldn't penetrate the gloom enough to tell if there was any movement or sign. But his hearing was better than the Elves', and he heard the faint rustle of many leather boots on stone. The Spider King's forces were coming . . . not far now. *Yes,* he thought, staring at Kat's silhouette, *during the melee she will breathe her last . . .*

Kat hated the earplugs. They made her want to jerk them out and scratch her ears. And from the sound of the grumbling thoughts whirling from the Elves around her, she wasn't the only one. She thought she heard Jimmy: *"Feel like I'm puttin' corks in me head!"* Another voice was Johnny's: *"Owww! Might as well stick an ear of corn in each ear."* But those were the only two clear thoughts. The rest were muddled. *"How much"* . . . *"Veil is"* . . . *"the Gwar behind"* . . . *"Yes, during the"* . . . *"boots are too tight—"* but nothing Kat could make sense of. Soon, she gave up trying and just stared out into the murk.

Kiri Lee was the first to see it. Flickers of green twirled above them, swirling against the night sky like sparklers on the Fourth of July. The effect was more intriguing than startling, and all of the Seven found themselves entranced by the brilliant display of oddly twisting lights. "What—what are they?" she asked aloud.

"Kyrin," Goldarrow whispered. "Death callers."

"Death callers?" Tommy had overheard. He joined them in looking up at the myriad of tiny green lights, getting closer now. "Um . . ."

"I'm not sure what you would compare them to," she said. "Large bats? Maybe something of a raven, too. They are night feeders with sharp beaks and long daggerlike forefingers at midwing, but their scream—that is the most dangerous thing."

"Ah, the earplugs!" said Kat.

"Yes," Goldarrow explained. "It will not drown out the pull of their wailing completely, but it will muffle the effects. Keep your head. They will be here soon."

"Should I ready my bow?" Tommy asked.

"Yes," answered Grimwarden. "But not for the Kyrin."

Tommy looked back toward the entrance to the Veil in vain.

"The enemy is coming," Grimwarden explained. "And they are coming with great stealth."

"What are we going to—?" Johnny started to ask.

"Be silent!" commanded Grimwarden. Then softly said, "Please, lord, remain silent. I need to time this exactly. Lord Jimmy, how close?"

"Not yet!" Jimmy said. The other lords turned to stare at Jimmy, but he was just one of many shadowy shapes.

Tommy watched the beady-green eyes descending closer and closer. *What is Grimwarden waiting for?* The wait was excruciating, the silence maddening until . . .

They all heard it . . . a high-pitched ringing that rose and fell in increasing swells of volume. As it grew louder, all made sure their earplugs were in place. Tommy felt something odd on his skin, kind of like pressure, kind of like electricity. It rapidly became uncomfortable, and pressure grew in Tommy's ears.

"Hold on!" Grimwarden shouted. "Jimmy?!"

"Almost there!" he cried, clutching his head from the throbbing pain. He wasn't exactly sure how his gift worked yet, but he prayed it wouldn't fail him now.

The Kyrin scream affected all of the young lords. Jett laid Autumn down and covered her ears with his large hands, but that left his ears exposed. He gritted his teeth. Kiri Lee winced as the sound took on more than just a spine-tingling jolt down her neck; within her mind's eye she saw jagged shards of glass splintering outward, each drawing blood from the skin of a dark sky.

"Come on!" Grimwarden growled. "Closer! Closer!"

Jimmy fell to his knees. "Just . . . a . . . few . . . more . . . seconds . . . *ahh!*"

Miss Finney dropped down to his side.

Lightning streaked overhead, cutting through the Veil with a brief but powerful flash of white light, giving the Seven their first look at the green-eyed beasts circling just overhead.

Featherless bodies with stretched flaps of black skin along the wing, the Kyrin resembled a bat more than a bird. But their heads were shaped like those of large crows. Luminous green eyes bulged on either side of their thick, razor-sharp beaks. And, with wings extended, their long fingers protruded like thorns on each wing. Their flickering green eyes had a dizzying effect as layer upon layer of the creatures drifted down, the night air now a swirling emerald vortex.

"Now!!" Jimmy screamed.

"Archers, FIRE!!" Grimwarden cried out as he began waving a long torch above his head like a madman. Quickly he slammed the torch to the ground again and again until it was extinguished.

Other fiery lights appeared in the distance. Too many to count. They streaked into the sky high over the Elves. A few struck the Kyrin cloud, but most continued their flight toward the Veil. Suddenly the Kyrins' deafening wails stopped as a battalion of Elven archers' flaming arrows found their marks on the approaching Gwar raiders. Then the Kyrin began a strange warble as the entire mass of green-eyed creatures swooped over the Elves and raced away toward the fires lighting the Gwar.

"The Kyrin are attracted to fire," said Grimwarden. "Thanks to Jimmy's timing and my hidden archers, we'll let the Gwar play with the Kyrin for a bit." He turned to see just how many Gwar had skirted the Kyrin attack and made for their position now. "Elven host, DRAW—YOUR—BLADES!!"

At their commander's summons, all the archers drew their blades and streamed out from their hiding places. Tommy couldn't believe how many there were. In a flash, they raced by the young lords and engaged the Gwar.

Grimwarden turned and quickly surveyed the Seven Lords who had journeyed from Earth to Allyra only hours before. The youths had surprised Grimwarden with their endurance, having survived not only the battle in Scotland but also the trip through the portal . . . a grueling ordeal for anyone—especially the first time. The screams of the Kyrin had lost much of their intensity in the maelstrom of clashing Elves and Gwar, and Grimwarden motioned for all to remove their earplugs. "Again we have a temporary advantage, but the Gwar will be on us swiftly. Prepare your weapons . . . your gifts. We may need to fight our way out of the pass. Jett, you have carried Autumn long enough. Let the healer Claris take her ahead of us, where it will be safer. We will need your strength here."

Though Jett would have carried Autumn all day, he didn't argue. He wanted to fight for his new friends . . . new family. As he gently placed Autumn in Claris's arms, Autumn whispered, "Thank you."

"Thank me by getting well," Jett said.

Johnny took his sister's hand. "I'll be right behind you," he said. "Soon as we finish here."

The assignment had seemed so easy that Gwar Commander Sorbin Heathmord had already begun mentally counting the vanadils he'd been promised. *I should have been rich. Simply backup Mobius's team at the last Earth portal. Mobius—the legendary Drefid warrior and strategist. How could he fail? All Mobius had to do was trap and kill the seven teenage lords and a ragtag bunch of Elves.* But clearly these were no ordinary Elves. *With more than a dozen Drefids, scores of Warspiders, and Cragon trees at his disposal, there was no way Mobius could lose. But he did. Worse than that, Mobius called half of my Gwar battalion and all of my Warspiders through the portal for support. Got them killed, too. Now I'm left chasing the Seven Lords. . . . Perhaps the Age of Reckoning is no more a myth than the might of my war hammer. Yet could their gifts be matured already?* Sorbin could just see his reward disappearing, coin by coin.

But all was not lost . . . not yet.

"Ferral!" he yelled to his subordinate. "Ready the reserves. I will lead them myself."

"Yes, Commander," Ferral replied. Ferral lumbered back across the uneven ground. He returned leading more than a hundred Gwar soldiers. These were not limber, cross-country Gwar like those who patrolled the Lightning Fields. No, these were the strong arms of the Bludgeoners—mace-, cudgel-, and hammer-wielding Gwar who knew nothing of pain except how to inflict it upon any who stood in their way.

Sorbin slammed two hammers together above his head and bellowed, "No mistakes! Make sure every Elf is dead!"

"Quickly!" Grimwarden shouted as he sprinted along the barely visible path. "Our escape lies just ahead!"

"Where?" Goldarrow asked, sprinting behind him. A sudden clamor from very close behind them caused her to stop and look back. She could see only a tumble of shadows. Then there came a single word cried out in agony and then strangled off: "GWa—!"

"Ellos, save us," Goldarrow said. "Grimwarden, the Gwar have broken through!"

"So fast? Jett, Johnny, fall back with me," ordered Grimwarden. "I know you're tired, but you must keep going. Brynn, lead the rest to the hidden gate! *All* of you, watch your backs!"

Flet Marshall Brynn forged ahead leading the others to safety, while Grimwarden and the two young lords stopped running.

As Grimwarden barked out orders, retreating Elves jostled between bodies and the rock walls. "Johnny, ready your flames, but wait for my signal. We must be sure the remaining Elves get past."

Grimwarden snatched a war hammer from the holster on his back. "Jett, I know you are better at hand-to-hand, but take this. Make your first blow to the stomach, then to the head. The Gwar are coming, and there are many."

"How can you see them?" Jett asked.

"I've spent more time in the Veil. My eyes have ad—LOOK OUT!"

There was no time for Grimwarden to intervene as a huge Gwar swept a wide-bladed axe toward Jett's neck. Jett ducked. Using the massive Gwar's momentum against him, Jett rammed the hammer head into the Gwar's shoulder, then swung the hammer at the creature's spine. The Gwar dropped to the ground and did not move.

"Johnny, ready your flames!" Grimwarden hollered.

"Right now?" Johnny answered nervously, wondering how he could work his gift with more accuracy.

"Not yet!" Grimwarden cried just as he swung his war staff into a Gwar's abdomen. The enemy doubled over, and the Elven commander brought his staff down on the back of the Gwar's skull, right on his tribal tattoo. The Gwar went down in a heap, but now the staff had a crack running through the center. "Hard-headed beasts!"

Elves, some fighting off Gwar as they ran, continued to race by. *What if the Gwar win? What would happen to Autumn?*

"Ahhh!" Johnny dove at a Gwar's legs. The creature rolled but clawed back to his feet. He turned, brandished a mace with curving thornlike spikes, and lunged for Johnny. The young man from the little town in upstate New York felt trapped. One moment he was safe in the comfort of routine—school, homework, bike riding—now he was face-to-face with a monster that he was sure would kill him if he didn't act. *Come on flames! Do your thing.* He raised his hands, more out of defense than aggression, and felt tingles on the rims of his eyes. Two white streams sputtered to life, flaring when they hit the Gwar. The engulfed enemy fell to the ground.

Still lying on the ground, Johnny stared at his hands, amazed at the strange power. So it *was* something he could control. But exactly how, he wasn't sure. The pure desire to survive was what did the trick now. Grimwarden shouted to his right and pointed to the cliffs. Johnny swallowed and aimed his hands skyward, firing jets of flame high into clefts of rock on the mountainside. He overshot at first, but then found a ledge, letting the liquid fire pool to provide them more light in which to see the enemy.

EEEEeeeee!! came the Kyrin scream as the flying creatures came once more en masse. A small cloud of them dove at Johnny. Again he aimed, held his breath, and raised his hands toward the birds. Nothing happened. For a moment he thought he might be out of gas or something. The Kyrin were racing toward him. He was so tired. He closed his eyes, then—*Whoosh!*—Johnny felt his shoulders press into the ground from the surge. The Kyrin fell, burning to the ground in black-charred pieces of bone and skin. But their kindred were not scared off, and they continued to attack. The Gwar pushed forward as well, and Johnny had too many targets to hit them all.

"Fall back!" Grimwarden yelled. "They are getting behind us! FALL BACK!"

At last, thought Mr. Wallace as he ran behind the lords. *The Gwar have caught up to us. All is turning to chaos. It's time.* He drew a slim dagger from his belt, but his grip felt weak. The dagger became slippery and awkward. He looked at his arms. They wavered in the twilight. *No, not now! Not . . . now!* He stumbled to one knee.

"Mr. Wallace!" Jimmy exclaimed. "I nearly tripped over yu. Are yu hurt?"

"I . . . I just need a minute," he replied, but his voice gurgled. "Go on, Jimmy! The only thing that matters is the lords getting to safety."

Jimmy hesitated a moment. It was terribly hard to see in the gloom, but something seemed very wrong with Mr. Wallace.

"Jimmy, come on," Regis called from the darkness ahead. Reluctantly, Jimmy left the stricken Sentinel.

But unknown to the others, Mr. Wallace was no Sentinel at all. *I must feed.* He was desperate now, shaking from head to foot. If any of the Elves saw him, it was over.

"Uhgg—ack!" Not six feet away, a Gwar fell flat on his back with an arrow buried in his eye.

Mr. Wallace vanished, leaving behind only a serpentine length of smoke. Invisible in the Veil's murk, the smoke traveled to the fallen Gwar and enveloped his head. A few seconds later, Mr. Wallace was whole again. He tossed an arrow to the ground and sprinted after the Elves.

"The enemy cannot be allowed to follow!" Grimwarden declared as he, Jett, and Johnny retreated. Now covered in blood and ash, the Guardmaster of the Elves was nearly spent.

Johnny had incinerated scores of Gwar soldiers. Using his lordly gift, he produced a near impenetrable wall of flame behind them. And try as they might, few Gwar could get through. Those who did fell at the feet of Grimwarden or Jett.

"I think that's the last of them!" cried Johnny. He willed the fire to stop and scanned the burning carnage behind them. "I think that's all. . . ." He swayed and would have fallen, but Jett held him up.

"C'mon, Johnny, I'll help you," said Jett, taking his new friend's arm.

"We'll help each other," said Grimwarden. "The secret gate waits for us. Let us hope the others have already passed through."

With a little effort, Kiri Lee went airborne and found herself dodging Gwar arrows and fending off Kyrin with her sword. She felt her steps falter in the air. Through the kaleidoscope of black wings, the hail of arrows, and the gray shroud of the Veil, Kiri Lee watched as three Gwar—massive, lumbering beasts—converged on the Sentinels. They slammed into Edward and Miss Finney from behind, sending the protectors sprawling to the ground.

Kat, too, had been tripped and tumbled to a harsh stop, rolling onto her back at the base of a hedge of stone. Kiri Lee thought Kat looked unconscious, but at least the Gwar had left her alone. She began to make her way toward Kat; then she saw him. *Oh, thank God. It's Mr. Wallace. He's coming to help her.* Kiri Lee watched the Sentinel stride purposefully toward the fallen teen. Mr. Wallace reached beneath his cloak and pulled something out . . . *a dagger? What's he do—*

EEEEeeeee! She saw a flash of luminous green eyes, then felt searing pain. A Kyrin had dug its claws into Kiri Lee's shoulder. It started to peck and slash at her face with its beak. Kiri Lee cartwheeled backward in the air. She tried to slash at it with her sword, but the effort took her focus off her wind walking and she started to sink.

Kat coughed and snapped awake. Pain throbbed in three different places. Something had hit her. *A Gwar?* There was sudden movement. Kat looked up. It was Mr. Wallace. He held a dagger in his right hand. The look on his face—Kat had never seen it before. *Furious . . . no, murderous.* Kat felt a sharp pain as she backed into the hedge of stone behind her, falling onto her elbows in a vain effort to escape. Mr. Wallace was almost upon her now. Kat screamed.

Just then a huge gray shadow filled her vision. There was a growling, guttural roar, and a massive Gwar soldier fell at Kat's feet. Mr. Wallace clung to its back and stabbed it repeatedly with his dagger. The creature struggled, but was losing strength. It made one last effort to reach around, but Mr. Wallace slid his blade under the creature's neck and gave a swift pull. The Gwar went still as if it were some electric thing that had been unplugged.

Mr. Wallace looked up at Kat his expression still fierce, but then softened. "Are you okay?" he asked. He started to hold out his right hand, but realizing it was covered in blood he held out his left. He helped Kat to her feet. "Kat . . . are you okay?"

"I . . . I thought . . ."

"Thought what?"

Kat blinked and looked at her former social studies and history teacher. "Nevermind. Yeah, I'm okay . . . thanks to you."

Kiri Lee twisted around so that the Kyrin clinging to her shoulder would be the first thing to hit the ground. Kiri Lee cried out from the impact. The crushed Kyrin let go of its intended victim, but quickly latched onto her forearm, claws sinking deep into her skin, forcing her to drop her sword. It pecked at the leather bracer on her wrist and dug its talons farther into her soft flesh. Not knowing what else to do, Kiri Lee reached with her free hand, grabbed the Kyrin by its neck, and squeezed. The Kyrin flailed its wings and claws, slicing Kiri Lee's arm, but she just squeezed harder. Soon the creature squealed and went limp. Kiri Lee tore it from her arm and tossed it aside, breathing heavily.

Jimmy, with Regis at his heels, raced back to find Edward and Miss Finney, bloody and exhausted, standing over three dead Gwar. "I saw them in me head," Jimmy said, "comin' for yu! And there was a fourth one, too."

"Mr. Wallace took care of it," Kat said as she and her Sentinel joined the others.

"Him," Mr. Wallace corrected. "Took care of him. The Spider King's Gwar are our enemies, but they are still beings."

"Quite right," said Edward. "Alas that they are enemies at all."

"But they are," said Miss Finney. "And I do not want any more of them to sneak up on us. We need to get moving."

Ferral had watched many of his kindred burn alive in the attempt to breach the wall of flames, including Sorbin, his commander. The Gwar soldier wondered if any survived at all. From his vantage point in a fissure of stone some forty feet up the mountainside, he could see nothing moving on the path below . . . except for pockets of Kyrin feeding on the dead. *Go after the Elves?* Ferral banished the thought from his mind. That was certain death. Foolish, too. The Spider King needed to know all that had happened. *Perhaps,* he thought, *I might get a handful of vanadils for my trouble.* The thought of the silvery-blue coins made him smile. Then he had another thought, and the grin that had begun to form vanished. *He might not believe me.*

Ferral clambered out of his hiding place. *Best get some proof.*

Rip Currents

THREE ELVES stood straining to see into the darkness as they waited in front of a peculiar fin of rock at the base of the mountain. Flet Marshall Brynn, Goldarrow, and Tommy had all but given up hope when they heard a familiar voice.

"Hail, Goldarrow!" Grimwarden shouted. "Look who I found!"

"Oh, thank Ellos," Goldarrow replied, seeing the large group of Elves returning.

Tommy saw as well. "Kat!" He ran to her but stopped short. *Whoa,* he thought. *I almost hugged her.* "What happened to you?" he asked instead. "You were behind me one second . . . then whoosh!"

"It's a long story," she replied, glancing at Mr. Wallace.

"We waited as long as we could," said Goldarrow, hugging Grimwarden, which earned curious looks from Flet Marshall Brynn and the other Sentinels.

"Probably too long," said Grimwarden, clearing his throat and squirming until she let go.

"Where's Autumn?" Johnny asked, looking around the group.

"Claris took Autumn through," said Brynn.

"Good," said Grimwarden.

"Mr. Grimwarden, sir?" Johnny said.

Grimwarden laughed. "Lord Albriand, ha! To think that a lord would call me sir. What is it, lad?"

Albriand? Johnny ignored the strange name he used, then pressed himself past the others. "My sister"—he said lowering his voice—"how far is she from wherever the help is?"

"Quite far," Grimwarden replied.

Johnny's tired eyes widened, panic starting to edge into his expression.

"If Claris and the others were taking Autumn by foot, then we would be right to worry, but they are not traveling by foot."

"They're not?" Johnny frowned.

"They're not?" asked Goldarrow.

"No," said Grimwarden with a hardly perceptible wink to Goldarrow. "And neither are we. I told you, this is a shortcut."

"Forgive me for before, Guardmaster," Goldarrow said, adding rather formally, ". . . for questioning your path."

"Elle," he responded, "do not waste another moment thinking of it. Thank Ellos the seven young lords are all alive. Thanks to Johnny . . . and the Kyrin, I don't think there are any Gwar coming behind us, but we dare not linger in this part of the world."

He led them behind the fold of rock and kindled a torch. Then he made a turn where it seemed there was no passage, yet disappeared into blackness. The others followed until all the Elves disappeared into the mountain.

Like a serpent of fire, a long line of torch-bearing Elves—flet soldiers, Dreadnaughts, Sentinels, and the lords—followed Grimwarden down into the winding depths of the black abyss before them. The path into the underground alternated between great high chambers and cramped tunnels with ceilings that were shoulder height at best. In some of the low places, Tommy noticed the rock above was stained with black soot from the torches. Their party was clearly not the first to have traveled this way.

After an hour or more of twists and turns, their war band entered a cavernous chamber. "What's that shushing sound?" asked Kat.

No one answered. And as they traveled on, the shushing blossomed into a full-fledged roar. "I don't like this," said Tommy.

"I hear you," said Jett.

"Where are we?" Kiri Lee asked.

"Wait here," Grimwarden commanded, moving away from the group with his torch in hand. They watched as he edged along a narrow ledge and eventually stopped beside a rope tied off to an iron ring protruding from the wall. He raised his torch, revealing what Tommy thought resembled a large, horizontal wagon wheel on the other end of the rope. Grimwarden set the chandelier ablaze and then released the rope from the iron ring. The brilliant light swung out into the middle of what was once a majestic hall, the ceiling held aloft by water-worn columns of sandstone that plummeted into a churning tumult of water. They all looked on in awe at the marvelous sight.

"It's an underground river!" Johnny exclaimed.

"An aquifer, to be more precise," Grimwarden corrected, now back from the ledge.

"Your shortcut?" Goldarrow asked.

Grimwarden nodded. Then he turned and addressed the Elves. "We'll break up into teams of no more than five. Any more and the cavesurfers will capsize."

"Cavesurfers?" Kat whispered.

"Sweet!" Tommy pumped his fist, but then turned red at the stares he'd earned.

"Each watercraft must be piloted by one of our trained cavesurfer flet soldiers or anyone with equal experience."

"I can pilot one," said Regis. "It's been awhile . . . but I used to be pretty good."

"It looks much like a rapid-runner," said Anna. "Do they handle about the same?"

"Precisely the same," said Grimwarden. "Even with five aboard, you'll turn at will."

"Then it should be no problem at all," said Anna.

"Seems we have more than enough qualified pilots," Grimwarden said with a smile. "Make sure each cavesurfer has a flet soldier who knows the way; these underground channels change frequently. You would not want to get lost, especially near the falls."

"Falls?" said Kiri Lee nervously. "I can't swim."

"What are yu worried about?" asked Jimmy. "Yu could just hop out of the boat and walk the rest 'a the way down."

"I guess I keep forgetting," said Kiri Lee.

"The falls are indeed perilous," Grimwarden explained. "But not with our pilots. We've not had a crash in fifteen years." He waited and watched the nods all around. Then he turned to Goldarrow and said, "Elle, recommendations for how we divide up?"

"I've never been much good at steering anything in the water," said Goldarrow. "I'm going with you."

Grimwarden coughed. "I meant how we divide up the lords."

"Oh, of course, right." She looked away and cleared her throat. "How about Tommy, Kat, and Kiri Lee come with us. Jimmy, Jett, and Johnny go with Brynn."

"Three Js, baby!" Jett high-fived the other two boys.

"Fine," said Grimwarden. "Follow me."

Anna tapped Kat on the shoulder. "Are you sure you don't want to come with me?" she asked with a hint of a smile.

Kat held up her hands. "Oh no, that's okay. Thank you, Anna, but . . . I've seen how you drive."

Anna feigned offense. "Crash once into a stone wall and no one trusts you. Goodness."

They followed Grimwarden down a circuitous rampart of smooth stone leading to the edge of the river. Tethered to any number of iron rings along the strand sat dozens and dozens of tiny raftlike boats, each shaped like an arrowhead, pointy in front and flat in the back. They were rather shallow crafts with two small bench seats spread through the middle, one near the bow for two people, a second along the aft for three. The boat itself was formed of a wooden skeletal system with rawhide stretched around the outside. The only other notable feature was a small tiller connected to a rudder, presumably where the captain of each vessel steered the craft.

"Oars?" Tommy asked as they boarded.

"Yes," Grimwarden replied. "Only for when we need to maneuver more than the remote tiller can manage. Or for the return trip. We will be riding with the current straight through."

"Cool!" said Jett. "How fast will we go?"

"Fast enough," said Brynn.

"Everyone in!" Grimwarden commanded, untethering lines and pushing their particular cavesurfer into the water. "I know it goes without saying, but keep your torchcells lit. Your life depends on them."

The entire war band made ready, pushing their crafts into the same still pool protected from the main artery's rapids by a natural jetty of sandstone. Jett stepped aboard with a steadying hand from Brynn, and sat beside Johnny and Jimmy in the aft. He watched Tommy, Kat, and Kiri Lee get seated with Goldarrow and Grimwarden in the lead surfer.

"Sentinel Brynn?"

"Yes, Jimmy?"

"Sittin' by yurself, are yu?"

"I suppose so," she replied. "We'd best put one of you up here to balance the—"

"No need," said Mr. Wallace, stepping agilely into the craft and sitting beside Brynn.

"Excellent," said Brynn. "Very good of you."

"It's the very least I could do," he replied.

The cavesurfers lived up to their name, carving through the currents with ease. The watercrafts weaved between the massive columns of the main hall, circling under the chandelier and positioning the boats so that they could dart out into the central stream of the river. Grimwarden's craft went first, followed by Brynn and the others. As the current whisked them out of the hall, each pilot lowered a torch to two different spots at the front of his or her craft. This ignited the cavesurfer's torchcells, pockets set like eyes in the front. The fire burned in the hollows of two crystal spheres that protected the flame from spray and intensified the light cast.

Each cavesurfer's captain maneuvered the craft around rocks, over small plateaus, and into side passages. The forks and splits in the path were many, and Grimwarden made numerous turns, all very controlled, very confident. In fact, the first twenty minutes of the ride were quite relaxing, the teens thought. Goldarrow and Grimwarden chatted in the aft with Kat beside them; more to the point, Goldarrow chatted . . . Grimwarden just nodded . . . a lot.

To Kat's growing aggravation, Kiri Lee fell asleep with her head on Tommy's shoulder.

"Hey," said Tommy, looking at Kat. "What's eating you?"

"What . . . why? Nothing."

"You look mad."

"Just tired," she said.

"Oh," he replied. For a few moments, the cavesurfer grew very quiet. Then Tommy asked, "Hey, can you read someone's mind while she's sleeping?"

Kat crossed her arms. "Why?"

"I was wondering what Kiri Lee's dreaming about."

There was an awkward silence before Kat answered. "You don't want to know." Kat's rigid posture made it clear that she did not welcome any further questions.

The currents picked up speed. Kat was staring straight ahead when she saw something shimmering in the distance. At first, she thought it was the torchlight dancing off yet another fork in the stream. But as the craft advanced, she realized that the hall itself was suddenly coming to an end. No hole. No little passage leading left or right. It was a solid wall. But the current kept moving.

"Um, Grimwarden?"

"Yes, Kat?" The Guardmaster's hand was steady on the tiller.

"Um . . . I think we're in trouble."

"What? Why?" His voice was still oddly unconcerned.

"Up ahead. There's just a solid wall. And we're heading"—she paused to look again—"straight for it!"

He turned his head and winked. "I suggest you hold on to something."

"What?!"

"Now would be a good time."

Kat screamed, Tommy yelled, and Kiri Lee woke up. Each one

clutched the nearest edge or railing as the surfer surged forward. The wall loomed just a few feet ahead, and the sound of the rapids grew to a deafening roar. All at once the craft tilted forward and plummeted. Grimwarden saw the look of exhilaration in Goldarrow's eyes and grinned. Tommy, Kat, and Kiri Lee held on as the craft plunged head-long down a tunnel, the ceiling not more than five feet above head level. Here the rapids turned into a water chute, the cavesurfer picking up unimaginable speed, the torchcells struggling just to stay alive.

"Lean left!" Grimwarden shouted.

Kat and the others clung to the sides and pitched their weight as the cavesurfer banked to port, making a wide, sweeping turn in the channel. Just ahead, the river careened up the side of the tunnel, where it had formed a glossy finish on the stone wall. Grimwarden's cave-surfer shot high along the wall, fishtailing slightly before pitching back into the center of the chute as the turn straightened out. It was then they all heard a long cry from the cavesurfer right behind them.

"Wooohooo!" Jett screamed. "Oh, BABY!" This was better than any dirt bike track he had ever ridden! He was dying to grab the helm himself and try some crazy trick, but he remembered he didn't really know the directions. That and he would have to contend with Brynn, an Elf it seemed best not to trifle with.

After more than four hours of navigating the relentless rapids, the entire flotilla of Elves finally came upon calmer waters. The current was still there, ever-present and irresistible, but the waterscape lev-eled out to a smooth sheet of black. Grimwarden, Brynn, Anna, Regis, and a few other surfer pilots navigated their crafts closer together in the wide and much more peaceful area.

"Incredible!" Jett roared. He slapped a high five across the water with Tommy.

"I wish Autumn had been here with us," said Johnny.

"She already went," said Grimwarden gently.

Johnny brightened at the thought. "She probably loved every

minute. Whenever we went to amusement parks, Autumn was always first in line at all the rides that make people barf."

"Uhm, speakin' of barf . . . ," Jimmy said, pointing.

"I don't feel so well."

They all turned. It was Kiri Lee, and even in the orange torchlight she looked a bit green.

"I think she's gonna toss her—"

Grimwarden glared at Jimmy. Then he leaned forward and handed a thin orange strip to Kiri Lee. "Nibble on this," he said. "It's a shoot from a hilthis mint sapling. It will calm your stomach." He paused a moment, seeing the uncertainty in the young lord's eyes. Then he said, "I use them myself."

Kiri Lee took a tentative bite. "Mmmm, that's not bad. I like it." She took another bite. "Wow . . . I think it's helping."

"Good, good," Grimwarden said tenderly. Then he faced the whole group. "You'll each need to brace yourselves for this last section. Daladge Falls can be a bit . . . troublesome."

"I thought what we went through earlier was the falls," said Tommy.

"That little slide?" said Grimwarden. "Nay. Daladge Falls lay ahead."

"Is it dangerous?" asked Kiri Lee, looking green again.

"It need not be," said Grimwarden. "So long as we stay to the left when we go over, and so long as we all remain in our cavesurfers . . . we should be fine."

"What if we don't?" asked Jett.

Grimwarden worked the tiller to keep their craft moving left in the channel. He exchanged glances with Brynn and Goldarrow. "I will speak plainly to you, young lords. Your pilots are all water-savvy, and the surfers tested and true. But in the unlikely event that you should fall out of the craft, you would perish."

"Why stay to the left?" asked Kat.

"There is a pocket in the water," Grimwarden replied. "At the bottom of the falls, near the right-hand wall . . . a whirling pool that will take a craft to the bottom . . . in an instant."

Daladge Falls

CAVESURFERS SPREAD across the surface of the underground river like fireflies on the side of a jar. The narrow passage to Daladge Falls had been peaceful enough. But as it widened, the Elves heard the pounding of the falls. It was less a constant roar and more like the percussive crashing of monstrous waves on an island of stone; the song of the falls made the young lords nervous. But they were not alone in their concern.

"Please tell me, Master Jimmy," said Mr. Wallace, "tell me with your foresight that we're going to survive this fall."

"I wish I could," Jimmy replied, squinting so hard that a stack of wrinkles appeared at the corners of his eyes. ". . . But I cannot see anythin' right now. Not since the battlefield. Think I'm tired."

"You've done this before, haven't you, Flet Marshall Brynn?" asked Jett.

"Dozens of times," she replied. All of her passengers relaxed a little. And then she added, "But each time it's different."

"Great," said Johnny.

"Tighten the straps around your waist," Brynn commanded. "We're getting close now." She leaned forward and plugged each of the torchcells with serrated pegs of crystal. "This'll keep the torches dry for when we go under."

"When we go under?" Johnny's eyes were as big as baseballs.

"At the bottom of the falls," Brynn explained, as if it should have been common knowledge. "Our momentum will carry us beneath the surface, but not far. These crafts are buoyant, and we will shoot up like dolphins."

"Okay," said Johnny.

"Are you sure you can't see what will happen, Jimmy?" asked Mr. Wallace.

"Not a thing," Jimmy said. "And I dunno that I want to."

"Fifty yards," said Goldarrow. "Hold on tight!"

"Ow! Kiri Lee," Tommy said, wincing. "Not that tight! I think I'm bleeding."

"I'm sorry," Kiri Lee apologized, pushing strands of her straight black hair behind her ear. "The falls, they terrify me."

Tommy swallowed. "We'll be fine. Grimwarden knows what he's doing."

Terrified? Kat thought. *You can walk on air.* She briefly attempted to read Kiri Lee's thoughts, but with no success. Kat didn't think she needed to anyway. *Of course she likes him. And of course he probably likes her. She's perfect. Perfect hair, perfect smile, perfect skin. Not a mutant . . . like me.* Kat looked away from Tommy. *Well, he can have her . . . for all I care.* She stared straight ahead . . . and wished she hadn't.

The walls of the cavern funneled to an opening more than fifty yards wide. There, the underground river rolled over an edge only visible due to the contrast in color between the water and the deep vault of space beyond. Grimwarden's cavesurfer was the first to arrive, and the current drew them relentlessly to the edge. Goldarrow shifted in her seat and glanced often at Grimwarden. If the Guardmaster noticed, he did not let on. He kept his eyes forward and continuously steered toward the left side. "Lean back and HOLD ON!"

The point of the cavesurfer went over the edge. The growl of the falls roared up. Their craft tilted down. And Tommy stared into a massive chute of turbulent water as the craft plunged into the yawning black mouth. Spray and chop pelted the craft and its passengers. Bouncing and careening against water and air currents, Tommy tried to scream, "We're all going to die," but the violence of the water drowned out his voice.

But it was here that the cavesurfers showed their true qualities.

Tommy, still certain his life was about to end, suddenly felt their craft skimming sideways—across the face of the falls. He stole a look at Grimwarden, whose arm and shoulder muscles were taut as he steered. The torch was only a small flickering light, but it was enough for Tommy to see the Guardmaster, who appeared to be enjoying the plunge as he expertly navigated the falls. Then Tommy saw him smile.

Tommy tapped Kat on the shoulder. "This is insane!"

She nodded and mouthed something Tommy couldn't hear. He looked over at Kiri Lee, and his heart stopped for a moment. She had ducked her head and bent her torso down so low that at first he thought she was gone. *It wouldn't be that hard,* Tommy thought, *to fall out.* He shook the image away and tried to focus on the positive. *Jett's got to be loving this.* Tommy started to turn to look for Brynn's cavesurfer, but heard Grimwarden: "HEAD DOWN! DEEP BREATH!"

The cavesurfer stabbed into the black water at the bottom of the falls. Tommy felt as if his stomach broke free from its lodging in his head, shot down through his neck, ricocheted around his shoulders and rib cage, and jettisoned into his feet. There was silence, but a deep churning pressure pulsed in his ears. All went dark until he saw stars and struggled against the urge to gasp for air. Tommy forced himself to relax and was rewarded with the feeling of ascent. Just when he thought he couldn't hold his breath anymore, he felt his back pop-up into open air, water filling the cavesurfer to his knees.

"You can sit up now," Grimwarden instructed, the rushing sound of water falling behind them.

"You mean, we're not dead?" Tommy asked.

"No, Tommy. But almost."

"That was—"

"HELP!" came a desperate scream half-choked with water.

Grimwarden jammed hard on the tiller and spun the surfer around. "Where?" he demanded. Other cavesurfers continued to plunge into the falls, only to pop-up seconds later. "Where?! Does anyone see?"

"Wait," said Kat. "Where's Flet Marshall Brynn's surfer? They were right behind us."

"They were," Goldarrow confirmed. "But I don't see them."

"HELP!" came the voice again. A flame leaped up from the water.
"It's Johnny!" Kiri Lee yelled. "Look there!"

They could all see Johnny now, flailing, his head dipping beneath the water. Just in time, Regis's surfer swept by him, and she grabbed his arm. Her flet soldier passengers hauled Johnny out of the water. "We have him!" she called.

"What of Jett, Jimmy . . . and the others?" Grimwarden called back.

Ice forming in the pit of his stomach, Tommy watched as Regis and the others scanned the water, each crying out, "Brynn! Jimmy! Jett! Can you hear me?! Mr. Wallace!"

Regis called again, waited, and then shook her head. "No sign!" Regis called back. She wheeled the craft around and raced immediately to Grimwarden. "Johnny says their surfer capsized," Regis explained, still looking out into the water.

"Flet soldiers!" Grimwarden called. "Rekindle the torchcells! Spread out and search. We have four in the water! Beware of the whirlpool!" Immediately more than a dozen surfers scattered.

"We need more light!" Goldarrow exclaimed.

A timid voice emerged from Regis's cavesurfer. "I think . . . I can help with that."

Those who heard looked over at Johnny.

"Nay, son," said Grimwarden. "Rest, get your strength back."

A gentle hand touched his shoulder. "Olin, we need the light."

Grimwarden frowned. He knew she was right. He looked across the water at Johnny. "Can you manage?"

"I think so."

"Flet soldiers, give him room!" commanded Goldarrow. Then to Johnny, she said, "Not too much, all right?" She indicated the lightly constructed cavesurfer and its occupants.

"Right," he breathed, remembering how far the flames traveled the last time. "Not too much . . ." Johnny held out his hands in front of him, staring into his palms as if studying every line on his skin. He furrowed his brow and worked his jaw. But nothing happened.

Ah, he is spent, thought Goldarrow. *He'd done so much in the Veil . . . and he'd been through so much.*

23

"You got this!" yelled Tommy.

"You can do it, Johnny," Kat entreated.

Johnny sat up a little straighter. Tension lined his brow, and he flexed his arms. He grunted and a small glow appeared in his hands. "It's working," he said. "I can feel it now!"

"Good, Johnny," said Grimwarden. "The roof of this cavern may be too high, but stalactites reach down—hit those if you can."

"Go ahead, Johnny," Nelly urged from her cavesurfer, her familiar voice giving him confidence.

Johnny took a breath, looked high above, and picked the center of the darkness overhead. He groaned, and the glow in his palms turned to a blaze. Twin streams of fire leaped up from Johnny's hands and stretched far into the darkness. He walked the flames about until he found a stalactite. Then it seemed he intensified the flow even more. The sandstone spike was enveloped in fire.

"WHOA!" Tommy exclaimed. Instantly half of the cavern was bathed in a brilliant orange glow, and at once the Elves began searching the waters.

Johnny turned around and shot another blast of liquid fire onto a second stalactite.

At last, Tommy could see just how vast and deep the cavern was. *They could park a battleship in here, he thought with dismay. How are we going to—?*

"We have Lord Hamandar!" yelled a deep voice near the turbulent base of the falls. "He is unconscious, but he lives!"

"Who?" asked Kiri Lee.

"Jett!" said Goldarrow with a cry of relief. "Oh, thank Ellos!"

"Commander!" called another voice. "We have their cavesurfer. . . . Wait, someone is in it! It is Brynn, and she lives!"

"Is there no one else?" Regis called.

The flet soldier shook his head.

"We should see the others by now . . . ," Grimwarden muttered, his voice trailing off. He spun the boat about and raced toward the back corner of the right side of the cavern.

"Where are you going?" yelled Regis.

"Keep searching!" barked the Guardmaster, rowing frantically. Tommy, Kat, and Kiri Lee held on once more. They couldn't believe how strong Grimwarden was—how he moved the craft so quickly. But he stopped just as suddenly and brought the cavesurfer around.

"We can go no farther," he said, speaking over the pounding water of the falls. "Beyond this point, the current will drag us in."

They all saw the change in the water ahead. It churned counter-clockwise in a vast water vortex . . . at least seventy yards in diameter. Closer to the center, the water rotated faster until it bottomed out to where no one could see.

Tommy blinked and stared. "There . . . on the edge. Do you see?"

"No . . . nothing," Goldarrow said.

"I see!" Kiri Lee cried out. "I think it's Jimmy!"

Grimwarden at last saw what the young lords had seen: the silhouette of an arm and a head barely above water. The arm was moving, but by the current or from life, he could not tell. Grimwarden stood up, rocking the boat. "Keep the craft steady," he told Goldarrow.

"What are you doing?" she shot back. "You aren't going to dive into—?"

"We have no choice!" he yelled.

"B-But . . . ," she stammered. "How will we get you back?"

"Think of something!" he yelled, and he dove into the black water.

Jimmy was disoriented and very close to drowning. The tumble he'd taken out of the cavesurfer had taken its toll, plunging him into the turbulent cauldron at the bottom of the falls. He swallowed more than his share of water as the swirling currents turned him 'round and 'round beneath the water. Suddenly the violent water released its grip on him, and Jimmy found himself floating in darkness on the surface. He'd called out again and again, but no one responded. Jimmy felt certain that Brynn, Mr. Wallace, Johnny, and Jett . . . were all gone, killed when their surfer capsized. Once or twice he thought he'd seen the flicker of light off in the unknown distance, torchcells from the other Elven pilots. They had plunged down the left side of the falls as instructed and now seemed so far away. He cried out once more, but realized he could barely hear his own weak voice above the explosive ruckus of the falls.

It seemed like an eternity he floated in the darkness, his thoughts all to himself. He was moving, slowly at first, but gradually gaining speed. Knowing he could only tread water for so long, he had almost resigned himself to the fact that he would indeed die here. But something inside Jimmy Gresham would not quit. Maybe it was the hardness he'd gained when he was very young from life in an orphanage. But there was sometone else, too. When he'd lived with the Gresham family, he'd hoped to have found a home . . . hoped to have found love. That had all vanished when Geoffry was born. But then . . . out of nowhere, Miss Finney and Regis had come and told Jimmy he was not a castaway kid, but someone quite special . . . royalty even. They'd told him there was a place where he belonged and an important job for him to do. No way he could give up now . . . NO WAY.

Then a brilliant burst of light exploded somewhere ahead. Jimmy turned, his senses coming alive. One of the giant dangling stalactites was now a raging inferno of flames, casting a warm orange glow throughout the cavern.

Jimmy felt a spike of energy, and he propelled himself hard against the current. But he could see his peril now. He could see the whirlpool: a monstrous spiral galaxy of water churning with slow but unstoppable progress. He was not in the outer bands but just thirty yards from the center.

"JIMMY!" a voice rang out. "Fight the current, Jimmy!"

Jimmy turned to face the voice. He couldn't quite make out the form, but someone was clearly telling him to swim for it.

Grimwarden splashed his way toward the whirlpool. Between spraying water and submerging for breaths, he saw Jimmy struggling. Knowing Jimmy was too far in to escape and in moments he would be, too, Grimwarden left their fate to Ellos and dauntlessly plowed on.

Then he saw Jimmy go under. "NOOO!" Grimwarden clawed at the water and kicked his feet with long, mighty strokes. The whirling current threatened to throw him off course, but instinctively he made the water flow work for him, curling with it to the side. Then he saw Jimmy's hand reaching up above the water.

Grimwarden jetted through the water, getting closer to the young lord.

"We've got rope!" Goldarrow said, raising the coil she'd found stowed beneath the backseat.

"Oh no," Kat cried. "Jimmy's gone under!"

Moving suddenly to see, Tommy and Goldarrow almost tipped the cavesurfer. They saw Grimwarden just as he dove beneath the surface. There were several breathless seconds until Grimwarden came up . . . empty-handed.

"Flet Marshall Goldarrow!" yelled a young flet soldier who had maneuvered his cavesurfer near. "You are too close to the pool currents! Row away!"

Goldarrow looked from the scene near the middle of the whirlpool back to the currents surrounding their vessel. She dropped onto the rear bench, grabbed an oar, and moved them back.

"Ah!" Kat screamed. "He's got him! Grimwarden's got Jimmy!"

Goldarrow jerked her head around. *Thank Ellos!* she thought. *But they are so far. How will I ever get this rope to them?* She thought about tying the rope to one of the oars and throwing it like a spear. No . . . Jett might be able to, but she couldn't. *Kiri Lee.* But she was too sick to attempt such a treacherous air walk. Then it came to her. *TOMMY.*

She grabbed the young lord's shoulder. "Your bow!" Goldarrow demanded. "String it! Have you any arrows left?"

"I think . . . one maybe—whoa!" Tommy fell on his rear in the bottom of the surfer, clambered back to his seat, and rummaged around looking for his quiver.

"Hurry!" Kat yelled. "Grimwarden's struggling. They're getting close to the middle."

"Ah, got it!" Tommy cried, holding up the quiver. "I've got one arrow."

"Give it to me," Goldarrow demanded. Her fingers moved faster than Tommy had ever seen, and she tied a very strange-looking knot onto the very back of the arrow. She had tied one loop of the rope tight right before the fletchings, another loop right behind them on the nock, and had left a very tight, tiny ball of rope hanging loose. "There," she said, handing the arrow to Tommy. "That ought to reduce drag from the rope somewhat. But still aim high."

"Got it!" Tommy said, his heart jackhammering.

Jimmy coughed, spat out water, and weakly gripped Grimwarden's arm.

"I got you, lad!" Grimwarden yelled, grasping Jimmy under his shoulders and pulling him close.

He's exhausted, thought Grimwarden. And now, holding the boy, he could not muster enough force to fight the whirlpool's massive current. They drifted with the current, Grimwarden struggling to see over the surface waves. "HERE!!" he yelled. "HERE, GOLDARROW!!"

Suddenly a new stream of flame stretched like a fiery tentacle to the roof of the cavern. Johnny had done well. Grimwarden could see much better, and that meant Goldarrow could as well. Bobbing up in the currents, Grimwarden saw a lot of movement on board his cavesurfer. It looked as if another cavesurfer was there as well. Then he saw Tommy stand . . . very tall . . . like he might be standing on the seats.

He has his bow! Grimwarden kicked as hard as he could and raised his hand to give Tommy something to aim for. But the way the current was dragging him it was impossible to stay in one place. Grimwarden worried that Tommy would only have time for one shot.

The arrow went up. *Good lad!* Grimwarden thought. *Plenty of height*. The thin rope trailed behind the arrow without weighing it down too much. The arrow fell at last, well within Grimwarden's reach. He turned his body to avoid dunking Jimmy, and just as the current pulled him away he grabbed for the rope. . . .

To their collective horror, Grimwarden's outstretched arm fell short of grasping the rope. He and Jimmy were tugged deeper into the whirlpool and were moving much faster now.

"NO!!" shouted Goldarrow. "Everyone, take hold of the rope. Pull the arrow back! Now!! Hurry!"

The whirlpool grabbed Grimwarden and yanked him backward. He splashed and flailed. He barely had the strength to keep him and Johnny above water, much less make any progress against the cursed current. "Hold on, Jimmy!" he growled. Then he saw the arrow skipping across the concentric waves, the middle and outer bands of the whirlpool. They were pulling the rope back for another try. "Hold on! We might have one last chance!"

Jimmy let his head fall back against Grimwarden's chest and looked up. "We're going to make it, yu know," he said.

Grimwarden's eyes opened wide. "You—you've seen it with your foresight?"

"No"—Jimmy laugh-coughed—"but I trust yu."

Grimwarden set his jaw. "Climb onto my back, then," he said. "I'm going to need both hands free."

"They're slipping below the surface!" yelled Kat, jerking back fistfuls of rope as fast as she could.

"No," Tommy shot back. "I can see them still . . . barely!"

"Yes!" she replied. "I see them now!"

Goldarrow couldn't look up. All she could think about was getting that arrow back as fast as possible. She saw it, skipping, practically flying across the black water. Just forty yards away, thirty . . . twenty, ten. "I've got it. Here, Tommy! Take it. May Ellos bless your aim!"

"I can only see Grimwarden's hands now!" said Kat. "What's he doing? He's doing something with his hands."

Tommy nocked the arrow and leaned outward. "Steady the boat!" he yelled. "I need to see!" Tommy watched Grimwarden's arms. He had one arm outstretched and high with his palm wide, fingers spread out. With his other hand balled into a fist, he was smacking it into the palm of the first hand. *What is he doing?* And then Tommy thought he understood.

Grimwarden smacked his fist into his palm. *Come on! Take the shot! Be true!* They were out of time.

"Grimwarden!" Jimmy yelled. "We're going under!"

"NOW, TOMMY!!" Grimwarden roared. "NOWWWW!!"

Tommy lined up the shot and fired.

A breath later and Grimwarden's hand felt as if a red-hot iron poker drove into his palm. He looked up to see an arrow shaft lodged halfway through his hand and blood pouring down his wrist. He grimaced and grunted, focusing on closing his fingers around the arrow. His arm jerked, elbow snapping, and he struggled to reach the arrow with his free hand. Then the current took them down.

"Did you . . . ?" Goldarrow's voice trailed off.

"I don't know," Tommy said. "They're gone! Pull!"

No sooner had the command gone out than the rope nearly pulled free from their hands. "Kat, hold on! Flet soldiers! GET THE ROPE AND PULL!"

The flet soldiers in the other craft took hold of some of the loose coils and added their might to the effort.

"They're . . . ah . . . they're still under!" yelled Kat. "Ah!"

"We don't have enough!" Tommy grunted, his arms burning. He felt as if he were engaged in a tug-of-war against an entire football team.

"We are fighting the teeth of the current," said Goldarrow. "But we will prevail! Endurance and Victory!"

Spluttering and puffing for air, Grimwarden and Jimmy broke the surface. Fresh blood pulsed out between the fingers of Grimwarden's hands. The pain was excruciating, but he clutched the arrow and the rope even tighter. They were moving, slowly—oh so slowly—but they were moving against the current. And they were alive.

"I-I-I told you," whispered Jimmy, slumped on Grimwarden's back.

Goldarrow, Tommy, Kat, and five flet soldiers heaved the rope with all their might. "Come on!" Goldarrow urged. "Pull harder! They're halfway now! Grimwarden, can you hear me?"

"Yes." His reply was audible but weak.

"You're hurt?"

"Thanks to that blessed archer of ours, yes," said Grimwarden. "Hurt . . . and alive."

Goldarrow saw the blood leaking out into the water. "Faster!" she demanded. "Let's get them in!"

Kat had never felt such a burn in her muscles, not even in gymnastics when she'd had to hang from the uneven bars until her coach said to drop. *Oh no!* she thought. *No, not now with everyone watching. No.* But it was too late. The pain was that intense. She could feel it building. Then she did it. *Squeak!*

"What was that?" Tommy asked.

"What was what?" Kat asked, fighting off another. *Squeak!*

"There it is again," said Tommy. "I heard a squeak."

"Get focused, both of you!" Goldarrow warned, the edge to her voice sword sharp.

"I'm sorry," said Kat. "It's just—" She never finished her apology.

"Aieee!" yelled one of the flet soldiers. "Razorfish!"

Grimwarden turned just in time. A glistening gray shape rose out of the water, a fin, curved and membraned like a bat's wing.

31

Grimwarden saw their peril immediately. He lifted his fists so that the fin could slide under the rope. He knew razorfish were quite blind, but they felt changes in water current, water temperature, and they could smell blood. The creatures didn't need to know exactly where their prey was, so long as they could bump some part of their fins against it. That dorsal fin could bite through leather armor, even light metal . . . to say nothing of what it could do to a man. It missed on its first pass, but Grimwarden knew it would be back. If it cut the rope before they were free of the whirlpool, then all had been for naught.

"There's another!" Goldarrow called out. "Behind you!"

Grimwarden spun around so that it couldn't hit Jimmy. The bulbous fish slid right alongside Grimwarden, its fin just inches away from his face. "Get us out of here!" he yelled.

Goldarrow and the others pulled in the rope, but it grew suddenly harder as if the current had intensified. "Come on!"

"They're both coming right for you!" one of the flet soldiers yelled.

"No, they aren't," said Tommy. His bow sang twice.

Pierced by Tommy's arrows, the two razorfish erupted in frantic thrashing. Their efforts were in vain.

Tommy dropped his bow and went back to helping the others pull Grimwarden and Jimmy toward the craft.

"Where'd you get the other arrows?" Kat asked.

"The flet soldier behind you," he said. "I reached between the boats and he gave me two arrows."

"That's good shooting," Kat said.

"Thanks," Tommy replied, feeling awkward and strangely happy.

Once completely free of the whirlpool's current, Grimwarden handed a sodden Jimmy up to Goldarrow and Tommy.

Kat thought Jimmy looked like a squirrel that had fallen out of a tree and drowned in a pond. "Is he going to be okay?" she asked.

"Yes," said Grimwarden. "We'll both be fine." Grimwarden swam over to the other flet soldiers and allowed them to help him aboard. "Mind the hand," he said.

Tommy glanced back at the struggling razorfish. A third had appeared. Tommy watched it head right for the others. It submerged partially and swam directly beneath one of the wounded fish . . . and cut it in half.

The two cavesurfers slid slowly back to where the others had gathered at the bottom of the falls. When they arrived, they found Flet Marshall Brynn and Mr. Wallace sitting in a boat together.

"Mr. Wallace!" yelled Kat. "You're alive!"

"Yes," he replied weakly. "Thanks to Jett for hauling me out of the water." He looked up and saw Jimmy. "Master Jimmy," he said. "You made it."

"Aye," he said. "Barely."

Kiri Lee sat up and said, "There aren't any more tubes or falls or whirlpools or ANYTHING ELSE DANGEROUS, are there?"

"No," said Grimwarden. "It's a smooth ride from here on out."

The cavesurfers raced along in utter darkness, the headlamps on each too damp to relight—even with Johnny's now limited power. The young lords sat listening in the darkness, the chill air whistling in their ears, and shivering in their damp clothes from the waterfall dunk. The Elves spoke in hushed voices as they deftly maneuvered the swift current of the underground river.

Tommy felt they were going west, far from the Dark Veil. *One wrong move might send us into a sheer wall or a ridge lurking an inch under the surface,* Tommy thought.

"I was thinking the same thing," whispered Kat. "I wish we could see a little." She turned around carefully to the cavesurfer behind them. "Johnny, how are you doing?"

"I'm thinking about Autumn," he said quietly. "With everything we just went through, how could she do any better?"

"She's way ahead of us," said Tommy. "I bet she's already there."

"The Sentinels told us she would get the best medical care in Allyra," said Kat. "That Claris lady sure seemed to know what she's doing. Autumn will pull through. I know she will."

"Yeah," Johnny replied with little certainty. It was silent again for several moments, and then Johnny said, "I might be able to make a little light again."

"NO," said Tommy louder than he meant to as an image of their boat in flames hurtling through the underground flitted through his mind. He didn't care that much for his curly locks, but he didn't want them singed off, either. "Uh, I mean, that's okay. I think the Sentinels want us in the dark."

"We are nearing the Nightwish Caverns," said Grimwarden, his whispered voice still somehow gruff and commanding. "Be silent and make no sudden moves."

At the head of the boat, a bluish spark kindled and for a moment illuminated Grimwarden's dark eyes, ragged long hair, and beard. The Guardmaster placed a glowing blue stone on the prow of the boat and sat down, showing his massive, broad-shouldered silhouette.

With the new light, Tommy could see just how narrow the aqueduct was . . . a thin channel between platforms of rigid stone and clusters of jagged stalagmites. Here and there, other byways appeared as shadowy cavelike holes. Then Tommy saw something he didn't understand: little flashes of light hanging ten feet in the air on either side of the channel. So many of them, evenly spaced, they'd light up as a boat passed and then fade out in the darkness left behind.

Arrowheads, Tommy suddenly realized. . . . *Razor-sharp arrowheads glistening like rows of sharks' teeth.*

Bowstrings pulled tight to their chins, arrows nocked and trained on the boats, an entire arsenal of Elven archers stood ready on either side of the river. Even if an enemy could navigate the pitch-black aqueducts and approach the caverns, he'd never make it past these archers . . . not without becoming a floating pincushion.

Light grew from some source far ahead. The boat rose in the water and began to slow. Tommy could see the archers better now. Two complete lines of bowmen garbed in dark gray and black, like the tunnel's walls, waited on the river's banks. As one, they removed the arrows from their bowstrings and expertly slid them back into their quivers. Then they crossed wrists and bowed. Grimwarden returned the customary gesture.

They're staring at us, thought Tommy. *All of them.*

The light grew stronger, and the boat emerged at last from the tunnel, floating slowly into a massive, vast expanse. Tommy's jaw literally dropped. Kat gasped. Even Johnny, who'd been so preoccupied with his thoughts of Autumn, couldn't help but stare.

"Behold!" exclaimed Grimwarden. "The Nightwish Caverns and the Remnant of Berinfell!"

An army of thousands of flet soldiers clad in rich browns and deep greens stood on either side of the river, their outstretched arms and extended rycheswords forming a celebratory roof above the newcomers. And beyond them, a teeming crowd, untold thousands of men, women, and children. Trumpets blared, thousands of voices rose in songs and cheers, and pure white flower petals cascaded down like fat snowflakes from the heights. And what heights there were! The ceiling of the Nightwish Caverns was hardly visible in the murky twilight so far above, but it was several hundred feet up at least. Great turrets and mighty bastions made of the strangest dimpled blue stone towered up on the left and on the right. And crafted upon these were many balconies stuffed with cheering Elven citizens. Bridges arched over the river in several places far ahead, and more deliriously happy Elves filled these.

"This is all for you," said Elle Goldarrow, turning to look at each of the teens as the line of boats emerged from the tunnel. Then she stood, raised her hands to silence the crowd, and announced, "We have won a great victory over the Spider King," her voice becoming loud, commanding, and resonant. "For today, the Lords of Berinfell RETURN!"

In the happy chaos that followed Elves leaped up and down, children shrieked at seeing the heroes, and more than one adolescent Elf swooned over the sight of the teen lords entering their domain. Banners fluttered, fists pumped, and swords rattled on the faces of shields as everyone welcomed what they had hoped for through so many years of darkness.

When Goldarrow sat back down, Grimwarden muttered, "It is not yet the final victory. There is much work to be done."

"Oh, don't be so morose," she replied. "Our people need this. It's their first real celebration in hundreds of years. Give them this day and the ceremony tonight. Then we'll go to work."

Grimwarden harrumphed and turned away. Goldarrow leaned toward the young lords. "With those wide, fearful eyes, you look like Gnomes." The teens didn't laugh, but Goldarrow was undaunted. "Smile at them . . . wave to them," she said. "They are your people."

Tommy, Kat, and Kiri Lee did as they were told. Their waves were tentative and slow, their smiles forced. As their boat drifted under a bridge, Kat whispered to Tommy, "They don't know, do they?"

"Know what?" Tommy asked. Kiri Lee leaned over to hear.

"They think we're heroes, like some great warriors come to save them. They don't know that we're just kids."

"No, Kat, you're wrong," said Kiri Lee. "We're not just kids. Not anymore."

Following their dramatic welcome into Nightwish, the Seven were given warm wraps before being served a quick meal and taken to their quarters—guys in one, girls in the other—two rooms at either ends of a long hall. They stripped off their still-damp clothes, donning brand-new night robes, and practically fell into bed, asleep in midair—except for Johnny, who worried about Autumn and why the Sentinels had refused his request to see her.

Sometime in the early morning, there came a knock at the door to the boys' quarters. Then a harder knock. Finally a knock so hard the ceiling almost caved in. Johnny leaped out of bed, feeling every muscle kink and pain, and opened the door. "Nelly!" he said. "And Guardmaster Grimwarden. What's going on here?"

"We're very sorry to wake you," said Nelly. Jimmy, Tommy, and Jett sat up, yawning.

"What time is it?" Jett rubbed his eyes.

"Early enough," said Grimwarden. "Had a ridiculously difficult time waking you, too. Almost took the door down. May we come in?"

"Just a sec," Johnny said, wandering away. "We couldn't figure out how to put out this candle-stone-thing, so I just covered it up." The room now lit in dim silvery light, Johnny let them in, and they sat at a small table in the center of the chamber. The other boys gathered around.

"Would you mind excusing us?" Grimwarden inclined his head, indicating that he wanted to speak to Johnny alone.

"No problem, Mr. Grimwarden, sir," said Tommy.

Jett nudged Johnny as if he might need backup. "We'll be right outside the door, dude."

"Just give us a shout," added Jimmy. Then the three boys shuffled out sleepily and closed the door.

"We have just been to see Autumn," Nelly began.

"How's she doing?"

"Good, very good," said Grimwarden. "Nelly, perhaps you would be better at this."

She nodded. "Johnny, tomorrow is the lordship ceremony. It is a very public thing where you will all be celebrated as the returning Lords of Berinfell."

"Even Autumn?"

"Well, we'll see how she's doing."

"So I may see her now?"

"It's best you leave her be," Nelly said.

"But she's my sister!"

Nelly looked to Grimwarden, then back to Johnny. "Regarding that. We were afraid that something will come as a bit of a shock to you."

"That I'm an Elf?" Johnny scratched his ear. "Well, I'm kind of over that."

"No, not that," said Nelly. "But it's related." She looked to Grimwarden, sighing. "See, Guardmaster, I'm not much better at this. Okay"—back to Johnny—"you remember how we told you that the Drefids took you and the others as babes, yes?"

"Sure."

"Well, when they brought you and Autumn out of Allyra and left

37

you on Earth, the authorities gave you to the Briarmans as brother and sister."

"But?" Johnny's sleepy mind didn't gather the implication.

"But you're not," said Nelly. "Not by blood, anyway."

Johnny sat back, eyes fixed in a blinkless stare.

"Your real name," said Grimwarden, "is Albriand Ashheart. Autumn is Miarra Swiftstorm. Two families. Two lordly families."

"We're very sorry to have to tell you like this," Nelly said.

"Does Autumn know?"

"Yes, she knows."

"I really can't see her?"

"No, not now," said Nelly. "She needs time to . . . to come to terms with this in her own way. That's why we didn't allow you to see her earlier. You'll have to wait until the lordship ceremony."

Grimwarden and Nelly bid Johnny good morning and left, letting the other boys back in. The four crawled back into bed, relishing the allowance of sleeping late. Everyone but Johnny, who, though quite exhausted, never did fall back asleep.

The Lordship Ceremony

"THIS IS the coolest thing I've ever worn," said Jett, admiring himself in a long mirror. "And that's saying a lot."

"You like the tunic, do you?" asked Brennath Eventide, a flet soldier assigned to help the young lords with their ceremonial attire. "I should say you might. The thread in these garments is worth more than the castle in which we now stand."

"Yur pulling me leg, aren't yu?" asked Jimmy, looking again at his tunic. Its design was the same as the others: black with ornate silver embroidery around the collar, sleeves, and waist. *What thread could be worth that much gold?* He turned and muttered to Tommy, "Yu think he'd be offended if I told 'im mine dunnot fit so well?"

"I doubt it," said Tommy. "I think they—"

"Offended?" Brennath laughed so hard his curly blond locks bounced on his shoulders. "You could scarcely offend me . . . a lowly flet soldier! I am at your service . . . bound to your service, actually. And because I am to teach you the nuances of our culture, let me begin by explaining that each one of the Seven Lords is in all things above my station."

Jimmy blushed. "Uh . . . well, that will take some gettin' used to. For most of me life, I've been rather second fiddle. Uh . . . more like tenth fiddle, really." Jimmy stared at the floor. "The tunic's all right anyway."

"It's not all right if it isn't just the way you want it," said Brennath. "Command me, m'lord."

"Uh, well then, I suppose mine is a wee bit loose."

"Well done, m'lord," said Brennath. "You will have to wear it for the ceremony, but I will have it altered before the council tomorrow afternoon."

"Thank yu," said Jimmy, still red-cheeked. "It is a great-looking tunic. And I do like the sword." Jimmy whipped the rychesword from his sheath, spun around, and slashed the air.

"WHOA, Jimmy!" Tommy leaped backward and blocked with his own sword just before Jimmy would have carved a gash into his upper leg. "Watch where you swing that thing. You could have cut off my leg or something."

"I knew yu'd block it," said Jimmy, quickly sheathing the sword. He winked but then whistled a nervous *whew*.

Jett laughed and cinched his sword belt a bit tighter. The triangular chamber in which they now stood, indeed the whole castle, was cut from the same dimpled bluish stone that the entire underground city seemed to be built from. Silvery light radiated up from clusters of icy-clear crystals in each of the three corners. Jett wandered over to take a closer look. "These crystal things are cool," he said.

"You are quite perceptive," said Brennath. "We call those cold lamps."

Jett laughed. "That's not what I meant by *cool*."

It was Brennath's turn to be red-faced. "I'm sorry, m'lord. What did you mean?"

"No need to apologize," said Jett. "I just meant these crystal, uh, cold lamps, they rock. They're sweet."

Brennath stared blankly.

"He means he really likes the way they look," said Tommy.

"Oh," replied the flet soldier.

"Right," said Jett. "C'mere, Tommy, Jimmy. Look at it. There's a tiny little fire burning down in the middle of these crystals. But it's weird fire . . . kind of silvery . . . like . . . ish." The others hustled over.

"Wow," said Tommy. "It's like fire made of mercury."

"That is a single ounce of dremask vein," said Brennath. "A peculiar metal to be sure—we discovered it at the bottom of some of the coldest underground riverbeds. Cold ignites it, and it burns cold."

"It burns in the water?" Tommy asked. "Then how do you put it out?"

Brennath regarded him gravely. "You don't."

Someone knocked at the door. "Are the lads dressed?" came a muffled woman's voice.

"The lords are garbed in their finery," said Brennath. "Do come in."

Regis strolled into the chamber. "Don't you all look dashing," she said, making a big show of looking over the young lords in their royal garb.

Jimmy stood up especially straight. Regis's dark eyes gleamed mysteriously out between long wisps of black hair. Jimmy sighed. He'd had a crush on Regis ever since she took a job at the tavern back in Ardfern. Now that he knew that she was actually an elite Dreadnaught warrior, well, that just made her all the more intriguing. *If only she wasn't hundreds of years older than me*, Jimmy thought.

"The sun is climbing high," said Regis. "It is time for the ceremony."

"What about Autumn?" asked Jett.

"Autumn . . . I cannot say if she will join us in Luminary Hall."

"Will Autumn be okay?" asked Tommy.

Regis's lips betrayed the slightest hint of a smile in one corner of her mouth. "Again," she said. "I cannot say. Maybe you shall see for yourself, if Lady Claris allows more visitors for her charge. Come now, lads, many are waiting."

"Regis?" Jimmy spoke up.

"Yes, Jimmy?"

"Would yu like t'know yur future?"

"Well, that depends," said Regis. She tilted her head, raised an eyebrow, and eyed him curiously. "Is it a good future?" Tommy, Jett, and Brennath looked on.

"I think so," said Jimmy, holding his arm in an L shape. "Yur future is to take me arm and walk me to the ceremony."

Brennath laughed. Tommy and Jett stared. Regis walked to Jimmy, took his arm, and said, "It is a good future indeed." She promptly led

Jimmy out of the room. Brennath followed, leaving two gawking young lords.

"I didn't know Jimmy was that smooth," said Jett.

Tommy just shook his head. *And all I can do is shoot arrows.*

Luminary Hall was cavernous and perfectly round. Braziers lit with dremask flickered brightly every seven feet around the perimeter wall. Their eerily beautiful silvery light glimmered on the ceremonial armor of flet soldiers posted at every door. Six of the seven young lords stood in front of seven high throne chairs arranged in a half circle near the middle of the room. Directly across from the thrones, seven smaller seats waited with a robed Elf standing statuesquely behind each one. Massive multitiered seats rose up around the center like a coliseum, and above those, wide balconies clung to the walls like caterpillars inside a jar.

"It looks like every single seat is filled," Kat said, staring.

"That's a lot of Elves," said Tommy. "Think they can even see us from way up there?"

"You can see them, can't you?" asked Jett. "This is great, like being in the Super Bowl."

"Just makes me nervous," said Kat.

"Hey, look a' that!" Jimmy exclaimed, pointing beyond the seven robed Elves to a low-level section of seats. "It's Miss Finney, Regis, Goldarrow, Grimwarden, and the others."

"Edward is there, too," said Kiri Lee.

"I wish this ceremony was just in front of them," said Kat. "I don't like being the center of atten—"

"Kat, look!" Tommy pointed to a section of Elves seated off to their left.

Kat gasped. What caught her eye was more remarkable than anything she had ever seen. Not their clothes. Not their hairstyle. It was their *skin.* "They . . . they're just like me." Kat held trembling fingers to her mouth. She remembered Mr. Wallace and Anna telling her about the Berylinian Elves, how they all had bluish skin like hers, but that had been back on Earth right in the midst of learning so many strange and unbelievable things. To see them in person filled Kat now with overwhelming joy, a kind of snuggling warmth that radiated through her body. Tears beaded and then rolled down her cheeks. *Blue men, blue women, blue children . . . different shades, too.* It was overwhelming. *I'm not a freak,* she thought. *If only Mom and Dad could see them.* She covered her face with her hands, shook with something like soft coughs, and cried tears that like a cleansing rain washed away years of silent suffering.

Anna appeared at Tommy's side. "What's happened? Kat, is she all right?"

"Yeah, she's cool," said Tommy. "Really cool, I think." He nodded toward the Berylinian Elves.

Anna understood immediately. She touched Kat's shoulders. "You see," she said, "you are beautiful. You always were."

And why wouldn't she think she's beautiful? Tommy wondered. Girls totally confused him sometimes.

Kat looked up to Anna with grateful, glistening eyes, but she couldn't find words. Then to Tommy. *Did she hear me just then?* He blushed.

In that moment, the young lords' attention was drawn to the center of the great room. A tall Elf wearing a long black robe with ornate forest green accents at the collar and sleeves strode forward. His hair was the color of iron, and his large, peaceful eyes smiled. He lifted his arms, showing the deep green lining of his cloak. When the hall became completely silent, he called aloud, "I am Alwynn Belkirith, High Cleric of the Tribes of Berinfell, successor of Elrain Galadhon." His voice was high like that of a tenor and as clear as a bell's toll at midnight. The acoustics of the hall carried his sonorous voice even to the highest balcony. "On this, the twenty-third day of Arduin in the year 1422, eight hundred years after our city and our hope were stolen from us, the Lords of Berinfell return at last."

Cheers and shouts erupted, but above it all, the Elves began to clap, everyone synchronized: *clap—clap—clap*—slow at first, then increasing speed. *Clap, clap, clap.* Thousands of Elves clapped in perfect rhythm even as the pace picked up. Faster and faster it went, until it was full-out applause, and the high cleric again silenced the crowd.

"Taken as infants and exiled to Earth where they would know nothing of their true lineage, today they have come here to claim their birthright." Alwynn slowly surveyed the entire room and lifted one hand. "Will you all witness their ascension and pledge your service to them?"

"WE WILL!" came the choral reply.

Alwynn walked in a circle and traced a fingertip around a sloping cone of gray metal that stood waist high in the exact center of the floor. "You, faithful Elves of Berinfell, wish to serve your lords, but you must meet them first. You must meet them ALL."

He turned and gestured toward an entrance to the far right of the young lords and their thrones. There, a shadow appeared in the doorway. This figure came forward, followed by two flet soldiers. They neared the center of the hall. Johnny squinted, saw the silvery dremask light in this person's hair. *It can't be. I thought she'd still be too weak to walk on her own.*

The figure came a little closer to the thrones. Johnny yelled, "AUTUMN!" And it was. She looked haggard and pale, but determined. She walked slowly across the hall, the two flet soldiers right behind her. As one, the other six teens raced toward her and embraced her. "Autumn, you're walking," Johnny said, holding her away from him.

"I'm still very sore," she said. "But I'm getting my strength back quickly. Claris says in another week, I'll be able to run. I mean . . . really run. But there are other things . . ." Her voice trailed off, and she and Johnny shared a sad and knowing glance.

What was that about? Tommy wondered.

Kat frowned as she read Johnny's and Autumn's thoughts. *"Poor Johnny and Autumn,"* Kat's thoughts replied in Tommy's mind.

What? Tommy's urgent question flashed back.

"They're not brother and sister . . . they just found out."

But no additional thoughts passed between them as the high cleric stilled the cheering audience and motioned for the lords to be seated, and then motioned for the audience to be seated.

Alwynn's eyes underwent a transformation. The quiet peace was replaced by vital confidence, almost ferocity. His voice matched his glare. "We, the Children of Light, have dwelt *far* too long in darkness," he said, the urgency of his words intensifying. "We, the founders of Berinfell and the caretakers of all of Allyra, have hidden in fear for *far* too long. We, the most ancient of the Great Races, have allowed ourselves to be driven near extinction. But NO MORE."

Cheers and more synchronized clapping. Alwynn gestured behind him, and the other six robed figures lowered their hoods. "Brethren of Elders, come forward. It is time to see our lords properly attired."

Properly attired? Kat looked down at her tunic and then over at Tommy and the others. *But we're all already dressed pretty elegantly.* She looked over to Kiri Lee who smiled back with confidence, used to being the center of attention.

Alwynn came first to Tommy. "You are Felheart, son of Lord Velaril and Tarin, his bride, of the tribe Silvertree. You were born a lord, but you must also choose to fulfill those duties by a pure heart. Your position requires stout leadership, but also . . . relentless service. Will you, before Ellos and all these you see assembled here, assume your position as a Lord of Elves? Will you honor our creeds? And will you serve your people?"

"I will," said Tommy.

Alwynn pulled something out of a deep pocket in his robe. "Then by virtue of blood and word"—he lifted a cord over Tommy's head— "I deem you a Lord of Elves. And I give you the amulet of the tribe Silvertree. You must wear it at all times, covering your heart, signifying your everlasting covenant to lead and protect your people, even at risk of your own life. Notice that the amulet itself is crafted from the most precious metals and stones, but the necklace is but a plain black cord. Remember, you—like the people you serve—are a blessed mixture of all that is precious and all that is common, and you must never stray from the right path. Now, sit, Lord of Elves. Sit upon the throne of your tribe."

Tommy nodded repeatedly and sat down. The high cleric stepped backward. Tommy looked at the amulet on his chest. It was round, about three inches in diameter, and seemed to be made of some kind of beveled crystal. Small irregular shapes were cut out of the field of the crystal, some wide enough that Tommy could fit a fingertip through them. The rest of the precious semi-transparent stone was divided into numerous sections by thin curving veins of silvery metal. Tommy held the medallion up closer to his face. In some of the smaller sections of jeweled stone, he could just make out a symbol or a letter of some kind. *Not English, that's for sure.* He squinted. *Goldarrow will know.*

A different elder came forward for each of the young lords, calling them each by their Elven name and tribe. To Kat: "Alreenia, daughter of Beleg and Lord Kendie of the tribe Hiddenblade." To Autumn: "Miarra, daughter of Lord Galadhost and Salura of the tribe Swiftstorm." To Johnny: "Albriand, son of Elroth and Lord Tisa of the tribe Ashheart." To Jimmy: "Thorwin, son of Lord Xanthis and Dreia of the tribe Valorbrand." To Jett: "Hamandar, son of Lord Vex and Jasmira of the tribe Nightwing." And to Kiri Lee: "Lothriel, daughter of Charad and Lord Simona of the tribe Oakenflower." And to each lord the elders gave a medallion, roughly the same size and seemingly crafted out of the same materials as Tommy's. But their interior shapes were very different, each as unique and intricate as a fingerprint.

The high cleric and the other elders moved to their seats, and for several moments the young lords and the elders were still and silent, enveloped in the atmosphere.

Seated in the first row of stands, Elle Goldarrow did not want to weep openly, but the gravity of all that had led to the young lords' rescue and arrival in Allyra—the waiting, the planning, the fighting, and the loss of life—came upon her in a rush. And at last she allowed herself to mourn for Charlie. She put her head in her hands. Grimwarden drew her to lean on his shoulder. "It was a terrible price," he said. "But it was worth it. Look at them, Elle. They have come, spanning time, from one world to another, to save us all."

She looked upon the seven lords, and through her tears, she thought of how they had matured ever so slightly. There was about them the look of warriors. It was as if she saw into the future right then. Suddenly they were tall and broad-shouldered. Matured. Wisdom was upon their brows, mission in their eyes, and unmatched power in their fists. And they even bore the scars of battle, the price paid for war, even the ultimate sacrifice. For loss. And for victory. She knew it was just her mind playing tricks on her. Or was it? Whether as kids or adults, the Seven Elven Lords of Berinfell had returned.

"We are the Children of Light," said Alwynn suddenly. "And upon this timeless occasion, we will dare to risk a little light."

A frenzied murmur rose in the hall, spiraling upward. Elle refocused, and the teens sat on the thrones once more. Young. Naive. *Oh, Ellos, spare them,* she prayed. But she knew it was in vain. *Or at least be merciful.*

The high cleric signaled to a pair of flet soldiers near the northern entrance to the hall. They worked at a locking mechanism, releasing a thin chain, and then they began to pull.

Alwynn stood and strode to the metallic cone in the center of the hall. As he removed the cone, he said, "May Ellos bless us with a clear sky and an unhindered path through the forest canopy." Beneath the cone was a large deposit of the same crystals used in the dremask braziers. But these were clearly crafted by the Elves' most gifted stonecutters. Ordinarily geometric, rigid, and sharp, these crystals were cut into the likeness of a lush flowering plant with seven star-shaped blossoms.

Alwynn returned to his seat. He and the other elders gazed upward.

The Elves stirred in their seats. Whispers filled the hall. And for many breathless moments nothing happened. In a repetitive cycle, Tommy looked from the crystal flowers to the elders to the roof of the hall and back again to the crystals.

Kat, also staring up, leaned over. "What do you—?" She never finished the question.

High above them all, a pinprick of light pierced the sea of murk in the hall's vast ceiling. A thrilled murmur grew from the Elves in the balconies. The excitement intensified as more and more Elves realized what was happening far above. The distant point of light became a beam, focused and narrow, traveling down through the dust. The noise level grew exponentially, but the Elves were not cheering or shouting. It was more like a spontaneous release of joy and wonder, like small children at their first fireworks display. Gasping. Giggling.

The ray of sunlight plunged down until it struck the sculpted crystal plant. In a split second, the single beam divided into seven. A thin ray of light blazed out of each of the crystal flowers and struck Tommy's, Kat's, Autumn's, and Kiri Lee's medallions. Taller than the others, Jett had to scoot down for the stream of light to hit his. By contrast, Johnny and Jimmy had to sit up a bit higher in their seats. Now the split rays of the sun struck each of the seven medallions, and for a few moments, each of the young lords seemed to have a captured star emblazoned upon his or her chest. Keeping their torsos still, the teens turned their heads this way and that, grinning and staring.

Alwynn, the elders, Goldarrow, Grimwarden, and the others smiled with deep satisfaction. A few of the oldest Elves had seen a similar ceremony before . . . but it was long ago when the Elves of Berinfell were still free to walk in the sun's light. In the underground, it was something more beautiful than they could have conceived.

Then there came a series of sharp gasps. The high cleric sat bolt upright in his chair. The sunlight blazing on the lords' medallions increased in intensity tenfold. Within the bursting brightness came sparkles of color. Suddenly needle-thin rays of light—deep sea blues, sunset reds and oranges, forest greens, amethyst purples, and sunflower yellows—fired out from each medallion and streamed in all directions. Crisscrossing strands of light filled Luminary Hall.

"Look!" Tommy exclaimed. "The light beams . . . they're hitting all the Elves . . . all of them!"

This the elders had not expected, and those assembled there had never seen anything like it. From the seven medallions, thousands of thin lines shot out in all directions, some striking the crystal flowers and reflecting toward the Elves seated behind the young lords. Every single Elf in the hall had a personal sunbeam blazing on his or her chest or face. Some laughed. Some wept. Some played with the light and ran their hands through it. Even the Elven children had streams of light.

"Alwynn, what does this mean?" asked Manaelkin Zoar, one of the elders.

Even Alwynn was unsure, but he answered, "It means Ellos smiles upon us."

The light flickered; each and every colorful strand blinked. And then it was all gone. Although the flet soldiers had not shut out the light, something had above the surface. Alwynn motioned to the flet soldiers, who quickly returned the mechanism to its original position.

The ceremony ended, and Elle Goldarrow and several of the other Sentinels led the young lords out of the hall, leaving the audience to their thoughts concerning the lords. From there, the Seven split up and made their way to their quarters.

"Go right to sleep," Goldarrow said to Tommy. "Tomorrow is the council, and many things must be decided."

"Things concerning us?"

Goldarrow put a kind hand on Tommy's shoulder. "Now that you have returned to Allyra, everything concerns you."

The High Council

THE SEVEN Lords waited at a large round table in the center of a well-lit chamber not far from Luminary Hall. Grimwarden was there, as were Goldarrow, the Sentinels, and Dreadnaughts who had survived the adventure on Earth, and a few other military leaders Tommy did not recognize. Surprisingly, even a few Gwar were in attendance. The Seven were taken aback at first, shocked that such villains would be allowed into the Chamber of Allegiance, let alone in Nightwish.

"Not all Gwar are evil," Goldarrow whispered to Tommy, seeing him wide-eyed. "Just as all Elves are not good."

He turned to look at her, brow wrinkled. "Really?"

"I expect it's no different on Earth," came a gruff voice from behind.

"Whoa!" said Kat, spinning around with the rest of the Seven. "You startled me—" She froze.

"Fulmooth Blandlard," said the Gwar. "Guard of the Aquifers, as of late." He extended a burly hand in greeting.

Kat looked to Goldarrow. A nod. "Pleased to meet you," Kat said as she tentatively grasped only one of his massive fingers. The Gwar did not smile; neither did he seem pleased at their meeting. *Great*, she thought. *Now I've offended him.* Fulmooth bowed his head in deference to the rest of the lords, then took his place among those who waited.

The uncomfortable encounter passed, and soon the room grew very silent. An ornate crystal chandelier, lit presumably by dozens of dremask flames, hung above the table. Tommy watched the flames dance and wondered just who exactly they were waiting for. He counted the empty chairs. There were seven. *Oh*, he thought. *The elders.*

As if on cue, the seven elders entered the chamber in a single line. They sat in the remaining seven seats. Jimmy leaned over to Jett and said, "Did yu notice . . . the high cleric didn' take the center seat."

"Yeah," said Jett. "Saw that. He didn't lead them in, either."

The elder in the center banged a gavel on the table. "I am Manaelkin Zoar, chief of elders and presider of this council," said the center elder.

"Oh," Jimmy and Jett muttered.

The chief elder lowered his hood, letting thin gray hair spill out on his shoulders. He looked to the seven young lords. "I apologize that we didn't have a more complete introduction last night," he said, tapping his chest with long, narrow fingers. "It was . . . a special evening. In fact"—he wiped the corner of his eye—"this is the first time we've convened the full council in eight hundred years."

Alwynn Belkirith nodded. "Every moment since the Seven have returned feels like a new blessing."

"Indeed," said Manaelkin. "For the benefit of the new lords, I'd like to start with an introduction. I am the senior member of the council, a dubious honor, since that means I am also the oldest Elf in the room." He paused for a smattering of soft laughs. "Nearly two thousand years of life—trial and much error—in Allyra has taught me a great deal. My wisdom, such as it is, I lend to this council. But I do not make the decisions. I am one voice among the many. That is all."

Manaelkin paused to let the assembly—especially the lords—ponder his words. Then with a sweeping gesture across the table he said, "Let us begin. Flet Marshall Brynn, you have news of the Spider King's movements?"

Brynn stood and crossed her wrists over her chest. Her wavy red locks bounced, and there was a gleam in her eye, but she was all business. "The Spider King's search parties continue in all parts of Allyra. We've spotted them as far west as Trulldore and as far north as the Hemlock Palisades. They are most numerous in the Thousand-League Forest of course, but they are wary and slow."

"They would expect us to create a stronghold among the trees," said Goldarrow for the benefit of the Seven.

"It has not yet entered his mind that we would stay below ground," said Grimwarden.

Kiri Lee raised her hand. Everyone stared at her curiously.

"I believe Lothriel has a question," said Miss Finney. "You're not in class anymore, Kiri Lee. You may speak freely here."

"Oh," she said, blushing. "Um . . . okay. I was wondering why wouldn't the Spider King expect the Elves—expect us, that is—to stay underground? Seems like a good place to hide."

The high cleric looked up sharply. Audience voices began talking. "Has no one told them?" he asked.

"There has never been a need," said Goldarrow, looking at Manaelkin. More murmuring. "On Earth, aboveground, there was no danger."

"Order!" Manaelkin rapped with his gavel until all was silent.

"I see." Alwynn nodded gravely. "Here, the danger is ever present. They must know."

Goldarrow stood and addressed the Seven. "Lords, you've heard us call our race 'Children of the Sun' or 'Children of Light'? These are not metaphors as one might think. Rather, there is an important reason for this." She paused. "Elves cannot live without sunlight."

"Whoa," said Jett. "You mean we'll die in the dark?"

"Only if you've had absolutely no sunlight for more than three days," said Goldarrow. "Even under cloud cover, you will still get enough of the sun through the clouds. On Earth, you knew this subconsciously. There were times when inexplicably you felt ill or weak. You probably felt drawn to go outside or at least to windows."

"Aye!" said Jimmy. "That's true. I canna' tell yu how many times in Ardfern, with the typical gloom, I felt . . . well . . . out of sorts."

"No wonder I like the beach so much," said Kat. "I always felt better there."

"That's right," said Goldarrow.

"But what happens now?" Johnny asked. "I mean, do we all go back to that hall and crank up the crystal?"

"No," Manaelkin replied. "We keep the opening above Luminary Hall sealed, except for special occasions. It is too risky to have anything for the Spider King's troops to discover so close to our main fortifications."

"How do we get sun, then?" asked Autumn. "It might help me heal faster."

"It would," said Grimwarden. "Just wait. You'll see."

"In the time we've been underground," Goldarrow continued, "we have increased our network of tunnels one-hundred fold. In various places beneath the Thousand-League Forest, we have constructed outcroppings and small clearings where the sunlight falls regularly. All Elves in our underground homeland have a scheduled time to sun themselves. We never use the same place twice in the same week, never for more than a few hours at a time, and never without a strong military escort nearby just in case."

An awkward silence descended. The young lords exchanged glances. Until the events of the past year, Tommy hadn't spent much time thinking about death. Then, with the attacks of the Drefids in Maryland, the fierce battles in Scotland, and the ambush in the Dark Veil, death had become a constant threat. One wrong step, one missed detail—it would all be over. But now . . . now there was another reason for fear. The lack of sunlight. Such a simple thing, really. *Not much different from water,* Tommy told himself. *Can't survive without water for more than a few days, right?* And yet, this was different. Every moment they spent underground, a clock was ticking. They can't bottle sunlight. It was then Tommy truly began to question if he should have come to Allyra at all. He knew it was a big deal, this whole *Lord of the Elves* thing and all, but he had no idea just how big. And that it might cost him his life? Well . . . maybe that was more than he could chew.

"Excuse me, Lord Manaelkin?" Tommy raised his hand. "But how long have we been underground, then? Like three days already, right?"

"Fear not, Seven Lords," said Manaelkin. "You have forgotten the glorious, colorful rays in Luminary Hall last night. Those will sustain you."

"Elder Manaelkin, if I may," said Brynn, standing. "There's more."

"Of course, Flet Marshall, please continue."

Brynn bowed her head. "As you know, the Spider King's forces have closed all of their usual portals into Earth. The last, of course, was the portal into Scotland. We've kept scouts in place to monitor them all, and they are still closed . . . abandoned, it seems."

"Surely the enemy knows of Sarron Froth's betrayal," said Ril Taniel, one of Grimwarden's esteemed generals from the Fall of Berinfell.

"I agree," said Grimwarden. "Sarron Froth provided us vital information for a time, but doubtless it will no longer be of any use."

"Pity we could not give him more in return," said Goldarrow.

"We gave him a chance to redeem himself," said Alwynn. "A place of friendship and peace when he drew his last breath . . . for Froth, there was infinite value."

The Gwar seemed especially moved by this statement, nodding their ascent.

Brynn nodded. "Every portal Froth mapped out for us has been closed," she summarized. "However, the Spider King has begun opening new portals."

"What?" Manaelkin started at the news. The Elves spoke openly among themselves now. The room buzzed. "Order!" The gavel banged again. "Why were we not made aware of this sooner?"

"My scouts from Vesper Crag have only just returned," answered Brynn. "All three of the new portals are in the Spider King's own realm. From our observations—perilous spycraft you should know—one of these portals is in almost constant use: Warspiders, legions of Gwar, cadres of Drefids. Many depart but few return."

"Where does this portal go?" asked Grimwarden. "Earth?"

"Likely," said Goldarrow. "Froth told us that the Spider King had yet to find another world with a suitable slave population."

"We've not been able to send a flet soldier through," said Brynn. "There is almost constant traffic there, and he keeps a legion of Gwar on station."

"We will need to monitor this situation carefully," said Manaelkin. "I do not know what the Spider King is doing, but I don't like it."

"Nor do I," said Grimwarden. "Brynn, increase the scouts entering Vesper Crag threefold."

"It is decided," said Manaelkin. "Thank you, Brynn. Your efforts, as always, are vital to our survival and our success. Endurance and Victory!"

"Thank you, Elder Manaelkin. I will personally see to the new scouts." Brynn bowed and took her seat.

There was some murmuring among the Sentinels until Manaelkin spoke again. "Now we turn to the primary reason for this hallowed gathering." He waited for full attention. "Beyond all hope, the young lords have returned to us. Long have we planned for this day. And as such, it is time to consummate our plans for rebellion. Guardmaster Grimwarden, as chief of the military, what is our timeline?"

Grimwarden stood. "Thank you, Elder Manaelkin. It is the recommendation of the Sentinels and Dreadnaughts that we take the young lords to Whitehall Castle to train them in Vexbane."

"Whitehall?" Manaelkin's eyes widened. "That is not an easy trek. Nor a secure location. . . . Why, it's aboveground. Have you lost your senses? Why there?"

Grimwarden made an attempt at diplomacy. "Surely you know. Whitehall is the birthplace of Vexbane, the combat style of our Dreadnaughts and our lords."

Manaelkin bristled. "Of course I know about Vexbane," he said. "Was I not trained by Aldarion Kel himself? But what need have the Seven of Vexbane? Their powers are waxing, and the enemy's surely wanes. You've fought two battles against the Spider King and won them both, have you not? What more should the Seven need to learn?"

Grimwarden ground his teeth. So much for diplomacy. "Has it escaped your notice, Elder Manaelkin, that there are far fewer Elves who have returned from those *stunning victories?* Has it escaped your notice that one of the lords was impaled on a Drefid's claw and nearly perished—precisely because her powers are raw? The lords must learn to hone their individual gifts so that they might use them together and thus be all the stronger. They are lords, yes, but lords raised in peace with no knowledge of war. They need training, time to adjust to our ways. They need the discipline of Vexbane. And we can only train them properly at Whitehall."

Manaelkin did not respond immediately. He turned questioning eyes to the other elders. Alwynn nodded in reply, but none of the others so much as twitched. Manaelkin turned back to Grimwarden. "Very well. Take them to Whitehall. How long?"

Grimwarden smiled. He didn't lose often. Not on the battlefield. And he wasn't about to be pushed around by a politician. "The training period depends mostly upon the lords," he said. "If they learn quickly, and we compress a year's worth of teaching—which I don't recommend, mind you—they may be fit for battle in six or seven months."

If Manaelkin's eyes had been volcanoes, they would have bathed everyone in the room in scalding hot lava, gas, and debris. "Six to seven months?! Have you gone completely mad? Eight hundred years of waiting, preparing, and training, and you want us all to wait longer? This . . . this is lunacy!" He threw his hands in the air. "One month. Nothing more. This is all you shall have. Do you contend?"

"Oh, dear"—whispered Goldarrow to Brynn—"this is not going well." Goldarrow knew the Guardmaster's quirks. She watched as Grimwarden's upper lip curled into a snarl, and his right eyelid twitched.

"Yes," said Grimwarden. "I contend." His whispered words were like the hiss of a drop of water flash vaporizing on smoldering plank.

"Very well," said Manaelkin. "Bring your witnesses. And be swift." Manaelkin banged his gavel.

Goldarrow was at Grimwarden's shoulder in an instant. "No, Olin," she whispered, holding tightly to his elbow.

"So help me, Elle, I'm going to take that gavel and—"

"Leave it be. See to your witnesses."

"You'll be one, won't you?" he asked.

She glared at Manaelkin. "I'll be first."

Stirring Convictions

GOLDARROW STOOD up behind the table and announced, "Elders, Dreadnaughts, fellow Sentinels, and Lords, we have come to a turning point in the history of Elvendom. The lords have returned, bringing us great hope to one day destroy our enemy and reopen the gates of Berinfell. The lords' returning is a gift . . . a gift that Elder Manaelkin would have us squander. For to push the young lords into battle before they are prepared is foolishness. The Spider King has not been idle these eight hundred years."

"I will answer!" announced the elder on Alwynn's left. He had bristling red eyebrows and a shaven head covered with reddish stubble. He stood and bowed. "I am Naramyn Sunfire and, along with Grimwarden, I have overseen our military preparations. We have not been idle, either, Sentinel Goldarrow. While you were away, we have grown our army to three times its greatest strength in Berinfell. We have improved our armor-craft. We have cultivated underground oceans of Nightwish flowers . . . for production of the spider weapons. And we have labored over war plans, detailed plans to invade the Spider King's stronghold in Vesper Crag and rid Allyra of his menace for good."

"I contend," said Goldarrow. "Elder Naramyn, have you seen the Seven Lords in action?"

Silence.

She waited.

He said nothing.

"Do you even know what their gifts are?"

"Well . . . I—I presume their powers . . . are the same as their forebears'."

"They are not, in fact, all the same," Goldarrow said, keeping her tone level. "All the preparations are meaningless if they do not include the lords; to say otherwise is blasphemy." A small tremor rippled around the room. "And all plans that include the lords are worthless unless they take into account the gifts of each lord, as well as how they work together. I yield my point for the next witness." Goldarrow sat down to a chorus of murmuring, but it was much louder on the elders' side.

"Your point is understood," said Manaelkin. "I am not against training the lords at all. But seven months? Now, listen, one and all. We cannot afford that kind of a delay. Our success—our very survival— could depend on the element of surprise. The Spider King has not reinforced his stronghold to prepare for a forward assault or even a siege. Up to now, he has not likely concerned himself with the possibility of an attack from Elves. In his eyes, he has beaten us down, scattered us, and left us without leaders. And in his mind, without hope. But he knows now that the lords have returned, and he knows that they were powerful enough to thwart his plans on Earth, as well as his ambush on the Dark Veil. At the very least, the Spider King will redouble his efforts to find us and fortify his stronghold. Every week we wait, he grows stronger."

"Wait," came a quiet voice from across the table. It was Autumn. "I mean, wait please." She looked to Nelly. "That is . . . if I can say something?"

Manaelkin's stony confidence softened. He said, "Of course you may speak, Lord Miarra. Please."

"Miarra," she echoed. "I love that name. It's so pretty. But it will take some getting used to. I'm still very much Autumn Briarman." With great effort and a squeaky kind of groan, she stood. "I want to tell you about something I did in battle back on Earth."

Nelly looked up. Johnny stared into his lap. The chamber became silent.

"The big battle," Autumn continued, "was in Scotland . . . outside Dalhousie Castle. Nelly, Johnny, and I . . . we got there late. Nelly told us to stay in a hiding spot while she entered the battle. She told us we weren't ready. But I didn't want to hear it. All those Elves . . . my family, sort of . . . and they were getting killed right in front of me. I couldn't just stand there and watch."

Manaelkin grinned knowingly. Indeed, Miarra had the blood of lords flowing in her veins.

"I didn't know what I was going to do," she went on. "But I went for it anyway. Nelly was already gone and far ahead. Johnny tried to stop me, but I wouldn't listen to him, either. I ran. And as I ran, something happened. I was moving faster and faster, but it took no extra effort. In a blink, I was in the midst of the battle. I found a sword, but more than that, I had found my gift. I used the supernatural speed and ran circles around the Gwar and Drefids. I . . . I think I killed a lot of them."

"We have heard your tale," said Manaelkin. "It was a valiant effort. And all the more reason we should—"

"No," Autumn said, her quiet reply shutting off the high elder like a slammed door. "No, I was not valiant. I was stupid. I should have listened to Nelly." She looked to Nelly, then to Johnny. "I should have listened to my broth—to Johnny. I used my speed the best I could, but it wasn't good enough. A Drefid got in my way. That's all he did. He just stood there, holding out his sharp finger blades, and I ran right into them. Thing is, I was going so fast . . . too fast. My eyes aren't used to that kind of speed. I didn't even see the blades until it was too late. Nelly was right. . . . I wasn't ready. I'm still not. And neither are the rest of us . . . not really. I'm sure Guardmaster Grimwarden here is a good teacher, and this Whitehall must be the perfect classroom for Vex-whatever-it's-called. But a few weeks, a month . . . well, that's just not going to be enough. We don't know what we can do . . . we barely know each other. Shoot, I can't even master everything they teach me in math in a school year. And that's ten months or something."

Autumn paused and scanned the room, everyone captivated by her. "I don't know how this vote is going to go. I'll . . . I'll do whatever you think is best. But I'd feel a lot better about this whole situation if I knew I had some time to adjust." She took a deep breath. "Thank you." Then she sat down.

Grimwarden beamed at Autumn. As did most of the Sentinels,

Dreadnaughts, and the other lords. The elders, for once, were not enveloped in murmurs. They sat placidly, eyes fixed.

Manaelkin seemed stunned. When he spoke again, there was little conviction and none of the confidence from before. "We have heard enough," he said. "I call now for the vote."

The quiet discussion and murmurs continued as attendants served each weighing member for the vote, handing them two candles. "The choice before you," said Manaelkin, "will likely determine the fate of Elfkind on Allyra. Light the purple candle if our people would be better served by the lords spending at least half a year at Whitehall. Blue if you believe one month of training and a swift and sudden attack on Vesper Crag will ensure our victory. Choose well."

Tommy leaned over to Kat once more. "Well?"

"Just a sec," she replied, staring and squinting. "Things have changed," Kat whispered. "I think." She was quiet a few moments more, listening to conversations in her mind. "Many of the Elves are remembering the Spider King's attack on Berinfell. It was a surprise attack. Some believe that was the only reason the enemy won. It seems like many are leaning toward Manaelkin's plan."

"Throw us right into war again?" Tommy shook his head. "I definitely don't like that plan."

"Yeah," said Kat. "Me, either."

"So what's going on now? Can you tell what they're—?"

"Shhh!" She shook her head. "I can't . . . hear . . . strange." Voices whirled in and out of her mind. She'd isolate one for a moment . . . and try to place the voice. Voice, that was what she called it, for most Elves subconsciously put their thoughts into their own voices. She'd heard Alwynn once. . . . *"But they're so young."*

She heard Manaelkin. *"Ridiculous. We shouldn't even be having"* . . .

But then, then a strange stream of thoughts pushed momentarily through the others.

. . . *"journey to Whitehall"* . . .

. . . *"fortunate turn"* . . .

. . . *"must not be seen"* . . .

. . . *"slaughter"* . . .

Kat sat bolt upright and scanned the room. *Slaughter? Who?* Her gaze fell in turn upon every Elf in the room, but she didn't recognize the voice. And no facial expressions revealed anything she could connect to those thoughts. Something about the Seven Lords going to Whitehall . . . had to be, but Kat didn't know what the last couple of thoughts meant. They might have meant nothing at all, just random words. Maybe even from several different Elves. No, not unless several Elves sounded alike. That handful of phrases had been uttered in one voice.

"You okay?" asked Tommy.

"Yeah, yeah," she replied. "Fine . . . I thought I heard something a little strange."

"Like what?"

"Ah, it was nothing," she said, still wondering. "I really need to learn to focus better." *Duh,* she thought. *Maybe the voice wasn't an elder at all.* She looked at the Sentinels, who, for the most part, were silent. Intense, but silent. Kat felt an odd weight on her left shoulder and whipped around. Mr. Wallace was staring hard, seemingly at Goldarrow. *But . . . was he staring at me?*

"Ignite the Flame of Conviction," Manaelkin instructed.

Each of the Elves with voting privileges put up a previously unnoticed metal screen, hiding the candles from others' view. Once these were in place, the Elves began to vote.

"Ah, this is going to drive me crazy," said Tommy.

"Uh-huh," said Kat, but she wasn't really paying attention to her friend or to the vote. Her mind was so intensely focused on trying to single out that one thought-voice again that she couldn't really attend to anything else.

Jett leaned over to Jimmy. "What's going to ha—?"

"I'm not tellin' yu," he replied quickly. "Those screens are there for a reason, yu know."

"That's just cold, Jimmy," Jett complained.

Seconds felt like hours as votes were cast. Finally, when all the Elves had looked up and given Manaelkin nonverbal assent, the council leader said, "Reveal your conviction."

Screens fell one by one. A blue candle lit. A purple candle lit.

Another blue. From his vantage, Tommy couldn't see all of the candles. Perhaps no one could except Manaelkin. Tommy thought that maybe it was designed that way. From what Tommy could see, the vote seemed very even . . . surprisingly even. The other lords gazed around the room as well. But Tommy saw Autumn close her eyes and bow her head. *What does that mean?*

Manaelkin's gaze seemingly followed the candles around the room, and at first, he began to smile.

"Oh no," Tommy whispered.

But then his expression hardened. Manaelkin hammered down his gavel and announced, "By three votes . . . the Lords of Berinfell will travel to Whitehall. There they will train and learn the art of Vexbane under the tutelage of Guardmaster Grimwarden for a period of no more than seven months. Your convictions have spoken. Let it now be done." He slammed down his gavel once more.

Polite cheers rang out. Goldarrow clapped Grimwarden on the shoulder. Most of the other lords surrounded Autumn in a group hug. Only Kat hung back. She was relieved they could train longer, but her enthusiasm was drained by the voice she had heard. *Slaughter. What did that mean?*

Grimwarden stood before the council in the final hour of the meeting, recapping the plans they had all drafted years earlier of an attack on Vesper Crag, anticipating the eventual return of the Seven. The meeting room had thinned somewhat, leaving only the lords, the most senior Sentinels, military leaders, and members of the council. While the young lords still required training, a full-fledged siege was still at the forefront of everyone's mind and needed to be addressed. "As you all are well aware, we've a sound plan for the initial attack and a prolonged blockade. However, I fear that what we really need the most is something we can no longer obtain." Grimwarden searched his memory, recalling his many conversations with Sarron Froth. Without the defecting Drefid's help, the portals would have remained a mystery to the Elves . . . the Seven would have never been found. But Froth had additional secrets, and the revelations of his most recent and final project might have proved invaluable . . . had Grimwarden only pushed the Drefid harder. He scolded himself now.

"Do not punish yourself further," Goldarrow spoke up. "What's past is past. We cannot change it."

Tommy leaned over to Kat. "What are they talking about?" he whispered.

Kat scrunched her face. "Something about . . . a map."

"Not just any map," Grimwarden said, startling them both. "*The* map of Vesper Crag." And with those words he withdrew a long cloth parchment from his belt. He laid it out on the table. The Seven all leaned in to take a closer look. The map showed a definite outline of a region, but only one corner of the map was filled in. Paths, symbols, codes—all sketched in rich black ink—no one but a master cartographer could have worked such fine detail and craftsmanship.

The Seven studied the parchment, each trying to understand the markings. Then Johnny and Autumn blurted out as one, "We know that map!"

All eyes went to the pair. Grimwarden's face changed in an instant to a mask of disbelief and . . . hope. "You know this map?"

Autumn looked to Johnny. "It's in our house," he said.

"Under my bed!" added Autumn.

"Impossible," Goldarrow said. "No one on Earth would have such a map as this."

"We found it in our backyard," said Johnny. ". . . In a field behind our house. Autumn picked it up."

"When we found the cave, with the book, and the weird wall," Autumn rambled.

"Weird wall?" Grimwarden begged.

"The book Nelly gave us"—Johnny looked at the map—"had a picture in the front that resembled a cave on our neighbor's land, Mr. Rizzo. So we went there and found the weirdest thing."

"Half a footprint," said Autumn. "Like a solid stone wall had cut it in half . . . like a person—"

"Had walked right through," finished Grimwarden.

Johnny smacked himself in the head with the palm of his hand. "It was a portal!"

"Yes, a portal!" said Nelly. "I told you that before, but you said nothing of finding a map."

"We didn't know," said Johnny. "Is it important?"

"Is it—?" Grimwarden half chuckled, half sighed. "Vital, but that's only if it is a map of Vesper Crag."

"Yes," said Manaelkin skeptically. "There are many maps that show many things."

"No," said Johnny. "I know that this is right. See, I thought the outline here and here was shaped like Sam when he lays down on the back porch."

"Sam?" Manaelkin inquired, his fiery eyebrows raised.

"Our dog," said Autumn.

"A dog is like a wolf," said Nelly, clarifying the strange word for the group.

Johnny frowned and went back to the map. "Yeah, but it's the same shape here . . . and here. Just like Sam's ears. And . . . up here, there should be a tower . . . or a platform or something."

Grimwarden was stunned. "That's right! That would be the Black Balcony near the pinnacle of the mountain. You could only know that if it was on your map. You . . . you found this in your . . . what did you call it? Back card?"

"Our backyard," corrected Autumn.

"Let me be sure I have understood you," Alwynn said, seemingly fighting back a grin. "You have the rest of this map secured back in your home on Earth?"

"Yeah," said Johnny.

"You're certain?"

"Absolutely!" replied Autumn. "I hid it myself. No one would ever find it."

Tommy raised his hand. "Excuse me. But why all the fuss about this map? I mean, I think I have a better idea here, one we're not thinking of."

"Go on, Lord Felheart," motioned Grimwarden to Tommy.

"If we're going to talk about bringing things back from Earth, we have weapons the Spider King could never dream of! Rifles, pistols! I'm sure some of the Dreadnaughts could help me find some machine guns on the black market."

"Black market, Tommy?" asked Kat doubtfully.

"Okay. Maybe online. You know, eBay. We could totally blast—"

"Lord Felheart," Grimwarden cut him off. "These weapons you speak of . . . are they made of metal?"

"Yeah, of course."

He smiled. "While they might be worthy additions to our arsenal, we could never bring them back."

"Some sort of time-space continuum issue?" proposed Tommy.

"Uh-no, Lord Felheart. Nothing inorganic, especially metals, can come through the portals. Conducting electrical currents in the gateways is not a good idea."

"Oh." Tommy's eyes lit up. "Kind of like putting a fork in the microwave. I did that once." The Elves didn't understand. In the awkward silence, Tommy leaned over to Kat and whispered, "I'd hate to be the Elf who first discovered *that* scientific fact. *Zzzap!*" Kat dipped her head and giggled.

Alwynn looked to Johnny and Autumn. "If this map is as you say, Lord Albriand, Lord Miarra, then we have no choice but to at least attempt a retrieval."

Everyone grew very quiet, looking one to another. Finally Johnny spoke up. "I'll go."

"Whoa!" Tommy exclaimed. "Johnny, there are soldiers there. You heard Flet Marshall Brynn. Lots of soldiers."

"Tommy's right," said Nelly. "But not just because of the soldiers. You, my young lord, need to train. I know the way to your home. I will go."

"With your leave," said Regis to Grimwarden, "I will go, too."

"What about the enemy?" asked Jimmy. "Yu could be takin' a great risk."

"An entire war host is a great risk," Regis admitted. "But, Jimmy, that map isn't just a general diagram like a street map of Glasgow. A map of Vesper Crag will show us the weak points in the Spider King's walls, the locations of his defensive war machines, armories, spider nurseries, and"—she paused, collecting her thoughts—"the slave camps."

"Slave camps?" asked Kiri Lee.

"Where he takes the people he's abducted from Earth to work, building his war machine. Some are taken as kids, so they are able to learn the trades of war and become more efficient when they grow up."

Tommy finally broke the silence. "We have to save them."

"Agreed," said Grimwarden.

"Without the map—," Manaelkin began.

"It would be impossible," finished Grimwarden.

"Still," said Goldarrow. "There's no guarantee Nelly and Regis will get through. Should we not send a battalion of flet soldiers and a rank of archers . . . storm the portal?"

Manaelkin shook his head. "You speak my mind as well, Goldarrow," he said. "I am a firm believer in overwhelming force. In this instance, however, stealth is our best hope. A frontal attack will only draw out the Spider King's interest. . . . He might even close the portal altogether."

"You will go blindly through the portal," said Grimwarden. "We do not know where on Earth you will appear. There's even a small chance that the Spider King has found another world to occupy. It could all be for naught. Nelly, Regis, are you certain you want to volunteer for this task?"

"I am certain," said Nelly.

Jimmy eyed Regis. *Please don't go.* The only one who heard his thoughts, of course, was Kat.

"As am I," said Regis.

Grimwarden raised his chin and nodded. "Very well. It does present its own set of difficulties, however."

Tommy waved his hands about. "You mean, besides sneaking through an entire war host set on killing them and having no idea where the portal spits them out?"

"Yes, Tommy," said Grimwarden, "besides those."

"Like what?" Tommy asked.

"Time." All eyes turned to Alwynn. "If Nelly and Regis are gone for but only one hour on Earth, that is almost three days for us here. Depending on where that portal 'spits them out,' as you say, it could be weeks for us. Maybe even months."

"Still, it is a risk we have to take," said Nelly.

Goldarrow sighed. "But it means—"

"We'll have to leave immediately," said Regis.

"Agreed," said Alwynn.

Grimwarden hesitated. He looked at the Seven. "Agreed." He stood up straight. "We base as much of our planning as possible around having that map in hand."

"And if it doesn't come back?" Manaelkin asked.

Grimwarden said curtly, "Then we will remain in hiding until it does."

"You mean a decision will be made by the council, don't you?"

Grimwarden turned his back and as he walked away said, "Of course."

Paying the Price

FERRAL DRAGGED his burden past six gates. None of the Gwar sentries offered to help. "Where is he?" Ferral asked. "The throne room?"

One of the guards emitted a wet snort. "Bah, throne room? Not hardly."

"Haven't seen him in the throne room since last Norander, heh-heh," said the other guard. "He's in his Plotting Chamber . . . practically sleeps there."

"Foul mood today," said the first guard. "I hope you've brought him good news."

Ferral inwardly cringed. He'd spent most of the long journey back from the Dark Veil thinking about how he'd break the news. *What does it matter? What is the worst the Spider King would do? He could lock me up and make me work in the pits. He might kill me.* Ferral shrugged. After what he'd been through, he was ready to die . . . if need be.

Ferral cast a derisive look at the two guards. "Lazy, the lot of you. After the leagues I've trod, you'd think one of you might lend a hand."

"What? And leave my post unattended?" asked the first guard.

"Perish the thought," said the other, laughing harshly.

Struggling for a better grip on the huge sack he was dragging, Ferral snorted and continued down the corridor. Just before he passed out of range, he heard a final exchange between the guards.

"He smells overripe, that one," said one guard. "Horrible."

"Yeah," the other replied. "Smelled like he'd been struck by a bolt in the Lightning Fields."

Ferral was half-tempted to go back and twist both their heads off, but he refrained for he had more pressing business. He traversed a tall arched hallway and found the stairwell he needed. It spiraled up, and Ferral found that dragging his burden was harder. The heavy sack slid from one step to the next, each one bringing with it a wet slapping kind of thud, until he reached the top and ducked under an arch to enter the passage.

Torches lit the right side of the hallway, and Ferral followed them to the Plotting Chamber at the end of the hall. The door was open, and the room was well lit by torches, braziers, and gigantic candle chandeliers. Ferral looked up to the high domed ceiling and wondered whose job it was to keep all those candles lit. *No thank you,* thought Ferral. He didn't care much for heights. That's why he'd volunteered for infantry. "Better get going," he muttered. "Or it will be my job."

It was a vast L-shaped chamber, and between the evenly spaced pillars on either side enormous steer-skin maps were stretched taut. Each of these, Ferral knew, represented one of the Spider King's victorious campaigns. Many battles against the Elves of Berinfell were there. And the slow, methodical annihilation of the Saer. Ferral had fought in the last battle against the Saer. The Spider King had commissioned the greatest fleet of warships ever assembled, and they'd at last taken the battle to the Saer's home island. *Now that,* Ferral thought, *was a glorious victory.* Having been a part of several such battles galled Ferral even more that his battalion had been ambushed so easily.

Somehow, his burden seemed even heavier now. Ferral slogged it across the floor, rumpling up several animal-skin mats. He turned the corner and saw the Spider King hunched over a table at the far end. He seemed so riveted, so utterly engrossed, that Ferral thought he might not have noticed he had a visitor. Still, Ferral wasn't about to break protocol and speak before being addressed. So he stood and watched his king, master of the Gwar race.

The sickle-shaped pupils of the Spider King's large half-moon eyes remained fixed, boring down on the map from their red irises. Like all Gwar, he was gray-skinned and mostly bald. But his skin was darker than most, more the slate gray of a tombstone or a thundercloud. And his fierce, dark eyebrows arched and then flared back over his scalp in a continuous strip that stretched all the way down to the back of his neck. A third strip of hair began like a sharp arrowhead above the center of his brow and swept all the way back like the other two.

Ferral watched and waited. The Spider King stared down at a map of the Thousand-League Forest. He never took his eyes off it but took out a stick of char and drew a painfully straight line, then another. When he was finished, the Spider King had drawn a diamond-shaped region, one of many such areas, Ferral noticed.

The Gwar ruler grasped a handful of figurines, Warspiders, Gwar, Drefids, and Wisps, carved from volcanic rock, and slammed them down one at a time—each with a sharp *thok!*—in the sector he had just outlined. Then, his elbows on the table, he dropped his head into his hands and went completely still.

"Ferral," said the Spider King without looking up, "where is your commander?"

The sudden voice so startled Ferral that he dropped the end of his sack. He bowed low to reach for it and said, "He is dead, my sovereign."

"Dead," he repeated, still not looking up. "*Mm . . . hum.* That . . . is unfortunate." The Spider King's voice was not as deep as some Gwar, but carried a resonant weight of its own. Even short responses sounded clever and calculated. To speak with the Spider King was to feel perpetually on edge and cautious, for undoubtedly the trap was already set.

"There's more," said Ferral. "Mobius . . . his plans failed. He even took half of our team for reinforcements. No one came back through the portal except . . . except for the Elves."

The Spider King stopped scanning the map. "The Lords of Berinfell . . . they have returned, then?"

"Yes," Ferral said in a half mutter, half growl. "It was by their hand that Mobius was laid low. We chased them to the Dark Veil, cornered them, and fought. But their powers were too much."

"Powers?" The Spider King swiped up one of the Gwar figures from the map. "*Hmmm* . . . they've reached the Age of Reckoning, then. Are you sure?"

"Certain, my king."

"Certain. Really?" With a flick of his thick thumb, the Spider King snapped the head off of the figurine. It bounced onto the tabletop and off onto the floor. "*Certain* is such a profound word. How can you be so sure?"

Ferral whisked out a tarnished dagger, slit the rope tie, and then upended the sack. The charred thing that rolled out onto the stone floor had once been a Gwar, that much was clear from its broad frame. But the figure was burned beyond recognition, a blackened husk.

"One of the Seven, the firehand, he sent forth streams of flame, flame that adhered to whatever it touched and would suffer no effort to extinguish it." Ferral growled under his breath.

"I have seen that sort of fire before," said the Spider King. He stood up straight at last, shrugged his massive shoulders, and—with a sudden twist of his pointed chin—cracked the joints in his neck. His eerie eyes fell on Ferral. "It is a devastating weapon. Tell me, Ferral— how then did you escape?"

"I hid," Ferral replied honestly, "in a cleft of rock beyond the reach of the flame. Someone needed to return to Vesper Crag, to bear you news."

"Did they now?"

"But I watched from that height. And I saw many things."

"Tell me."

Ferral smiled inwardly. He knew his information would prove valuable. How valuable? He had no idea, but he wasn't going to throw it out all at once, but rather let the Spider King ask for it. "One of the Seven is injured, perhaps mortally," he said. "A girl . . . she was car- ried the entire time by the Berylinian lord."

"If she dies," said the Spider King, "the whole group will be diminished. I suppose that's too much to hope for. What else?"

"The Elves have compromised the Dark Veil."

"Yes," said the Spider King. "That is how they defeated your battalion."

"What I mean, my king, is that the Elves had a garrison of archers hidden within the Veil."

"They did not alert our border guards?"

"No, they were there already . . . waiting for us. And when they were convinced that we were finished, they disappeared with the Seven into the canyon."

The Spider King's eyes narrowed for a moment. He stroked his dark goatee all the way down to its carefully trimmed point. He looked down at the map of the Thousand-League Forest. "Of course," he said. And then he began to laugh. The chiseled muscle in his upper chest flexed as he laughed, deep, hearty guffaws that filled the room with sound. He arched his head back and roared with laughter. His mirth stopped abruptly, and the Spider King swept his hand across the map, sending figures skipping across the table and tearing three-jagged rifts in the animal skin.

"My king?" said Ferral tentatively.

"My good Ferral," said the Spider King, "you have just solved the greatest mystery of this age. Where have the Elves of Berinfell gone? Thousands fled the city, this we knew. But in eight hundred years of searching, we were never able to determine their new location."

"And . . . now you know? Surely not the Veil?"

"No." He laughed out the words, "Not the Veil. Underground, Ferral. There are catacombs beneath the Dark Veil, running far to the west. Did you know that?"

Ferral shook his head.

"Yes, we used to mine a dremask vein there . . . before we found a better source. We never did explore those twisting passages beneath the ground. That was a miscalculation. We all believed the Elves would go to their strength—into the trees. There they could oppose us with some success or . . . lose themselves for hundreds of years. No . . . instead, they went to their weakness."

"I still don't understand," said Ferral.

"The Elves cannot bear to part with the sun . . . it will kill them, if they remain secluded in darkness long enough. But they have gone beneath the surface . . . and they have access to this place via the huge storehouses of water—aquifers—beneath the Veil. I will send a thousand scouts to investigate. But in the meantime I must alter the scope of our search."

"How so?"

"We must catch them in the sun," said the Spider King. "They must come up. They must. As they have been for quite some time, it seems. We need to search the clearings in the forest, shelves of rocky mountains, the high branches of the tallest trees. Anyplace where they might soak in the sun."

"But we have not wings," said Ferral.

"No," said the Spider King. "Not yet. But we will."

Ferral scratched at his own briar patch of beard. "I am not sure what you mean, my king, but we may not need wings after all. There's one more bit of news."

"Go on."

"There is a Wisp among the Elves."

The Spider King tilted his head to the side and raised an eyebrow. "A Wisp? How could you possibly know that?"

"I saw one of the Elves dissolve into smoke and then re-form."

"You saw this . . . in the Dark Veil? Even with the ambient gloom in that place?"

"There was a great fire behind him. I could see him plainly. The Elf stumbled, dissipated into smoke, and then re-formed. He, in Elven likeness, ran off with the others as if he were one of them."

"The beauty of those creatures," said the Spider King. "And how useful. They can vanish as fast as thinking only to materialize moments later in the guise of anyone. For all you know, Ferral, I might be a Wisp."

Uncomfortable silence hung between them. A flickering shadow fell over Ferral, and when he turned to look, he nearly jumped out of his skin. A hooded Drefid stood behind Ferral. *I am going to die,* Ferral thought as he looked up into the Drefid's cold white eyes.

"Good to see you, Asp," said the Spider King. "I hoped you'd come today."

"I have much news," he said, his voice like ice scraped across rough stone. Asp lowered his hood. From Ferral's angle it looked like the Drefid was crowned with fire. But it was only the candle chandelier hanging behind him.

"There's been quite a lot of news shared here today," the Spider King said, gesturing at Ferral.

"You know about Mobius, then?" asked the Drefid.

"Yes, and much more," said the Spider King. "But I have many things to discuss with you. The muster on Earth proceeding as planned?"

"Of course," said Asp.

The Spider King nodded. "As I thought." He came around the table and stood beside Ferral. "Wait here then, would you?" he said to the Drefid. "I have some things to show Ferral. He has been of great service to our cause."

Asp nodded. "As you say."

The Spider King led Ferral out of the Plotting Chamber and down a dimly lit auxiliary hallway toward the rear of the fortress. It smelled of old metal and something else, a pungent, stinging aroma. In silence, they came to a large arched door made of blackened iron. The Spider King reached into the collar of his tunic and pulled out a thick key. He held it up for Ferral to see and then slipped it into the keyhole and turned it. There was an echoing metallic click.

When the door swung open, a wall of heat washed over Ferral . . . heat and stench. "You possess more wisdom than the average Gwar infantryman," said the Spider King. "I wish to expose you to more of our operation, our ultimate plan. Would you like that?"

"Yes, my sovereign," said Ferral, amazed. Things had worked out much better than he'd hoped.

"Then follow me and listen."

The first eighty yards of this narrow tunnel were completely dark. Ferral walked cautiously behind the Spider King, listening to his master's voice and taking great care not to accidentally cause him to trip or stumble. The scent was menacing, bringing tears to his eyes.

"Yes, Ferral, it was incredibly shrewd of you to escape from the Elves at the Veil. The news you brought has left me breathless with new plans. Underground . . . who would have thought the Elves would go underground, so far from their precious sun? Children of Light, *bah*!"

Red light from far ahead began to illuminate the passage, and soon the tunnel walls vanished as the Spider King and Ferral emerged into an enormous cavern. The heat was more oppressive, and there was a peculiar deep throbbing, more felt than heard. But it was the myriad of sights that stopped Ferral in his tracks.

The path upon which they now stood stretched hundreds of yards across the cavern. Curving ramparts, some going up, some down, branched off from the main path like dozens of arteries from some massive organ. The vast floor area was lined with octagonal sections like honeycombs. These were all sizes, and some of them were covered with white filaments of webbing. And moving among them were beings whom Ferral mistook for Elves. They were everywhere. Some wheeled wooden carts full of sickly yellowish orbs. Others carried crinkled spider skins on their backs. Still others were on their hands and knees dipping cloths into barrels of some clear gelatinous substance and wiping it onto small sections of the honeycomb. And everywhere Ferral turned, there were Gwar taskmasters roaming the ramparts. Their whips, cudgels, and polearms were busy keeping the slaves focused and busy.

"Humans, Ferral," said the Spider King as he began to walk again. "They are tending to the spider fields, building our army, a force powerful enough to conquer two worlds."

"Two?" Ferral squinted. The air burned his eyes. "You mean . . . Earth?"

"You are most assuredly officer quality," said the Spider King. "Yes, Earth. It is fertile ground for our expansion. They are simple, reliant on their technology, and very, very soft. Even now, we are planning an invasion of their pretty world. Slaves used to be enough. But not anymore."

They had traversed more than half of the main passage. Ferral saw much larger honeycombs here, many covered in a thin drape of webbing. Warspiders teemed within. Then he saw something that made him turn away. Quick as lightning, one of the larger Warspiders darted over its chamber, impaled a slave, and dragged him back.

"Unpleasant, isn't it?" said the Spider King. "Horrible way to die. And you know, I heard that spider's thoughts. It was ravenous, like so many here."

As far as Ferral was concerned, the sooner they arrived at the other side of the cavern, the better. Timidly he asked, "Sir, do you think I might play a role in the conquest of this other world?"

"Yes, I do," he replied. "That's why I brought you down here. You needed . . . a broader perspective."

They reached the other side and left the cavern behind. Climbing a curling, torch-lit staircase burrowed deep into the heart of the mountain, the Spider King spoke over his shoulder to Ferral. "Earlier, Ferral, you said Mobius's plan failed. Do you remember?"

"Yes, my king," puffed Ferral, out of breath from the climb.

"Good . . . then you should know that Mobius had no plan of his own making. It was my plan. And, Ferral . . . my plans do not fail. They can be improperly . . . *executed* . . . and that is what happened, I assure you."

"Of course, m'lord." Ferral swallowed and warned himself not to get too comfortable around the Spider King. *I've already put my foot in my mouth once . . . best keep quiet.*

The stairs ended at yet another iron door, and they entered an oval chamber about thirty yards across. Torches lined the interior, interspersed with a variety of statues in shallow alcoves. In the center, two throne seats looked out through a large window into a cavern of unguessable depth. The Spider King stood in front of the thrones and stared into the darkness. He seemed to be waiting.

During the silent pause, Ferral found himself wondering about the thrones. Two seats carved from white stone by a masterful artist, they rose up from the floor like living things. Grooved milky-white bark, marbled through by slender black veins, these seats looked like trees that had grown into the shape of chairs. Curiously, the left-hand throne was dingy and scratched, its white stone smudged as if by years of use . . . and the clinging ash of Vesper Crag. But the right-hand seat, this appeared newly hewn and polished with great care. It almost glowed with its stark, ghostly white.

"You've shown great initiative, Ferral," said the Spider King, gesturing for Ferral to join him at the gaping window. "Initiative and wisdom. Perhaps I should make you an officer, a commander even. What do you say to that?"

Ferral bowed low before answering. "I have no words, my king, only thanks. I am at your service in whatever capacity you see fit."

The Spider King nodded eagerly. "I believe you are even more than commander material, my good Gwar. I have in mind a special distinction for you."

Incredulous of his good fortune, Ferral bowed again. "Sir?"

"In my army, there are many commanders . . . many more officers besides. But very few, save the Gwar and Drefid elites, earn such an honor as I am about to bestow upon you." His dark cloak spreading like a bat's wing, the Spider King laid his heavy arm on Ferral's shoulders. "As you know, Ferral, I do not spend very much time in my . . . more formal throne room. I linger in my Plotting Chamber, and . . . I come here to meet with my queen."

Ferral looked up. *Queen?* This was the first he had ever heard of her.

"Would you like to meet my queen?"

"If it pleases you, lord . . . I would consider it an honor above all rank."

"You are well-spoken," said the Spider King. With a sudden, irresistible thrust of his arm, he shoved Ferral forward, over the edge of the window. Ferral's body skidded off the slick stone. He scraped and flailed for a hold . . . and fell.

"See if you can talk your way out of this," said the Spider King. He backed away from the window and sat in the unclean throne. He let his head fall into his right hand and absently stroked the clean throne with his left hand. Then he waited for the inevitable.

"WHAT HAVE YOU DONE?" Ferral shrieked in agony. His left leg was broken. And he felt something warm oozing down his face. Blood most likely. He lay helpless, his back to the same sheer wall of stone he had slid down moments before. Ferral had nowhere to go. "WHY DID—?" He heard movement just beyond. "There's something down here!" He clawed at the slate behind him. But the twisting of his body jarred his leg, sending a jolt of pain up his spine. "Let me out! LET ME OUT!!"

There was gray light above but only black ahead. And yet, there was something there. At first, he heard a faint clicking sound. Then a harsh scrape, like someone dragging a pickaxe across stone.

His heart beat wildly.

Ferral lunged awkwardly to his side, hoping for escape, and put his hand in something sticky. He recoiled, jerking his arm backward. There was something on his hand, crawling across his fingers. He shook his hand violently, then froze. A loud, undulating hiss came out of the darkness. It was close.

Very close.

Safety Above

THE EVENING after the Elven High Council Meeting, Nelly and Regis slipped away from Nightwish Caverns under cover of darkness. On foot, this Sentinel and Dreadnaught, respectively, were known to be among the most woodcrafty and stealthy of all the Elven military leaders. But for the sake of speed, they were willing to take some risks. They rode rangesteeds, a curious cross of a bull and swift-tailed deer, and galloped east through the Thousand-League Forest. They would give the ruins of Berinfell a wide birth and make haste across the valleys before abandoning their mounts and picking their way across the Lightning Fields to Vesper Crag. There, by Ellos's hand, they would sneak into the portal and vanish from Allyra.

Later that same night, Grimwarden found Mr. Wallace pacing outside of Autumn's room in the infirmary. "How is she?" asked the Guardmaster.

"I wish I could tell you," Mr. Wallace replied. "Claris won't let me in to see her. I've been waiting more than an hour."

"Good heavens! Is something wrong?"

"Judging by all the inane giggling I've been hearing, I don't think so. Ah, I cannot wait any longer. I will come back some other time." Mr. Wallace departed by the winding hall, vanishing in the flicker of dremask torches.

Grimwarden was not nearly so patient. He had to see Autumn. He knocked briskly on the chamber door and announced, "Grimwarden here to see Lord Miarra." He put his ear to the door and heard a staccato burst of laughter. That was too much for Grimwarden. There was very little that made him angrier than being forced to wait. One exception was being laughed at. "Now see here—!" he said as he barged in. He stopped short as Autumn cartwheeled by, missing the door by only a few inches. Grimwarden watched her land with a perfect round-off near the far side of the chamber. "Autumn?" he asked absently.

"It is," said Claris, sitting on the edge of Autumn's bed.

"Remarkable!" Grimwarden exclaimed. "Autumn, do you feel quite well?"

"I feel much better," she replied. "Did you see my tumbling run? I can do a handspring. Wanna see?"

"Um, no thank you," he said. "I've seen quite enough, I think." He turned to Claris. "There's no one among the Elves whose medical opinion I value more than yours, Claris, but are you sure Autumn ought to be doing such things as . . . handsprings?"

"I know how this must look, Guardmaster," Claris answered, standing out of respect. "But all that remains of her wounds are healthy pink scars. What perplexes me the most is Autumn's internal healing. When I first dressed her, I was more than a little afraid that the Drefid had pierced her liver . . . her stomach, too. She was in great pain, and the region looked an ugly purple as if infection had already begun. Now, she seems as fine as can be. My salves and medicines have never worked this quickly. Perhaps we have witnessed a healing by Ellos?"

"Perhaps," said Grimwarden. "I mean . . . any healing is by Ellos's hand. But I would have thought the wound would have required much more time to heal, especially after all that bouncing around with Jett and, of course, the turbulent waters of Daladge Falls."

"Do you suppose Autumn has a dual gift?" asked Claris. "Could it be that she is also a quick healer like Jett?"

"If she is," Grimwarden replied, "it would be the first time that gift manifested in that bloodline. . . ." His words trailed off and he remained thoughtful for a moment. "Well, whatever the reason, I am delighted to see Autumn"—he paused as Autumn cartwheeled by— "doing so well. I came to find out how soon Autumn will be in shape enough to make the journey to Whitehall."

"She could leave tomorrow," Claris said.

"Tomorrow? That is spectacular news!" said Grimwarden. "We'll leave tomorrow night, then."

"We?"

"Yes, Claris. I want you to join us. You have staff enough here." He thumped a meaty fist into his open palm, then winced because of his wound. "Given the nature of Vexbane, combined with the young lords' gifts . . . accidents are bound to happen."

After more than two hours of twisting, turning tunnels—always rising, sometimes steeply—the Elven party bound for Whitehall entered a wide cave. Its sides seemed coated with thick moss. It smelled of the deep woods, of leaves decomposing into mulch, and of damp earth.

"Did you feel that?" asked Kat.

"What?" asked Kiri Lee.

"A breeze," she replied. "Just a whisper. It felt cool. Nice."

"Aye," said Jimmy. "I felt it. Smelled it, too. Fresh, like the moors in Ardfern . . . in the mornin'."

"We're nearly out," said Grimwarden. "Our stonewrights have done a magnificent job venting Nightwish and its myriad passages, but still . . . the air of the underground is never as clean . . . never as sweet."

The Seven had been given short swords just in case, and Tommy—though his gift was still far from mature—was given an extra quiver of arrows for the journey. Grimwarden led the way, followed by Goldarrow, Claris, Brynn, Mr. Spero, and the Seven. Anna and Miss Finney stayed behind to tend to their duties in Nightwish. Mr. Wallace and a thick-calved female Elf called Mum Bathers, or simply Mumthers as she liked to be called, brought up the rear. Unfortunately for Mr. Wallace, Mumthers liked to talk.

"You just wait, dear," she said to Mr. Wallace. "When we make camp, I'll fix us such a stew! Taters, I have, golden and savory. Rubbages and climbing garlic, too. We'll throw in some salted pork. Oh, my mouth is watering already."

Mr. Wallace did not reply.

Mumthers waited. And waited.

"Oh," said Mr. Wallace at last. "I'm sure your stew is delicious."

Mumthers smiled, gratified. "Oh, it will be," she replied, taking a very deep breath, which was very deep indeed due to the barrel-like nature of her rib cage. "Why, this stew recipe comes down three generations, it does. My great-gram learned it from an old Taladrim trader out west of the forest, and . . ."

To Mr. Wallace's great discomfort, Mumthers's tale went on for quite some time. But even the history of Taladrim stew had to pause when they passed out of the cave into the cool of the night.

"It wasn't a cave at all," gasped Tommy. He stared in disbelief at the massive fallen tree from which they emerged.

"Like the redwoods," said Kat. "My parents took me there when . . . when I was younger." Her thoughts drifted back to California and the Redwood National Park. She wondered if her parents missed her the way she missed them.

"These are the Silver Mattisbough," said Grimwarden. "The oldest trees in this world. Sadly there are few left alive, and fewer still seedlings to replace those."

"When I was a child," said Claris, "I would come to this part of the forest and play with my friends for hours on end."

"As did I," said Goldarrow. "The forest has always been a playground for the Elves."

"Should be," said Brynn.

"Grimwarden," said Mr. Wallace, staring thoughtfully into the blue-green twilight of the deep woods. "By what route will you lead us to Whitehall?"

"The North Strand," he replied. "Our scouts report the trail clear as far as Amberwood, but there is a Gwar encampment in Bellhollow. We'll need to duck well east of that."

"No argument from me there," said Mr. Wallace.

"If we make good speed, we'll reach the Spine by sunrise, and follow that craggy hidden path by day . . . at least until the ruins. From there, it's a more-or-less straight march beneath the pines north to Whitehall."

Goldarrow stood between Tommy and Jett and put an arm around each of their shoulders. "I wish we were making this journey under different circumstances," she said. "The Thousand-League Forest . . . well, there is so much that we could see."

Grimwarden loosed his war staff from its backhanger sheath. "Let us pray that we can all return during happier times."

Warbling, trilling, chirruping sounds surrounded the Elven party as they trod, the creatures of the deep wood settling in their roosts for the night.

Music in the air, thought Kiri Lee. They had been walking at a brisk pace through the forest for more than a few hours. She wondered what strange crickets, frogs, and birds there might be out in this Elven world. The sounds were all so mesmerizing; Allyra held one magical experience after the next, each an adventure waiting to unfold. *Dangerously beautiful,* she thought.

"Seems like it's gettin' a wee lighter," said Jimmy.

"We're still several leagues from the Spine," said Grimwarden. "A solid day's walk. We'll need to find shelter and make camp."

"Why?" asked Jimmy. "I'm not a bit tired."

"You have all held up well, considering the terrain," said their leader. "No, . . . lack of endurance does not yet hinder us, but we will soon lose the blessing of darkness. All it would take is one Gwar scout to note our presence."

"Just one?" asked Jett. "I know it's just fourteen of us, but I'm pretty sure we could smoke most any old Gwar scouts. Uh . . . no pun intended, Johnny."

Autumn laughed out loud. "Get it, Johnny? Smoke?"

"I get it," he said, yawning. "Very funny."

"This is no laughing matter," said Grimwarden, his words tightly clipped and stern. "These Gwar scouts are the enemy, but we will never take pleasure in killing." He walked away muttering, "May it never be."

Goldarrow put a heavy hand on Johnny's shoulder. "Take no offense," she said. "Grimwarden is quite sick of war, and rightly so. His flesh bears the scars of too many battles to name. He is the greatest warrior in Elven history, but to him that simply means he has lived long enough to witness more horrors than anyone else."

"Still," said Jimmy. "Why can we not keep goin'? We can fight if we must."

"No, Grimwarden is right," said Goldarrow. "A scout may do irreparable damage in more ways than one. He could belong to a much larger force nearby and cause them to descend upon us like locusts. Or he could be far from aid and simply escape to tell his master where we are . . . where we are going. We might not even see the scout if he has any skills at woodcraft. The lethal damage would be done . . . and we might never know. And then there are the spiders."

"Spiders?" Kat got the chills.

"While you might dispatch any number of Gwar well enough, you will miss the tiny specks that serve as spies."

The young lords cast their eyes at the ground. The sounds of the forest grew momentarily louder. How many spiders crept around their feet at this very moment?

"This way," Grimwarden commanded from up ahead. "I know of a place where we can camp."

A little later, they stopped to make camp. Tommy thought they'd pitch a ring of tents full of comfy sleeping bags, or at least find a deep cave where they could have a hearty, crackling fire going. Now, more than fifteen-stories high in the top of a swaying tree, Tommy stared frightfully out at the sleepy morning forest and realized just how wrong he had been.

Theirs was not the tallest tree, but, at this height, that didn't matter much. Still far above the main forest canopy, their treetop allowed a dizzying, panoramic vista of a patchwork quilt made with every shade of green, yellow, and brown. The sky was blue steel. Shreds of dark gray clouds moved slowly across the distant horizon. The horizon . . . where the farthest reaches of the Thousand-League Forest met the sky.

The wide flet upon which the Elves now stood was roughly rect-angular with rounded corners, the massive Mattisbough trunk growing through its center, leaving thin walkways on two sides and large open platforms on the other two sides. Waist-high closed railings protected the entire perimeter, and a slanted roof covered it all overhead. Every part of the full structure seemed a natural part of the tree, beams and platforms sanded and cunningly joined to the trunk so that no seams were visible.

Standing on the edge of the flet with just one hand on the railing, Jimmy called back, "Sure'n this is a grand tree house! I canna' believe how high we are! What say yu, Tommy?"

Tommy slumped down against the trunk wall—as far away from the railing as possible—and mumbled, "Yeah . . . cool."

Kiri Lee knelt down beside him. "Are you afraid of heights?"

Tommy sat up a little straighter. "No, well . . . yes, but not like normal heights, like on the roof of a house or a normal tree."

"It's not so bad," said Kiri Lee. "You know the Elves are amazing builders. This hidden flet is probably sturdier than most buildings back on Earth."

Tommy put on a brave smile, but thought, *Easy for you to say. You can walk on air.*

Kat stood near the trapdoor entrance and watched Tommy and Kiri Lee talking.

". . . is completely hidden from below," Goldarrow was saying to Kat. "It moves and flexes with the wind, but it would take more than a hurricane to knock this—Kat, are you listening to me?"

"What?" Kat startled. "Oh . . . I'm sorry. I was just thinking about something."

Goldarrow glanced left and nodded knowingly. "I see," she said. "Well, I wouldn't worry too much about that. Tommy looks as green as you look blue."

"Thanks," said Kat. "That helps . . . sort of."

"Whoa, Autumn!" exclaimed Johnny. "Don't get too close to that rail."

"Quiet!" Grimwarden hissed. "We may be hidden from view, but Gwar have keen ears."

Uncowered, Johnny escorted Autumn away from the flet's railing. Autumn tried to shake his hands from her arm. "It's okay," she whispered.

He looked at her doubtfully.

"Really," she insisted. Finally he let her go.

"Wow, Johnny," said Jett, looking over from across the flet. "And I thought my ma was protective."

"Let it go," Autumn whispered. This time she put her hand on Johnny's arm.

"He better not be calling me a mama's boy," muttered Johnny.

"He's not," she urged. "Relax."

Grimwarden went to the rail, reached up to the eave, and released a dark, leaf-patterned tarp that dropped down. He tied it off at the rail like a window shade. As he walked the perimeter, repeating the process, he said, "Young lords, Commander Brynn will give you each a fletroll. You are in great need of rest. And Mumthers will give you something to eat, nothing too heavy. The stew can wait until Whitehall. Sleep well and do not fear anything on the ground beneath us. We have left no sign of our coming, and are unseen from below. Lady Claris has the first watch. We are . . . quite safe. *Elloset nyas.*"

Brynn brought fletrolls to each of the lords and bade them find a place to rest. She came last to Tommy. He unrolled the mat. Made of tightly woven vines and only an inch and a half thick, the fletroll was surprisingly long and surprisingly soft. Tommy spread his roll out as close to the trunk as possible and lay sideways upon it.

Goldarrow patted Brynn on the shoulder to move her along, then knelt beside Tommy. "Are you going to be okay?" she asked. "You were looking very uncomfortable earlier."

"I don't like heights," he said.

She laughed softly, brushed back a few locks of golden hair, and said, "An Elven Lord afraid of heights is a bit of a . . . a . . . what do the humans call it . . . an *oxymoron*. This fear will pass, Tommy. You are pureblood from the line of lords. One day soon you will dance upon the treetops."

Tommy couldn't imagine doing anything in the treetops except clinging mightily to the thickest branch and holding on for dear life. "But . . . what if we're attacked? What if"—Tommy swallowed—"the Gwar try to cut down the tree?"

Goldarrow smiled and gently patted Tommy on the shoulder. "On the backside of the tree, there is a tethered line. It descends a thousand feet into the forest. If necessary, we will escape that way. And should the enemy find our tree and attempt to cut it down, we would all be long gone before they cut halfway through a mature Mattisbough trunk."

She started to stand, but Tommy reached out for her arm. "Mrs. Galdarro . . . I mean . . . Sentinel Goldarrow? What did Grimwarden mean, just a minute ago, when he said something . . . it sounded like a different language. He said Ello-ny-something."

"*Elloset nyas*," she replied. "And yes, it is different. It is old Elven First Voice, we call it. Not the oldest of our languages, but still not spoken much in these later days."

"What does it mean?" he asked.

"It means God rest you."

Rest, Tommy thought. *Right*. Even with his eyes clenched shut, he could feel the slow sway of the tree. He opened his eyes and glanced at the other young lords, just grayish-blue lumps spread across the floor. They were all asleep, and Tommy thought he heard snoring. *Probably Jett*, he thought. *Too deep to be a girl.*

None of the others seemed frightened. Tommy tried to convince himself that he had no reason to fear, either. He was among friends, right? But were they really his friends? They'd fought together and traveled together. But really, they'd all just been thrown together. If it all went away . . . all the Elvish stuff . . . and the seven of them were somehow transported back to Earth to the same school, would they still be friends? Tommy didn't think so. Jett was a football star. He'd have his jock friends and endless stories of game-day highlights. Tommy didn't think Jett would have time for an average kid.

Kiri Lee was drop-dead gorgeous. She'd be so far out of his league at school, he'd need a ladder just to catch a glimpse of her shadow. Tommy frowned and rolled over to face the tree trunk. No, Kiri Lee would be untouchable.

Johnny and Autumn might be friends. They seemed pretty down-to-earth. They liked afternoons of exploring creeks or fishing or riding bikes. *Yeah*, Tommy thought. *I could probably be friends with them.*

Jimmy? *Maybe.* He had a good sense of humor. But he was moody and seemed too much of a loner, like one of the kids who wore black all the time . . . and eye makeup. Tommy laughed quietly. He couldn't picture Jimmy wearing eye makeup. But still, there was something about Jimmy that warned you to keep your distance. It was like hearing a snake's rattle every time you got too close. *Jimmy might be a friend,* Tommy thought. *But not a close one.*

That left Kat. Tommy rolled back around to face the others. *She'd still be a friend,* Tommy thought. In fact, he couldn't think of any of his friends back on Earth who had seemed so genuine. Kat was on his mind all the time, too. He wasn't sure why, then immediately shook the thought out of his mind.

A brief change in the ambient sound, a flash of light. Tommy turned his head and saw Claris emerge from the trapdoor, where nearby there was a pile of ropes and timber. *She didn't use the rope ladder?!* Just the thought made Tommy feel sick.

Mr. Wallace and Grimwarden met her there. They whispered, but Tommy heard them.

"All clear?" asked Grimwarden.

"Not quite," she replied. "We're safe enough. But two miles east there is a Gwar search party. They are organized and systematic. I watched them map out a fair stretch of the wood before I returned."

"Even if they come this way," said Mr. Wallace, "they will find nothing."

"Agreed," said Grimwarden. "Still, we will need to alter our route to the Spine."

"There is something else," said Claris. "They have spiders with them."

"Warspiders?" Grimwarden kept his voice low in spite of the revealed threat.

"Yes," she replied. "But they are young, not a third of their mature size. Still."

Grimwarden nodded. "Understood," he said. "We will be wary." He turned to Mr. Wallace. "You have the next watch. Be careful."

"I will," he replied. "Should I monitor the enemy's movements?"

Grimwarden nodded. "From a safe distance."

"Of course."

Tommy watched the Sentinel descend. Mr. Wallace didn't use the rope ladder, either. Tommy shivered, but not from cold. When the trap-door closed, a breeze rustled one of the shades so that Tommy saw a crack of the afternoon sky. Once more he was awed and frightened by their height. He rolled back to face the trunk again. *What am I doing here?* he thought sadly. Hundreds of feet up in a tree . . . in another world? His stomach tightened and churned. He thought of his parents, his home back on Earth. *What have I done?* All at once regret poured over him like a dark waterfall. He'd made an awful, awful decision. *I don't want to be a lord. I just want to be a normal kid. I want to go home and play catch with Dad. I'll even eat Mom's meat loaf . . . and love it.* The tree shuddered. *And she can be as overprotective as she wants.*

But the pangs of regret were made all the more miserable by the certainty that he could not change his decision. It was too late. Exhausted both mentally and physically, Tommy fell into a hard sleep. So deep was his slumber, in fact, that he didn't hear Mr. Wallace come back, nor Brynn when her turn at the watch was over, nor when Mr. Spero's turn began.

Outside the flet, the sun had dipped below the eastern horizon. Night had come swiftly.

High Treason

"KIRI LEE," whispered Goldarrow, gently shaking the young lord. "Kiri Lee, wake up, you're having a bad dream."

Startled, Kiri Lee opened her eyes wide. She gasped and frantically crawled backward until her back hit the trunk of the tree. "No, no!" she whispered urgently. "You stay away! You're not real. You're . . . not . . . her!"

"Not who?" Goldarrow asked, cautiously approaching. "Kiri Lee, it's me, Goldarrow."

Just then Mr. Spero opened the trapdoor and emerged. Kiri Lee screamed, "No! Not him, too! Stay away from me!"

Shocked and dismayed, Mr. Spero held up his hands in a pleading manner, rooted at his spot by the trapdoor. "Keep her quiet."

Claris and Brynn rushed over to Kiri Lee. The other lords began to wake up.

"Kiri Lee, there is no danger here," said Grimwarden from the other side of the flet. Mr. Wallace stepped away from the group gathering around Kiri Lee, but froze when Grimwarden lifted one of the shade tarps and proclaimed, "*Vex lethdoloc vitica anis. Senesca, mi'jena, baden wy feithrill adin ny!*"

The moment the Guardmaster spoke the First Voice phrases from ancient Elven scriptures, Kiri Lee snapped out of the waking dream and began to weep. And Mr. Wallace fell to his knees and shook as if struck by sudden cold. But Grimwarden had not seen. He had joined the others around Kiri Lee.

Still rattling the sleep from his mind, Tommy sat up on his fletroll. "What's all the noise about?" he asked, squinting at the light from the now raised tarp. Ignoring the hushed conversations to his left, Tommy stared with drowsy fascination at the opening just above the rail. There seemed to be something there, a small patch of prickly-looking black. It reminded Tommy of one of the stickerballs from the sweet-gum trees in his grandmother's backyard. That or a small sea urchin.

A sea urchin . . . in a tree? Tommy thought. With eerie quickness, it moved, coming into full view—an adolescent Warspider about the size of a basketball. Motionless on the railing it sat, glassy black eyes staring in all directions at once.

"SPIDER!" Tommy yelled, at last free of the sleepy trance. He tumbled across his fletroll, grabbed and strung his bow, and then loosed an arrow into the cluster of dark eyes.

Screee! The creature tumbled backward over the rail. Two more took its place. All at once, shadows skittered across the tarps on the three other sides. Forelegs appeared in the cracks. Something clattered above.

"We are found out!" Mr. Spero yelled. "Guardmaster, to arms!"

A great spider leaped just as Grimwarden wheeled around. His axe flashed and split the spider from fangs to spinneret. The pieces of its ruined carcass fell on either side of him. But more spiders sprang up to confront him.

Meanwhile, Goldarrow flicked out her rychesword and impaled a gray arachnid that had just appeared over the solid railing. Grimacing, she used her free hand to push the ruined creature off her blade. She watched it tumble over the edge and plummet. Then she gasped. "Grimwarden, there are Gwar, more than a hundred rallying at the base of the tree! Some are climbing!"

The Guardmaster finished bludgeoning one of the larger spiders. "Goldarrow"—he shouted, wiping gelatinous green muck from his face and beard—"you and Mr. Wallace, take the Seven. Hit the chute!"

"Right!" she called back, already moving.

Near the trunk, Tommy spent his last arrow felling yet another spider, but there seemed no end of the creatures. Two raced along the flet floor toward his feet, but Jimmy was there in a flash. He leaped on top of one, crushing it with his full body weight. The other snapped its fangs and lunged for Tommy, but it didn't get far. Jimmy had grabbed one of the creature's back legs and now held it fast. Tommy had a hard time getting his short sword out of his scabbard, but at last managed to pull it free. Then, just as Jimmy lost hold of the spider's leg, Tommy plunged the blade into the creature's eyes. The sword stuck deep and wrenched from Tommy's hands. The spider thrashed about until flipping over in the corner, its dead legs curling inward.

"Come on!" Goldarrow yelled. "Follow me!"

Jimmy ran on, but Tommy spun on his heels, searching. He spied Kat, ran to her, and pulled her along.

Keeping more spiders at bay, Mumthers stood on the trapdoor, the strong latch broken loose. At the same time, she swung a long-handled cast-iron skillet and dueled a slightly larger spider with striped fangs. The creature lunged, but each time, Mumthers gave it a clanging blow that sent it reeling backward. Finally, it caught the skillet in its fangs and began to pull. Mumthers fell forward, off the trapdoor. Up it popped and immediately a spider began to climb in. Still engaged in a tug-of-war with the other spider, Mumthers didn't see the one coming up behind her. "Let go, you wee beastie!" she yelled. "Or I'll make a soup of ya!"

The skillet came free suddenly. Mumthers raised the heavy pan over her head and brought it down like an axe, crushing the spider's head. Then, hearing a loud crunch from behind, Mumthers jumped and spun around. She found Jett standing on the trapdoor with a half-smashed spider beneath it. "Oh, that's a good lad," said Mumthers. "I owe you a pie."

"Jett, come ON!" Goldarrow yelled from across the flet.

"I'm not leaving yet!" Jett yelled back.

"Jett, what are you doing?" demanded Grimwarden.

"There are too many spiders," said the young lord. "You need me to stay and fight."

Grimwarden thrust the bludgeon end of his axe into the face of a charging spider and yelled, "What I NEED is for you to get out of this tree! We will take care of the spiders! Now, go!"

Jett hesitated another moment and then ran past Grimwarden, Brynn, and Mr. Spero.

Johnny had Autumn pinned behind him against the trunk. He held his hands up, and licks of flame appeared in his palms.

"NO!" shouted Goldarrow. "Johnny, you can't use fire here. It could trap us and kill us all. LORDS, this way! Wallace, take the rear guard!" Her blond hair whipped as she rounded the bend and led the lords up the corridor on the narrow side of the trunk.

Mr. Wallace did as he was commanded and pushed the lords to follow Goldarrow. Tommy, Jimmy, Kat, Kiri Lee, Autumn, Johnny, and Jett—they all went by. *At least one of them should have died,* Mr. Wallace thought. He charged after them.

On the other side of the tree, Tommy and Jimmy raced across the flet and burst through a tarped doorway out onto an uncovered deck area. "Whoaaaa!" Tommy slid to a stop at the edge of the flet, clinging to a vertical post, feet dangling over open air. Jimmy saw Tommy nearly go over the edge and grabbed his shirt just in time. Tommy stood mumbling, looking down at the seemingly endless fall from their high perch into the forest depths below.

The others crashed through the door, immediately bumping into the back of the person who preceded them as the line halted. They found Tommy clinging to a railing post, panting. "OH—*huff, huff*—MY—*huff, huff*—GOSH!" gasped Tommy. "I almost died!"

"We're trapped," said Kat. "We can't get down."

"It's not over yet," said Goldarrow, rushing past the gawking lords.

Mr. Wallace came around the bend last. Sword drawn, he turned to intercept anything that might have been following them.

"This is our way out," said Goldarrow. She cast a quick concerned glance at Tommy and then reached up into the air above her head. She grabbed something no one could see, gave a great tug, and then released. Puffs of shimmering powder appeared directly overhead and continued like a wave along a cord that sloped from the top of the flet's roof far into the forest.

"Look at that," said Johnny.

"Did you just make that cable . . . appear?" asked Jett.

"Elves are not sorcerers," she replied. "We coat it with crystamine to keep it hidden. I'll explain later."

"Are we going to do what I think we're going to do?" asked Autumn.

"I think I'm going to be sick," muttered Tommy.

Screee! More Warspiders. "Let's get moving," said Goldarrow.

"What about the others?" asked Kiri Lee.

"They are fighting so that we can escape," said Goldarrow.

"But will they get away?" asked Autumn.

"They had better," said Goldarrow, her last glimpse of Grimwarden flashing in her mind. She knelt by a large chest, fumbled with a key, then flipped the chest open. From within she drew several bundles and began tossing them to the lords. "Unwrap them," she commanded. "They are harnesses."

Screee!

Goldarrow hurriedly took one of the bundles, unlatched a metal clasp, and unwound several loops of material. She hooked loops around her arms beneath the shoulders and one around her waist. "Do as I have done—EXACTLY as I have done. Quickly!"

Tommy was at it in a heartbeat. He unwrapped his harness, put it on, and turned around in front of Goldarrow several times until he was absolutely certain he had it on correctly.

"I will go first," said Goldarrow. "Follow my lead."

"Um, Sentinel Goldarrow," said Johnny, "we *have* to follow your lead, don't we? We're all on the same wire, right?"

She looked at him affectionately. "Yes, of course, my lad. But there may be places ahead where tree limbs or clefts of rock poke out. We may need to swing ourselves one way or the other, so it is best that I face them first. Each of you keep your eyes riveted to the one in front of you. Do as they do!"

"Uh, I'm not sure I want to do this," said Tommy.

"Tommy," Goldarrow said, "you have no choice." She looked to Jett and said, "Only if you have to."

Jett nodded.

"What?" Tommy asked, but he got no answer.

"You'll be fine, Tommy!" said Goldarrow. She grabbed the chute line, pulled it down, and attached the metal clasp. "Count to ten after

I'm gone and leave the platform." With that, the Sentinel leaped off the platform and sped away down the chute line.

Tommy clicked his hook onto the cord and gave it a hard yank. It seemed like it would hold. He stepped to the edge and made the mistake of looking down. A twisting vertigo of dark limbs and green foliage rose up to meet him and he stepped back.

"Tommy, you need to go," said Jett. "Goldarrow's going to get too far ahead."

"I know," said Tommy. "But I'm—hey, whoa, stop!"

But Jett pushed Tommy off the flet as easily as a father might push his toddler on a swing.

"WAAAAaaaaaaaa!" And Tommy was gone.

Jimmy went next. Then Kiri Lee, Johnny, and Autumn.

"C'mon, Kat!" said Jett. "Ladies first."

"No, you go. If there are any Gwar down there, beat them up for me!"

Jett laughed. "You got it." He secured his hook to the line and teetered a minute on the edge, staring hard at the tree trunk behind them.

"What?" Kat asked, but the sudden clamor made any answer impossible.

SCREEE!

Three larger Warspiders, four to six feet in diameter, came around the bend. Mr. Wallace killed two, but the other got by him and lunged forward.

Kat slashed it with her short sword, but it leaped . . . right onto Jett. Grappling with the spider, its massive curling fangs inches from his face, Jett fell backward off the flet. His harness cinched tightly around him as he and the spider were whisked away.

"JETT!" Kat screamed, but there was nothing she could do.

"AAAAAAAAaaaaaaaaaaa—Mmph!" A fat paw of foliage smacked Tommy across the face, filling his open mouth with bitter-tasting leaves. He spat them out, shut his mouth tight, and strained against

the wind in his eyes to see Goldarrow racing ahead. Full branches *whoosh*ed by above and below. Forest sounds—frogs, insects, birds, wind—all melded together in an undulating rush of sound. There was a curious high ringing, too. Tommy realized the creepy tone came from the friction of the hook on the chute line as he blasted through the treetops. It was like being shot through a green tunnel, and Tommy constantly ducked or raised his feet, trying to avoid another blow.

There she is! He saw her, just a shadow among shadows up ahead. His eyes were watering profusely. He tried to call out to her, but it felt like a powerful, invisible hand had grabbed his words and thrown them hundreds of miles behind him. *What is she doing?* Blinking constantly, he watched the Sentinel start to swing out sideways. *Oh no.*

Piercing the green in the distance, great gray fangs of stone rose up among the trees on either side. Some were fat and mountainous with gaping caves and ruinous jagged ridges. Others were narrower like monstrous stalagmites. It occurred to Tommy that they looked like the jaws of some colossal undersea beast . . . and he was heading straight for them.

Mr. Wallace joined Kat at the edge of the flet. "The spider went with Jett!" she cried out. "Do something."

"I cannot. I have no bow," he replied.

SCREEE!

More spiders were coming. A lot more.

Kat raced to the chute line and clicked the latch. "Get your line, Mr. Wallace, hurry!"

Mr. Wallace ran to the chest, looked into it, and then stood up. "It's empty," he said. "Go on without me."

"No . . . I can't leave you," she said, pulling at the leather straps.

"You must," he replied, trying desperately not to think of what he had in mind—lest she read his mind.

"No," said Kat. "I won't. This harness, it's made of leather . . . or something. It's very strong. It can hold us both."

SCREEE!

"Come on!" she demanded, working at the harness.

There came the sounds of spiders again, closer now, and then the voice of one very angry Elven commander. "LORDS, GET THEE GONE!" Grimwarden shouted.

Mr. Wallace and Kat had tried several methods to get into the harness but found the only way was for them both to put their legs through the straps. But they immediately realized that their upper bodies had no support from the harness. They'd have to cling to the strap that descended from the attached hook.

"Ready?" Mr. Wallace asked.

Kat nodded. She glanced back over her shoulder at the Sentinel. He smiled back, and they stepped off the platform.

Screee! All fangs and mandibles, the Warspider gnashed at Jett and, with all eight legs, clung to his body with astounding strength.

"Get off me!" Jett yelled. "You nasty . . . *uhg* . . . thing!" He used his powerful upper body and arm strength to push against the critical joints of the spider's midsection, all the while kicking at the creature's segmented legs, but it would not let go. Tangled with each other and swaying violently, they sped down the chute line. The pair crashed through tree limbs, the wood slapping their bodies with enough force to break an average man's back.

"*Ah! Grrr . . . ah!*" Jett grunted. The Warspider still would not let go. He tried a different tactic: pushing with both his legs at the spider's underside, but that met with far worse results. The creature raised its abdomen and its twitching spinnerets and sprayed tendrils of gray web on Jett's legs. He soon found his legs webbed together as if bound with steel cords.

Wriggling and twisting at the waist, Jett could only use his abdominal muscles to distance himself from the underside of the spider. All at once, the creature began contracting its legs. Jett felt himself being pressed inexorably toward the spider's gaping jaws. If it pierced him with those fangs . . . He had to kill the spider. He had to do it now.

Flexing his triceps and chest muscles, Jett pressed the creature just far enough away. With reflexes faster than man or Elf, Jett released the spider's torso and grabbed its fangs, one in each hand. *Screee!* The beast's eight legs crushed Jett up against it, but Jett did not let go of the fangs. Instead, he began to pull them outward.

The spider shrieked and fought, slamming its forelegs against Jett's back. Jett just pulled even harder. Its fangs were strong, rooted deep in its maw just beneath a cluster of black eyes. But without the threat of venom, the fangs were no match for Jett's lordly power. Wider and wider he pulled them, the spider beginning to flail, its grip loosening. Jett didn't stop. He pulled as if he was using the posthole digger in the backyard in North Carolina. He could feel the internal membranes begin to snap. He growled, a deep roar turning into a violent yell. Two horrific cracks and the fangs ripped free, spattering Jett with something dark and hot. He flipped the spikes around, and then jammed them back into the spider's face, venom filling its head. In a trembling seizure, the spider let go and fell away.

"See ya, Spidey!" Jett yelled, exultant. But he felt something pull sharply at his legs. *Oh no. The web.*

The spider had wrapped up Jett's legs and was swinging like an enormous anchor beneath him. Jett screamed. The pain was immense. And then Jett saw it: a rocky cleft jutting into the path of the chute line.

Rocketing down the chute line, Tommy felt his insides quaking as he narrowly missed the first protruding stony ridge. He kept his eyes glued to Goldarrow to try to mimic her movements. She rocked to the left. Tommy did likewise. She swung back to the right to miss an outstretched limb. Tommy followed suit. It wasn't that hard actually . . . just a matter of twisting your hips until a little momentum got you swinging back and forth. The trick was controlling the sway so that he wouldn't swing the wrong way at the wrong time. *If I miss, I'll be*

smashed on the side of a cliff like a bug on a windshield, Tommy thought just as—

WHACK!—something slammed into Tommy's feet and he was spinning out of control. He felt the harness tighten on his legs and chest as he spun 'round and 'round. Speeding down the chute line, being squeezed by the harness, and rotating too fast to see, Tommy yelled for help. All he heard in reply was the roar of forest sounds and wind.

Exposed rocky ridges were coming up fast. It looked to Jett like there were some big trees reaching out into his path as well. *The dead Warspider must weigh three hundred pounds,* thought Jett. The first cliff came up fast. Too fast.

Jett could do nothing. He closed his eyes, feeling a heavy difference in the wind as if the air pressure had suddenly changed. He started to rotate a little, but twenty seconds later he opened his eyes to realize he'd missed the rock face.

But there were more ahead. Jett knew he would be at the mercy of anything in his path as long as the spider's corpse was attached. *But maybe . . .* if he could just get his legs close enough to one of the branches or a sharp edge of stone, maybe it would saw through the webs and free his legs. *Or maybe it would tear my legs clean off,* thought Jett despondently. *I heal fast, but not that fast.*

There was no time. Up ahead . . . stone and limb. Jett cringed, barely missing a branch and swaying to the right. Too far. He was heading for the rock face. The spider struck the stone first, slamming into the rock with a loud crunch. The recoil from the blow kept Jett from being dashed as well. He looked down at the Warspider . . . or what was left of it. It weighed less without four of its legs. Now Jett could flex his abdominals enough to bring his webbed legs up, causing the spider to swing. Jett grinned.

Another rock ahead, this time on the left. He timed it perfectly, leveraging his lower body so that the tethered Warspider swung forward like a pendulum. The spider crashed into the ridge of stone, splitting the creature's bulbous abdomen and tearing two more legs free from the rest of its body. The impact spun Jett around, and he had to whip his lower body the opposite direction to slow the spin.

Some legs, the thorax, and a half-ruined head were all that remained of the Warspider. Jett could now move his body with ease, controlling his sway such that he could avoid the branches and rocks at will. Soon he had careened the spider-corpse into so many obstacles of wood and stone that all that was left was a pumpkin-sized hunk of spider goo.

But Jett relaxed a little too soon; just up ahead something hung from the chute line. It was an irregular shape . . . with many legs.

Tommy felt himself jerk to a stop. Not a complete stop. He was still spinning, but something grabbed at his legs. He screamed and kicked.

"Tommy!" called a voice. "Be still! I can't help you if you won't stop struggling."

"Goldarrow?" Tommy opened his eyes, and as his spinning slowed, he saw the Sentinel directly ahead. "How did you—?"

"Brakes," she said, smiling wide. She lifted her legs and showed Tommy her nearly shredded boots. Then she looked up abruptly. "Oh, Tommy," she said. "Hold on."

"LOOOOOK OUTTT!!" came a voice from behind. Something crashed into them, setting them to swinging every which way, and once more sailing along the chute line at full speed.

"Sorry about that!" yelled Jett. "I tried to slow down, but the cable kept burning my hands."

"You use your feet," Goldarrow said as she stopped her own spin. Scrutinizing Jett and especially Tommy, Goldarrow saw that both were unharmed. She laughed. "See," she said, holding up her ruined boots once more. "Like me."

Jett and Tommy joined in the mirth of the moment, but in truth Tommy felt a little nauseous.

Suspended together in one harness, Mr. Wallace and Kat streaked down the line.

"Do you miss your parents?" asked Mr. Wallace. He wanted to keep Kat talking, keep her thinking so she wouldn't perceive his thoughts.

"You know, it's funny," said Kat, closing her eyes and letting the wind wash over her. "I missed them more when I was living with them . . . more than I do now."

"What do you mean?" Mr. Wallace asked. He shifted slightly and reached for the handle protruding from his boot.

"It's hard to explain," she said. "But seeing their faces everyday at home . . . it just made me miss the way things used to be. We used to be close, used to go to Newport Beach . . . Dodgers games . . . Surreau's Pizza Grotto. But more than that. It was the way they were around me: tender, caring. There was love I could feel—even if they were just pouring me orange juice." Kat emitted a kind of laugh-sigh. "It was all before the poly."

He had the dagger halfway out of his boot now. "The . . . poly?"

"I know what you're trying to do," said Kat.

Mr. Wallace froze. "Wha-aat?"

"You're trying to keep my mind off how high we are . . . how fast we're going." Kat laugh-sighed again. "It's okay though. Heights don't bother me. But they seem to freak Tommy out."

Mr. Wallace exhaled. "I am glad you are comfortable," he said, his hand going back to the dagger. "But I am really interested. Why . . . why don't you miss your parents now?"

"It's not that I don't miss them now," she said. "But here, I don't see them . . . and there are so many things going on . . . strange things . . . wonderful things. It all still feels like a dream."

He hadn't expected her to finish speaking so quickly. He'd been thinking dangerous thoughts. But had she noticed? He lifted the dagger, the point inches from her lower back, aimed at her kidneys. He didn't know how long it would be until they reached the end.

"But you know," she continued, her mind racing, "I worry about how much they miss me. They don't know where I am, they don't know anythi—AAAaaaahhhhhh!" Kat arched her back and screamed again.

The dagger fell away from Mr. Wallace's hand. Beginning to shake, he looked down at the sword blade sticking into his gut. Then he looked up. "How dare you!"

Kat twisted the blade even harder, yelling just inches from his face.

"This . . . isn't . . . over!" he hissed. Spasms wracked his body. Armor, clothing, flesh began to change . . . becoming coiling, luminous vapors. A mocking, jeering face appeared over Kat's shoulder, then vanished. And like that, Kat sat alone in the harness.

Taking Stock

A WEARY and somber collection of Elves waited in a densely wooded dell at the bottom of the chute line. The Seven had survived. As had Goldarrow, Grimwarden, and Claris.

"I canna' believe it," said Jimmy, pacing. "Mr. Spero, the others, they died fer us."

Grimwarden sat on a stump, shaking his head and muttering. "I failed you, Brynn. Poor Mumthers. And Mr. Wallace? How could I not have known?" As he spoke, fresh pain writhed in his words. "I should have seen it. I should have done more."

"As for Brynn and Mumthers," said Goldarrow, "you did what you could. You cannot be everywhere at once, no matter how hard you try. Brynn and Mumthers will be sorely missed, but not in a thousand years would either want to be a burden to you. And as for Mr. Wallace, the Wisp must have slain him in Scotland," said Goldarrow. "Then he came through the portal with us. You could not have known."

"Ah, Elle," he replied. "But so much might have been avoided had I but interpreted the clues. In the Dark Veil, on Daladge Falls, and the ambush here—how clear it seems to me now."

Kat sat next to Tommy on a fallen tree. "You mean, in the Dark Veil, when Mr. Wal—when that thing killed the Gwar . . . he was actually going to kill me then?"

"Yes," said Grimwarden.

"I knew it!" exclaimed Kiri Lee. "I saw him from above. It didn't seem like he could have seen the Gwar, but then, well . . . it seemed different."

"And on the falls?" Jimmy asked. "He caused that, too?"

"If he had his way," said Goldarrow, "he would have killed all of you. He had chances. I wonder. But he must have had a change in plans."

Grimwarden stood up, grunted ferociously, and heaved a stone into the woods. "He knows the location of Nightwish Caverns . . . and Whitehall . . . and he knows our plans."

"But I killed him, right?" asked Kat.

"Your sword thrust was well aimed," said Claris. "But you cannot slay a Wisp with steel alone."

"They are altogether evil creatures," added Goldarrow. "You must combine your blade with the word of Ellos. Only in this way may a Wisp be dispatched."

It grew very quiet. Jett had his broad back turned to the group. He made no sound but trembled like a mountain quaking. Kiri Lee placed her slender white hand on his shoulder. "Mr. Spero was your teacher, wasn't he?" she asked.

Jett didn't turn around, but she heard his answer.

"I'm so sorry, Jett," she said.

No one replied.

"You—you know what I'd like to be doing right now?" Jett asked, his chiseled square chin trembling. "I'd like to be home with my ma and dad, sitting on the big old couch in the den, watching a movie, and eating a big bowl of popcorn with real butter! Thing is, I can't. I can't even hop on a plane and go home. None of us can. We're in some other world! We're trapped. Who is this Spider King anyway? Why's he have to go stirring all this up? Why all the hatred? Why?" Jett reared back and kicked a fallen log twenty yards into the wood. He crouched low and fell to a seat on the leaf-strewn forest floor. He put his head in his hands. "I'm tired," he whispered. "So tired."

"Jett," said Jimmy, standing behind the strongest member of their team. "Yu spoke well, my friend. Yu spoke for us all, I think."

Tommy wasn't sure why he got up. He was spent. Every part of him wanted to just fall over and sleep forever, but he went over to Jett. "Look at me, Jett," he said. Jett looked up, his violet eyes rimmed by red lids. "You're so right that all this—ALL OF THIS—is messed up. But Earth's no better. Every time you turn on the news, all it is . . . is someone got shot, this plane went down, some politician got caught doing something illegal. But look, we're here to do something about it." Tommy looked from face to face. "Right now, we need to take all of this pain and let it burn itself in. 'Cause we've been given a mess of power . . . and good leaders." He looked for a moment to Grimwarden and Goldarrow. "I feel funny quoting my dad—I mean, the one back on Earth—but he would always say to me, 'To whom much is given, much is required.' We've got something to do here, something big. And if this Spider King is bent on messing things up, then I say we take him out."

Grimwarden leaned over to Goldarrow. "We've found their leader," he whispered.

"I should say so," said Goldarrow.

Before Tommy knew what was happening, the other lords surrounded him and Jett.

"We're in this together," said Kat.

"Together," said Johnny.

One by one they all said it. And they all meant it. "Together," Jett said at last, nodding.

"Oooooohhhhhh, deeeeeeeeaaarrrrrrr!" came a voice from somewhere above and behind. "Look out below!"

A large shadow came tearing through the canopy above them, and with a loud "Ooomph" and a thud, Mumthers was there among them. She got up, picking leaves out of her hair.

"Mumthers!" yelled Jett. "You're alive!"

"Yes, me lad," she replied. "Spider bit me in the leg. I passed out straightaway. The beastie probably thought I was dead and moved on. Thought I was dead meself. But when I woke up among a bunch of dead spiders, I figured I must still be in Allyra. Weren't no heaven leastways. Good thing I hung around, too, as me family spices were littered about. Wouldn't do for the Spider King's minions to go off enjoying those, now would it."

Jett coughed out a laugh, ran to Mumthers, and hugged her.

Seeing in the Dark

DEEP IN the northwestern corner of the Thousand-League Forest, carved into the living rock of Mount Mystbane and shrouded by the fearless cliffhanging trees, Whitehall Castle stood as a monolithic achievement of carved stone. Its various arches bounded down the slope and through the woods like the trails of skipped stones, racing to intersect smooth columns and suspended porticos. Ivy scaled the walls and wrapped the towers, further folding the ancient architecture into the forest. Abandoned for an age, well-camouflaged, and far away from the Spider King's stronghold in Vesper Crag, Whitehall was the one place the Elves thought it safe to conduct the secret warfare training of the returning lords.

Tommy was still exhausted from the arduous journey and the ambush the night before last, but seeing this place in the morning light and after some sleep energized him. Whitehall held a power, he felt, something left behind by Elven warriors of ages past.

And now, as Tommy stood at his window and watched the morning fog drift slowly through the valley below, he could hardly believe such a place existed. A babbling stream ran just beneath the railing and rushed out into thin air, dropping into the mist far below. The stonework all around his room had been carved with the antediluvian pictographs of the Ancients, the Wise Ones who had first constructed this place. Fashioned as a place for reflection and solace, Whitehall was still a marvel despite centuries of neglect.

Tommy walked slowly down the staircase that led from his bedchamber to a large chamber. Adorned with dusty paintings and cobweb-encrusted fixtures, the room was capped by a domed ceiling of glass, now hazy from lack of cleaning. Stretching his arms, Tommy continued through the chamber to yet another hallway that opened up to a columned courtyard on one side. It was here that he found Grimwarden twirling a long staff and looking thoughtful.

The famed Elven warrior followed the age-old forms of his people, moving the wooden weapon through the air in perfect rhythm to the counts of an invisible drum. Left and right, legs bending and stepping, the staff flipping over and under his arms—it was an act of beauty to behold. The motions would culminate in a sudden thrust in front, succeeded by a jab behind and a swift about-face, jarring an unseen enemy with the length of the wood.

When the exercise had reached its end, Grimwarden addressed Tommy, who stood awestruck beside a column.

"Good morning, Lord Felheart."

"Morning," he replied out of habit, a glazed look of fascination still in his eyes. "Just *Tommy* is fine."

"Tommy. Right." Grimwarden winced at the Earth name. "Did you find your bed comfortable?"

Tommy didn't answer the question. "Can you teach me how to do that?"

Grimwarden smiled. "In time. All in due time. But first, your bed?"

"Oh, sorry." Tommy took a step forward. "Yes, it was fine. A little musty smelling, but I guess I should have expected that."

"The long, hollow years weigh heavily upon this place . . . it is as you say." Grimwarden laid the staff against a stone bench and walked forward. "Shall we eat? The others are in the refectory."

"Sure thing! I'm starving."

Grimwarden looked at him curiously. "Tommy, I know our path was not the easiest, but did you not sup yesterday, and the day before?"

"Uh, right. It's just an expression." Tommy rubbed his face. "Let's go eat."

The two walked back into the corridor Tommy had come out of and continued farther down the hall before turning left at an intersecting hallway. Fingers of light worked through a large filthy window at the far end, accenting an open door. It was in here that Tommy and

Grimwarden greeted the rest of the lords, all assembled at the large board in the center of the room.

"Good of you to join us, Master Felheart!" came a loud voice from the other side of the mammoth kitchen. It was Mumthers. Already beloved by the Seven, she was jovial in speech and action, a whirlwind of activity—in and out of the kitchen. She was as wide as she was tall. *Perhaps a little too fond of testing her own food,* Tommy thought. And who wouldn't be with cooking like hers? Her apron was permanently stained by any number of ingredients, and despite her largish form, she carried herself in her blue dress much like a ballerina, light on her feet and twice as nimble. Her effusive hand gestures and waves of her spatulas kept people out of her way and eagerly awaiting whatever sumptuous meal she had prepared.

"Come, child! Sit! Sit!"

"Thank you, Mumthers." Tommy dipped his head. "Hey, every-one."

The others gathered around the table greeted him and made room on one of the benches. Goldarrow gave him a warm smile.

"You, too, old Grimwarden," Mumthers added. "Warriors need to eat as well."

"No quarrel with you there, Lady Bathers." Grimwarden smiled, his eyes dancing with anticipation. "What have you cooked for us this morning?"

"Considering no one has stocked this hole for a wee while, I was forced to use some of our rations. But the garden, though profusely overgrown"—she waved a spoon through the air in a grand arch—"still had a number of goodies that the rabbits overlooked."

And whatever it is, Tommy noted, *it smells wonderful!*

She turned to the hearth where a large cauldron bubbled, and beside it an iron pan sizzling with, well, something. *Sausage?* Tommy wondered.

"Been up since well before dawn to gather what I needed for these scrumptious goodies, I was." Mumthers produced a lined basket with two loaves of freshly baked bread, and poured everyone a mug of springwater and honey warmed by the fire. Next, she scooped the meat out of the skillet and onto a trencher proclaiming it to be rabbit sausage. The seven young lords winced.

"Thus the reason the rabbits have left the garden alone?" Grimwarden laughed. Everyone chuckled.

"Don't mock me until you try it. I added my family goods," she said. Her family goods—Tommy would come to find out—were the secret spices of her great-great-grandmother that she had rescued from the flet during the ambush, a concoction that could turn even a piece of bark into a delicacy. After this, she produced a stack of bowls, passed them out, then filled them with soup from the steaming cauldron. "Asparagus, leek, and a little of the leftover ham. An egg and some cream to thicken it."

"Where'd you get the cream?" Tommy asked.

"It would be wiser not to ask, Tommy," Grimwarden whispered. "Just let your mouth enjoy and your mind relax."

Tommy smiled and looked at his bowl, his spoon hanging over it. But Grimwarden couldn't have been more correct; his mouth enjoyed it, every mouthful. Mumthers had made a feast out of a famine, and every bite seemed better than the previous. He had never had rabbit before; even the thought made him a bit queasy. But as Mumthers had prepared it, he wondered why he had never tried it before.

"Watch the biscuits," said Jimmy without looking up from his bowl.

"What?" asked Kiri Lee. "What bis—?"

Just then, Mumthers tripped, launching more than a dozen biscuits into the air. They descended like meteors, exploding with flaky goodness all over the table and all over Kiri Lee. One biscuit hit the back of Kiri Lee's spoon, catapulting a glob of gravy right at Jimmy. Again, without looking up, Jimmy lifted a cloth napkin, perfectly intercepting the gravy that would have splattered him in the ear.

"Okay," said Kiri Lee, "a little earlier warning would have been nice."

"The question is," said Kat, "did Jimmy know what would happen earlier but just waited to warn you? Other than Jimmy, only I know the answer to that question."

Much like the biscuits beforehand, the table exploded in laughter.

When the kids had cleaned the trencher of sausage and had exhausted their capacity for bread and soup, Mumthers declared their first meal in Whitehall a success and hugged each of them, including Grimwarden. Everyone else stifled laughs as she slapped his back like a baby being burped.

"I'm so full I don't think I could eat again for a day," Tommy finally said.

"That's spectacularly good to hear," Grimwarden said when he had broken free of Mumthers's embrace, "because you won't be."

The kids looked up to him in shock. "What do you mean?" Autumn inquired hesitantly.

"Your training starts now. And your first lesson is to learn how to master your appetites. First physical, then emotional."

"What's our second lesson?" Johnny asked.

"How to run," Grimwarden said, to which the kids rolled their eyes. Then Grimwarden added, "In the dark."

"I can't see anything," Kat declared.

"Hey! Watch it!" Johnny whined, giving Kat a push. "You stepped on my foot!"

"Sor-ry!" Kat spat back. "Like I could see it."

"M'lords, please," came Grimwarden's voice from up ahead.

"Grumpy," Kat whispered at Johnny.

"Geek," he spat back.

"It seems you've met your match, Johnny," Autumn stated.

Up until now, Tommy realized their relationships had been built on seemingly surreal circumstances, ones that did not truly reflect the normal everyday issues of *being human*, as Tommy put it. It was one thing to escape from school, fly across the globe, and flee through Gwar-invested territory, but it was quite another to, well, get along. As he had thought before, who among them would actually be friends given normal circumstances? Would they pick each other first at kickball? Would they sit at the same cafeteria table? Would they invite one another over to birthday parties? By the looks of things now, probably not. And it was about to get a whole lot worse.

"All of you, enough. You are a team," Grimwarden continued, "at least you will be." Though they could not see him, Kat and Johnny knew he was staring at them. "Becoming a team means that you rely on one another . . . that you trust one another in everything, even with your very lives. Your destinies are not your own, but are intertwined with those of your people."

With his voice echoing down the cavern beyond them, Grimwarden emphasized just how deep they had journeyed beneath Whitehall, and just how helpless they were when there was no light, not even the flicker of a torch.

"Everything I will teach you, from tactics of battle and skills with your weapons, to the history of your people and the legacy you carry, will be for naught if you do not know how to work together. And I can think of no better way to start than here, where all you have are your ears."

"Sir? What do you mean?" Jett asked.

"Your ears, Lord Hamandar, so that you can listen to others more than you listen to yourself. It is an easy thing to speak. Anyone can do that. But it's quite another thing to listen, and even further, to *hear*."

"But I thought you said we'd be running. How can we run in the dark?" Kiri Lee asked.

"By listening to one another," Grimwarden said. "Before you lies a tunnel that stretches deep into the heart of Mount Mystbane and under the Thousand-League Forest. It goes on for miles. Somewhere along its path I have placed a clay jar.

"Now the rules: At least one of you must be moving forward at all times. Break the jar and you will start again. But bring the jar back to me and you will be allowed to have another of Mumthers's delicious meals."

"Do you mean we can't eat until we find the jar?" Johnny asked anxiously.

"You are correct. Thus why you will run rather than walk—as the jar is, how can I say, not as close as you might prefer."

"I don't like this at all," Johnny interjected.

"All the more reason for you to complete the task in a timely fashion, Johnny," Grimwarden said. "If you don't like this, believe you me, what is coming will make this one of your fonder memories."

The young lords were already uneasy, what with the pitch-black dark around them. And now they were supposed to journey farther into this cave? Without lights? Though no one dared speak out, Johnny wasn't the only one who thought this was crazy. Cold fear began to wrap its tentacles around their chests.

"Now"—Grimwarden's voice came from behind them—"I'll leave you to your chore."

The teens spun around. "Hey, how'd you get back there?" Johnny asked.

"You weren't listening," Grimwarden said.

"I still don't get how we're supposed to do this," said Kiri Lee.

"Let's just think about it, Kiri Lee," Tommy spoke up. "We'll need to work together." They couldn't see it, but Tommy was running his fingers through his curly hair, as he did anytime he was deep in thought. "We could stretch out in a long line, evenly spaced. Then the person in the back will run all the way forward, using the voices of those in front to guide them. After each gets in the lead position, he or she could take four steps or something feeling around for the jar. Then the leader could yell back to the person in the rear. That person runs forward and does the same in front of you. When we actually find the jar and head back to Whitehall, the person in the rear always carries it, passing it off when it's his or her turn to run forward."

"Almost like a type of relay race," Autumn said.

"Seems kinda silly if you ask me," said Kat, trying to act as though she wasn't impressed. Then she looked to where she thought Grimwarden stood. "Silly, right, Mr. Grimwarden?"

"The lord does offer a workable solution," answered Grimwarden.

"But that's going to take forever," Kat said.

"Then I suggest you get started. And remember: break the jar and you start over."

"This is impossible," Johnny added.

"Young Lord Johnny, when you start listening as much as you protest, you will begin to *do* the impossible instead of *complain* about it, I assure you."

"Yeah, Johnny," Autumn chided him.

Grimwarden responded, "And Lord Miarra"—she could tell by his tone Grimwarden was glaring at her through the darkness— "provoking your friends doesn't become you."

"Yes, sir," she replied softly.

There was no reply.

"Commander Grimwarden?" Autumn's voice echoed down the cavern. An eerie silence befell them all. "He's gone!"

The first hour was terrifying. And downright frustrating.

None of the Seven had experienced utter darkness; most people rarely do. The feeling pushed all of them into a state of claustrophobia. Kiri Lee and Johnny had mild panic attacks, and Jett—despite his manly gift of strength—remained absolutely quiet.

The pack followed Tommy's idea to a tee: the person in the rear ran up the side of the pack, each member of the line making a ruckus and reaching out to guide the runner, until he or she arrived at the front and took four more steps, arms held out. But the speech was far from encouraging, each individual spouting off about how this was stupid or how it would be easier if they were just left alone to do it by themselves. As soon as the leader tripped—effectively stalling the progress while the leader recovered from a bloody knee or a scuffed hand—the entire group bickered. And then the tirade of insults *really* began as each new leader passed by, fumbling toward the front.

"If you weren't so clumsy"—said Jett, picking himself up off the tunnel floor—"maybe we'd have found the clay pot by now!"

"Me?" cried Johnny, unable to see but glaring in the direction of

Jett's voice. "You stopped without any warning. I'm not the mind-reader, you know." He groaned aloud. "Mannn, I think I broke my nose on your back."

"Ah, come on, it's probably just a scratch," Jett grumbled. "If I was doing this alone, I'd be back in the kitchen already."

"Of course you would," said Autumn. "It takes a lot of food to feed that ego!"

And so it continued: the lords tripping, stumbling, arguing, yelling, insulting each other as they searched for the clay pot Grimwarden had hidden in the tunnel. Until finally, frustrated, tired, and hungry, Autumn pronounced, "This is pointless!" Five voices agreed. . . .

"Wait," said Kat. "Where's Tommy?"

"Oh my gosh," said Kiri Lee. "Tommy?"

"C'mon, Tommy!" yelled Johnny. "Quit messing around."

"Guys, I think we lost Tommy," said Autumn.

"You sure did," Tommy finally spoke up.

"Tommy?" Jett asked. "You okay?"

"You know, Jett, that's the first caring thing anyone has said since we started this challenge." No one replied. "Look at us!" Then he thought better of it. "Nevermind." He shook his head. "Here we are, stuck down who-knows-how-far underground, given the simple task of returning a jar to the surface, and we can't even encourage each other. What's up with that?"

Again no one replied. For the first time in more than an hour, the Seven were utterly speechless.

"Yeah, what's up with that?" Kat finally admitted.

Though none of the others could see it, each of them nodded.

"Sorry, guys," Johnny offered up first.

"Me, too," said Jimmy.

Stepping on each other's words, they all apologized at once, offering hands blindly for high fives, handshakes, or pats on the back.

"Okay," Tommy concluded. "We cool?"

"Yeah, we're cool," said Jett on everyone's behalf.

"Now let's go get this done. No more slams, got it?"

"Got it," they all said.

"If what they say about us is true—and I tend to believe it is— then we're like family. And we'd better start acting like it. And not the bickering kind."

"We got ya, Tommy," said Kat. "Family."

"Family," echoed all the others.

"All right then," Tommy said. "We have a jar to find!"

In the next hour the Seven learned to work together, even encourage each other.

"Keep it coming, Johnny. You're doing great."

"On it, Autumn," he replied.

"Right here, Kiri Lee. I'm right here. Yu just give me yur hand."

"Okay," she replied. "Don't let me fall."

"You all right, T-man?" asked Jett.

"Fine, thanks," said Tommy. *T-man. That's kinda funny,* he thought. *But I like it.*

Under Tommy's direction, they formed a kind of chain of Elves, navigating the twists and turns as one. They began to eat up the darkened terrain, moving much faster than before and making much better time. Of course they weren't keeping track of the time, but someone else was.

Tommy was in the lead and felt the floor slope sharply upward. "Hold on, guys," he said. "The floor shoots up here . . . I just want to check and make sure that—" His hand brushed up against the smooth lines of a glazed terra-cotta vessel, pushing it over. "Whoa!" he exclaimed, reaching out to keep the jar from crashing. "It's the jar!"

"Don't drop it!" Autumn hollered. "You got it?"

"Do yu got it?" Jimmy asked.

"I got it!" Tommy finally exclaimed, hugging the earthen vessel close to his chest.

The Seven gave up a mutual cheer and surrounded their friend. They patted his back and then reached out to feel how big the jar was. It was no more than two feet tall and about twelve inches wide. It was adorned with two handles below the mouth, one on each side.

"You did it!" Kiri Lee hugged Tommy.

"We all did it," he corrected her. "Our team. Our family. To us! The Seven Elven Lords of Berinfell!" Tommy yelled.

"All right!" they all exclaimed, clapping loudly. All, that is, except Tommy, who clung tightly to the earthen jar.

When the revelry calmed down, Tommy took a few steps forward, back the way they had come. "All right, gang. Who's hungry?"

With victory sweet in their chests, and the smell of Mumthers's next meal swirling in their heads, the Seven made their best time yet, covering the same ground as before, but in less than two hours.

They took even more care to guard the precious prize this time. Not a single team member fell, and again the jar didn't endure so much as a scratch. By the time Kiri Lee first noticed the tunnel warming in both temperature and the faintest of glows, they were operating like an efficient machine. In less than five hours the team seemed just at home in the dark—relying solely upon their friends' voices—as they did in broad daylight.

Squinting painfully, they stepped into light. It was then that Grimwarden appeared . . . directly *behind* them.

"Well done," he said, clapping slowly. "Well done, indeed."

"Hey!" Autumn pointed. "How'd you get back there?"

"Yeah," the others joined in.

"Back here? Why, I've been behind you the entire time."

"The entire—" Tommy thought it through. "So you heard—"

"Everything," finished Grimwarden.

The revelry the Seven had felt just moments ago suddenly vanished, replaced now by the smothering grip of shame.

"I was deeply moved by how much you care for one another," he added. The Seven were sure he was being sarcastic. "Your encouraging words no doubt made all the difference. To date—as I have been training Elven soldiers for some time—you have accomplished this task in record time."

"Wait, so you're serious?" Kat asked.

"Absolutely. I always put the jar in the same place. You were the fastest to bring it back."

Johnny decided to ask what they were all thinking. "But what about all the bad—?"

"Yes, but when that strategy didn't work, you tried a different path. You are my greatest pupils yet. And will make fine leaders in battle when you are through here at Whitehall." Grimwarden strode forward and took the jar from Tommy. "You picked it up, eh, Tommy?"

"Yes, sir."

"Very good. Very good indeed." He studied the boy's face a moment longer, withdrew something from within the jar, and stuffed it inside his tunic next to his chest. "Now, to Mumthers's hearth fire!" He swung his hand at them. "Off with you!"

And as they raced back up through the sprawling halls and staircases of Whitehall, they each reveled in the valuable lesson they saw in Grimwarden's praise: it's anyone's game to criticize, but it's kingly to see only the good in others.

The Art of Discipline

THE SEVEN found their first few days in Whitehall spent much like the first. Grimwarden had them embark on various exercises that he called team building, each of them holding the same reward: more of Mumthers's delicious food. It was a trivial tactic, but it worked nonetheless. Quite well, as a matter of fact: a hungry stomach was good motivation for budding teenagers . . . especially the boys.

The pupils slept in two rooms, boys in one, girls in the other. The furnishings were sparse—just a bed for each teen, two chairs beside a dusty writing desk, and a wardrobe shared by all. Large windows provided a commanding view in at least two different compass directions, overlooking the thick forest treetops that surrounded their mountaintop hideaway.

The Seven found themselves awakened each morning by the sound of the most annoying forest bird they had ever heard. Much like a rooster crowing at the first rays of the sun, the *stunted pigmy albatross*—a much smaller and uglier cousin to the famed, large-winged flyer—cackled. And cackled. And cackled. The Seven thought the sound resembled something of a laughing hyena they'd seen on the Discovery Channel combined with a cat choking on a hairball. The irritating sound was unpleasant enough to rouse anyone from slumber, no matter how deep.

They stumbled from their beds only to find themselves led down the barracks corridor by the aroma of freshly baked bread and frying bacon from a wild boar Mumthers had killed earlier that morning. They convened as before in the refectory and shared in light conversation, settling into the routine that the first week demonstrated. Each morning after breakfast, they were met with a new challenge by

Grimwarden, testing their ability to work together—and to follow orders without compromise—while simultaneously developing their physical stamina and strength.

They had races around Whitehall's grounds, pairing off into teams and searching for hidden objects; they carefully maneuvered through the treetops in elaborate ropes courses, assisting one another and coming close to falling on more than one occasion; they even took a few trips to a nearby waterfall, swimming back and forth across the rapids just above the headwater. But in each exercise, they learned a little more about the history of their people, and about one another.

In the mornings Goldarrow sat the Seven down after each challenge and debriefed them, talking them through the finer points of the exercise—where they had excelled, where they had failed, and most importantly where they had overcome their fears and worked together. But always the conversation came back to lessons learned by the greater race of Elves, with Goldarrow sharing one of a thousand stories from the rich heritage of their people, most often setting a heavy tome of a book on the table and turning its ancient pages. She would read a passage, cite a particular tribe, and then point to a young lord and explain how he or she was related to the tribe in the story. The students grew more deeply connected with the history and the land than they ever could have imagined.

The afternoons were not so exciting. Whitehall hadn't been inhabited for almost a millennium, abandoned with the Fall of Berinfell and left to the hand of nature. Vines had crept into every available nook, splitting rock and allowing water to run its course, eroding mortar, and inspiring mildew. Heavy dust covered nearly every facet of the sprawling castle, and bird poop and rodent feces adorned places of prominence in every room. Grimwarden saw fit to make this the Seven's post-lunch, pre-dinner ordeal. He passed out lye soap, buckets and bristles, spades and cement, and makeshift wheelbarrows, then sent the Seven on their way.

For what felt like weeks, the teens worked their fingers raw, scrubbing and rinsing, lifting and dumping, hauling and fixing. It was tedious work, and eventually their complaints reached Grimwarden's ears.

"It's just that we thought we were training to be warriors," Jett protested in a group meeting. "Not janitors."

Grimwarden looked at him silently for a moment.

Now you've done it, thought Tommy, feeling a little angry himself. He well remembered Mr. Charlie.

When Grimwarden finally spoke, his voice was low and powerful. "Never mistake service for anything less than the highest form of nobility, Jett. Dictators and tyrants lead without serving; only true kings use their place of power to lead in the most humble of ways."

The subject was never broached again.

While the days were consumed with constant lessons and active labor, the evenings were the lords' refuge. After cleaning the grime from their hands and clothing themselves in fresh linen tunics, the Seven would meet in the dining hall and feast on whatever exquisite repast Mumthers had thrown together for them. Except on the rare occasions that Mumthers would point out their reliance on comfort as a crutch and bring them some grainy, dry food they might find on the trail in times of battle, or give them an ancient nutritional supplement when other food sources couldn't be found, which one would only eat in desperate situations.

It wasn't long until each of the Seven felt they were becoming close friends . . . family. The shared experiences, the connection to their ancestors, and the excitement of what lay ahead all forged a bond that they realized was more valuable than any they had ever known.

It was in these late-night gatherings that a new tradition was incorporated into their ever-widening schedule: music and dancing. After the trenchers had been cleared and the goblets returned to the kitchen, Grimwarden would pull out a hand drum and Mumthers her wooden flute. Lively music filled the grand hall within moments. Goldarrow and Claris would gather the Seven in the center of the room, just in front of the hearth fire, and demonstrate the tune's required steps.

At first the boys were far from enthusiastic, contesting with a wave of their hands, moving toward their seats. But Grimwarden would have none of it and stopped playing at the first sign of their resistance. "Goldarrow has told me that men care little for dancing in most of your modern Earth cultures," he said. "Here, you will find yourselves among the chickens and the barn animals if you decline a lady's hand." The boys could practically feel the girls glaring at them. "Real Elf men *dance*."

The small, closely-knit group carried on long into the night, dancing and laughing. The girls twirled through the dining hall as if it were a grand ballroom; the boys did their best to pick up the steps from Goldarrow, and tried not to disappoint their fearless leader who watched on from his drum, betraying more than one grin at their folly. By the second week, the boys had at least six different dances memorized and actually began to enjoy themselves and dancing with the beautiful company that whisked around them.

It was in this second week that something else began. . . .

Just after chores, and just before dinner, Grimwarden escorted the Seven down a corridor of the castle that they had previously traveled only to clean off dust and rodent excrement. Here he stopped at a large door. The lords remembered it because it had been locked, frozen shut either intentionally or, more likely, through lack of use. But when Grimwarden produced a long and rather ancient-looking key, the teens knew whatever was behind this door was important. And it was apparently meant for them.

"Today, my young lords," Grimwarden said with his hand resting on the iron handle, "you will be introduced to a world of secrets known only to a chosen few." A silent wave of exuberance rippled among the Seven.

"Behind this door lies the courtyard of the Seven Oaks, birthplace of Vexbane, and training heptagon of the Kings of Berinfell."

"Hepta-huh?" Johnny asked.

"A seven-sided polygon," Autumn explained.

"Right."

Grimwarden continued. "From now on, you will rise one hour earlier." A soft moan rippled through the group. "During this hour you will conduct physical training of my bidding: running, push-ups, sit-ups, pull-ups, and swimming."

"Gym," Tommy muttered.

"I hate gym," Kat said, but not too loud.

"When you have broken fast and cleaned, you will report here at once . . . in these." Grimwarden pulled a set of clothes from behind his back: black breeches and a matching tunic, each with silver stitching and strange knot work that reminded Jimmy of artwork in the Celtic tradition.

"Uniforms!" Kiri Lee exclaimed, probably the first time she was ever enthusiastic about the idea. "Like a work-out version of our ceremonial robes."

"Those are really cool, Guardmaster," Jimmy replied, asking to hold them.

"Nike's got nothing on us now," said Jett.

"I'm not sure about this *Nye-Kee* you speak of, Lord Jett. But these are the training uniforms of all who endure the Vexbane path," said Grimwarden, handing the garments out. "A badge of honor to all those who recognize their design. And they will serve you well."

"Endure?" asked Kat. "What do you mean?"

"Have you noticed that *not* every Elf in Allyra is a Sentinel or a Dreadnaught? Why is that?" he asked.

"Because they didn't sign up?" answered Jett.

"Because they would never pass," corrected Grimwarden. "It is an arduous affair, and only a few ever prove themselves worthy."

"And the Lords of Berinfell?" Tommy spread his arms.

"Have no choice. It is your destiny. But as with all others who have walked out from among these trees with the Vexbane ring on their finger"—he brandished his right hand on cue and flashed a single-jeweled ring on his index finger—"you will have to contend for it, fighting only yourself for the honor."

Autumn broke the silence with, "Whoa."

"But what you find behind here"—Grimwarden tapped the wood—"is not for the faint of heart, nor the weak in spirit. For you will be tested in ways unimaginable, tried to the point of breaking . . .

and then some. If it weren't for the noble blood that runs in your veins, I would advise each of you against passing through this door." He paused a moment, looking at the Seven and remembering when he was called to service. . . . *No one would say* yes *to the call, if they knew the cost ahead; such is the blessing of ignorance and the reason for many an unanswered prayer.* "Once you have entered, there is no going back."

"Still interested?" Kat nudged Tommy, knowing she was the only one who actually knew what Grimwarden was thinking.

Bring it on! He winked.

"You will learn the secrets to your powers and face a test unlike any other."

"Test?" asked Jimmy.

Grimwarden eyed him, staring hard into his face. And with that he turned and walked back down the corridor with his key.

The lords stood awestruck.

"Um, where are you going, Mr. Grimwarden, sir?" asked Kiri Lee.

"To the kitchen."

"And the door?"

"Who said you were going in now?" Grimwarden was nearly to the end of the hall.

"Uh, well . . ." Kiri Lee and the others stood dumbstruck, and rather let down.

Grimwarden stopped and spun back around. "Oh, stop moping, we start tomorrow morning! You all can stay here if you like, but Mumthers's cooking is calling me!"

The next morning, after a long run through the lower valley, a quick bath, and a bowlful of cream and oats, the lords converged in the hallway. As before, Grimwarden was standing with the key in hand, this time with Goldarrow right beside him. They huddled around the door dressed in their uniforms, eager to see what was behind it. Grimwarden twisted the key through the archaic mechanism within and unlatched the iron handle. Then pushing forward, he led the teens out into a lavish courtyard as Goldarrow checked the hallway a final time and latched the door shut behind them.

Seven white oak trees lined the perimeter, creating a large, green canopy overhead. The ground was polished marble, white overall with black lines running from the trees to a black center circle, creating seven distinct pie pieces. The entire space was encircled by a high wall now drenched in thick ivy and not overlooked by a single window from the rest of the castle. It was by all means hidden.

Grimwarden instructed each of them to be seated among the white sections. They hesitated a moment, each pupil mesmerized by the courtyard's beauty. Despite the rest of the castle's utter disrepair, this place seemed vibrant and well kept.

Grimwarden instructed them to close their eyes. And then he began to talk. Softly. "Here," he said, "everything is about the one we call Ellos. Everything." He let the last word hang, and Tommy found himself immersed and somewhat overwhelmed by the sweeping claim. *Everything?*

"From the distant stars," Grimwarden went on, "to the roots of the mountains, and beyond, to the very heart of this world—it is all a testament to Ellos. He created, he sustains, and he renews. And why? For his good pleasure. You, too, young Elves, are his pleasure." He paused. "This is no small detail. You are the joy of he who created everything, and so you have a reason for being alive. All power flows from him. Without him, we have nothing . . . are nothing. In him, we have all we will ever need and are all we were meant to be."

When he stopped speaking, none of the young lords moved.

The last few minutes had taken them all by surprise, drawing their collective mind's eye on a journey to an undiscovered country. But it was more than just their teacher's words or their own youthful imaginations. There was something else. Or *someone* else. It was almost as if Ellos himself had showed up in their midst, walking among them in the training circle.

The lords sat and looked at each other. Staring.

"I think we just had church," Jett said, remembering going with his parents to church every Sunday in North Carolina. He always left there feeling inspired . . . but nothing like this.

Tommy had been to church before, who hadn't? Stained glass, smelly hymnals, and the lady with the blue hair behind the organ. But this . . . this was something altogether new. An experience unlike any other . . . like, instead of hearing *about* God, he had actually *met* God. *If that's church, I want more*, Tommy thought.

"Me, too," said Kat.

Tommy snapped his attention to her. "Oh, right." *Cool.*

They all wanted more.

Grimwarden stood, gathered something from among the trees, then prompted the teens to sit back off the circle. He moved about in the middle of the Seven Oaks, wielding a long staff. Their teacher seemed oblivious to the lords now, his body spinning through the plane of the fighting circle as if he were dancing with the staff, much as Tommy had seen him do on the first morning. He twirled it about his head one moment, only to thrust it forward the next, followed by a lightning-fast change in momentum as he lunged backward. Each movement, each action, was an intentional thought practiced over years and years.

The teens moved forward, more than a few with mouths agape, lining the fighting circle's perimeter. Grimwarden jumped and rolled, twisting through aerials like a gymnast. Faster and faster he went, yet all the while as agile as a wildcat bounding through the jungle.

"That is so cool!" Autumn remarked.

"Can you teach us, Grimwarden?" Jett asked.

Grimwarden stepped away from Johnny and lowered the staff. "Places, each of you." The lords wasted no time stepping onto the seven sections.

"Guardmaster Grimwarden?" Kat raised her hand.

Grimwarden looked to Kat, and then to Goldarrow who stood against one of the oaks. "What's she doing?"

"Kat," Goldarrow stepped forward. "You don't need to raise your hand here." She looked back to Grimwarden. "It's an Earth thing. In class they do that to ask a question."

"Right," said Grimwarden, looking back to the young lord. "Yes, Kat?"

"I thought we were here to learn how to use our gifts?"

Grimwarden looked to her, then studied each of their faces for the briefest of moments. "Before you learn about what makes you unique, you must learn what makes you common. It is not what differentiates you that binds you together, but what you share. So before we learn to cast fire, or read minds, or heal others, we learn this." He spun the wooden shaft through his fingers with the ease of a skilled baton twirler.

Grimwarden walked over to Jett. "They say you're the strongest one, Jett. Do you feel strong?"

"Yes, sir. I do."

"Step forward." Jett took a step forward as Grimwarden handed him the staff. "Hit me."

Jett stared at him blankly.

"Hit me."

"But I—"

"Hit me before I hit you." Grimwarden raised his fists. But still Jett hesitated.

Grimwarden threw a punch aimed right for Jett's face. Jett barely avoided the blow, but it sent the message: Grimwarden was not playing. Feeling a surge of anger mixed with fear, Jett lashed back. He held the staff with two hands and swung the long end straight down on top of Grimwarden's head. Only the staff passed right through the space where Grimwarden stood and collided with the ground, sending a jolting rattle up Jett's arms. "Owww!" he stammered. A second pain came from a hand slap on top of his head. "Double owww!" He rubbed it.

"Swing again!" Grimwarden ordered, this time backing out into the middle of the circle. Jett followed, now sizing up his opponent. "Come on, purple eyes, I have lunch waiting for me!"

"Not unless I get to it first!" Jett lunged forward with the end of the staff, driving it hard at Grimwarden's stomach. But Grimwarden sidestepped as Jett nearly fell flat on his face. Another smack to the head. "Hey!"

"Mmmm, that was a good lunch, Mumthers." Grimwarden rubbed his stomach in mock form.

Jett spun around and leaped toward Grimwarden again, this time trying a combo, throwing each end at his target: one jab toward the face, the other toward the groin. But both Grimwarden avoided. Then Grimwarden grabbed the staff in the middle, twisted it so quickly that Jett lost his grip, and twirled the weapon around so that one end was but an inch from Jett's cheekbone.

"That was so cool!" Tommy wailed.

While Jett's pride was more than a little bruised, Grimwarden was too preoccupied with Tommy's language. "Lord Tommy, why would you ever say that was coo—?"

"Um, Grimwarden," Goldarrow waved to get his attention. She mouthed the word *Earth*.

Grimwarden shook his head. "I'm not sure I will get used to any of this." He turned back to Jett. "Well done, Lord Hamandar—I mean, Jett. You fared quite well."

Jett, feeling far from worthy of any praise, followed Grimwarden's gesture to return to his place.

Grimwarden searched the circle again. "Lord Miarra," he said to Autumn. "You are the one gifted with speed, are you not?"

"I am," she replied with a wide grin. Visions of what she had done to the enemy at Dalhousie Castle filled her mind's eye. But those were instantly replaced by the devastating carelessness she had displayed . . . carelessness that almost cost her life.

Grimwarden saw the change in her countenance. "Do not be afraid. There is no shame here, and what's past is past. You are good to remember your mistakes, but wiser still to learn from them."

Autumn hesitated for the slightest of moments, then took the staff he offered and walked forward into the circle.

"Go ahead."

"You *want* me to use my gift?"

"Do your worst."

She took a deep breath. "If you say so."

Autumn raised the staff and all at once became a blur of motion.

The wood whizzed past her body, arms hardly discernable. The Guardmaster stood very still as Autumn moved forward. Everyone was sure Grimwarden had met his match. A blow at this speed could be fatal. Grimwarden reached out his hands. All at once the staff stopped in front of Grimwarden's face, between his two palms.

Autumn stood, eyes wide. "How—how did—?"

"What your eyes cannot see, your ears can sometimes hear," Grimwarden said. Suddenly all the lords in the circle spontaneously high-fived each other. Grimwarden glanced over to Goldarrow, slightly uncomfortable from the look of it.

"They like you," she yelled. "It's all right. Relax!"

Grimwarden raised his eyebrows and turned his attention back to the circle of faces. *Strange customs.* He lowered his hands to silence their praise and sent Autumn back to her place.

"Lords of Berinfell, you have learned your first lesson. Skill and talent are two different entities. Skill by itself lacks inspiration, while talent alone will yield mistakes. But together they are a force to be reckoned with. The difference is discipline and desire. Each fuels the other. If you desire to do what you saw just now, then you must discipline yourself."

Goldarrow, still leaning against the tree, marveled at the Guardmaster's words. She had heard this practiced routine countless times before, even remembering when she took her first class from him when they were but a few decades old. He was still amazing. Lost in thought, it took Grimwarden a few times of calling her name before she realized he was asking for her.

"Are you listening?"

"What? Oh." Goldarrow reached a hand to her face, slightly flushed. "Yes, sir. What?"

"The *staffs*," he said for the third time.

"The staffs? Right. Yes. Right here, sir." She reached down beside the oak and carried the bundle of poles to the center of the circle. Grimwarden took them and turned away.

"Each of you, step forward," he ordered.

One at a time, the Seven came up to him and received a stout length of oak, sanded as smooth as the countertop in their kitchen back on

Earth. "The staff does not leave your side for the next week," Grimwarden ordered. The students weren't sure exactly what Grimwarden meant. Reading the look in their eyes, he went on. "Let me be precise. When you eat, it is with you. When you run, it is with you. When you bathe, it is with you."

"Bathe?" said Kiri Lee.

"Bathe," replied Grimwarden. "And if Goldarrow or Claris catch you without it, that's extra training."

The Seven reasoned they could live with a little extra running for their apathy.

"And no food for a whole day."

"Bathe," said Kiri Lee. "Check."

"One!"

Seven *swooshes* graced the air of the circle as seven staff ends met the upper-right-hand corner of an invisible square in front of each pupil.

"Four!"

Again, the staffs raced to the space at their lower left with a rushing of air.

"Two!"

A quick pass to the upper left.

"Three!"

Seven staffs whistled to the lower right.

"Very good," said Grimwarden. "Now focus. Each movement is a deliberate action. Intentional. But never the end of your thinking. Only the beginning." He waited as each of the students held in the *three* position.

"Four! One! Two! Four! Three!"

The staffs crisscrossed the air again, only this time more than one missed a mark, and two staffs struck one another accidentally.

"Stop, stop, stop," Grimwarden said, frustration mounting in his voice. "I said, focus!"

"Why don't you let me take them?" Goldarrow asked, resting her hand on Grimwarden's shoulder.

"That's not a bad idea," Grimwarden replied. "I'm thirsty anyway." He walked from the circle, leaving Goldarrow in the middle.

"Everyone, hold your staff like this." Goldarrow had her hands shoulder width apart, palms down, staff level at chest height. "Similar to what Grimwarden taught you, the *five* position is here." She raised it to just above her head. "*Six*"—down to her waist—"*seven*"—left hand over the right, staff standing vertically to the right—"and e*ight*"—right over left, vertically to the left. "Now: all together. Five, six, seven, eight. Again . . . five, six, seven, eight." They repeated the form several times. "Tommy, pull your elbows in. Five, six, seven, eight. Kat, a little higher." Goldarrow counted through over and over. "Johnny, watch the bend in your arms. . . . Jett, lower. . . . Autumn, Jimmy, bend your knees."

"Oh, got it," Tommy said. "One is here," he swept the tip of his staff to the upper-right-hand corner.

"Like we're attacking," Jett added.

"Precisely," said Goldarrow. "One through four are offensive forms, while—"

"Five through eight are defensive," finished Kat.

Goldarrow looked to her. "Did you cheat?"

"No, no! I figured it out! Honest!"

Goldarrow laughed. "I was just kidding."

"So it looks like this?" Jimmy asked, moving his staff while he counted out loud from one to eight.

"Well done," said Grimwarden, walking back into the midst of their circle. He carried a long bundle of fabric under his left arm. "Well done indeed. After a few more weeks like that and we'll start you sparring one another. And then, something new."

"Something new?" asked Tommy.

"Aye, something like this." With *this* came the sound of steel ringing in the air: a magnificent blade drawn out of hiding from its scabbard and brandished in the morning light.

Playing with Fire

AUTUMN HELD her sword in low guard, eyeing her opponent across the Vexbane Circle. Jett, likewise, circled slowly to the right, edging carefully around. Any sudden moves would be interpreted as an advance, and he could not afford to mess up with Autumn on the other side of any weapon. When at last Jett felt in control, he lunged forward. Autumn instantly disappeared from his view, but he anticipated this, sank to his knees, and spun around to face the opposite direction.

The moment Jett raised his sword up to parry, a series of hard blows hammered down on it like a woodpecker drilling a tree. Sparks lit up the circle. He absorbed all the hits and then lunged toward Autumn, ceasing her speed attack and knocking her on her back. He pinned her hands to the ground and she dropped her sword.

"Get off me!" Autumn yelled, struggling under his inescapable grip.

"Say 'uncle' first."

"Just get off, okay?"

"'Uncle' first!"

"Yeah, right! No way!"

"Then I'm not getting up."

"Autumn, Jett," interrupted Grimwarden, "might I remind you this is a sparring exercise in weaponry, not verbal bickering."

"Then tell him to stop using his strength on me!" Autumn contended.

"Well, you used your speed! How am I supposed to counter that?"

Grimwarden harrumphed. "Well, I can see we need to move to the next level."

"The next level?" Tommy inquired. "What's that?"

"Come with me . . . and bring your weapons." And with that Grimwarden turned from the training court and entered the castle. The Seven quickly picked up their swords, staves, and bows and followed Grimwarden.

When Grimwarden finally stopped deep in a seldom-traveled section of Whitehall, the Seven stood before a dead end. A solid stone wall. Grimwarden didn't seem about to say anything, so Jimmy piped up. "So . . . what're we here for?"

"Your new training lair," replied Grimwarden, a subtle smile creeping across his face.

"I hate to sound ungrateful, but it's an empty corridor," Kiri Lee said, looking back down the way they had come.

"Oh really?" Grimwarden said, leaning lazily up against the stone wall before them. He stood there for a second; then all of a sudden the wall began to move.

"Whoa!" the teens cried out.

"What'd you do?" asked Jett, pointing at the wall sliding away from them. The receding surface revealed an opening on the right-hand side of the corridor. "Check it out!"

"A new door!" Kat exclaimed, walking toward it. "Can we?" she looked to Grimwarden.

"Be my guest," he said.

The Seven walked through the door and continued down a very narrow passage, roughly cut from the bedrock of the mountain. A few sharp turns lit by torches on the wall eventually led to a descending staircase. And upon clearing the last step, the Seven emerged into a massive hall aglow with a hundred torches at least. From wall to wall, the room was filled with every kind of training apparatus imaginable. Ropes interlaced one another and crisscrossed from floor to ceiling; wooden planks rested on fulcrums like giant seesaws; knotted ropes hung from the ceiling every few feet in long lines, while telephone pole-like beams stood straight up in the middle of the room; there were balance beams, suspended stepping platforms, even floating pads in a long pool of water. And all about the room were wooden boards cut out in the outline of men, hinged at the bottom—targets, from what the Seven could tell.

"This, m'lords, is the lair." Grimwarden stood back, allowing them to look on in awe. "Created thousands of years ago and seen only by those who built it . . . for one purpose."

"It's incredible!" said Johnny.

"What purpose?" Tommy asked, turning to their teacher.

"You."

They all turned to look at him in wonder. "Us?" "What did you say?" "Huh?"

"That's right," he went on. "The architects of Whitehall knew of the Berinfell Prophecies, just as all the ancients did. Our land would be rescued by Seven Lords. But they also knew such leaders—such warriors—would need more than just the Vexbane Circle. To be greater than any other conqueror in our history, they'd need to train more than any other conqueror in our history."

"So *that's why* you contended so strongly for us to come here in the council meeting," concluded Kat.

"Among other reasons, yes."

"So let me get this straight." Tommy worked it through in his mind. "This lair has been sitting here, unused, for hundreds of years waiting for us?"

"Thousands of years is more like it, but yes. While you were busy cleaning up the castle these last three months, I've been busy replacing lines, swapping out rotted planks of wood, lubricating the gear mechanisms, and reworking the torches. But it's mostly just as they left it. Untouched. Unused. And waiting to train the elite of Allyra."

Kat walked forward to touch one of the old planks of wood. "I can't even believe . . ." Suddenly a thousand voices filled her head at once. Singing, laughing, shouting orders.

She let go.

The sounds stopped.

"What is it, Kat?" Kiri Lee asked. But Kat intentionally ignored her. "Kat?" asked Jimmy.

"It's the ancients," said Grimwarden. "How do you train a thought-reader? You impart your memory into your work. For you, Kat," he said, stepping forward, "there are millions of memories here. Every song that the workmen sang, every order given during the construction, they're all in here for you to discover . . . to sort through . . . to learn from. Our history. Our traditions. It was rumored that the women who lived here would bring their infants in here just to sing them to sleep, knowing that the melodies would be captured . . . for you."

Kat could feel hot tears filling her eyes. The fact that she had been the center of attention for a group of her people so many years ago was profoundly moving. They would never meet her, and she would never meet them. But somehow, they would connect over the ages of time and share life together: one looking forward to hope, the other looking backward to love.

"For all of you, this place will be your world for the next several weeks. You will take the skills you have learned in Vexbane—of communing with Ellos, of sword and spear, of staff and of bow—and you will marry them to your own unique gifts. Foresight. Strength and healing. Air walking. Speed. Marksmanship. Thought-reading. Fire.

"You will be the most elite warriors in all of Allyra when I'm done with you. And you will be an unstoppable team when united in action and in heart. Here, it is not only the individual we will train—as we have aboveground—but the team. How to work as one. And if Ellos blesses us, we'll have you done by the time Nelly and Regis return from Earth."

It was only Kat who heard his thought, *If they return from Earth.*

The next several weeks were some of the most exciting, most exhilarating the young lords had ever experienced in all their lives. Their daily cleaning chores were cut down to mostly just cleaning their rooms and washing dishes; all other activities took second place to their training in the lair. When they weren't in the room physically, they were dreaming about it at night. Every challenge they could not best in the day became their nighttime puzzle, turning it over in their minds, wrestling with it through the midnight hour. They would awake eager to try out their new strategies and please their teachers.

But more than anything, they were excited to learn about their unique gifts. Grimwarden would spend time with each student, explaining the disciplines needed to master the most foundational aspects of their talents. Sure, each of them had dabbled with their skills when no one was looking—who wouldn't! But to actually know the history behind the power—where it had come from in their family line—and then how to focus, train, and control the gift was a spectacular feeling. No longer just untamed whims within them, their talents began to be honed to something of an unconscious response, summoned with the slightest thought, subdued with a passing whisper. Their powers and the deep respect they had for the teachers magnified exponentially.

"Are your eyes closed?" Grimwarden asked Johnny.

"Yes, Guardmaster."

"Now, tell me how many targets you saw."

"Nine. Three along the floor, two on the tower to the right, another on the tower on the left, two on the bridge"—he hesitated, searching his memory—"and one hanging from the ceiling."

"Well done." Grimwarden scratched his beard. "Think you can do any better than yesterday? I spent all night repairing the bridge."

Johnny winced slightly. "Sorry."

"Do it again and that's no dinner for you."

Although the other lords were busy with their own training regimes, they all *ohhhh*-d him from around the lair. "I won't miss this time," Johnny replied.

"You'd better hope not!" Autumn yelled from the ropes.

"Very well." Grimwarden turned to look at the target range. "The Gwar are attacking . . . NOW!"

Johnny spun around, blindfold still in place, and raised his hands.

From his right hand came three bursts, another three from his left. Then a final massive blast from both hands held together. The streams of fire shot forward, illuminating the entire room like the sun. The other lords covered their eyes against the brightness. In quick succession, the wooden targets vaporized into plumes of smoke and ash.

As Johnny lifted the blindfold, Grimwarden began clapping. "Well done, Lord Albriand . . . Johnny."

Johnny blinked and counted the smoldering piles of rubble . . . *eight, nine,* . . . *ten!* "I did it!" He tossed the blindfold up in the air.

"Fine work," Grimwarden high-fived him awkwardly, much to Johnny's shock. The other lords laughed, happy to see Grimwarden making the attempt, then congratulated Johnny.

Leaving Johnny to the rest of his physical training regime, he called Jimmy to one side of the room, standing below a very small raised platform two feet square. It hovered directly over a pool of water about ten feet deep. "Lord Thorwin, what say you? Ready to get wet again?"

Jimmy took a deep breath. "Not this time," he smiled. "I'm ready."

"Good then. Up you go." And with that, Jimmy placed a heel in Grimwarden's cupped hands; the teacher thrust him skyward, Jimmy doing a front flip and landing on the platform. "And you'll need this." Grimwarden threw him another blindfold, something he never seemed in short supply of in the lair.

Jimmy wrapped it around his eyes and tied it off behind his head. "Ready."

"Tommy, Jett," Grimwarden gestured them over. Together, the three of them reached into a wicker basket and each removed two smooth stones. "You first, Tommy. Then Jett."

"You ready, Jimmy?" Tommy yelled.

"I already said I was a second ago!"

"I just don't want to hit you like last time."

"Enough, Tommy," Grimwarden placed a hand on his shoulder. "I think he learned that lesson."

"Okay," Tommy replied, saying it more like a question. He looked to Jimmy.

"Here it comes!" Jimmy yelled.

"Hey, I was going to say that!"

"I know," Jimmy replied. Tommy hesitated. "Would you just throw the stones?"

Tommy, finding he was accurate with any weapon—not just the bow—wound up and threw the first stone, followed quickly by the second. Right behind him came Jett, wheeling his arm back and drilling Jimmy with his first and second stones. Grimwarden was last, throwing with all his might.

Jimmy stepped to his right, catching Tommy's first and second stones, one in each hand. As Jett's next two whizzed at his head, Jimmy used the ones in his hands to deflect Jett's, the stone projectiles flinging off into the far wall. Grimwarden's stones were next. Jimmy threw Tommy's first stone back at Tommy, the second back at Jett, and caught both of Grimwarden's, winging one right back at Grimwarden. The last he kept for himself.

Tommy, Jett, and Grimwarden ducked or jumped out of the way. "Whoa!" said Tommy. "That wasn't in your training scenario!"

"I know," Jimmy grinned, removing his blindfold. "I improvised."

Week after week the Seven grew stronger, testing their skills against every new challenge Grimwarden could throw at them . . . in many cases, literally throw at them. But none of them would ever forget the day they walked into the lair and it was pitch black.

"Grimwarden?" a few of them called out. Their voices echoed throughout the vast chamber.

"I'm here," came a reply from across the room.

Tommy leaned over to Johnny, "Want to light things up?"

"Yeah, sur—"

"Belay that, Johnny," Grimwarden yelled back. "You'll have your chance." Johnny stood in the darkness, his hands poised to set fire to the pitch-black darkness. "All of you, listen to me. Before you lays a new course, one you have never encountered before. But unlike your previous challenges—where each of you tested with me individually—this one requires something more. It requires all of you to work together. As one." Though the Seven could not see a hand in front of their face, they each looked to where one another stood, taking in Grimwarden's next instructions with care. "No clues today. No advice. You must figure this one out on your own. Now, a few rules."

"Rules?" Kat echoed.

"Yes. Kat, you may only read the objects painted in red."

"Red? Hey, wait a sec! I can't see a—"

"Johnny, you may only cast fire on what Kat tells you. Jett, your strength can only be used on anything painted blue. Tommy, no throwing, only the bow you find on the course may you use. Kiri Lee, you may not take more than five steps in the air at one time. Autumn, you may not leave Jett's side for more than two seconds, which I will be counting. And, Jimmy, you may only use the words *yes* and *no*. Am I clear?"

The Seven stood blinking in the darkness, going over the rules in their minds.

"Your objective is simply to get to me. Failure on any front and you cook for yourselves for a week." And their previous failures with such contests proved he was not joking. But a week? "You have until the sand runs out in the glass beside me."

"Starting when?" asked Tommy.

"When Kat questioned my saying there would be rules."

"What!" the Seven cried out.

"I suggest someone does something shortly," Grimwarden chided.

"Quick, what do we do?" asked Autumn.

"I can't see a thing!" said Jett. "This is crazy. We need light."

"But, guys, I can't do a thing until Kat gives me a target."

"Kat?" asked Tommy.

"I'm thinking—I mean—"

"Well, just starting feeling around," cried Jett. "You're bound to find something!"

"But she can't read just anything," Kiri Lee put in. "It's got to be red."

Thanks, Queen Obvious, Kat thought and then immediately wanted to kick herself.

"Kat, over here," Autumn suddenly called out. "I've found something right in front of us here. Feels like four candles on a table."

The six of them shuffled forward, letting Kat to the front. "You're right, candles. But which one can I read? Which one is red? I can't just tell Johnny to light them all. He's supposed to light *one* of these."

"Take a chance, I guess," said Tommy. "There's no way to be sure."

"Yes!" exclaimed Jimmy.

"Yes?" Tommy turned in the direction of his voice.

"Yes!" Jimmy said again.

"He can't say more than yes and no, remember?" said Kiri Lee.

Tommy thought quickly. "'Yes,' there is a way to be sure?"

"Yes!"

"How?"

"He can only answer yes-or-no questions," Kiri Lee restated. "Jimmy, can you tell if Johnny is about to light the candle that Kat can read? One that she might instruct Johnny to light in the future because it's red?"

"Yes," but his response was not as confident as before.

"Well, let's give it a shot," tried Kat, reaching for the first candle. "Johnny, light this one."

"All right," he said, stepping forward and grabbing it.

Jimmy didn't make a noise.

No one moved.

"Jimmy? Is it working?" Tommy asked.

"No," replied Jimmy. This whole yes-and-no thing was harder than he thought.

"Why not?" Kiri Lee inquired openly.

"You're frustrated," said Autumn. "Right?"

"Yes!"

"Wait a sec," Tommy thought for a moment. "Johnny, did you actually try to *light* the candle?"

"Well, no, not really."

"So there is no future for Jimmy to see," surmised Tommy.

"YES!" hooted Jimmy, excited that someone else put it together.

"Jimmy"—Tommy grabbed him by the wrist—"put your hand on Johnny's arm here. If he starts to light the wrong one, yank his arm away. Johnny, small flames, dude. Okay?"

"Got it," said Johnny.

"Here we go," said Kat. She lifted the candle as before.

Johnny took a deep breath. The thought of missing out on Mumthers's cooking for an entire week did not sit well with him. Not at all. "Here goes." But no sooner did he lift his finger to light the candle than Jimmy yanked his arm aside, the small flame snuffed out from the sudden breeze.

"No," Jimmy spoke.

Everyone let out a deep sigh. It seemed to be working.

"Next one," said Kat. Johnny took it from her and did the same thing. Again Jimmy yanked his arm away suddenly, the flame just barely avoiding the wick.

"That was close," said Tommy.

"Too close," amended Johnny.

"Okay, Johnny. Third one." Kat offered the candle. She could feel his fingers shaking slightly.

"You can do this," said Jett. "Stay focused, guys."

Johnny took a deep breath and produced a small flame from his fingertip. At first he thought Jimmy had spaced out, forgetting to yank his arm away, until he realized the candle he was holding had a red smear across the wax.

"You did it!" Kat exclaimed. She clapped her hands a few times and then said, "Here, let me read the candle. Must be instructions."

But no sooner did she take the candle than Tommy interrupted her. "Guys . . . would you look at that!"

Kat raised the single candle and the Seven of them stared out into the lair. . . .

Leaps and Bounds

"I HOPE you're not going to let all this sand run through the glass simply while gawking," came Grimwarden's voice, echoing through the lair. Yet still the Seven teens stood, amazed at what they saw. All but the stone landing they stood on had been submerged by water, the entire room flooded. Their lone candle cast only a little light, but it was enough to see that they stood on the only dry patch for quite some distance . . . and all the hanging apparatuses that normally clung to the ceiling and walls had been removed, leaving only a barren lake in front of them.

"And now that you can see," said Grimwarden again, "there's one more rule. No one gets wet."

"Grrreat. So now what?" asked Johnny, letting out a deep sigh.

"We'll figure it out," replied Autumn. "Don't worry."

"There goes my dinner."

"I'd say you have about seven minutes," came Grimwarden's voice again.

"Everyone, search for clues!" Tommy said, now looking every which direction. "There's got to be something."

"Hey, look over there," said Kiri Lee. She pointed to the edge of the landing in front of them. She asked for the candle and then knelt down. "There's a small patch of red paint."

"Hey, you're right!" said Tommy. "Good eyes! Kat, you wanna read this?"

"Mind-reader, coming through," she replied, pushing herself deliberately between Kiri Lee and Tommy. Sure enough, a small red patch of paint clung to the edge of the stone as it dropped down into the water. She placed her finger on it and closed her eyes. After a moment, all Kat could say was, "Huh."

"Huh? What is it, Kat?" asked Tommy.

"I think it's a riddle."

"A riddle?"

"Yeah. *Hanging bows fly like doves, when sent by flaming strands above.*"

"*Huh* is right," added Jett. "Any takers?"

"There's something above us," Autumn surmised. "Hanging. From the ceiling, I think."

"Totally. A bow for me?" suspected Tommy. A few of the others nodded.

"But I can't see a thing. Not with this candle," said Kiri Lee.

"Then Johnny will need to light it up," suggested Kat.

Tommy shook his head. "But only what you tell him, remember?"

"But how am I supposed to see what is up there?"

Tommy looked to Jimmy. "Try again?"

"Sure." He shrugged his shoulders. "Johnny, do your thing."

"You got it. But . . . uh . . . where?"

"Pick a spot, I dunno. Just remember, you really have to shoot fire."

"Right." Johnny took a deep breath and raised his arms.

"Wait!" Kat interjected. "Just not a lot. If there really is a bow hanging up there, we don't want to burn it up, too."

Johnny stared at her. "You do realize you're asking me to shoot fire up into the air blindly, don't you?"

"I'm just saying, don't do like a big *whoooosh!*—just like a little *swish.*"

Jett laughed. "I do believe that's the first time I've heard a girl use two sound effects in one sentence."

"And I believe you're letting Mumthers's next meal slip away," said Grimwarden.

"Okay, Johnny, like she said," instructed Tommy. "Just a little shot."

Johnny raised his hands and felt the familiar surge of power rise within him. He aimed toward the ceiling when suddenly Jimmy knocked his arms down. But it was too late. Fortunately the stream of fire shot out a little ways into the watery floor, erupting in a thick blast of steam.

"That was close," said Johnny.

"Too close," added Kat.

"Did anybody see anything?"

"Yeah, Tommy," said Autumn. "I think right over there." She pointed to a spot overhead about ten or fifteen feet away from the platform. "Like something dangling from the ceiling by a rope."

"A bow?" asked Tommy.

"Could be. Hard to tell."

"Johnny, aim where she pointed."

"Roger," he said, extending his arms once again.

"But wait a sec," Autumn stopped him. "If he burns through the rope, and that bow drops—"

"*Splash!*" said Kat.

"That's three sound effects," said Jett. She winked at him.

"Kiri Lee! Of course!" exclaimed Tommy. He turned to her. "Run over the water?"

"All right, Johnny." Tommy put his hand on Johnny's shoulder. "Just enough to burn through the ropes. And aim high. Kiri Lee will do the rest." He looked to Jimmy. "Stop him if it's the wrong target." Jimmy nodded.

"Time's wasting," Grimwarden hollered.

Johnny took a deep breath and looked up, aiming into the darkness. "Here goes nothing."

The blast of fire came uninterrupted this time; either Jimmy had zoned out, or Johnny had hit his mark. The Seven tracked the fireball as it lofted through the darkness and lit up the rest of the room. Suddenly the orange glow connected with something just below the stone dome above. A flare of white light. And then the steady glow of flames on a hemp rope.

"Nailed it!" shouted Jett, pumping his fist.

"Good job, dude!" said Tommy. "Check it out!" There, suspended over the water in the approximate location Autumn had indicated, swung a longbow, suspended by a burning cord, and bound to it, a quiver of arrows.

"There's more stuff over there!" Autumn pointed out into the room, the rope's fire-light illuminating even more of the lair's submerged obstacle course.

"Not now, Autumn!" Johnny shouted her down. "That bow is about to fall!"

"Kiri Lee!" yelled Tommy.

"I'm on it!" She stood on the edge of the platform, shaking her hands as if she were warming up for a music lesson.

"It's going to fall in the water!" Kat yelled.

"Her timing will have to be perfect," said Autumn.

"I'm on it!"

Tommy piped up. "Use Jimmy!"

"Yeah, Jimmy!" said Jett. "Tell her when to go!"

"This is so cool," Tommy replied.

No sooner did they look to her than Jimmy yelled, "Yes! Yes! Yes!"

"*Yes*, like as in now, yes?" Jett asked.

"YES!"

All at once Kiri Lee took flight, one foot higher than the other, walking out into midair. The other teens counted her steps for her. *One . . . two . . . three . . .*

She extended her hand just as the rope snapped and the bow descended from its holding. As it fell, the orange embers marked its flight. The lords gasped. It would be too far away, and Kiri Lee could not risk another step farther out or risk not being able to come back within the allotted five steps Grimwarden had mandated. She stretched out her hand, then closed her fist.

Her hand grabbed the trailing length of burning rope as the bow plummeted beneath her. Without even thinking, she yanked up, and then threw the weapon behind her, turning in the air and using her last two steps to leap back toward the platform. She sailed through the air, but she was short.

"Gotcha!" Jett exclaimed as he caught her just two feet from the ledge, feet dangling over the water.

She smiled and looked up at him, a bit nervous. "No sweat."

"No sweat," he grinned back.

While the fireball had illuminated the hall for a few moments, the darkness crept back in once more, saved only by the flickering candle that Kat held.

"I can smell Mumthers's dinner cooking," Grimwarden said lazily. "Wonder if you'll have the chance to savor any of it?"

"Quick! What's next?" Jimmy hollered. "Come on!"

"Easy, Turbo," Johnny held up a hand. "We'll get there."

"Kat," said Tommy, holding up the bow. "Look here." A red smear crossed the leather-wrapped handle of the bow. "Read it."

Kat took the bow lightly with two hands and closed her eyes. "Targets. Two of them."

"And just three arrows," Tommy held the quiver up.

"Not much room for error," Autumn replied.

"And I can hardly see." Tommy looked to Kat. "Sure there's not anything about letting Johnny light something up?"

Kat closed her eyes once more. "Nope."

Tommy sighed. "*Great.*"

"Wait!" Kat grabbed the quiver, nearly knocking Tommy into the water. "The arrows!"

"What about them?"

"Hold on." Kat clenched her hand around the shafts.

"But, Kat—" Kiri Lee made to warn her, but Tommy waved her off.

"Look," he pointed. Sure enough, the feathers on the ends were dyed red. Everyone watched.

"Come on, Tommy! That's your cue!" said a few of the teens, eager to be done with this challenge.

"Guys, chill," said Tommy. "I'm not shooting anything until I'm sure what I'm aiming for."

"Johnny, light the arrows." All looked back to Kat.

"You sure, Kat?" Tommy took one arrow from the quiver.

"I'm sure. Johnny, light it up."

"Will do!"

Tommy nocked the arrow and held up the tip to Johnny. Using just his fingertip, Johnny set the shaft ablaze. As Tommy drew the arrow back, he hesitated. "But I still don't know how this helps—"

"Of course!" Kat exclaimed. "There aren't three arrows because you might miss one. Tommy, think of it. You're the best! Grimwarden knows you won't miss. The third one is to light the room. Sink it into the stone above and you'll have a few moments of light to see by."

Tommy looked at her wide-eyed, saying, "You are brilliant," to which Kat blushed. But no one else could see it in the candlelight. Tommy aimed for a spot in the darkness and let the arrow fly. An orange flame streaked through the lair like a shooting star in a midnight sky.

Crack-thunk!

The missile found its mark, sinking deep into the rock ceiling above, bits of stone flittering into the water far below. And at once the shaft burned all the brighter, giving off a sizeable blast of light.

"Whoa! Check it out!" said Autumn.

"I see it! I see it! Kat, another arrow!" She passed him the second shaft, and in two heartbeats, the arrow was sent flying through the room. The sound of smashing metal blistered through the air, sparks flying; the third and final arrow caused the same result, two shackles now blown apart, loose chains falling from the ceiling. But no splash. The Seven listened as a strange grating noise began, and with it came a return to black as the arrow in the ceiling was extinguished. The grating sound increased, metal sliding over metal.

"Something's coming," Jimmy said. "And fast."

Kat held up the candle.

The scrape of metal was getting closer. Picking up speed!

Jimmy screamed, "Look out!"

All at once a heavy metal gangplank plowed into the stone ledge, sending chunks of rock splashing into the water. The Seven jumped back with a start, the candle blowing out.

"Quick!"

"Relight it!"

"Over here, Johnny!"

"Kat! Where are you?"

"Here, take my hand."

"Oh, gotcha!" Johnny took the candle and in a moment it was alive again. He raised it, and there in front of them was a long walk-way stretching far over the water and angling up.

"Autumn, to the top," Tommy pointed. "See what's there."

Autumn was gone in a second, racing up the bridge. Then, "Owww!"

"What is it?" the others blurted out.

But in keeping to Grimwarden's command, she was back in another second, standing beside Jett. Autumn rubbed her forehead. "A stone wall is what it is! Bashed my head right against it!"

"Are you certain?" said Tommy.

"Take the light up, and I'll prove it to you."

The Seven clambered onto the metal scaffolding with Johnny leading the way with the candle. Their footsteps echoed off the water below. With no handrails, one wrong step meant a trip into the drink, and no dinner. As they neared Autumn, still rubbing her head—a trickle of blood running into her eyebrow—they noticed that it was not a wall at all.

"It's a boulder," Tommy said, amazed. "On top of a tower from the training course."

Autumn stepped forward and looked at it in the light. "A boulder? But what's a—?"

"I'll move it," Jett said, stepping forward. "But not before I heal that," he pointed to Autumn's forehead.

"No, really, it's just—" But before she could finish her sentence, Jett placed his hand over the wound on her head, held it there for not more than three seconds, and then withdrew it—a smudge of fresh blood on his palm. On Autumn's forehead, the cut had vanished.

"I still don't get how he does that," Kiri Lee said. "So cool."

"Jett, the boulder?"

"I'm on it, Jimmy," Jett said, annoyed. He walked up to the boulder and pressed both hands firmly against the enormous rock. Then, bracing himself on the tower platform, he pushed.

At first, nothing seemed to happen. More than one of the others wondered if maybe Jett's powers had diminished in some way . . . maybe from healing Autumn. But those thoughts were short-lived as the rock began to roll forward, and a beat later, plummeted off the tower. A giant splash erupted from far below as water shot upward. The Seven clambered onto the platform so as not to get sprayed, remembering Grimwarden's firm warning. A moment later, all was still, save for the flickering candle and waves lapping gently against the sides of the lair far below.

"I would say you have about three minutes left," came Grimwarden's voice. "Maybe a little more. Almost here?"

"Three minutes?" Jimmy threw his hands up. "I canna' *believe* this!"

"Hey, look at that!" Kiri Lee pointed to a post protruding vertically from the far right side of the platform. Attached to the top was a rope descending out and away from them, and on it was a pulley with a handle set horizontally.

"It's a trolley!" Johnny yelled.

"A what?" asked Jimmy.

"A trolley. We built them all the time in our backwoods. Grab the handle and off you go. Just like on our way here to Whitehall in the forest."

"So that's how we get down," surmised Kat.

"Problem," Tommy interjected. "There's only one trolley. Once someone uses it to get down there, how do we get it back up here?"

"Aw, mannn! He's right," said Jett.

"It looks way too far for me to air walk," said Kiri Lee.

"Johnny, shine the candle over here," said Autumn. "I think I see something." The two neared the opposite corner of the platform. Coiled in a neat pile was a thick rope.

"We'll tie one end of this rope onto it," Autumn held it up. "Then pull back the pulley each time."

"That might take forever," said Jimmy.

"Not if I'm pulling it," replied Autumn, a sparkle in her eye.

Tommy set to tying the rope onto the trolley and then asked who wanted to go first. The only person to volunteer was Jimmy. "I got nothing to lose," was all he said, which no one really understood at the time. He stepped in front of the post and grabbed the handle. He tested the strength of the zip line with his weight a little, then lifted up his legs. A breath later he was sailing down the rope and vanished out of sight. The others heard a loud "*Woohooooo!*" echo out into the room as the pulley *whizzed* faster down the line. Autumn held the tail of the trailing rope, watching the coil unravel over the side of the platform like an endless snake hurling itself into midair.

All at once Jimmy's progress seemed to slow as the *whizzing* of the zip line decreased in pitch. His course was bottoming out, reaching the end of the line. And then, silence.

Everyone held their breath.

"I'm here!" Jimmy yelled. "And Grimwarden is, too!"

"Autumn!" Tommy yelled.

"I'm on it." It was just that fast that the pulley suddenly appeared back at its starting point, the line and wheel smoking.

"Who's next?" Tommy asked.

"Might I suggest two at a time?" Kat said, stepping forward. "We'll never make it in time."

"Good thinking." Tommy looked over. "Ladies first."

Kat stepped up, followed by Kiri Lee. Kat didn't even look up. Once situated on each side of the handle. They were off and flying.

Next came Johnny and Jett, Johnny handing Tommy the candle.

Jimmy went by himself as Tommy insisted that Autumn not go alone. Then Tommy and Autumn leaped out into total pitch black, hollering all the way down.

When all Seven were at last assembled on the landing far below—having traversed nearly the entire hall—Grimwarden produced a brilliant flash of light that settled into the steady blaze of a torch. And beside his smiling face he held a timing glass . . . the final few grains of sand slipping through the narrow center.

"Who's hungry?"

15

The Scarlet Raptor

ON THOSE rare occasions when he was free from the brutal training schedule, Tommy spent nearly all of his time exploring the labyrinthine passages of Whitehall Castle. The intricate network of corridors, keeps, tunnels, and towers was an irresistible puzzle waiting to be solved . . . and Tommy loved puzzles. Most often, he'd make a wrong turn and wind up at a blank stone wall or, worse, right back where he'd started. But every once in a while he'd follow a passage and discover spectacular settings like a chamber full of sunlit water fountains or a hall strewn with intriguing artwork. Or, like yesterday, a secluded balcony high on Whitehall's central tower. Why he hadn't found it earlier, he wasn't sure. But Whitehall was vast indeed.

Tommy had spent several hours reclining on the balcony's curving stone bench and quickly made it his own. Eyes open or closed, he found the spot relaxing and entertaining. Colorful birds crisscrossed in the air and disappeared into the dark green shadows under the canopy. Braided mimots—the striped, ghost-faced monkeylike creatures that lived in the treetops—hooted and cackled as they leaped branch-to-branch after each other. And numerous driftworms—thumb-sized, fuzzy purple caterpillars—descended from the upper branches on gossamer parachutes of silk to land wherever the breeze carried them. It was as peaceful a place as Tommy had yet seen in Allyra.

After a particularly exhausting long sword session, Tommy couldn't wait to get back to his new special escape. Traversing several large halls, climbing two flights of stairs, and racing blindly down a dark passage, Tommy turned a corner and . . . came to an abrupt stop.

Kat was sitting in his spot.

She looked up at Tommy, her bluish skin purpling with a blush. But there was no smile. Just a sigh.

"You're kidding," they both said.

"I just found this place yesterday," said Tommy.

"I found it a month ago," said Kat. She saw his shoulders fall and didn't even need to read his thoughts. "It's okay," she said. "There's room for two."

Feeling somewhat disappointed and very awkward, Tommy sat. He crossed his arms and leaned on the balcony rail. He didn't look at her but could feel Kat's stare. When she finally looked away, Tommy felt somehow lighter. He relaxed a little and absently watched the driftworms.

"I come up here to work on my First Voice studies," Kat said, trying to think of something interesting to break the awkward silence.

"You and Kiri Lee with your First Voice stuff," said Tommy. "Beats me."

"Languages can be a lot of fun."

"I suppose," he looked away. "If you're smart."

"I'm sure you could learn quickly, Tommy. You're smart." But Tommy didn't answer, and another awkward silence filled the time.

"Oh, look," said Kat. Tommy turned. A small purple piece of fuzz was crawling down her forearm. "It tickles."

"Reminds me of woolly bears back at home," Tommy said. "Except they're not so purple."

Kat smiled and held up her hand. The driftworm traveled the length of her index finger and seemed perplexed as to where to go from there. "Have you seen the moths that these things turn into?"

Tommy shook his head.

"Claris says they're as big as both your hands . . . and they glow."

"Cool," said Tommy. He envisioned the forest canopy at night, alive with hundreds of luminous moths. "Way cool."

Suddenly Tommy and Kat stiffened and looked up. They had heard a sound, a haunting . . . alien sound. Like a bird's cry, but it gradually phased into a screaming voice. It trilled and then faded.

"What was that?" Tommy asked.

"Shh, there it is again!" Kat looked at him wide-eyed. "Did it . . . did it speak?"

"So you heard it, too?" Tommy gasped. "It said—"

"*CoO-oMmMm-mme.*"

"It's in the castle somewhere!" Kat said.

"Where?"

"This way!" Kat leaped from the stone bench and tore through the doorway. Tommy sprinted after her. Hearing the sound again, they followed the echoes farther into the castle, and then veered off down a passage they had never taken before. The haunting call led them deeper and deeper into the mountainside. Several twists and turns later, Kat held up a hand for Tommy to stop. The passage they were in was lit only from windows at either end. They stood in the shadows between.

"Why'd you stop?"

"That last—whatever it was—it's here. I feel like we should see it."

Tommy pointed to the far side of the corridor . . . . a dead end. "Maybe you just heard it echo."

"No, it was right here."

"But it's just a wall."

Kat let out a yelp and jumped back. Something moved at the base of the wall.

Something with eyes.

Tommy and Kat edged backward, squinting in the dim light. It was hard to see whatever it was, but something snakelike emerged, apparently squeezing between two stones just above the floor. It slithered toward them and squeaked.

"Oh, it's a frake!" said Kat. She stepped forward and, to Tommy's astonishment, picked the thing up.

Tommy looked at it curling around Kat's wrist and up into her hand. "A what?" he asked.

"A frake. Well, that's what I call it at least." She gave him a goofy smile. "It's like a furry snake. Fur-ake—get it? Nelly called it some Elven name I can't remember. So I just call it a frake. Here, hold it."

She let it slither into Tommy's cupped hands. Indeed, its body was like a snake's, but completely covered in soft, shorthaired fur. It had huge eyes and a small pink nose. It squeaked again and then emitted a low purring sound. Tommy looked at Kat. "No chance this is what made that sound."

"No," said Kat. "No way." She walked over to the wall, eyeing the stones. "But that little guy just came out of the wall. Which means . . ." She pressed her palms flat against the stone. "I bet there's something behind here." She pushed in several places.

"Yeah, right, Kat," he said. "That only happens in the mov—"

"Ah! This one." Kat found a stone that slid inward and then fell, revealing a gaping black hole.

"I don't believe it." Tommy stepped forward. "What's in there?"

"I can't tell. Hey, put the frake down and help."

"Oh . . . right." Tommy placed the still-purring creature on the passage floor and pulled at the edge of the hole until he dislodged another stone. It was no little effort, but soon Tommy and Kat had an opening they could crawl through.

Kat looked at Tommy. "Think we should?"

"Why not?" he asked, sarcastically adding, "I mean, if you hear a scary bird-scream-ghost-voice coming from a black hole in a stone wall, the only thing to do is investigate." Kat whacked him on the shoulder and then disappeared through the wall.

It was a little more awkward a fit for Tommy. When he was through, Kat said, "Stairs."

Still wiping dust from his tunic, Tommy looked up. About seven feet away, just visible in the inky dark, gray steps spiraled up and to the left.

"Come on," Kat said.

Placing each foot carefully and bracing themselves on the cold, dusty walls, Tommy and Kat began their ascent. "*Phew!* There's a ton of dust," Tommy said.

"Been a long time since anyone's gone through here."

"I wonder why it was bricked up."

None of the answers that suggested themselves were very comforting. They continued to climb in silence, Tommy assuming the lead and Kat right on his heels. Up and up and 'round and 'round it went. Ethereal, gray twilight filtered down from somewhere far above.

The dust was powdery and thick. How many years had it built up? Tommy wondered. But he noticed that there weren't any cobwebs . . . not a single one. That was good. Tommy had had enough of spiders. In fact, he—

Kat squeezed his shoulder like a vise. "Did you hear that?"

"No," he whispered back, his heart kicking into thrash-metal mode. "What?!"

"It sounded like . . . scratching."

"I don't hear any—" He stopped short. He did hear something. A scraping . . . or a scratching sound but not very loud. What it lacked in volume it made up for in creepiness. Tommy pictured a zombie locked away in a stone crypt and, though the flesh of its fingers had worn away long ago, it still kept scratching.

"Stop thinking stuff like that," Kat whispered. "Yikes."

"Sorry."

The scratching grew louder as they climbed. Tommy went around a bend and stopped. Kat bumped into his back. Tommy whispered urgently, "STOP, don't move."

"What?" Kat looked over his shoulder. The spiral staircase ended at a tower chamber, the entrance of which had once been bricked up like the opening far below. Now it was a jagged hole and on the other side, with the Allyran sky darkening behind it, was a large solitary window. In the window was an immense bird. At least nine feet tall, the avian creature had a raptor's profile, like a hawk or an eagle, only it was covered in brilliant scarlet feathers, and its fierce eyes were gold. It stood on a dark marble dais in the middle of the room with a small curved set of stairs leading up to it. The dais itself was strewn with countless parchments that spilled all over the chamber floor. Aside from the window and the perch, the only other feature in the room was a stone bookshelf behind the bird, filled with very dusty, very large books.

Tommy blinked. It seemed to be staring directly at him.

"I think we should go back," Kat whispered from behind.

The bird screamed. Every tiny hair on Tommy's neck and arms

stood straight up. And it was so loud it made both their ears ring.

The bird released Tommy from its gaze. It hopped down onto the floor and lifted one of its long, taloned claws and began scratching at the dark stone of the chamber wall. Its talons had to be ridiculously sharp to gouge the stone like that. Several strange symbols, scratched in white, were already there, and the creature was finishing another. It almost looked like a language of some sort.

Screech! The bird had apparently finished writing on the wall, and it turned its golden eyes on Tommy. It made a kind of deep chirp and bobbed its head in the direction of the symbols on the wall. It chirped again, louder and more urgent this time.

Tommy took a step forward.

"What are you doing?!" Kat clutched at his tunic. Tommy didn't answer, but she knew what he was thinking. "Tommy, come back! I don't think you should get near it!"

Tommy looked back over his shoulder. "I think it wants me to look."

"I think it wants to eat you! Tommy!"

But Tommy didn't listen. He turned and kept going. As dangerous and strange as it appeared, there was something about the bird that felt . . . right. The creature watched Tommy intently, staring down its beak with unblinking eyes.

Tommy stepped through the ruined entrance to the chamber. It happened too fast for him to react. The bird's claw shot out and raked Tommy's forearm. Kat screamed and watched him fall backward, blood dribbling from the new wound. She reached Tommy's side just in time to see the fierce scarlet raptor spread its vast wings and leap toward them.

"Anyone seen Tommy?" Jett asked as he walked into the study.

Johnny and Autumn were deep into a game of *Tawlbwrdd*—an ancient Elvish version of chess, but with two unequal teams both with different objectives—so their eyes never left the board.

Jimmy peered over the edge of a book called *The Precepts of Vexbane.* "No, why?" he asked.

"I carved a football out of that spongy wood they call celura, and I wanted to see if he'd throw it around."

"Football?" Jimmy's coppery eyebrows rose comically. "Yu carved a football? I canna' believe it. I love football. I'm a striker, yu know. I can bend the ball and—"

"Not that kind of football," said Jett. "I mean my kind of football."

"Oh," said Jimmy. "That American rubbish."

"Harrumph," said Jett. "Don't knock it till ya try it."

"Don't mind if I do," said Jimmy, closing the book.

Kiri Lee entered the study next. "Have you seen Kat?" she asked.

"No," said Jett.

"Nay," said Jimmy.

Johnny and Autumn said nothing, but Johnny moved one of his assailants six spaces to the north.

Jimmy looked from Jett to Kiri Lee and said, "We canna' find Tommy or Kat, huh? A wee bit odd, don't yu think?"

This time Johnny and Autumn did look up. They filled the study with a chorus of *"Awwwwwwwwwww!"*

RaaaAAAA! The fierce scarlet bird bore down on Tommy and Kat as if they were two helpless hares hiding at the base of a shrub. The raptor's wings spanned the entire tower chamber. It wheeled about at the last second but extended a talon so that it sliced across Kat's shoulder.

"Kat!" Tommy yelled, drawing his sword.

She yelled and fell to one knee. Blood ran down her upper arm. Meanwhile, the huge raptor landed back on its perch among the parchments.

"You okay?" he asked.

"It stings," she said. "But it's not deep. C'mon, let's go while it's not looking."

"How do you know it's not looking?" asked Tommy. Even though it was clearly focused on something in the bed of scrolls, Tommy thought it very likely that those huge golden eyes could still easily track their movements.

"I don't know," she replied. "But we've got to try. That thing will kill us."

She pulled Tommy toward the stair, but again, he stopped her. "Wait," he said. "Look at it. What's it doing?"

"Who cares what it's doing?" But even Kat, scared as she was, couldn't help but be captivated by what she saw. The towering scarlet bird of prey stood, balanced upon one foot, on an outstretched scroll. It bowed its regal head low and stared as if concentrating. Then it stretched out its other foot, extending first one talon and then the other, daubing blood from each in turn on the scroll. Once there were two small blots of blood on the parchment, the raptor lowered its head even more, and the whole creature became stone still.

Tommy and Kat couldn't help but stare. Birds weren't supposed to act like this. Of course, they knew very little about birds in Allyra. But this creature seemed so focused, so . . . knowing. The way it scrutinized the blotches of blood, it seemed to be thinking about them, thinking carefully . . . deciding.

The raptor looked up suddenly. Tommy and Kat stepped back a pace. It screeched, but it was no mere caw or cry. It was something with syllables, something spoken. In an instant, the great bird turned its back on the two teens and mounted its perch. When it turned around again, it had a large book clasped within one of its clawed feet. It held the book out toward Tommy and Kat.

"Are you kidding me?" exclaimed Tommy.

"I think it wants us to have the book," said Kat.

"Not sure if that's a good idea," said Tommy. "The last time I took a strange book from someone, I found out I'm an Elf and ended up in another world."

Kat almost choked with laughter. "Be serious," said Kat. "I'm going to get it."

"You were the one just telling me to stay away." He shook his head. "Take my sword!"

"No, I don't want to look like a threat."

Look like a threat? Tommy didn't understand girls at all. "Just be careful."

Eyes locked on the bird, Kat stepped forward. It made no move but held the book out with seeming ease. Three wide, rounded steps led up to the perch. Kat climbed them very slowly. She stood now within reach of the book, but being so close to the creature, she realized just how large it was. It towered over her. Its thick, tufted breast and shoulders were well muscled, and its wings—even while folded—looked massive. Its beak was long and curved down at the end, finishing with a sharp point.

It was a powerful creature and very beautiful in its color and strength. Kat looked at its nest among the scrolls and wondered how long the bird had lived in Whitehall. That was when she looked a little more closely at the unrolled parchment near the bird's foot, the one the bird had daubed blood upon. There were four blotches. Two of them glistened, still wet. The other two were very dark . . . very old.

Rawwwaaawwwk! The bird shook the book and extended it a bit farther.

Her mind reeling, Kat looked away from the scroll and back to the bird. She wished she could read the raptor's mind. *Not that I'd understand bird thoughts.* She smiled in spite of the potential danger and reached for the book. The scarlet raptor stared down at her as she took the book, and bobbed its head. The book was so heavy Kat needed both hands to keep from dropping it.

Rawwwaaawwwk! The bird bobbed its head some more and flapped its wings.

"What's the book?" asked Tommy, wind buffeting his body.

"I don't know," she replied, wiping dust from the thick volume. "There's nothing on the cover."

"Think it's another copy of *The Chronicles of the Elf Lords and Their Kin?*"

"If it is"—Kat measured its thickness with her thumb and forefinger—"then it's the extended director's cut."

Sheathing his sword and shaking his head, Tommy joined Kat at the first step. "Open it," he said.

She did and was met with a pungent but not unpleasant old-paper smell. There were a few blank pages of parchment paper and then what seemed to be a title page. "*Elfkind: The Histories and Prophecies of Berinfell.*" She shrugged. "Maybe it is the same. Our books were histories, also."

"Maybe," said Tommy. "It is handwritten, too. But it looks older . . . smells older."

"And '*prophecies*'? That wasn't part of my book."

"Mine, either. Let's bring it back. Maybe Goldarrow will know what it is."

"Good idea," she said, but as she turned to leave, the gigantic bird did something very strange.

Rawwwaaawwwk! Rawwwaaawwwk! Still bobbing its head, the raptor leaped down from its perch, landed on the chamber floor next to the teens, and laid its long wing at their feet.

Tommy marveled at the intricate spread of feathers—long and short, wide and thin—spread majestically before him. "Is . . . is it bowing?" he asked.

Kat shrugged. "I don't know what to think."

The scarlet raptor cocked its head sideways, looking directly at Tommy. It squawked, flapped the extended wing a few times, and then sidled over so that its wing actually lay over the tops of their boots.

"It wants something," said Kat.

"Seems like," Tommy agreed. "But what?"

Before Kat could answer, the bird shifted to the side, knocking both teens off balance. Tommy fell directly on the creature's back. Kat toppled right behind him and almost lost the book.

Rawwwaaawwwk! Its cry sounded almost jubilant compared to the piercing screeches from before. So quickly did the raptor rise up on its legs that Tommy and Kat had to scramble up and straddle the creature's back—that or fall off. And it was supremely good that they did not fall off, for the scarlet raptor leaped up onto its scroll-strewn perch, and with a mighty push from its strong legs, it dove out of the chamber window.

"Did yu hear something?" asked Jimmy, picking up the hand-carved football from the grass behind him. He and Jett stood in the grassy courtyard on the northern side of the main castle. The sun had gone behind the trees, casting Whitehall in the gray of twilight.

"Just the sound of the ball hitting your brick hands," said Jett.

"Nay, I'm serious," said Jimmy, scanning the darkening skies. "It sounded like screamin' or somethin'. I canna' explain it."

"You sure?" He looked up. "'Cause I don't hear anything."

Tommy and Kat stopped screaming as the raptor pulled out of the dive and leveled out just above the treetops. Its speed was still remarkable, and the wind washed over the two teens as they clung to the giant bird's back. It turned and glided swiftly around the contour of a jutting cliff, and then beat its wings and sped out over the vast ocean of green foliage. The sun was setting red on the far eastern horizon, and a misty blue shroud was creeping up on the forest below.

"You still have the book?" Tommy yelled over his shoulder.

"Yeah!" Kat replied, most of her voice swallowed by the airflow. "It's smashed between us!"

"Oh!" Tommy could feel it now, pressing into his back. That was okay. He shut his eyes, desperately trying to think of something other than how high up they were.

"Are you okay?" asked Kat, but before Tommy could answer, the bird brought its wings in close to its body and plunged into a dive once more.

Tommy cracked his eyelids open just a bit and was immediately sorry he had. The raptor was taking them almost straight down, diving toward the canopy. *We are going to die,* Tommy thought with some sense of irony; they'd made it through battles, portals, more battles, and even careened down a thousand-yard zip line. Being smashed to death by a suicidal bird wasn't at all how he expected to go out.

But the raptor had no intention of killing itself. It blasted through the leafy canopy and seemed to slam on the brakes just before hitting the ground. Kat heard a sharp agonizing scream as the bird pulled up, but it wasn't Tommy. And it wasn't the bird. Tommy had heard it, too, and the two teens peered down along the side of the bird. Between wing beats, they saw clutched within the mighty raptor's claws a large Gwar warrior. He was struggling mightily and shrieking out words that Tommy and Kat didn't understand.

"How did the bird see him?" exclaimed Tommy.

"It's a bird of prey!" answered Kat.

The creature beat its wings harder, and soon they were climbing above the trees again. Upward the bird soared. Tommy's heartbeat banged against his chest like a boxer's speed bag. He wouldn't look. He couldn't look.

There came a fresh round of snarls from below, and they looked down. The raptor suddenly let go of the Gwar. Screaming and flailing, the Gwar disappeared from view.

"That's going to hurt!" yelled Tommy. "The Gwar's a goner!"

"I . . . I think this giant bird is a friend!" Kat yelled over the wind.

"Yeah, but where is it taking us?"

The Age of Chains

THE THOUSAND-LEAGUE Forest seemed even larger and vaster from above than it did from beneath its canopy. Convinced that the scarlet raptor meant them no harm, and to his own surprise, Tommy had kept his eyes open much of the long flight. There was a dizzying variety of trees below, but after more than an hour of flight, the scenery seemed to blend into one endless pattern with no landmarks in sight.

Tommy felt Kat's head on his back. He gave her a slight shrug. "Don't fall asleep, Kat!" he called back.

"Ummm," Kat mumbled groggily.

The raptor reduced its airspeed, and Tommy was glad not to have to yell. "I was afraid if you fell asleep, you might fall off."

"That would make some heroic story, huh?" Kat laughed aloud. "The great Elven Lord Alreenia Hiddenblade survives countless battles only to fall off a giant bird."

Tommy laughed, but only politely. No matter that she was joking, Tommy didn't want to think of anything bad happening to Kat.

Kat didn't mean to eavesdrop on Tommy's private thoughts. It just kind of happened. "Aww," she said almost involuntarily. "Thank you."

"Thank you? For what?"

"Uh, well . . . for keeping me awake, right? I could have fallen off."

"Uh . . . sure," Tommy replied, but then he exclaimed, "WHOA!"

Kat looked over his shoulder and saw that the immense forest had come to an end. A sprawling gold vista stretched before them, a lush, hilly grassland, carpeted in some tall waving grain with a few trees

standing tall and alone here and there, as well as thatches of rich bur-
gundy flowers.

The raptor glided between the hills, back and forth, swaying on
the wind. Soon the last sliver of sun on the horizon disappeared, and
night descended over Allyra. Still, the two teens had no idea where the
giant raptor was taking them.

"Look," Kat said, pointing to the sky. "The stars . . . there are a lot
more blue ones."

It was a clear night. Without glare from the big-city lights, the
heavens looked immeasurably more vast and deep, but closer. Tommy
felt if he could just stand up on the bird and leap, he might be able to
grab a star. And Kat was right; there were a lot more blue stars, very
few white ones.

The raptor banked left and rose on a draft over a tall hill and a
grove of trees. On the other side a menacing shadow loomed, a
structure of many tall towers and sprawling castle keeps. Knowing
Kat could not know, Tommy still found himself muttering, "What is
that?"

Kat's grip on Tommy's shoulders tightened. "I don't know," she
said. "But I think it's our destination."

"Vesper Crag!" Tommy gasped, his hand instinctively moving to
his sword. "I should have known . . . this bird's a spy. It's bringing us
to the enemy!"

"I don't think so," said Kat. "Vesper Crag, that was far to the east.
We've been traveling north, away from the setting sun. And look at
this place. It's all dark. If this were an enemy fortress, there'd be
torchlight or bonfires or something."

"Okay, but I still don't like it."

Fields of that same tall grain surrounded the building, and as the
giant bird cruised low above them, there seemed an ever-present
whisper, like a multitude of ghosts trading secrets. The raptor rose up
to a half-wrecked wrought-iron gate and set down softly on the other
side. Behind them, a high fence encircled the entire fortress.

Tommy and Kat did not dismount immediately. In fact, they didn't
want to get down at all. But the raptor had other ideas.

"Whoa! Hey!" The raptor rolled its body hard to the left, extending its left wing like a ramp. Tommy and Kat toppled off, hitting the ground rump first. Adding insult to injury, the thick book of prophecies slid down the wing after them and thumped Kat in the back of the head. "Owww! Oh, come on!"

The two teens had barely gotten to their feet when the raptor leaped ahead, toward the building, turned, and squawked. Kat said, "I think it wants us—"

"I know . . . it wants us to follow it," said Tommy, shaking his head. "Of course it does."

Wishing he'd brought his bow, Tommy put his hand on the pommel of his sheathed sword and set off after the bird. Cradling the book, Kat followed after. Seeing the teens behind it, and apparently satisfied, the raptor continued forward, leaping ten yards with every bound.

There was no clear path through the tall grain, so they walked through it.

The building loomed up before them, and a sliver of moon had risen to bathe it in pale white light. Walls of differing heights encircled the structure, and tall towers with black windows at the top peered down on Tommy and Kat. A ruin, it seemed, for the walls were damaged, great sections caved in places. Broken chunks of wall and single stones littered the ground and were blotched with moss and surrounded by tall grass. The main entrance was just ahead, a yawning black mouth locked open to receive its meal. The raptor waited there and jerked its head with a beckoning motion.

Tommy and Kat approached and looked at each other. "No way," said Tommy.

"What choice do we have?" asked Kat.

"Lots of choices. We can run away."

Rawwwaaaawwwk!

"Right," said Kat. "Don't you remember how the bird swooped down and plucked that Gwar right out of the tree? How far do you think we'd get?"

"Good point," Tommy said. "But look at this place. Anything could be lurking in there."

"If this bird wanted us dead, he could have already killed us." Kat entered the shadows of the building.

Reluctantly, Tommy drew his blade and went in after her.

"It'd be nice to have some light," said Kat. "I left the arc stones back in Whitehall."

"Wait," said Tommy, shifting his sword under his arm and drawing two stones from his belt. "Ah, knew it. I've got a couple. Here."

Kat received the small clear stone and immediately scraped it on the wall. It sparked once and kindled bright blue light inside. Tommy did the same, and soon they had plenty of light—eerie though it was—to find their way. Tommy glanced back to the opening behind them. The raptor waited there, cocking its head curiously side to side.

"I guess it's not coming in," said Kat.

"Smart bird," said Tommy.

They made slow progress up the main hall, which was what it seemed to be. Wide enough for five adults to walk side by side and with a high ceiling, the hall went on for a dozen paces before the first passages opened up on either side. "Which way?" asked Tommy.

"Lots of choices," she replied, holding her arc stone high. "There must be ten lefts and ten rights up there."

"Well?"

"Let's try the first left."

"Why?" Tommy asked.

"It's what I do when I play video games," said Kat. "Process of elimination. We take this to the end, come back, and take the first right and so on."

"Except this isn't a game," said Tommy.

Kat didn't have an answer for that, but they took the left-hand path anyway. Arc stone in one hand, sword in the other, Tommy led the way. This hall felt cold and drafty. And a foul smell permeated the air . . . sweet in a sickening kind of way, like meat that had spoiled. Cobwebs wavered above and in the corners like ghostly garments. The walls were a mere eight feet across and felt closer than that.

I don't like this one bit, thought Tommy.

"Me, either," whispered Kat.

They soon came to a portion of the passage where there were arched openings on either side. As Tommy and Kat drew nearer, they realized that these openings were sealed off from the passage by thick black bars. Each cell had its own gate, and some of these were torn from the hinges and lay in mangled heaps.

"It's a prison," said Kat. "Or was a prison."

"Why would the bird bring us here?" asked Tommy as he wandered into the cell on the right. "Smell's stronger in here," he said. The arc stones cast creepy shadows through the bars. "Kat, come look at this."

Kat came in and found Tommy looking at a low gray slab of stone near the wall. He held up his arc stone and said, "Look."

There were scratches in the wall just above the benchlike slab. Hundreds, if not thousands, of scratches in sets of six vertical lines scratched through by a seventh diagonal line. "Looks like someone was here for a *lonnng* time," said Tommy.

"Look out, Tommy!" Kat shone her arc stone on the slab where a jet black spider the size of a child's fist had dropped and was moving toward Tommy.

Tommy took a step back and smacked at the arachnid with the flat of his sword. Again and again he missed until he gave up and used the heel of his boot instead. *Crunch!* "I hate spiders," he said.

"Don't we all . . . now," said Kat, scanning the cell for other threats. She held her arc stone high, near the back corner of the cell. "Awww, I don't want to know what this is, do I?"

Tommy joined her there and looked down at the hole in the cell floor. He held his light directly over it and leaned over. "Looks like it goes down pretty far . . . and—*whew*—I think the smell's coming up from there." He looked up at Kat. "No, I don't think you want to know what this is," he said.

"Come on. Let's look farther down the hall."

Cell after cell they passed, and each one was the same: thick black bars, a wide slab bench, and an ominous hole in the back corner. There was something at the end of the passage; something there on the ground. Cautiously, they drew near and found that the strange, squat shape was a large chest. *Treasure!* thought Tommy. *So that's why the bird brought us here.*

"I hope so," Kat replied. "You want to open it?"

"I do, but—"

"I'll do it," she said. "Here, take the book . . . and watch for spiders."

As Kat went to the chest and looked for handholds on its lid, Tommy couldn't help but picture thousands of little black spiders pouring out of the chest.

"Nice mental image, Tommy. Thanks."

"Just be careful!" he urged.

Kat nodded. She found two metal clasps, wiped off the cobwebs, and forced them to unlatch. The lid groaned open.

Tommy winced, but spiders did not come streaming out. Kat muttered, "No treasure."

He joined her to look down at the chest's contents: piles of heavy-looking chains and hook-shaped shackles. In spite of the discomfort he felt at the discovery, Tommy couldn't help but pick up one of the chains. Or . . . at least he tried to pick one up. He handed the book back to Kat and put his arc stone on the ground so that he could use both hands. "*Uhhnnnh*, this is really heavy," he said, holding it up. "I feel kinda bad for the prisoners who had to wear these."

"Hold it up a little higher."

"Okay, but like I said, it's heavy."

He lifted the chain so that one of the shackles dangled in front of Kat's face. She held up the arc stone to get a better look. "There's writing . . . numbers: 6025 . . . and a strange little three-dot thingy."

"Three-dot thingy?"

"Yeah, it's like a triangle with a dot at every angle but no lines to join them. Seems like a punctuation mark maybe."

"Great," said Tommy. "Can I put this thing down now?"

"Yeah, yeah, put it down."

He let it drop back into the chest. It hit with a series of dull metallic thuds. He closed the chest and took up his arc stone once more. "Seen enough of this hall?" he asked.

Kat nodded. "Let's go back."

They had passed several cells when Kat spotted something. "Wait, what's that?" She held up her light. There were some peculiar white posts sticking up toward the back of the cell, but it was hard to see due to a hunk of the cell wall that had fallen in.

"Looks weird," said Tommy. "You want to go see what it is?"

"No, I did the chest. Your turn."

"Great," said Tommy. He had to open the cell door for this one. It moaned a protest but opened enough for Tommy to get inside. Sword ready, he entered the cell and moved carefully around the rough, fallen stones. The white posts caught the light of the arc stone and reflected back brightly. The posts were bowed slightly, and Tommy squinted at them. He recognized the shape, but the concept didn't fully materialize in his imagination.

He took another few steps and stepped around the largest hunk of stone wall. Then he froze.

"What is it?" Kat asked. "Tommy, what's wrong?"

He didn't answer.

Bones. A full skeleton. The posts were actually ribs of a massive, barrel-chested, humanoid figure. And then there was the skull. Much larger than an Elf's, especially the eye sockets, black and empty, and the jutting jaw filled with jagged teeth and fang incisors.

Gwar.

Unnerved by the discovery, Tommy backed away. He backed hard into the cell door, sending a shooting pain down the middle of his back and slamming the door shut with a thunderous clang. An image filled Tommy's mind so ferociously that he cried out. He saw himself, shackled and chained, thrown into the cell, and the door slammed shut . . . forever.

"Let me out!" he yelled, pushing hard on the cell door and becoming all the more frantic when it wouldn't budge.

"Hold on," Kat said. "It opens the other way."

But Tommy didn't listen. In a frightened rage, he began to slash at the cell door.

"Tommy, stop it! I can't open the door with you swinging that sword around!"

At last, Tommy lowered the sword and backed away from the door. Kat kicked open the cell door, grabbed Tommy's wrist, and yanked him out of the cell. "Tommy! Tommy, what's wrong?"

"I'm sorry, Kat. I don't know what happened. I just kind of lost it in there. I thought . . . I thought I was trapped in there, trapped forever."

"What did you see in there?" she asked. "What was it?"

"A dead Gwar . . . or at least that's what I think it was. I've never seen a skeleton like that. It was old and kind of twisted up. But the skull is what really freaked me out. Wait . . . how did you do that?"

"Do what?"

"You told me to stop slashing the door," said Tommy. "In my head."

"No, I didn't," said Kat. "I was yelling at you."

"You were loud all right," said Tommy. "But it wasn't out loud. I'm telling you, I heard your voice in my mind."

Kat was silent for several moments. "I can hear your thoughts," she said. "But . . . I've never even tried . . . hold on." She stared at Tommy and concentrated. She saw his thoughts floating before her, and focusing all her efforts she placed one of her thoughts. "Well, what was I thinking about?"

"Um," Tommy looked at her strangely. "You want ice cream?"

Kat laughed aloud. "Oh my gosh! It works! I put my thoughts in your head!"

"Okay, see," said Tommy. "But, you know, that's kind of weird."

"Grimwarden told us the gifts would get stronger," said Kat. "I wonder what yours will do."

Tommy did not reply, but looked up and down the hallway. *So many cells.* "I don't like this place, Kat," he said. "It's different from before. Before I was just scared. Now I feel heavy inside. Almost sick."

"What about the other hallways?"

"Let's just go," he replied. "I think we know what this place is."

Other than the constant whistle of the wind, the flight home was silent. But with her newfound ability, Kat was able to communicate with Tommy by projecting her thoughts and then receiving Tommy's.

"Why would this bird take us to a prison?" thought Kat.

And what's that prison doing out in the middle of all that tall grass or grain, or whatever it was? And why us? Tommy answered inside his mind.

"I think I might know that last bit," thought Kat. *"Remember when the bird cut us both?"*

Yeah, it still stings. Why?

"Well, I got a closer look at the parchment the bird seemed to be writing on with our blood."

Okay, what was it writing? asked Tommy.

"It wasn't writing. It was matching samples."

"Huh?" Tommy exclaimed out loud.

"That parchment was very, very old. When I looked there were two fresh bloodstains—ours and two old, dried-up bloodstains. Remember when the bird was staring so hard at the parchment? I think he was comparing our blood to the Old Ones."

Like a test?

"I guess, maybe to see if we are really Elves."

Or to see if we're really Elven lords, Tommy added.

"I wonder what the bird would have done if we weren't."

Remember the Gwar? I don't think it would have been pretty.

A few hours before dawn, the scarlet raptor landed lightly on its scroll-filled roost. The creature allowed Tommy and Kat to clamber down. They left the bird's chamber and returned to the main gathering room in Whitehall. A fire still burned in the huge fireplace near the stairwell, but no one else seemed to be awake.

"Should we wake someone up?" asked Kat.

"Nah, especially not Grimwarden," said Tommy. "He'd probably knock us into next week."

"Best not to surprise the fiercest warrior in Elven history."

"I'm not going to be able to sleep," Tommy said.

"Are you thinking what I'm thinking?" asked Kat.

"You ought to know," said Tommy.

The two plopped down on a bench and set the book on a long board.

"Where should we start?" asked Kat, opening up the book.

"I don't know," said Tommy. "Prophecies sound cool. Never liked history much."

"Me, either," said Kat. "Mr. Wallace would be angry if he heard me say that." She felt a pang as soon as the words left her lips.

Tommy turned a few pages past the title page. He found the strange series of dates like in the book Mrs. Goldarrow had given him. He was about to flip past it when something stood out from the page.

9680 Founding of Allyra

8015 Golden Age of Elves

7252 Construction of Berinfell

6866 The Age of Chains

5807 The Nemic Wars

4297 Alliance with the Saer

4021 The Bloodless War

3927 Invasion of the Taladrim

3811 The Gwar Revolution

3108 Age of Peace

2222 The Fall of Berinfell

2220 The Age of Hiding

"Why'd you stop?" asked Kat.

"Something's different," he said. "I don't remember this Age of Chains, do you?"

She shook her head. "I might not be remembering it right, but I thought I remembered there being an awfully big gap between some of the dates."

"Like something was missing," muttered Tommy. "It's got to be this."

"What are you waiting for?" she asked. "Turn there."

Tommy found the page and they started to read.

"Wait a minute," said Kat. "What are we doing?"

"What do you—oh, right, touch the ink."

Tommy put his finger down on the opening line of the page. Nothing happened. He touched various places on the page. Still nothing.

"Let me try," said Kat. But her touch elicited the same response. "It must not be written with the same ink as the books we saw."

"Or maybe . . . it was written before that ink was invented?"

"Looks like we'll have to read the old-fashioned way."

Eyes greedily devouring the words, Tommy and Kat soon found that the story being related in this chapter tasted foul . . . tasted of misery and . . . treason.

After reading for a long time, Tommy slowly closed the book. He fought back tears and refused to look at Kat. Something about the shared experience . . . he knew if he looked at her and saw her crying, he'd lose it, too.

"The Gwar," whispered Kat. "They weren't prisoners of the Elves. They were slaves."

The Prophecies of Berinfell

JUST BEFORE breakfast, Tommy and Kat gathered all the young lords together for a meeting. It meant giving away the location of the special balcony high up on Whitehall's main tower to the other teens, but it could not be helped. They needed a place where they could talk discreetly.

A pile of ridiculously large muffins waited on a platter on a shelf near the inner wall. Jimmy, Johnny, and Jett eyed them greedily.

"Don't make me smack your hand like Mumthers," said Tommy. "Those are for after we talk." But as good as the muffins looked, he couldn't think of eating with his stomach so twisted in knots.

"What's all this about?" asked Jett.

"Yeah," said Autumn. "Why all the secrecy?"

"Wait," Jimmy interrupted, standing dramatically and extending his arms like a surfer. "Don't tell me, yu are both secret agents."

This bit of drama was answered with nervous laughter, except for Johnny, who laughed aloud—until Autumn glared at him. "What?" he asked. "It was funny."

"Where were you two yesterday, anyway?" asked Kiri Lee. She cleared her throat. "Goldarrow was worried."

"Yeah, Tommy," said Jimmy. "I canna' believe yu left me to play silly American football with Jett."

Kat had been sitting on the bench nearest the edge of the balcony. She stood up and said, "It's about where we were yesterday. And, guys . . . this is serious." Her voice cracked slightly at the end, and the smiles around the room vanished.

Jimmy turned red and slid to a seat on a stone bench along the inner wall.

Kat began, but she and Tommy told the story together, filling in each other's thoughts, sometimes interrupting to add some critical detail, . . . other times lending a nod or a somber shake of the head. They told about their discovery of the secret tower and the scarlet raptor. They told of the creature's testing their blood and giving them the ancient book. They told of the raptor's taking them on a long flight north. They told at last of their exploration of the abandoned fortress . . . and, upon their return to Whitehall, their reading the missing age of Berinfell history.

When Tommy and Kat finished, they met expressions of confusion, shock, anger, and sadness.

"They started it." Jett shook his head. "All this fighting . . . all this death and pain, and the Elves started it."

"Why?" asked Kiri Lee. "Why would the Elves try to enslave the Gwar?"

"From what we can tell, fear," Kat explained. "Elves and Gwar lived together, kind of neighbors geographically. There was often trade between the two groups, and when the Elves wanted to put down roots and build their kingdom, it was partially on the backs of the Gwar that they built it."

"But even then, the Gwar were willing to help," said Tommy. "They were friends."

"Right," Kat went on. "But the Elves saw how strong the Gwar were and how they were becoming more and more advanced in the use of powerful stones and minerals. They feared the Gwar would turn on them and overrun them. And when a really harsh winter came over the land—"

"The Fell Winter of 7066," Tommy chimed in. "It snowed so much that much of Berinfell was paralyzed. The Elves went to the Gwar for help, but they refused . . . the Gwar cities had their own problems."

"This shocked and infuriated the Elves," Kat explained. "The Gwar had never turned them down before. A faction of the Elves stirred up the rest saying that this was the first sign of a Gwar rebellion—that they needed to take decisive action. The Elves still had superior weapons and tactics, so they invaded the Gwar capital city, took the Gwar by surprise, and forced them to clear Berinfell of ice and snow."

"After that," said Tommy, "the Elves bought and sold the Gwar as property, like pack animals only worth as much as their muscle."

"It got even worse later," said Kat. "The Elves found a region where a valuable food grain called gildenfleur grew naturally. And they wanted to build a trade center there, a fortress."

"But to do that," said Tommy, "they needed stone, and the nearest quarry was eighteen leagues away."

"A league is like three miles, right?" asked Autumn. "So that's fifty-four miles?"

Tommy nodded.

Kat continued the explanation. "The Elves made the Gwar mine the stone and then transport it. They had to build a fortress to be a center for their own slave trade. The Elves called it Cairn Umber, but the Gwar had another name for it: Fellmarch, after the long, bloody journey the Elves forced the Gwar to take. Thousands of Gwar died on that horrible road and in the construction of that fortress."

"What's it mean?" asked Johnny. "Are we fighting on the wrong side?"

"Our ancestors did," said Tommy. "We're all related to Elven Lords who either did hateful things or who did nothing while all this was going on."

"But that doesn't mean we're on the wrong side," Kat explained. "Many of the Elves were against slavery of any kind to begin with. For two hundred years they fought with the council to end it once and for all, to pay reparations to the Gwar, and seek peace."

"Did it work?" asked Kiri Lee.

"According to the book," said Kat, "the Elves signed a treaty with the Gwar in the spring of 5807. All Gwar were given unconditional freedom, land, titles, technology, crop stores, and gold. The Seven Lords issued a formal apology and requested forgiveness."

"But then the Nemic invaded," said Tommy.

"Nemic?" blurted Jimmy. "Who're they?"

"Whoever they are or were," said Tommy, "they were fierce,

superior to the Elves in many ways. They would have destroyed Berinfell if it weren't for the Gwar aiding them against the invaders."

"Wait, wait, wait," said Jett, pacing between the balcony and the wall. "After all that? After the killing, after the slaving . . . the Gwar still helped the Elves?"

Tommy nodded.

"Mannn," said Jett. "That's just crazy."

"What I don't get," said Kiri Lee, "is if the Elves and Gwar signed a treaty and then fought together against a common enemy, why are they still fighting now?"

"That's where things get interesting," said Kat. "See, not all the Gwar were willing to sign the treaty. In fact, about two-thirds of the Gwar were led away by one, Palor Irethrall. They broke away from the Gwar nation and settled in Vesper Crag."

"You mean"—Jett wrinkled his brow—"the Spider King?"

"One and the same," said Kat.

Tommy finished. "The Elves and the Spider King's Gwar have been at bitter war ever since."

"So what do we do now?" asked Johnny.

"If you want my opinion," said Tommy, "I think we should confront Grimwarden and Goldarrow about this."

Jimmy stood up. "Yeah, why didn't they tell us this in the beginning?"

"But the books they gave us didn't have all that in them," said Autumn, wearing a pained expression. "Did they lie to us?"

"That," said Kat, "is a very good question."

"You are late for training," said Grimwarden. At first, he stayed focused on the sword blade he was sharpening in the lair's forge. But when the Seven walked in without saying so much as a good morning, he put down the sword and looked up. "You're not dressed for training, either."

"We may not be training today," said Jett curtly.

Grimwarden had seen more carnage in war, more overwhelming attacks, and more treachery than almost any living Elf, but something about Jett's cool pronouncement sent rivulets of ice down his spine. "Before I assign you twenty-one cords of wood to cut as punishment, can you defend such arrogance?"

"Tommy, you want to answer his question?" asked Jett.

"I think Goldarrow should be here as well," Tommy said. "Guardmaster, we have some questions. Something . . . something has changed."

"I see," he replied, the ice beginning to form on his spine once more. "Then I will go myself to get her. She is tending the garden on the windward hills."

Grimwarden returned a lot faster than the young lords thought possible. A startled Sentinel stood at his elbow. "Lords," Goldarrow said, "what's wrong?"

Kat looked to Tommy. They both found themselves speechless at first. Tommy finally stepped forward and placed the book in Goldarrow's hands.

Upon glancing down at the book, Grimwarden and Goldarrow wore expressions of confusion . . . of nervous curiosity. But when Goldarrow began turning pages, both their faces paled. Goldarrow's hands trembled.

"Where did you get this?" Grimwarden demanded.

Mistaking his tone for suspicion and anger, Kat responded in kind. "Why?" she asked. "Were you keeping it hidden from us?"

"Hidden?" echoed Goldarrow. "No Elf has laid eyes upon this manuscript for more than three thousand years."

"I want to believe you," said Tommy. "I really do. But we read the histories, Kat and I, and it's the same history that was in the books you gave us."

"The same histories you've fed us here," said Jett.

"The same except for more than seven hundred years of slavery," said Kiri Lee.

"You led us to believe bogus histories," said Jett, his face now more anguished than angry. "The Elves started all this! . . . You made slaves of the Gwar!"

"And I thought fer once," said Jimmy, "that I might do somethin' good . . . be some kind 'a hero." Jimmy's voice went high and thin. "We're not heroes. We're the bad guys in this story!"

"In the past, yes," said Grimwarden. "But we will not be ruled by the atrocities of the past."

"Jimmy, Tommy—all of you," said Goldarrow, her own voice strained with sorrow. "I am sorry that you had to find out in this way. But please understand, the full history of Elves has been lost to all but the Old Ones for thousands of years."

"The Old Ones?" several of the lords asked.

Grimwarden strode forward. "Manaelkin is not the oldest Elf to survive the sacking of Berinfell," he said. "There are others, Elves solely devoted to Ellos who fled the corruption of our people. They keep scriptoriums—vaults of vital Elven documents—hidden in the safe places of this world. The Old Ones still teach and practice the customs prescribed at the founding of Allyra. Some of us, Goldarrow, Alwynn, and myself, have had the opportunity to learn from the Old Ones. Because of their teachings, we know much. But not all . . . far from it."

"But you knew about the slavery," said Autumn.

"And you knew that our histories were incomplete," said Kiri Lee.

"Yes," said Goldarrow. "We knew about the Elven enslavement of the Gwar. But we did not seek to deceive you."

"That's what it feels like," said Johnny.

"You were to be taught as much of the original history as we know," said Grimwarden, "as a part of your lore studies here at Whitehall."

"With all due respect, sir," said Tommy, "that's easy to say . . . now."

"Tommy!" Goldarrow said sharply. "Have you not already learned enough about the Guardmaster to grant him the benefit of the doubt? Have we, prior to this misunderstanding, given you any reason—any reason at all—for such suspicions?"

Tommy stared at his feet. In fact, of the Seven, only Jett and Kiri Lee still looked on.

"Having read the histories in this rare and ancient volume," Goldarrow went on, "you now know more of our history than we do. But, THINK, if we had shared even our limited knowledge with you, would you have come back to your homeland with us?"

"I can answer that," said Jett, undeterred. "No, I wouldn't have come. And I'm not going to stay, either. I don't want to be a part of any civilization that takes slaves."

"You are not thinking clearly," muttered Grimwarden fiercely. "For that, I forgive your rash words." A blink and he stood directly in front of Jett, towering over the young lord. "But allow me to provide you with clarity. What began in 6866 is a bloody gouge in all of Elven history. But that ended thousands of years ago. Hear that, Jett. All slavery ended. It is over, in—the—past. And we are not the villains. Our ancestors confessed their atrocities and were forgiven . . . by many of the Gwar nation. But not so, the Spider King. He chose and continues to walk the path of bitterness."

"Maybe he should still be mad," said Jett. His voice was taut, but his posture less certain.

"Tell me, Jett," said the Guardmaster, still directly in front of Jett. "How much blood will it take, then?"

"How much . . . what do you mean?"

"If, as you suggest, the Spider King—the Gwar nation even—is justified in their retribution, . . . their revenge war, how much Elven blood must be spilled to pay the debt in full? One Elven life for each Gwar life taken? What of the slaves who survived? Must one Elf die to make up for the life stolen away from a Gwar as a slave?"

"I . . . I don't know," said Jett.

"And just how do we take these Elven lives?" asked Goldarrow. "Do we let the Spider King raid Elven villages until the debt's paid? Or would the Sentinels choose who lives and dies? Jett, don't you see the lunacy of this? The Spider King may have once been a respectable Gwar. The enslavement of his family, maybe his own parents, surely wrought havoc in his life. But he *chose* this. And he has departed from reason if he believes he will ever quench his thirst for vengeance with more blood."

There was a long pause. "I never thought about it like that," said Jett.

"You are young," said Grimwarden. "Your emotions run hot, especially yours."

"And beyond the usual trials of your teenage years," Goldarrow went on, "you've had your entire world turned upside down. You've seen death. You've fought and bled in war. You've left your Earth homes behind and so much more."

"Yes, you've suffered more than anyone should have to at your age," said Grimwarden. He stepped away from Jett, and one by one his gaze fell upon each of the Seven. "But that is no excuse to call evil that which you have known to be only good. If we have wronged you, it is out of benevolence, not deceit. Do you all understand that?"

"Yes, sir," they together replied.

And that was the end of it. Muttering as he left the room, Grimwarden said, "To think I should live to see the day when I reprimand all Seven Lords of Berinfell."

A few shell-shocked minutes after the Guardmaster departed, Tommy looked sheepishly to Goldarrow. "We really screwed up, didn't we?"

"Well . . . yes," she replied. "It is this very error that divides so many good children from their good parents."

"What do you mean?" asked Kat, her stomach churning.

Goldarrow said, "All too often, especially in your world, teenagers flooded with passions begin to second-guess their parents, even to the point of distrusting those who love them most." Kat began to cry. Goldarrow embraced the young lord and said, "That struck very close to the bone."

"I'm sick of crying," Kat growled.

Goldarrow rubbed Kat's back and said, "As a very wise person once told me, 'not all tears are evil.' Let it go, Kat."

Kat's body seemed to convulse. Her words came out in an anguished moan. "I wish I could see my mom. I wish . . . I wish I could tell her I'm sorry."

The other six lords looked on and wrestled with thoughts of their own.

Warm yellow light from a trio of oil lanterns fought with shadowy corners and tall, dusty bookshelves for control of the North Study's atmosphere. The light won, casting ruddy light on the cheeks of two elite Elven warriors. Grimwarden and Goldarrow sat so close together they were almost one being. So riveted were they to the book Tommy and Kat had found that they'd completely ignored Mumthers's call for lunch . . . and dinner.

Having finished the complete *Histories* section, they went on to read the rest of the book: *The Prophecies*. Page after page, they'd come across passages that filled them with wonder, hope, horror, or confusion. The section they read now flooded them with all of these, and more.

Having read the dense text four times already, Grimwarden read it aloud.

"'It shall come to pass in the years of plenty that the Sunchildren will forsake the old ways. Great glory will they ascribe to themselves, glory stolen from Ellos, Maker of All. And in those times, their eyes will be darkened. Just as the eclipse blots out the sun, they will see no more than their closed hearts reveal. In their wickedness, the Sunchildren, yea the very same offspring of Ellos, will forget the gifts of mercy and freedom given them of old and will dare to fetter another race.

"'Speak now the cries of Genesset! Wash in floods of water and blood! The long winter will end, but barren, bitter gray will remain in their hearts. Mountains will vomit despair. Rivers will course with frigid tears. And the rain that falls will not quench or cleanse. Marred will be the Sunchildren and the captive Stonechildren both. Deep will that splinter drive. Even so——'"

Goldarrow's touch interrupted. "Stonechildren?" she repeated. "The Gwar?"

Grimwarden nodded. "There can be little doubt." He was quiet a moment. "You understand the repercussions . . . what this means." It was not a question.

Even the tired expression on her face told the tale. She understood fully. "Even in the Golden Age of Elves . . . we were wrong about the Gwar. They, too . . ."

"Are children of Ellos," Grimwarden finished.

"What about the Saer? The Nemic? The Taladrim?"

"Enemies and allies alike," said Grimwarden. "All created by Ellos. And all his children." He breathed out a heavy sigh and his shoulders relaxed. "May Ellos forgive us for our arrogance. We must get word to the elders."

"Wait, Olin," Goldarrow said, her brow beetled in concentration. "The Nemic and the Taladrim have other gods. And what of the Saer who name no god?"

"Between the two of us, Elle, I am not the most wise. Give me a spear and an army, and I'll know what to do. But all this thinking makes my head hurt."

"But surely the other gods they name, they are not the same as Ellos?"

"Nay," said Grimwarden. "*Nyas nai necro arwis elloas aberne my. Llyas ca vex vespris mara logis. Wy vala e' Genesset ca cerrath a' llyam.*"

"Now here you have wisdom well beyond mine," said Goldarrow. "I have not kept up in my studies of First Voice. You said, 'Never be God,' and something about 'the doors of Heaven.'"

"Hmmm, that is surprising," said Grimwarden. "You understood more than you think. It is translated: 'You must not have any other god before me. They are ignorant and powerless. The doors of Heaven are closed to them.'"

"But see," said Goldarrow, "they cannot enter Heaven, so—"

"Many have interpreted it that way," said Grimwarden. "But the text does not say that these races cannot enter Heaven. The only reality implied is that while they are following other gods, they may not enter Heaven. If they follow Ellos—"

"Like the Gnomes," muttered Goldarrow.

Grimwarden felt a strange exhilaration at this new realization, like ancient bonds had been broken and at last he could inhale a full breath. He smiled as he said, "It seems Ellos has no prejudice toward race or culture. It is only the condition of our hearts that matters."

"If they are turned toward him," Elle sat back.

Grimwarden paused a thoughtful beat. "If only our people had known long ago."

Goldarrow covered half her face with her slender hand. "No, Olin," she said. "We knew. We've always known. But we chose our own way."

Grimwarden's joy vanished like the sun behind a very dark cloud. "There it is," he said. "Spoken plainly in the open."

"All is not lost," said Goldarrow, leaning forward and pointing to the page. "See what it says here:

"'Even so, a seed of light is sewn. A remnant will forsake the dark path. Chains will be broken. Light will again sparkle on the towers of the City of the Sun. Berinfell will rejoice in new freedoms, and once more Elves will look for Ellos the Mighty. And they will find him. Ellos will go before the Sunchildren against their enemies, and they will win victories such as will be made into song, and be sung through the ages. There will be such a peace as Allyra has never known.'"

"When?" Grimwarden asked hungrily . . . desperately. "When will that be?"

Goldarrow stared at the text. "Alas," she said, recognition dawning on her face. "That peace has already come and gone."

"Why do you say that?" Grimwarden asked.

"Read the very next line," she said.

Grimwarden read:

"Then will come the Plague of Spiders."

"I'm telling you," said Kat, in her customary seat on the secret balcony. "It's all about us."

"What?" Jett blurted out from his customary place by the pile of muffins.

"Come on," said Jimmy, pacing near a window. "What yu're sayin' is that a three-thousand-year-old prophet knew what we'd be doin' now? Funny, that."

"I don't think it's that funny," said Tommy. "But I think Kat's right. Read it for yourself."

"You have the book?" Jett nearly spat muffin crumbs out of the window.

"No," said Kat. "Grimwarden and Goldarrow have it. But I wrote down some of the prophecies. Look."

Jett took a look at the parchment roll. "You wrote ALL that?" he asked.

She nodded proudly.

"I can't read your handwriting," said Jett.

"Oooh," Kat growled. "Then listen." She read an excerpt from the page where she had scrawled her notes.

> *"Seven Elven Lords in their halls of light.*
> *Lords of Berinfell, beware the Spider's bite.*
> *Seven will be old and Seven will be young,*
> *When the Spider King's onslaught has begun.*
> *The walls will shiver. The walls will shake.*
> *Under his staff the walls will break.*
> *Children of Stone and Children of Night,*
> *Empty the throne of the Children of Light.*
> *Not to slay but something worse.*
> *For even his minions fear the Curse.*
> *Allyra weeps for its fallen Elves.*
> *Where once lived light, now darkness dwells.*
> *For an Age and an Age, the black stain will spread.*
> *As a new world falls into the Spider's web.*
> *From tunnels long and caverns deep,*

The Children of Light will rise and seek
Their own who were lost but never slain,
They return to end the Spider's reign.
But malice broods in mountain's heart.
And menace is born by forgotten art.
As storm clouds fill the eastern sky,
All hope will flee and courage die.
Lest the Rainsong be heard o'er both mountain and field,
The Spider will reign and the line of Lords shall yield
Bound by jaws of rock, discovered by no Lord alone,
The Rainsong lay dormant upon the Keystone.
One will be found, and one will be lost.
For travelling this path requires a cost.
Power unmatched and victory assured.
Secrets revealed and tempest endured.
Seven Elven Lords in their halls of light.
Lords of Berinfell, beware the Spider's bite.'"

"Okay," said Jett. "So maybe that is us."

"So we can't win?" asked Autumn.

No one answered at first, but then Johnny spoke up. "You were always the smart one," he said. "And I'm not much for books and all. But I don't think it says we can't win. Sounds more like we won't win without this Rainsong thingy, whatever that is."

"Brilliant," Jimmy said, patting him on the back. "That's right brilliant."

"Okay," said Tommy. "I can see that. Kat?"

"Yeah, that seems right. And if we find this Keystone, then we find the Rainsong . . . whatever either of those things are."

Tentatively hopeful, they nodded one by one. "Well, I think we now know what we need to do," said Tommy.

"Uh-huh," said Jett. "We need to get that Rainsong and go kick some Spider King butt."

Invasion of Nightwish

"IT'S BEEN nearly three months, Alwynn," said the elder called Danhelm, slamming his fist down on the council table. "The Spider King could attack at any moment, and we sit here shaking in our burrows like field mice. But we have accrued a sizable army, outfitted with the very best of weaponry and supplies, and our people are strong. Yet you're content to let the Seven remain in the care of Grimwarden, mastering outdated fighting styles and cooing to superstitious myths? How can you even consent to such folly? Is it because"—the council member paused, drawing all eyes for his final blow—"you are a dissenter?"

An audible gasp went up around the room, Sentinels speaking behind their hands, Dreadnaughts mumbling with heads bent low.

"Order!" Manaelkin bellowed, slamming his gavel down numerous times. "Order, I say!" When the room was brought back to yet another uncomfortable calm, Manaelkin eyed Danhelm. "My dear friend, the words you utter forth against our brother are quite . . . bold."

Not that you haven't fed them to him yourself, Alwynn replied behind an expressionless face.

Manaelkin continued. "Yet still, it would seem that certain attitudes, shared by more than one among us, would see our people— through apathy and inaction—fall once more . . . to the Spider King."

"I contend!" Alwynn stood and pushed his chair back, and with him dozens more Elves raised their voices. The council chamber burst into a shouting match, Elves just inches from one another's faces, veins bulging, fists clenched.

"ORDER!" Manaelkin demanded, striking his gavel so hard that the handle broke and the head skittered across the stone table. But it was just a show. Appear to mediate the discussion, appear to be appalled by the reactions, and most of all, appear not to take sides—that was Manaelkin's way. While Manaelkin had held to the controversial vote taken half a year before—agreeing to let Grimwarden have the time he needed to train the young lords—he had done everything in his power to undermine it from the inside. A true politician. And seeing his work now manifest in the foul tempers of his compatriots, he contented himself to sit back down, letting the arguments unfold before his very eyes . . . his smiling eyes.

In all the commotion not a single one of them noticed the chamber door fling open and a pale-looking errand boy enter. He struggled to gain the nerve to speak, eventually waving an arm. Then he resorted to yelling, but still his dire plea went ignored, added to the throng of violent words spewing forth like poison. Desperate, the youth reached for one of the dremask stones, held it aloft, then shielded his eyes. He cast the luminous crystal onto the council table where it exploded, the dremask vein splattering across the room like bits of flaming lava. Instantly, the males of the council brushed the flaming puddles of silvery fluid from their clothes and leaped back, searching for the cause of the explosion.

"What in the name of—?"

"Reports from our scouts, both in the aquifers and through the tunnels, a large army approaches. The Spider King has come!"

Ages beneath the surface had given the Elves time to hone their defensive procedures to a point sharper than their razor-tipped arrowheads. Quietly and efficiently, the elderly, the infirm, nonmilitary males and women, and all children were evacuated into boats and shepherded through canals by flet soldiers to emergency shelters west of their underground refuge.

The Elven military, too, had made constructive use of time, conducting invasion and defense drills and preparing fortifications and weapons. Thousands of flet soldiers lay hidden. The invasion of Berinfell left a fiery red brand on the mind of every Elf. They would be ready . . . this time.

Now, Nightwish Caverns held its collective breath. Massive dremask torches burned in the highest towers, illuminating the stone city in waving hues of blue and gray and casting long shadows. The central aquifer shimmered like a vein of incandescent blood, running slowly between the towering structures—fortresses, keeps, and turrets— where no fire or light burned in any window. There were only darkened sockets, lidless, empty eyes staring at everything . . . and nothing. A city of ghosts.

"Perhaps he will think the city abandoned"—whispered Alwynn, leaning on a cold balcony wall overlooking the city—"and return to Vesper Crag."

"You'd like that, would you?" asked Manaelkin, standing behind him.

"If it means saving Elven lives, yes," replied the high cleric.

Manaelkin sniffed loudly. "Even you must realize this battle cannot be avoided forever."

"Alas that it cannot," said Alwynn, scanning the upper gates for any sign of the enemy. "So deep is his bitterness, the Spider King is bent on rooting us out. Yes, even I know we must fight. But I fear the time is not right . . . not without the Seven Lords."

"So we agree at last?" said Manaelkin. "That is the very thing I have been striving to avoid. It was a fool's errand to send our strength to a place as remote as Whitehall. The lords should be here . . . here to lead us to greatest victory."

"Nay, Elder," answered Alwynn. "And think twice before you tarnish the name of Allyra's greatest commander. Were it not for Grimwarden, there would be no remnant of Elves to resist. Fool's errand!" This time, Alwynn sniffed. "He is no fool who seeks to do what is right."

"Indeed?" Manaelkin scoffed, stroking his beard. "But where is Grimwarden now?"

Alwynn did not respond. Manaelkin would not see, would not relent. He would go on arguing even as brave Elves bled to death on the streets below. It made Alwynn sick to his stomach. So Alwynn remained silent. Vigilance was needed.

Manaelkin turned to one of his runners. "Send two companies into the catacombs, spearman in front. Tell Travin to speed his retreat. Archers to their positions. And ready the layadine cannons." The runner crossed his forearms and bowed slightly, then turned on his heels and disappeared.

"Layadine? Already? You think . . . Warspiders?" Alwynn asked.

"You wouldn't?" Manaelkin's face was etched with cynicism.

"But what if the Spider King has not brought his full force? What if, as before, he has only extended one arm? He himself may not even be—"

Manaelkin turned sharply. "I warn you, Alwynn: oppose me here and I will have the guards put you under lock and key. And when we are victorious, I will see to it that your name is remembered only for wishing to betray our people, content to watch them beaten into oblivion."

Alwynn raised his chin ever so slightly. "And if we lose?"

The council chief thought for but a moment. "Then . . . I will be vindicated. Grimwarden himself will realize he never should have separated the lords—again—from their people. But being right will bring no joy to the dead."

Commander Travin led the foremost legions himself; it was how Grimwarden would have done it . . . how Grimwarden had taught him to do it. *"Never ask a man to go where you yourself will not go first."* The burly warrior led his flet soldiers to the far side of the city. Leaving the last of the dwellings behind, he and his men crossed the South Bridge and began the short hike up the stone steps, finally arriving at the entrance of the gated openings of a series of tunnels.

With a single wave of his hand, three thousand flet soldiers—spearmen, archers, and infantry—seemed to disappear, blending instantly with the forest of stalagmites that covered this end of the cavern. Travin smiled. What a surprise it would be when the Spider King's forces burst through these gates . . . only to find the seemingly empty city. Disoriented and wary, the enemy would seek to traverse the stalagmites and WHAM! the trap would be sprung.

Travin massaged the thick muscle on his bare forearms. He was tense. Not just for the anticipation of battle. He was half Elven, half Gwar. Ever true to the forces of Berinfell, he still felt torn. *Why had it come to this? Why was the Spider King so intent on spilling blood?*

Travin loosed his heavy mace from his back holster and watched the gates. Any minute now.

Manaelkin and Alwynn had watched Travin's forces vanish into the stalagmites. Alwynn was pensive, wringing his hands half the time, rubbing his temples the rest.

Manaelkin would not admit it, but he, too, was very worried. In Grimwarden's absence, he had directed their defensive plan. It was a sound plan to be sure. But the Elves were best suited for forest warfare. They had learned through many hard years how to adapt to Nightwish Caverns, but still, they were not natural cave fighters like the Gwar.

A high, haunting sound from the south snapped Manaelkin from his thoughts and snatched their gaze to the south.

Screee!

Screee! The keening sound made the hair stand up on Travin's forearms. *SLAM!* A tremendous blow shivered the gate directly in front of Travin's spearmen. *They're here,* Travin thought, swallowing back bile. Another crash into the gate. Other percussions sounded from the other gates.

Steady, lads, Travin silently willed his soldiers. The slams continued, blasting the iron gates in a strange rhythm, like the heartbeat of a mechanical beast. *Steady.*

The blows to the gate echoed throughout Nightwish. Alwynn hoped that the Elves evacuated from the caverns could not hear. He could not shake the image of tiny Elven children clinging to their parents and weeping. *Please, dear Ellos*, Alwynn prayed, *keep them safe.*

Travin jumped. New screams, but not from the gates, and not from the Warspiders. These were agonized cries of Gwars echoing up from the aquifers. Those who dared to come by watercraft were now feeling the sting of legions of archers' arrows. Hundreds would die before the first Gwar entered Nightwish by water.

KERRR—RACK! The center gate fell from its hinges. Massive hammer-wielding Gwar poured in, followed immediately by Warspiders. Travin watched them come to a halt a few yards from the stalagmites. Then he watched them slowly begin to advance.

Wait, Travin continued to will his troops. *Wait until they are committed.*

And they were. The Gwar soldiers and Warspiders began to gather steam as they plunged forward, clambering over the spikes of stone.

"Curse them!" Travin growled under his breath. The other gates fell, one by one. And Warspiders were climbing to the cavern ceiling and advancing above the Elves. *Leave them to the archers and cannons,* he told himself. *Watch the—*

A huge, red-legged Warspider bearing a Drefid plunged its foreleg down a mere foot from Travin's position. The Elven forward commander shrugged. His spear was meant for a spider, but the opportunity was too good. He heaved the weighted shaft right at the Drefid, piercing his side and lifting him bodily from the saddle. "NOWWW!!" Travin yelled. He lifted a war horn to his lips and loosed several blasts.

His spearmen responded, and suddenly it seemed to the enemy as if the stalagmites had come to life. Gwar, spider, and Drefid fell dead in bunches, their wide-eyed corpses never realizing what had killed them. But more and more enemy soldiers vomited from the gates. Travin's archers did their duty. Hundreds of Gwar fell, but several hundred followed. And the Warspiders, blast them, continued to take to the ceiling.

Travin could only hope the layadine cannons were ready. He clambered up to the top of his stalagmite and yelled, "Infantry, collapse . . . NOW!!"

The enemy forces that still lived and continued to meander through the stalagmites found themselves suddenly caught in the jaws of an Elven vice.

Glisith had been trained to use the layadine cannon only three years prior, shortly after his enrollment in Berinfell's army. Being among the many Elves born and raised solely in Nightwish Caverns, having never seen the Land of the Sun—as it was called—for more than a few hours a week, he was eager to be rid of the enemies of his forefathers and get topside, for good. But having rarely seen the outside world, he had also never seen the enemy, knowing them only through the stories told to him by his parents at table. But what his eyes saw tonight from his perch on one of the watchtowers made his finger slip from the trigger.

Bursting from the tunnel entrances on the south side of the city like an entire colony of ants erupting from a flooded anthill came a black wave of Warspiders emanating in all directions. Glisith could only gape as wave upon wave spread out from the black hole, the beasties covering the walls like a plague.

"What are you doing, flet soldier?!" The authoritative voice of a frantic Elven commander snapped young Glisith from his stupor. "Fire! Fire! FIRE!!"

Suddenly recalling the practiced form of his rank and duty, Glisith lowered his goggles, took aim down the long barrel, centering on the very middle of the tunnel, and held his breath. Then he squeezed the trigger.

Though the cannon was anchored securely in the floor of the watchtower turret, the blast rattled his jaw and made his ears ring. Glisith sat stupefied in his gunnery chair, watching his charge zip clear across the cavern and explode in a spray of white ash deep in the heart of the tunnel. He had never actually fired live rounds before. A thunderous resounding of dozens of other cannons joined his own, charges exploding in the tunnel, the entire space shaking with explosions.

"Reload!"

Glisith's ears were ringing. He followed his commander's orders and took the wrapped load from his spotter below. He spun open the hatch wheel, working the gears as quickly as he could, and then shoved the round inside the chamber. *Layadine in the front, propellant in the back.* Then he slammed the door shut, and with uncommon efficiency he screwed back the gears, sealing the housing.

"Fifteen degrees!" ordered his commander.

The spotter worked a giant winch below Glisith that moved the cannon's vertical angle. Slowly, the cannon adjusted, Glisith now aiming at a patch of unaffected Warspiders and their riders climbing up the wall, nearly out of reach of the dremask lights. The shock of the first round over, Glisith felt his training take over, and he grabbed the trigger intentionally . . . then squeezed.

Travin ducked as Gwar tumbled from their dissolving Warspiders, many falling to their deaths from the heights above, smashing into the South Bridge, others broken on the stairs or drowned beneath the weight of their armor in the river below. Still other Gwar rolled down the steps as their mounts squealed, collapsing underneath them, the Warspiders' innards hissing and popping as the deadly layadine powder went to work on the one thing it was harvested to kill: spiders. Any Gwar who managed to live through the ordeal met a swift end as Travin's forces laid waste to everything in their path.

19

The Taste of Blood

THE LAYADINE cannons continued to pound away at the gaping hole in the far wall, through which wave after wave of Warspiders poured into the giant, subterranean home of the Elves. But no sooner did the Warspiders crest into view than the white powder rendered them helpless, their bodies bursting, wracked with horrific tremors. Likewise, their Gwar, and now Drefid riders, tumbled into the spear-armed flet soldiers. Row upon row of the warriors jabbed and skewered the disoriented enemy combatants, dashing Gwar and Drefid bodies into the rocks and river below. In the first thirty minutes of fighting, not a single Warspider, Gwar, or Drefid made it into the heart of the city.

Alwynn stood in awe, watching his brethren hew the Spider King's forces and doing so with so few losses of their own.

"Why so surprised, cousin?" Manaelkin mocked. "Where is your faith?"

Alwynn turned to address the chief council. "In Ellos," he replied. "Where it has always been. We are witnessing providence, divine intervention."

"Ellos—" Manaelkin stopped his words. It wouldn't do to blaspheme with other soldiers around. Still, he could not remain silent. "Of course Ellos the Mighty is always our source of . . . *inspiration*. But now we see the might of Elves at its finest. We have anticipated the Spider King's every move. They are coming as swine to the slaughter."

Alwynn winced. He was glad to see the Elves triumphing, but it was not a joy to see the enemy die. And there was something troubling him. "Manaelkin," he said. "Does it seem at all to you that this victory is too easy?"

"P-p-what?" Manaelkin faced the high cleric. "Too easy? Victory is victory!"

"I wonder," said Alwynn. "And I'm worried. Have you ever seen such a force in all your life? Not even Berinfell saw such numbers."

"And yet you question—"

"It is a massive army, but why wouldn't the Spider King himself lead this army? This should be his most glorious victory."

"He didn't lead the Berinfell invasion, either," retorted Manaelkin. "So what then?"

"He attacked Berinfell when we Elves were our strongest," Alwynn explained. "Perhaps he let his Drefids command out of fear for his own skin. But an attack here on a sun-deprived remnant of hiding Elves; wouldn't he come to glory in his final triumph?"

Manaelkin for once did not have an answer.

"And yes," Alwynn went on, "this is a massive enemy army, but what if the Spider King's forces have grown and increased in the same percentages that ours have? Then the troops he sent today into Nightwish would amount to little more than a finger of his prodigious hand."

Manaelkin eyed him, suddenly realizing his fellow councilman's logic. But he was too proud to express it. "So what if this is a small number," he said. "Today we have lopped off these, tomorrow the rest."

"Again, I wonder," said Alwynn. He paused and then asked, "Do you ever tire of your own ploys, Manaelkin?"

The council chief eyed him narrowly. "No, because I'm right."

Alwynn looked back to the battle; *massacre* was more like it. "You manipulate your own mind to make sure you're always right," he mumbled. "Until you have nothing left to manipulate."

As the mass of dead continued to rise, Travin ordered entire units of flet soldiers to leave their posts and start casting corpses into the river where the current would carry them to a subterranean lake far away from the protected water supply of the Elves. There, razorfish and other sightless carnivores would feed for months to come.

The layadine cannons pumped out the white powder, filling the entire cavern with a thick film of the stuff. And with it, the invasion slowed. Flet soldiers farther back began to lift their voices as they noticed fewer and fewer Warspiders come through the hole. Soon Travin realized the entire city was caught up in euphoria as the unthinkable became reality: they had defeated the Spider King's attack.

When the echo of the last cannon blast died away—and nothing stirred beyond in the catacombs—Travin gathered his troops and plunged up the bloodied steps, pursuing the retreating enemy army back to the surface. Travin hoped that the most recent scouting reports had been accurate, that there would be no ambush waiting above. But even if all the scouts had been captured or killed and the enemy waited above, Travin knew they had to take the battle to the end, had to make sure.

Travin and his forces chased the remaining Warspider right out of the catacombs and back into the gleaming light of the morning sun. Once above, there was no other attack, no ambush, no reinforcements.

The flet soldiers, cheering in victory, soon felt a new surge of emotions. Here they stood completely free of fear for the first time in centuries. No cowering behind carefully erected screens, waiting for some search party to happen upon them; no counting seconds by passing shadows to keep groups of sunning Elves from being topside too long. Those days, it would seem, were over. Here they were, shouting and raising a ruckus, their most feared enemy now tucking its tail and running back to its hole.

"Well done!" Travin awarded them. "WELL DONE, I SAY!"

When Travin had finally returned, leaving behind a company of flet soldiers to guard the point of entry aboveground, he presented the details of the battle in full to the council. Manaelkin was practically gushing with pride, though he tried his best to remain collected and not betray the overwhelming sense of accomplishment he felt.

"My men will alert us at the first sign of a counterattack," Travin finished up. "But I suspect the Spider King will be found nursing his wounds for quite some time, and think twice before engaging us again."

"Here, here!" the elders replied, pounding their fists in agreement. All but one that was.

"See here," Manaelkin said when the praise finally subsided. "It would seem our brother, Alwynn, still does not share our enthusiasm."

Alwynn sat stoically.

"What would you say, Alwynn?" said Danhelm.

"What would I say?" Alwynn drummed his fingers a few times. "Commander Travin"—he looked to the warrior—"would you say the layadine cannons contributed to our success?"

"Aye," replied Travin, "more than that. They were our saving grace."

"And the layadine?"

"Surely a gift from Ellos himself."

"Here, here!" replied the rest, pounding the table yet again.

"It is a wonder that Ellos would send us to the only place where the Nightwish flower grows, and in it our key to victory," said Danhelm. Another round of support thumped across the room.

"And I would ask you, Travin, have your gunnery commanders accounted for what has been used in today's massacre?"

At this question, the commander grew a bit uneasy, as did the rest of the council.

"There is no need to dwell on such—"

"Yes, Manaelkin, there is." Alwynn leaned forward now, his hands gripping the table. "I most heartily agree that layadine if a gift from Ellos, one that takes decades to cultivate, and even more to stabilize." His voice was strenuous now. "*Hundreds of years*, brothers. So I would ask our beloved commander again . . . how—much—is—left?"

An uncomfortable silence fell over the room as all eyes fixed on Alwynn, and Alwynn glared at Manaelkin. When Travin spoke, there could be no doubt that whatever means had secured victory this time, it would not happen again . . . at least not for another few hundred years.

By the time the council had reconvened the next morning, Alwynn felt as if his point had been but a minor inconvenience, now over-shadowed by a far more dynamic prospect: the Seven Elf Lords.

"While I appreciate the concerns that some have brought to light"—Danhelm paused in regard to Alwynn—"I would propose to this assembly that layadine, and its providential existence, has served its purpose: to gain us this one victory and in turn speed momentum in our favor, and nothing more." The notion had somehow gained great favor among most of those present. "Are we to rely on such a tactic in the future, as some have come in the habit of relying upon? Or are we to look to new windows of opportunity, ones that far outweigh flowers and powders?"

"Say it!" some of the Elves demanded. "Out with it!"

"Brothers of the council"—Danhelm's voice rose—"I say it is time we retrieve the Seven Elf Lords from Whitehall and make good our siege of Vesper Crag!"

The council chamber erupted with cheers and clapping. It was the very notion they had all been holding to themselves. And, truth be told, Alwynn, too, hoped to put an end to the still-looming threat of the Spider King. But what Alwynn also knew was that the Seven were entrusted to a man far wiser than any of the councilmen at this table. Grimwarden would return the Seven to their *people*—not a council—when he thought they were ready, and not a moment before. Anything less would be reckless at best . . . suicide, if Alwynn's suspicions were well founded. Alwynn felt powerless—and even more, he felt betrayed that his own compatriots would turn against the very man they installed to advise them on all things military: Grimwarden. Oh, it was a noble cause, to be sure. Who among them did not dream of freedom? Did not long for the days of walking freely beneath the light of the sun once again? But just because a prophecy foretells something, doesn't mean a particular generation will live to see it.

Move too fast, gentlemen, Alwynn thought to himself, *and I fear you will not find the Seven as you so desire them. And then not even a thousand years of layadine could help you crush your enemy.*

Grimwarden sat beneath his favorite oak and took a large bite from a fresh ketelo fruit. The papery reddish skin of the oblong fruit dissolved on his tongue, and he enjoyed its distinctive tart taste. He stretched his heavy limbs, relishing the cool shade that the leaves provided him against the afternoon heat. It was a pleasure he had long forgone, knowing he must suffer with the rest of his people in their underground plight. But being here in Whitehall these many months, this spot, . . . this practice, had become his one respite. And he allowed himself the pleasure. He tossed the core into a thicket and closed his eyes, feeling the soft breeze blow across his face and rustle the leaves above. Grimwarden sprang to his feet and summoned his blade. "Speak!" he commanded. "While you can."

"Commander Grimwarden, is . . ." Grimwarden recognized that voice. ". . . is that—*ugh!*" Someone was clearly struggling in the undergrowth.

"Who goes there?" Grimwarden replied, now lowering his sword. Whoever this was, he was none too skilled in stealthy movement.

"Is it safe?"

"Safe?" Grimwarden chuckled. "I daresay you scared off any creatures for many a league. In any case, show yourself. Or do you need help to escape the bracken?"

"Nay," said the stranger. "I can manage—whoa-ah-whoa!" Nearly tumbling out of a thick briar bush—thorns still pulling on braided hair and knit cloth—emerged High Cleric Alwynn.

"Alwynn, my friend!" Grimwarden sheathed his sword and walked swiftly to meet the man. "What in Allyra brings you all this way?"

Alwynn was still busy trying to wrest himself of the woods. At last he smoothed his cloak and pressed his shoulders back. The two Elves crossed wrists over their chests and bowed. "Grim urgency brings me," said Alwynn.

There was no mistaking Alwynn's tone. Grimwarden stood back. "Go on."

"The Spider King invaded Nightwish."

"*WHAT?*" Grimwarden rocked as if struck. Suddenly all his private misgivings about taking the lords and leaving Nightwish surfaced anew. "When?"

"Four days ago. A full invasion. Through the catacombs."

"So they finally discovered us."

"Yes. Our enemy sent a larger force than that which toppled Berinfell, but we repelled them."

"Truly?" Grimwarden thought quickly. "Travin?"

"Yes, yes," said Alwynn. "He was valiant. But, Grimwarden, the Spider King did not lead this force. I believe he was testing us."

"Did we pass?"

"We defeated them utterly," replied Alwynn. "Only a handful of casualties."

"Only a handful? I don't under—"

"They used almost all of the layadine, by Manaelkin's order."

"Fools!" Grimwarden slammed his fist into his palm. "How often have I advised the council of sparing, strategic use of our layadine stores? Bah, the council leader has won us a great battle. Pray he has not forfeited the war."

"I have, and I will," said Alwynn. "But do not say that it was not strategic use of the layadine. Winning such a decisive victory has earned Manaelkin great authority, authority to follow through with his original plans."

"He demands we return the Seven Lords to Nightwish?"

"Worse," said Alwynn. "He comes to take them back, by force if necessary."

"Manaelkin was always calculating, but now I fear he has gone entirely mad! How much time do we have?"

"I left as soon as the council concluded. His plans were to gather his detachment of flet soldiers and depart just hours later."

"Then he is near?" Grimwarden gazed into the woods over Alwynn's shoulders. "I'll need to sound the warning bell. Who knows where the Seven have scattered on their afternoon off. I—"

"You have more time than that," said Alwynn. "Two days, or a little more."

"You put two days between you?" Grimwarden looked on Alwynn with new wonder. "Forgive me for the implications of my question, but how could someone of your age and modest woodcraft gain that kind of time on able-bodied soldiers?"

"I flew," said Alwynn. Seeing the bewilderment in his friend's face, he explained, "I sought aid from the Old Ones. They lent me one of their scarlet raptors. Wind-swift, they are."

"Scarlet raptors," Grimwarden muttered.

"Yes, the Old Ones maintain a secret eyrie in the Bristlethorn Hills, more than a hundred of the rare birds."

"Do they?" Grimwarden asked, almost to himself. "Do they indeed? I will remember that. You see, this is not the first time I've heard of Elves riding the raptors. One lives here in Whitehall, or did. We haven't seen it for weeks now."

After a pensive silence Alwynn asked, "What will you do?"

"Get the lords as far away from here as possible. And then confront Manaelkin myself." Grimwarden found himself absently fondling the pommel of his sword. Then he looked up to Alwynn. "And you?" The question was a good one as Alwynn was clearly a council member; by now his absence was duly noted, with more than one of his brethren having their prejudices confirmed, and when they realized he had gone to Grimwarden, there would be no question as to where his sympathies lay.

Alwynn gave a funny smirk. "Well, if you're going to pick a fight, you might as well have a crotchety old politician in your corner."

20

Puddle Jumping

"REMEMBER"—NELLY whispered, her back against the cold stone of a dead end—"keep a contact point at all times."

Nelly edged two barrels out away from the wall. "I've got the barrels. Five count on the crates . . . make them six feet out for a launch point."

"Agreed."

"I hear them." Nelly crouched behind the barrels. Backlit from the other end of the passage, at least seven large warriors approached. The Gwar leading them was absolutely massive. He carried a wide shield, but Nelly couldn't see his weapon. If she waited longer, she would lose any small advantage. Her back once more against the wall, she put one foot on each barrel and drew her knees back to her chin. She kicked the barrels launching them forward with a thunderous force. They careened down the passage toward the approaching warriors.

Five seconds later, Regis slid the crates into position, and the two Elves lunged up on them and sprang toward the enemy.

SLAM! THUD!

The towering warrior in front had leaped over the rolling barrel and swung his shield like a bat. He smacked Nelly out of the air, and she landed in a heap by one of the crates.

Graceful and lithe as she was, Regis could not do any harm to the smaller Gwar. He rotated his body outside of her fist strike and blocked her knee upstroke with his own well-muscled leg. Then he spun Regis inside his iron arms and held a dagger blade to her throat. "Peace, Elf," he whispered urgently. "I am one of your kindred."

"I ain't seen moves like that for a long time," said the larger one. "That's Vexbane. Good thing I'm pretty fair at Vexbane my own self."

Nelly sat up groggily and tried to shake the cobwebs out of her mind. She thought sure she'd heard that voice before. *Wait! There's only one Elf I know who likes to use that odd human dialect.* "Merrick?" she called out. "Merrick Evershield?"

"Yes, ma'am," he replied. "But I prefer Charlie."

The large warrior strode over to Nelly and offered his thick hand. Speechless and gawking like a child at a parade, Nelly took his hand and allowed him to pull her to her feet. "I don't believe it," she said. "Charlie?" She brushed her fingers along the dark skin of his cheek and stared into his violet eyes. "We thought we'd lost you. When you didn't come through the portal . . . we thought . . . ah, Charlie, it's so good to see you, even dressed as a Gwar!" She threw a clumsy hug around his neck.

"Wisp got me good," he said, patting her awkwardly on the back. "Stabbed me in the gut and left me for dead. Fortunately for me, some of our folk were still on that side. Like Orli here."

The smaller Elf holding Regis said, "Yes, my group of Sentinels came a little late to the party in Scotland. A snowstorm in Austria, you understand."

"Um, can you let me go now?" asked Regis, squirming.

"My apologies, darling," said Orli. He released her and sheathed his dagger.

Mr. Charlie took a step backward and said, "You know, I was beginning to wonder if somethin' happened to Grimwarden in Allyra. Figured for sure he'd have found the portal by now."

Nelly shook her head. "By now? We only just learned there was an open portal," she said. "But, Charlie, how did you know we'd be here?"

"Didn't. Been watching this portal. Figured we'd find a way back through it or someone would come over with orders for us, unless—"

"We made it back, Charlie—with all the lords."

"Why are you here then?"

"We are trying to get to Autumn and Johnny's house in upstate New York."

"Where is here, anyway?" asked Regis.

"Canada," said Orli. "Northern Quebec actually."

"That explains the cold."

"Why do you need to get back to the Briarmans' place?" asked Charlie.

"Before they knew who and what they were, Johnny and Autumn found a map, hid it in their room. A map of Vesper Crag."

"Vesper Crag?" Charlie echoed. "Well, if that don't beat all. The Spider King's probably none too happy about that."

"Still," said Orli, "what good's a map of Vesper Crag? It's not very likely that we'll be invad—"

"We're planning an invasion," said Regis. "You've been away for a long time. The lords are training under Grimwarden and Goldarrow. We have amassed an army three times the size of anything we had in the past. And we've developed new weapons as well."

"Truly?" replied Orli. The other Elven warriors behind them buzzed with excitement.

"Yes. But we haven't much time to locate the map and return to Allyra."

"If memory serves," said Nelly, quietly, "Quebec is just over the St. Lawrence River from northern New York, right?"

"If by 'just over' you mean seven hundred miles, then yes," said Charlie. "We're deep in the wilderness up here."

"We've got to get that map," said Regis.

"There I can help," said Charlie. "We've got a little seaplane stashed away in a cove on a lake . . . two-mile hike east of here."

"Gassed up and ready to go," said Orli, nodding to Nelly.

"Take us there," said Nelly.

"That might not be so easy," said Charlie. "Muster is nearly over."

"Muster?"

"Asp Bloodthorne, the Drefid commander here, assembles the strength of his army every day at dusk. Once he releases them from the muster . . . well, this place'll be flooded with ten thousand Gwar."

"Ten thousand?" Nelly gasped.

"And that does not count the legions on patrol or on training missions," said Orli.

"Just what are they doing here?" asked Nelly.

"I think you can guess," said Charlie. "But there is much more we can share. It'll have to wait. The horns haven't sounded, but it won't be long."

"Lead the way," said Nelly.

They went back the way Nelly and Regis had come.

"Here!" yelled Orli as he passed a wickedly curved short sword to Nelly and one to Regis. "You might need these."

The nine Elves hurtled down the passage, looking for the next branch. But not ten yards from them, an endless line of marching Gwar crossed their path.

"Down here!" beckoned Charlie as he diverted into a narrow opening on their left.

Praying they hadn't been seen, the Elves followed. It was an access way, not meant for much travel. In fact, some industrious Gwar had decided to use it for storage.

Nelly tripped over a crate and would have sprawled if it weren't for Orli's swift assistance. The ribbon of passage curled this way and that, up and down, and finally there was a light at the end.

Charlie went through first, but stopped as the others barreled through behind him. They'd entered a chamber teeming with no less than forty Gwar, a kind of mess hall.

Charlie nodded and motioned to the other Elves to follow. There was another door in the back right of the chamber. If they could just get through without—

"Wait!" commanded the Gwar leader. "I don't think I've seen your tribe mark. Come round, let your heads breathe so I can see your mark. Maybe I'll put you in for a commendation."

Charlie stood very still. Inside his helmet, he shut his eyes tight. He'd hoped to avoid confrontation, hoped to avoid notice. But now there were few options. "Looks like it's time to kick the hornet's nest," he muttered.

"What's that you say?" asked the Gwar.

Charlie ignored the question, turned, and approached the Gwar. The other Elves were ready to follow Charlie's lead. He stood now directly in front of the Gwar. He began to remove his helmet. "A commendation?" Charlie asked. "Do you think?"

"Perhaps," said the Gwar, watching with keen interest. "You captured spies . . . and you know how Asp feels about ELVES."

Charlie whipped off his helmet and slammed it into the Gwar's forehead. Charlie had his shield up in a flash, raised it horizontally, and beheaded the enemy in one swift motion. Then with a roar, he lowered his shield and barreled into a group of Gwar, knocking them down like bowling pins.

Orli sprang into action next. He removed an odd Y-shaped blade from his belt and flung it at a Gwar near the back of the chamber.

Outnumbered four to one, the Elves quickly evened the odds. The battle was over in minutes. Dead Gwar littered the chamber. Two Elves had perished as well.

"We have to go," Charlie said.

"Must we leave our friends here, among the Gwar?" asked Orli.

Charlie's posture sagged. "We have no choice. They will slow our escape."

The seven remaining Elves raced through the door at the back of the chamber. Their path of escape was full of twists and turns, sudden blocks, and hasty detours. But they avoided conflict and seemed to be making progress, when Charlie stopped them and said, "I thought that last turn was wrong. Orli, I think we've gone underground by a level or two."

"Yes, yes, I think you're right. We don't want to be down here."

"Why?" asked Regis.

"They breed the spiders down here . . . and do worse things." Orli pointed to a dim, wavering light some sixty yards ahead. "Come, Charlie, I have spent more time in this place. Follow me." Swiftly, they escaped the mountain and fled into the night. 🗲

21

Conflict of Interest

"CHANGE OF plans," Grimwarden started off. He paced in the formal dining hall as the Seven sat around the board, along with Goldarrow, Claris, Mumthers, and Alwynn. The team had just finished dinner, and Grimwarden asked them all to remain, even insisting that Mumthers be seated—a habit she never entertained. "As you can imagine, Alwynn's presence is unexpected, and far more than a simple inspection of our progress. It would seem that unforeseen events have initiated a move among part of the council of elders to take you"—he indicated the lords—"from Whitehall prematurely, and by force if necessary."

"You mean they want us to march with them on Vesper Crag?" Autumn asked, remembering the tumultuous council meeting so many months before.

"Why not wait a little longer?" questioned Tommy.

"The Spider King attacked Nightwish Caverns," Alwynn interjected. An audible gasp went up around the table. "However, the Elves of Allyra have won a formidable victory, albeit costly."

"Costly in lives?" asked Kiri Lee.

"Materials," Grimwarden corrected. "Layadine, the valuable extract of the Nightwish flower, is lethal to Warspiders."

"Spiders of any kind, really," said Alwynn.

"The stuff you used back in school to kill that one spider!" Tommy pointed to Goldarrow.

"The same," she replied.

"The elders made the decision to use the powder during the siege," continued Grimwarden.

"So we won! Good choice!" Johnny pumped his fist. "Sweet!"

"Except that they extinguished nearly our entire supply." Grimwarden let the ramifications settle over them.

Tommy raised his hand, still not comfortable with his place as royalty. Grimwarden shook his head and Tommy spoke up. "Why is that so bad? Can't we just make more?"

Alwynn answered this question. "Tommy, the process of extracting and making it suitable for use is a highly dangerous process, one that requires great skill, and one other invaluable commodity."

"What's that?" he asked.

"Time."

"Oh. Like how much?"

"Three hundred years, on average."

"Three hun—!"

"Time that we do not have," Grimwarden interrupted.

"So"—Jimmy sat up a little in his chair—"are we ready? I mean, aren't we close to being done with the Vexbane training?"

"Close?" Grimwarden eyed him. "Perhaps. Finished? No. But I fear we may never have that luxury. As I see it, our only choice is to get you all as far away from here as possible, and complete what little training I can manage in a different location. The council is right: we do need to raze Vesper Crag, and you are essential to that process. No one would argue that. But there is still much you need to learn." Grimwarden looked to Elle for her support. Surely, she felt the same. "But this brings up a greater matter. Vesper Crag itself."

Alwynn spoke next. "The elders, while bent on securing you as an invaluable asset to war, have no formal battle plan. We are councilmen—politicians at best—not warriors. And while Travin has surely won us a great victory with his planning, he is no Grimwarden. Our battle strategy lies here in this room, among all of you."

"Us?" mouthed Jimmy, trying to hide his astonishment. "Attack Vesper Crag?" *And I canna' control my gift yet,* Jimmy worried. They knew how to swing a sword, knew how to slay an opponent in two moves. But plan an entire invasion?

"We must produce a battle plan," Grimwarden said, placing his hands on the table and leaning forward. He looked at each of them, taking his time. "And I need each of you to contribute. While you have little experience on the battlefield, you are the royal Seven Elven Lords, and you know more than you think you do. Each of you carries answers to clues that must be answered—keys to unlocking doors to the battle. The time is coming when we will unleash the full power of Berinfell upon Vesper Crag. But not here. Not now. We must focus our attention on keeping you safe," he motioned to the lords.

"One thing I do know," he went on, "I will not surrender the Seven to a council of elders bent on taking Vesper Crag at any cost. Win we shall, but not before Ellos grants us divine wisdom to proceed. And not before we have exercised discretion." He looked to Claris and Mumthers. "You are to return to Nightwish; Mumthers, Claris will be your escort." Mumthers dipped her head respectfully. "Alwynn, Elle, and I will stay here to intercept the council and buy as much time as we can for the rest of you."

"And us?" asked Tommy.

Grimwarden placed his weathered hand upon a huge tome that lay on the table before him.

Alwynn brightened immediately. "Is that—?"

"Yes," he replied. "The Berinfell Prophecies."

Alwynn nearly leapt from his seat. "The Old Ones, are they here?"

"Nay," said Grimwarden. "But they were once. Remember the raptor I spoke of? It nested and stood guard over this book in a long-forgotten tower deep in the recesses of this castle. Tommy and Kat stumbled upon it, and I daresay, not by accident."

"I wonder," said Alwynn, trembling, "if I might read it."

"Of course," said Grimwarden. "In time. For now we seek Ellos's guidance from its pages." He turned to face the lords once more. "Goldarrow and I have scoured the prophecies. Best we can tell is that the Keystone is hidden away in a fortress to the far north. Precisely where, we cannot be sure. It is best that you head in that direction. The seven of you will follow the Tricin River, then go northeast along the Spine until you come to our rendezvous point, a dell with over-grown ruins right at the end of the Spine. You'll leave tomorrow, taking the tunnel off the garden courtyard."

"You mean the one where we did the first exercise?" asked Jimmy.

"With the jar! When we first arrived, yes!" added Kat.

"Aye, that's the one. It will get you far from Whitehall without ever being seen. It opens up at a curl of the river. From there you know what to do."

"I wish we had a flock of those scarlet raptors," said Johnny. "Seems like the best form of transportation, if you ask me." He wasn't the only one who didn't relish three days on foot.

Grimwarden glanced at Alwynn. "Ah, if only we had just four such flying mounts. Unless the raptor Tommy and Kat rode has returned, we have only the one the high cleric rode in on."

"Ah, I meant to mention that to you," said Alwynn. "The willful featherbrain flew off the moment I got off it."

"Seems Ellos has decided for us. Use your feet. Use the tunnel. I will find you in three days' time. Take shelter and wait for us in the deep wood."

"And then?" asked Tommy.

"And then, Lord Felheart, we seek the Keystone."

"Lower your bridge and open your gate!" Manaelkin cried out. "By order of the High Council of Berinfell! We have urgent business with Guardmaster Grimwarden!"

"I greet thee, Manaelkin," Grimwarden said, his head suddenly appearing between a crenellation in the wall above the drawbridge. "But one moment with the gate. It is some doing for just the three of us." Grimwarden disappeared from view.

Manaelkin mumbled to Danhelm, "What does he mean, 'just the three of us'?"

"I do not know," Danhelm replied. "Perhaps the others are off on training missions."

"Hmmm," Manaelkin muttered. "Perhaps."

Inside, Grimwarden turned to Goldarrow and said, "I want you to remain up in the gatehouse."

"What? What are you talking about?" she asked. "You'll need my help, if not with the gate, certainly with the bridge."

"We can manage," he said, motioning to Alwynn. "I don't expect any trouble beyond my arrest. But just in case, should things go badly, you watch from up here, descend the rear stairwell to the tunnels, and follow the lords. Understood?"

Reluctantly, Goldarrow nodded. "But I'm none too happy about it, mind you."

"Noted. But we cannot afford the risk of no one to help the lords." And that was the end of it.

Grimwarden descended to the gate. He and Alwynn raised the portcullis and opened the gate locks holding the bridge in place.

"GRIMWARDEN!" Manaelkin screamed from outside. "Open the gate this instant!"

"We are!" he bellowed back. "Had you ever lifted a finger at a gate in Berinfell, you might know this is no—*ahg!*—easy—*urgh!*—task! Grimwarden grasped one of the turnpegs of the massive iron wheel on which the drawbridge's release chains were wound. "Alwynn, a bit of help!"

Together, they moved the wheel enough to dislodge the thick stopping peg and allow the chain to roll outward. "Slowly!" Grimwarden yelled, straining against the weight. "Slowly!"

Alwynn could not help any longer without losing consciousness. He let go. Grimwarden couldn't hold it by himself. The drawbridge fell the remaining six feet and slammed into the ground below, sending up a cloud of debris. As the dust cleared, Grimwarden and Alwynn stood in the entryway, side by side.

"Alwynn," Manaelkin seethed. "I should have guessed."

"Guessed?" inquired Alwynn. "You've known where I stand for a long, long time."

"Yes," Manaelkin replied. "I suppose I have. You stand against Elvenkind, against our final victory."

"I am not the one defying the high council's original vote and bringing an army to make certain his own will is done."

Manaelkin drew out his blade and started across the board, but when Grimwarden drew out his own blade, the council chief thought better of it and held fast. "We're here for the Seven Lords," Manaelkin said plainly.

"Oh, so you didn't come for tea and cakes?" Grimwarden mocked.

"Give me the lords!"

"They are not yours to take, Manaelkin!" Alwynn spat back.

The chief council was furious, intolerant of what he deemed insubordination. He looked behind him. "Flet soldiers! Bring me the Seven Lords! And let no one stand in your way!"

The flet soldiers were called to attention and began to march, passing to either side of Manaelkin and crossing the drawn bridge. But as they neared the far side, their march slowed to a halt.

It was Grimwarden.

These were the men he had trained. Raised from boys into men. And despite the most hellacious triads of the chief councilman, they would not be disloyal to him. Not now. Not ever.

"Yes," Grimwarden said, waving his hand. "Do come inside. You, too, Manaelkin, so we can discuss this as is fitting." Grimwarden turned his back and started to walk back under the gatehouse. Alwynn remained a moment, wondering what Manaelkin would do.

"What are you doing?!" Manaelkin screamed. "Attack him!" He started forward now, shoving his way between his soldiers and brandishing his dagger. "BRING ME THE SEVEN!"

"Grimwarden, defend yourself!" Alwynn cried. "He has a blade!"

Grimwarden started to turn, but not in time. Manaelkin dove.

A bright blue light exploded in the center of the drawbridge, shattering the thick board into oblivion, as well as all those who stood in the middle of it. Manaelkin's splinter-riddled body slammed into Grimwarden and saved him from the most direct force of the blast. Alwynn was similarly spared by the corpses of more than one slain flet soldier.

Grimwarden slowly heaved Manaelkin's lifeless body to the side and blinked, his ears ringing from the blast. *Only one weapon has that much power. Arc rifles. But how?* He propped himself up on an elbow, head spinning. Dazed. Scores of dead flet soldiers, some still burning, lined both sides of the ditch between the castle and the far bank. Outside of the castle wall remained hundreds more flet soldiers, each reeling from the blast they had witnessed. And beyond them came a sight that made even Grimwarden shudder.

Appearing among the trees like ghostly apparitions came a wide front of Warspiders and their Gwar riders. *Pop! Pop!* More arc stones were fired as the enemy poured through the trees.

"Olin! Get up!" It was Goldarrow's voice, but heard as if through a tunnel.

Grimwarden looked up. She was running down the front steps of the gatehouse. He tried to call out to her. *Elle . . .* but he wasn't sure if his mouth actually spoke the word.

By his side now, she said, "Olin, you're bleeding!"

Grimwarden stood on unsteady legs. He quickly assessed the attack. Flet soldiers were valiantly trying to form up lines. Archers had taken to the trees, but they had no leadership.

Kah-booooom!

More explosions shook the grounds outside Whitehall.

Grimwarden summoned all his strength. "Get to the Seven!" he spat. "The tunnel!"

"I'm not leaving you, Grimwarden," she choked back tears.

"NOW!" he roared at her. She grimaced, closing her eyes. "I'll come with Alwynn if we can. But our lives"—he coughed—"are irrelevant now. I will stand with our soldiers here! But you must go with the Seven, see their journey through. Too many—"

"But, Olin, I—"

"GET AWAY FROM HERE!" He shoved her back.

Going It Alone

THEY HAD been running all morning, having finally emerged from the underground tunnels into the light of day. Even in top condition as they were, the pace was grueling.

Kat bent over, hands on her knees, gasping for air. "I have to stop."

"Can't," Jett said. "Not yet. Keep going."

But she shook her head. "It's too much."

"Me, too," Kiri Lee joined in. "Can't we rest for just a minute?"

"For all we know, the elders have half of Berinfell's army on our heels," Johnny suggested. "Grimwarden said not to stop. Only at night."

"He also said it was a three-day journey by foot," Kat reminded him. "We can't keep this pace forever. Come on. Just a few minutes." She looked to Tommy for support.

He puffed out his cheeks. "Fine," Tommy said, glancing at Jett. "But just enough to catch our breath."

"Ah! Thank you," Kiri Lee said, putting a hand on Tommy's back. Kat glared.

The seven of them wandered down to the edge of the river they'd been following. Grimwarden called it the Tricin, running due north. They knelt and splashed the cool water in their faces, taking in deep drinks out of their cupped hands. Refreshed, they walked back and found places to sit among the shade of the woods, some atop small boulders, others leaning against tree trunks.

"How d'yu think it's going back at Whitehall?" Jimmy asked to no one in particular.

"I think Grimwarden is thrashing those guys," said Autumn,

"sending the elders all the way back to Nightwish with their tails between their legs."

"Oh yeah!" said Jett, making a fist. "See ya, wouldn't want to be ya!" The rest chuckled.

"What about the army?" asked Kat. "Do you really think they would hurt Grimwarden and Goldarrow? Alwynn?"

Tommy sat up a little taller. "I think the elders would give it a pretty good go, but in the end, I can't ever see the army—his army—turning on Grimwarden."

"The dude would pummel them," Jett said, smashing his fist into his other palm, and making a *poof!* sound with his mouth.

"Still," said Tommy, "I wish we knew what was going on back there."

"I could run back," said Autumn.

The thought hung in the air.

Finally, Johnny leaned forward. "No way."

"I'm serious," Autumn retorted. "I could be there and back before you'd even miss me. And they'd never even see me."

"Forget about it."

But Tommy stared at her with the slightest grin on his face.

"No way, Tommy. She's not going," said Johnny.

"Zip down there, scope it out. Zip back." Tommy scratched his head. "I can't see the harm in that."

Johnny was on his feet walking toward Tommy and Autumn. "I forbid it!"

"Forbid it?" Autumn sat bolt upright.

"Dude, easy," said Jett, also standing to meet him.

"Yeah, I forbid it. She's my sister—"

"Your fellow lord of Berinfell, ruler of Allyra," Kat corrected.

"Whatever."

"And I'm going," Autumn concluded.

"No!"

"You can't stop me, Johnny."

"Autumn, but what if you—?"

"What if I what, Johnny? I die?"

He hesitated. "Yeah. What if you die?"

"What if we all die?" she spat back. "Haven't you realized that we've been training to fight? For war? People die in wars, Johnny. But what we've been taught to do is use our gifts to keep others from dying. To learn what we can, when we can. To be faster, smarter, stronger, and braver than our enemy. And maybe, just maybe, this scouting trip would work to our advantage. Give us a lead on our pursuers."

Johnny just stood there, mouth open, but no words. He glared at her but could find nothing to say. He glanced at Tommy, then Jett.

"So I'm going."

"No more than ten minutes looking around, Autumn," instructed Tommy. "No unnecessary risks. Johnny is right about one thing: we definitely can't afford to lose you. Not now."

"Not ever," said Johnny.

Autumn smiled, and then walked up to hug him. While he might not be blood directly, he would always be her big brother. "Thanks," she whispered. And a moment later she let go, vanishing in a swirl of leaves.

Autumn felt the forest passing by her in slow motion, picking her course as easily as a child skipping through a park. But she knew in reality her body was traveling at unimaginable speed, seen only as a blur by any forest animals that saw her. Her feet never stumbled once, clearing rocks, running along downed trees, and bounding over shrubs. She followed the river all the way back to where it wound around the base of a slowly rising hill, the one upon which Whitehall sat. And it was then she came to an abrupt halt.

Towering high above her was a thick plume of black smoke, rising like a damp chimney fire from a white stone woodstove . . . Whitehall!

Autumn covered her mouth with her hand, gasping. "It can't be," she whispered. Something moved in the woods behind her. She spun around. A Gwar was traipsing through the underbrush. The warrior had not yet taken notice of her, so Autumn darted to her left, hiding among a stand of oaks. The Gwar continued to lumber through the wood, obviously not concerned with stealth. Autumn connected the fire above with the scouting Gwar in the same time it took her to race up the hillside and stop just beside a giant boulder not one hundred yards from the main gate.

The drawbridge was nowhere to be seen; only a blackened, yawning hole remained in the ditch that separated the main path from the fortress's entrance. But more surprising was the sight that filled the entrance: hundreds of Gwar soldiers, and even more Warspiders. They milled about aimlessly, dismantling the main courtyard and heaving stones from the upper ramparts above.

"They're bored," Autumn said to herself. She watched them, each disconnected, unconcerned. Whatever had happened here, it was long over.

She heard Tommy's warning in her head, but it hadn't even been close to ten minutes. Two; three at best. . . . Autumn zipped out from behind the boulder and ran to a short hedgerow about fifty yards up. She needed a closer look. And that's exactly what she got. As she crawled on her hands and knees to the end of the brush, she peered around the corner hoping to see farther into the fortress's main entrance; but just twelve inches in front of her was the corpse of a flet soldier, extremities blackened by fire, face marred.

She screamed, scrambling backward.

A dozen Gwar heard the noise and spun around, instantly engaged.

Autumn looked up, heard shouting.

"Time to go."

And when the group of investigating Gwar got to where the noise had come from, Autumn was long gone.

"It's bad." Autumn pulled her windswept hair back into a ponytail.

The others stood. "How bad?" asked Tommy.

"Whitehall has been invaded."

"I knew it!" shouted Johnny. "Manaelkin is evil!"

Autumn shook her head. "It wasn't Manaelkin." The others looked on. "Not unless he has a new fascination with Warspiders."

Tommy was stunned. "The Spider King?"

"What?" they gasped.

"But how?" asked Kat.

"I don't know. B-but I did see"—she shuddered—"bodies. Elven bodies. Everywhere. I think the elders arrived, just as Alwynn said. But they were surprised. In any case, the place is crawling with Gwar and Warspiders. They've let anything that could burn, and are now destroying whatever they can with their hands."

"I can't believe it's all gone," said Kiri Lee. "Just like that."

"It was a good home for us," Tommy nodded. "But it is not why we're here."

"Agreed," said Jett. "We have a job to do."

Tommy looked to Autumn. "Any sign of—" But her solemn look and a gentle shake of her head cut him short. No one said anything for a whole minute, each pondering the fate of their teachers. A heavy weight fell on their shoulders, the air becoming hard to breathe. Surely Grimwarden and Goldarrow had escaped. They would have found a way. Wouldn't they? But if the attack truly had been a surprise, perhaps there was no way.

Kiri Lee looked to their leader. "So what do we do, Tommy?"

Tommy looked to Jett. "Jett's right. We have a job to do, and we've got to find that Keystone. If Grimwarden were here, he'd want us to find it. Without it, we are not equipped. And that's what he is"—he corrected himself—"*was* all about."

"Yeah, but where do we even start?" Johnny asked. "I mean, it could be anywhere." The others nodded in agreement. The task did seem overwhelming at best.

Tommy thought for a moment. "Grimwarden didn't send us three days north for nothing. He must have known there was something up here. Something that might help us. So"—he looked north along the river—"I say that whatever *that* is, we look for it."

"A wild-goose chase, then," said Autumn.

"Except we know our goose is a Keystone," corrected Tommy. "So that's at least *something*."

"I'm still not too sure about this," said Kiri Lee. Johnny also nodded. "I mean, what if Grimwarden is on his way here now? He said to wait for him after following the Spine-thingy for three days. Shouldn't we give him time?"

Tommy shook his head. "That plan was made under the assumption it would only be Manaelkin and some flet soldiers. I fear that everything has changed now. Most likely, Grimwarden is—"

Kat reached up and put a hand on his mouth. "Don't say it." She suddenly realized how forward the gesture was and pulled her hand away, blushing slightly. "Sorry."

Tommy continued. "I was just saying that every moment we waste thinking about *what-ifs* is a moment we waste going after the Keystone. And if anyone would know how to find us in the Thousand-League Forest, it's Grimwarden and Goldarrow."

Tommy walked around in a circle, collecting his thoughts. They all waited, knowing he was working on something. A gentle breeze rustled the leaves overhead, and a few birds called out from their roosts. When Tommy finally addressed the other lords again, he had a marked air about him . . . a new boldness in his speech. Something was changing in him. In them all.

"We move on. We have been trained for this, and now is our time to step into the light. We were born for greatness, and have miraculously been brought here, to another world, to do one thing: save its people. Our people. We are no longer followers. We're the leaders now. And what happens next rests on *our* shoulders. *Ours.* I don't like that feeling any more than you do, but it's just the way it is. And for whatever reason, I have to believe Ellos's hand is in this. He will not give us anything we can't handle. He's with us. Always."

While no one had ever heard Tommy talk quite like this, they all believed him. Believed he was right. That he knew what he was talking about. And while his clarity of conclusion did seem a bit lofty, they would have been lying if they said they didn't feel the same thing. They *were* born for this. And they had a choice to make. Here. Now.

"Are you with me?" Tommy asked, putting his hand out, palm down.

The others looked to each other, knowing they were about to take matters into their own hands . . . matters of Berinfell . . . of tens of thousands of their Elven kindred, as well as the human slaves in the catacombs of Vesper Crag . . . of the fate of their very existence . . . of living and dying.

"I'm in," said Jimmy, placing his hand on top of Tommy's.

"As am I," said Jett, stepping forward.

"Me, too," Kat smiled.

"Me five," said Autumn with a wink.

"*Moi, aussi.*" Kiri Lee placed her hand on top of the growing pile. She got a few funny looks. "It's French. Me, too. What?"

The last hand was Johnny's. "Count me in."

"Endurance and Victory!" Tommy proclaimed.

"ENDURANCE AND VICTORY!" the others shouted, pumping their hands as one and then throwing them in the air.

"We go north," said Tommy. "Then northeast along the Spine."

"Until?" asked Kat.

"Until we find something."

"Or get found," said Jimmy. And they all turned and looked at him.

Elle's emotions swung between fits of weeping and surges of aggression. One moment she was mourning for Grimwarden, whom she was quite certain had not survived—nor had Alwynn—the next she was bent on finding the Seven and storming the Spider King's lair personally. She had run by torchlight through the underground tunnel leading from Whitehall, only to emerge into broad daylight, eyes bloodshot, gasping for air. The reality was that she was more exhausted from anguish and desperation than she was from sprinting.

Yet as much as she knew she loved Grimwarden, it was the mission that mattered more. Should the Seven fail, all hope of life beyond these next few days and weeks seemed pointless. The Spider King would regroup and assault Nightwish again. She knew it was only a matter of time. And without the Seven, without this Rainsong, there was no hope. Her secret love would remain so forever, locked in her heart, bound in her grave.

No, she must find the Seven. And search she did. For days. Until she found the rendezvous point near the overgrown ruins and found no sign of the Seven. Ever the optimist, she refused the conclusions of loss or capture. Rather, her thoughts turned to the seven young teenagers she had helped become warriors. Each of them a force to be reckoned with; each of them vibrant and hopeful.

"I am too late. They have gone on," she muttered to herself, feeling a cool breeze waft across her face. She turned her head and looked about the forest, realizing she was not meant to find them. That they had indeed stepped into their destiny and were safely on their own now. At least, that's what she told herself. ❧

23

Fighting with Fire

"NORTHEAST," SAID Tommy, out of breath but refusing to slow their pace. They'd left the Spine just hours before and sprinted through a dense forest toward a very uncertain destination, dusk now descending around them. "That's all I know."

"It'd be nice if the book had a map in it," said Johnny, puffing along just behind Tommy.

"Or maybe Grimwarden could have given us some more specific directions," said Jimmy.

"Even Grimwarden didn't know," said Kat. "I saw his thoughts before he sent us away. Northeast of the Spine was all he could interpret from the prophecies."

On and on they went, ducking low branches and leaping fallen trees. They went at full speed heedless of exhaustion and heedless of the possibility that the enemy could lurk nearby. Each of them drew strength—and courage—from their months of training under Guardmaster Grimwarden. When before they would have fallen on their faces and begged for rest, now they gritted their teeth and charged forward. When before they would have quailed at the sight of a scouting party of Gwar, now they felt confident that working together they could strike down most any foe but, perhaps, the Spider King himself.

The Thousand-League Forest had lived up to its name and then some. From Nightwish Caverns, northwest to Whitehall, and now northeast . . . the deep forest seemed to have no end. Even Tommy and Kat, who had seen the end of the forest from the air, found themselves wondering if the woods would ever end. The forest floor had become uneven, too, making the run even more treacherous. Rising to steep hills, opening suddenly to reveal a swift-flowing stream, or falling away into little dells or hollows, the trail kept the Seven focused.

The afternoon turned to evening and the evening to night, but under the canopy it was much the same: greenish-blue twilight.

Tommy saw that a few of the Seven were lagging well behind, so he made the decision to stop and rest at the bottom of a dell—where by sheer chance, several trees had fallen forming a kind of ring of benches.

Eventually they all joined him, and with the exceptions of Jett, whose strength and healing abilities made exhaustion nearly impossible, and Autumn, who felt as though she were walking at any pace less than lightning-fast, the lords sat staring at each other and did nothing else at all but breathe. Jett and Autumn spent the time gathering logs for a cooking fire.

Jett threw an armful down in the center of their ring of fallen trees and said, "There you go, Johnny. Do your thing."

"I don't think we should," Johnny muttered.

"Why not?" asked Jett. "We gotta eat."

"For one thing," said Johnny, "a fire will show the enemy right where we are."

"He's right," said Kat. "You remember what Grimwarden told us. The Gwar have keen eyesight, especially at night. Remember on the Dark Veil?"

Tommy shivered. "That was close to the end for us. Still . . . I was looking forward to mixing up some of the stew ingredients Mumthers gave us. I thought I saw a stream back there."

"Oh, stop," said Kiri Lee. "You're making my stomach growl. I'm starving . . . just not enough to want us to risk a fire. It's not just the Gwar, you know. Who knows what kinds of creatures there might be this deep in the woods."

"Creatures?" Jett laughed so hard he snorted. "Shoot, there's nothing out here but squirrels and owls." As if on cue, an owl hooted loudly somewhere outside of their little hollow. "See?" said Jett.

"I don't know," said Tommy. "We've already seen spiders a bit bigger than we're used to. Gwar, Drefids, Wisps, and Cragons, too. For all we know there could be patches of those awful trees right near here."

At that, Jett fell silent. He'd had more intimate experience with Cragons than any of the Seven. Even with his great strength, something about those immense trees sent a chill down his spine. They were all silent for a time, nervously glancing up at the trees around them, just black silhouettes against the deep forest and the night sky.

"Okay," said Jimmy. "Let's stop all this monsters-in-the-woods nonsense, right? Let's use our heads, not our imaginations."

"What do you mean?" asked Tommy.

Jimmy grinned and tapped his temple with a finger. "Elementary, my dear Bowman. Yu can have yur stew without lighting a fire—or at least without lighting a fire that would bring enemies or beasties. Johnny's gotten quite controlled with his fire. What's say he just holds the pan in the palm of his hand and lets out just a bit of flame? Could yu do that now, Johnny, without it burnin' yu?"

"Yeah, sure . . . I guess," he replied. "Why didn't I think of that?"

"Because," said Jimmy, "I'm the brains of this operation."

An awkward silence lingered. Then everyone but Jimmy burst out in hard laughter.

"Well, it's true," Jimmy contended, but that only intensified the situation.

Johnny fell backward off his log and rolled in the dead leaves.

"That's enough," said Tommy, wiping away a tear. "It's a great idea. Jett, you have the pans in your pack. Let me have a couple. I'm going to get some water."

"I'll go with you," said Kiri Lee.

Those same words were right on the tip of Kat's tongue, but she managed to be a few seconds too slow.

Tommy was grateful to have Kiri Lee's company. The stream was quite a bit farther back than he'd remembered and, powers or not, he didn't feel too comfortable being in the dark woods so far from his powerful

friends. Shooting a bow with ridiculous accuracy was great for a battle, but not when you couldn't see.

"It's just a little farther," he said.

"That's what you said five minutes ago," said Kiri Lee.

"This time I'm sure," he said with a chuckle.

Fortunately for Tommy, they found a dark ribbon of stream a few
moments later. Tommy took one of the pans and knelt on the edge of
the bank. He stretched every which way but couldn't reach all the way
down to the water level. "Shoot!" he grumbled. "I'm gonna have to go
down there."

"No, I'll do it," said Kiri Lee. She picked up the second pan and
took the first one out of Tommy's hands. She stepped off the edge of
the bank, trotted along the air until she was just above the water. She
dipped and filled both pans and then walked on invisible steps back
to Tommy's side.

"I wish I could do that," Tommy said, shaking his head. "Looks
like so much fun."

"It is," Kiri Lee replied. "But you have a gift."

"Yeah, but archery, well . . . it's just not as cool."

"Cool," said Kiri Lee. "What a silly concept. Here we are in the
middle of a thousand leagues of forest in a mysterious world, and
you're worried about being cool."

"Well, when you put it that way."

"Ah, it was that way on Earth, too. We all worried so much about
being cool, but no one really knew what cool was there, either. It's all
made up, in people's heads. Like I said, silly."

Tommy chewed on that for a moment, listening to the gurgle of
the stream and the chorus of night frogs. Then Kiri Lee spoke again.
"When I said you had a gift, I wasn't talking about your skill with the
bow."

"Okay," said Tommy, "now I'm lost. Where's Jimmy and his brains
when I need him?"

"You're a leader, Tommy. A natural. People look to you for decisions . . . advice. That's kind of why I wanted to come with you to get
the water."

The hair on the back of Tommy's neck prickled. "You wanted to come with me because I'm a leader?"

"No," said Kiri Lee. "I need some advice. See, I really like one of the members of our team, but I'm not sure how to tell him."

"You mean LIKE like?"

Kiri Lee nodded.

"Oh," said Tommy, feeling suddenly very warm. He thought that perhaps he could boil the water with the palms of his hands. "I, um . . . I don't know much about romance."

"He's that way, too," said Kiri Lee.

Could she be more obvious? Tommy wondered. *What do I tell her?* He decided on the direct approach. "I figure the only thing that can mess you up is if you keep quiet about it. If he's got any interest in you, then you telling him would be a good thing, right? And if not, you still need to know, right?"

"Thanks, Tommy," she said. "I knew I could count on—what was that?"

Tommy's heart raced as he strained to listen. He'd heard something tramping around in the leaves. "Probably just a squirrel," he said.

"What you are doing in our woods?" came a high, squeaky voice from the darkness.

"That's no squirrel," said Kiri Lee, drawing twin daggers.

Tommy's sword flashed out with a loud ring. "Who are you?" he demanded. "Show yourself!"

"Aiieeeeeee!" squealed the same voice, followed by diminishing footfalls in the leaves.

"Should I go after it?" Tommy asked.

"I think you scared it away," said Kiri Lee. "Besides, it didn't sound all that threatening. We need to get back to the others."

"So what do you think it was?" asked Johnny, a pot of stew simmering in each of his hands.

Tommy and Kiri Lee shrugged. "No idea," said Tommy. "But it said we're in its woods."

"That doesn't make much sense," said Jett.

"Could it have been a Gwar?" asked Autumn. "Like a spy?"

"I've never heard a Gwar speak like that," said Kiri Lee.

"And a Gwar spy wouldn't give away its position," said Tommy.

"Probably wouldn't run away, either," said Jett. "Ah, I wouldn't worry about it, man, you did the right thing."

"Thanks, Jett," Tommy replied. "But I wonder."

"Hey, how long on the stew?" Jett turned to Johnny.

"I think it's done," Johnny replied, shaking his head. "You know, with my gift, I thought I could get a cool superhero nickname. Maybe the *Man of Fire* or *Flame Man*. Now"—he glanced at the simmering pots—"now, they're going to call me the *Elf Stove*."

That started up a chain reaction of furious laughter, amplified again and again as each of the lords took a turn teasing Johnny.

"How about *Potman*," suggested Jett.

"No," giggled Autumn. "He's not a man yet."

"Hey!" complained Johnny, but he took no insult. "Of course I'm not a man. I'm an Elf!"

"*Skillet Boy!*" suggested Kat, smiling at last.

"That's good," said Tommy. "I was thinking *Stew-pendous Guy!*"

"Oh," said Jimmy, "that's horrible. Really. I think we should call him *Captain Crockpot*."

"You guys should stop," said Kiri Lee, trying hard not to laugh. "We should be encouraging each other, not insulting."

"No big deal," said Johnny. "It's actually kind of cheering me up."

"Well," said Kiri Lee. "In that case . . . I dub thee *Sir Soups-a-lot*."

"Booo," hooted Jett. "That's worse than—"

A rumbling sound rolled out of the darkness, followed by a shrieking, "*Aiieeeeeee!*"

"It's that voice!" shouted Tommy, stringing his bow.

"And something else," said Kat.

"It's not far away," said Jett.

The growl intensified to a roar. The shriek became desperate.

"Come on!" urged Tommy, and he fled into the trees. Autumn whooshed by Tommy. "Wish she wouldn't do that!" he grumbled. He broke into a clearing and stumbled to a stop right next to Autumn. Jett and Johnny ripped through next with Kat, Kiri Lee, and Jimmy close behind.

"We're not going to like this," said Jimmy.

They looked up and saw what Jimmy had glimpsed with his inner foresight seconds earlier. Half crouched in a thatch of crushed bushes and shrubs, a massive four-legged beast scratched and clawed at a tree on the far side of the clearing.

Thick bodied, with a long neck and tail, powerful limbs with long, slothlike talons, and an arrowhead-shaped skull—the creature's form was that of a dragon such as each of the lords had read about in story-books on Earth.

But this beast had no wings, and its glistening scale armor looked something like shingles of wet tree bark. Down the center of its neck and tail grew a whitish ridge of cartilage, and it was covered with irregular patches of dark green moss. The creature looked as if it had been knit together from the forest floor and risen like a woodland nightmare to terrify all who beheld it.

And so the Seven stood transfixed, watching the creature scratching and, at times, shaking the tree. Its luminous yellow eyes peered ever upward, casting eerie light into the higher branches.

"Aiieeeeeee!" came the shriek once more. "Help meee!"

The fearful plea woke Tommy from his trance. "Where are you?"

"Here!" cried the voice.

"Do you see anything?" Tommy demanded.

"No," they each answered.

"Wait," said Kat. "There's something up there with thoughts like ours . . . and it's out of its mind with fear."

The tree that had only been swaying slightly before now rocked back and forth from the creature's violent thrusts.

"Oooooooooh noooooo," cried the voice. "Get me, do not let it! Pleeeeeease!"

Tommy had heard enough. He had an arrow nocked in a heartbeat and fired the shaft into the hollow behind the beast's right forelimb. The arrow was right on target, but the shaft sprang back and fell harmlessly to the ground.

The creature did not seem to notice the arrow, but intent upon its purpose, it opened its jaws and belched forth a billowing stream of green fire. The plume rose like an oily explosion, and little licks of the wispy green flame danced on every branch and leaf.

"Ahhh, aiieeeeeee, ah, ah, ah!" Whatever was up there seemed to be crying.

"We've got to do something!" yelled Kat. "He's in pain."

"Tell him we're coming," Tommy commanded.

"I don't know if I . . . well, I'll try," she said, staring into the tree's upper limbs.

"Jett, Johnny, Autumn, . . . distract it," Tommy ordered. "Jimmy, tell us its moves. Kiri Lee, standby to get up in that tree. I'll cover you all."

Kiri Lee raced into the woods on the right. Jett vaulted to the left and wrenched a massive stump from the ground. Johnny stepped into the middle of the clearing with Autumn behind him.

"We'll handle this, Autumn," said Johnny, whirling balls of flame in his palms.

"No, you don't," she said, whacking him affectionately on the shoulder. "Remember what Grimwarden taught us."

"I know," he grumbled. "Every part matters. I guess you'd better go, then."

Autumn drew her axe and, in a blink, stopped next to the tree, a little farther than she'd meant. At high speed, she backed up, raised her axe, and went full throttle for the creature's left foreleg. Her momentum added weight to the blow, and the axe bit into the creature's shin bone.

"FIRE, right at yu, Autumn!" yelled Jimmy. "Go fifty meters to yur right!"

Incensed, the beast growled, turned, and fired a burst of green flame at Autumn, but she was already fifty yards into the woods.

Perplexed, the creature swung its neck back toward its business at the tree. Jett was there. He swung the stump like a comically large baseball bat and hit the dragon so hard that it rolled away from the tree and lay stunned for a moment. But only a moment.

"Look out, Jett!" yelled Jimmy. "DIVE right!"

In the span of a breath, the creature curled into a ball, used its tail as a lever, and propelled itself toward Jett. He hadn't heard Jimmy's warning, and the creature slammed into Jett like a freight train. A huge briar bush broke his fall. He could feel the new wounds healing, but he knew they would not mend fast enough. Jett looked up as the beast uncoiled and sprang.

"Now!" said Tommy. "The fires in the tree are burning out. Go!"

Kiri Lee was already climbing the air. She sprang up unseen stairs and strode across the clearing into the tree. "Where are you?" she called.

"No, no! Stay you away!" came the shrill voice, still higher in the boughs.

"I'm a friend. I'm here to help you! Where are you?"

"Be I here!" it said.

Kiri Lee had little but the flickering fires below to give any light. Stare as she might, she could see no creature, no being up in that tree. *Wait!* There was an odd clump in the crook between the topmost branches. The shape was strange, but its surface looked virtually the same as the tree's bark.

"I still don't see you!" she said. The words were hardly out of her mouth when, *"Oomph!"* something heavy thudded into her shoulder.

"Drop me not!" the shrill voice warned. The thing was clinging to her for dear life.

Kiri Lee twisted her body to regain her balance and stop from sinking. She felt the sudden heat from a great burst of fire that flared beneath her. Whatever was on her shoulder felt it, too, and scrambled to climb, getting no farther than the top of her head. "Oh, stop squirming!" she exclaimed. "Or you might fall."

Kiri Lee stepped out and gained some altitude once more, moving quickly back toward Tommy's position.

"How walk you on air?" asked a voice in her ear.

"Long story," said Kiri Lee.

"Long stories, Migmar likes."

Ten descending strides later, Kiri Lee set her feet on the forest floor. "Down put me, please!" came the voice.

"Did you save it?" asked Tommy, but because he was aiming his bow, he did not look to see for himself.

Kiri Lee grabbed whatever it was at her shoulder and, with some effort, placed it on the ground. A burst of light from the fires at last showed her what it was.

A tsunami of flame crashed into the airborne dragon, engulfing it in hungry, flickering tongues of red and orange. Johnny's burst propelled the beast sideways against the trunk of a thick tree, and it slid to the ground. The forest floor and all the surrounding woods kindled immediately. The fire did not quench, but the creature was not defeated. Like something demonic, it rose, a monstrous dark shape wreathed in the inferno. Fierce yellow eyes glared out of the maelstrom and locked on Johnny.

"Come on!" Johnny baited it, making sure that it wouldn't turn its attention back to Jett. "C'monnn!" He flared the fire on his palms.

The creature roared and vomited a spurt of green flame. Johnny's orange fire met the beast's burst, and the two fires strove against each other between them. The bright flames tangled and writhed, but the orange flame was mightier.

Johnny took a huge breath, felt the tingling above his eyes, and pushed the heat to an entirely new realm. The orange flame went white and overwhelmed the green, sending a sharp blast into the dragon. This time, the fire bit into its scales and found flesh beneath. The beast rolled, flailing its neck and tail, trying to put itself out.

Still burning, the giant lizard came to its feet and looked to charge. But it fell limp as if something had pulled its plug. One of Tommy's arrows had put out one of the beast's glowing eyes and plunged deep into its skull. It did not get up again.

24

The Moonchildren

"WHAT IS it?" asked Tommy, staring at the thing Kiri Lee had rescued from the tree.

"I've never seen anything like it," said Kiri Lee.

"It looks like a person . . . made of tree roots," said Jimmy. "Look at it. It's got arms and legs."

At twenty-five inches from head to foot, the small being stood with its gnarly rootish hands pressed indignantly into its gnarly rootish sides. Green acorn-shaped eyes glared out from its gnarly rootish face. "Am not a person I," it said. "Am not an it, certainly either. Am Gnome! Am Migmar!"

"A Gnome?" Tommy repeated, his eyebrows raised.

By this point the other young lords had joined the circle surrounding the Gnome.

"One of the Seven Highborn races," said the Gnome. "Know you surely?"

"You mean like the little guys we use for lawn ornaments?" asked Johnny. "My uncle had a couple of them in his garden, but he never liked them. He'd have me take my slingshot and—"

"Probably best not to finish that thought," said Kat.

The Gnome's eyes narrowed, and one of his knobby hands reached into a knotholelike pocket. It pulled out something the Elves could not see and plopped it into a crevice of a mouth.

After chewing audibly for a few moments, the Gnome began to shake. Pearl white droplets bled out from all over its flesh. It began to trickle and pool, giving rise to still more trickles until it seemed the rootish texture of its flesh was melting away.

"What's happening?" cried Autumn. "You didn't hurt it, did you?"

"No," said Kiri Lee. But she began to back away. Gnome or not, the transformation happening before her was nothing short of alarming. Too much like a Wisp.

"Well, would ya look at that?" said Jett, wonder written in his eyes.

Where there had stood a diminutive figure made of root and bark just moments ago, now there stood . . . a diminutive figure with flesh, hair, and clothing. A proper Gnome. The eyes were still the same acorn-shaped green eyes. But everything else had changed. This little fellow, for fellow he seemed to be, had a hay-colored shock of hair and long sideburns that stopped just short of his shiny chin. Resting like clouds over his eyes were bushy brows that seemed to be made of just three or four single strands curling and curling and curling around each other. He had ruddy cheeks like a schoolboy just home from sledding and tiny lips that, at this moment, were pressed in a taut frown. With perfect balance he lifted up one of his stubby legs to look at his foot.

"Awww," said Autumn. "It got burned."

"Not it. Migmar! Come sooner, if you had," said the Gnome, "burn me not, that forest dragon."

"So that's what that was," said Jett. "Makes sense. That thing looked like it came right out of the ground."

"Yes, came from the ground, he did," said Migmar. "Nasty thieving things, they be."

"But I thought dragons have wings," said Johnny.

"Huh?" Migmar's eyebrows seemed to leap off his forehead. "Is fire boy not too smart? Be burrowers, dragons. Need wings not." Migmar stopped rubbing his singed foot. When he stood upon it again, a strange look came upon his face . . . a mixture of confusion, deep thought, and then . . . relief.

"Thanks be to you," said Migmar. "Owe you life. Come you to my village. Celebrate."

"Is your village far?" asked Tommy.

"No, not far," said Migmar. "Standing, you are, on Gnome special land."

"I don't know if we should," said Kat, but she didn't say aloud what she thought she'd heard in the little person's thoughts.

"Thank you, Migmar, for the invitation," Tommy said. "I think we'd all welcome a village right about now. But we're on an important mission north."

"Going where?" Migmar asked.

The Seven looked at each other nervously. "Honestly," explained Tommy, "we're looking for a, well, some sort of *object*. But . . . uh . . . it's kinda hard to explain, and . . . uh . . . we don't exactly know where it is."

"Interesting. Come then to Appleheart," said Migmar. "Experts in maps, Gnomes are. Wander far and wide. Help to you. A big help."

Tommy looked to his friends, received many nods, and said, "Okay, Migmar, lead the way."

The Gnome smiled broadly and raced into the woods. The Elves followed as quickly as they could.

"Do you smell something?" asked Johnny.

"Yeah," said Jimmy. "Horrible, really. Probably just the burned-up dragon."

"I don't think so." Johnny glanced at Migmar. Then he scrunched up his face and tried to hold his breath. And like that, the Seven followed the little Gnome into the woods.

Where the Seven had stood in the clearing just moments before was now filled with smoldering dragon remains. The violence over, birds settled in their roosts, cicadas started singing, and small animals darted along the forest floor. The full moon cast a pale light into the clearing, permitted by a clear evening sky full of stars. And passing over the grass came an immense black shadow, shaped like a massive bird, and on its back the silhouette of a lone figure with weapon drawn.

It was a longer tangent than Tommy expected. For two solid hours they marched, but Migmar certainly seemed to know the forest well. He led them across deep gullies where there at first seemed no crossing, through rock faces where at first there seemed to be no passage, and over a swift-moving stream where at first there seemed to be no ford. At last they came to a strange and beautiful glade. In this wide place only two kinds of plants grew: tall, graceful trees with smooth white bark and red leaves and waist-high, feather ferns with yellow flowers shaped like stars.

Migmar stood at the edge of this sea of ferns and said, "Wait you here. Be me back!"

Before any of the Elves could ask a question or say, "Hey, wait!" Migmar was gone into the ferns. Here and there, moving away from them, the Elves saw the ferns jostle or sway, but otherwise they saw no sign of Migmar's departure.

"Do yu think he ditched us?" asked Jimmy.

"I don't know," said Tommy. "He seemed a good little fellow. Kat, you had some concern about him. Did you pick up his thoughts?"

Kat nodded. "It's a little hard to explain," she said. "Gnome thoughts aren't like people thoughts—er . . . Elf thoughts, I mean. They think of a single topic, sometimes a single word. And all around this word, a hundred phrases and sentences whirl like moons around a planet. Emotions come rushing in around it all like an endless wave. It's confusing . . . and noisy."

"But you thought you heard something . . . something that bugged you?"

"Yeah," she said. "It was that central word . . . well, it kept coming up 'lawbreaker' or something like that. But the emotion was what worried me. It was fear."

"Come you forward!" came Migmar's high voice from up ahead. A patch of the ferns quivered ahead. "My village is this way. Come on."

Tommy looked at his friends and shrugged. They marched together, into the ferns, hearing the stems snap beneath their boots. An unseen bird cawed overhead. Choruses of crickets, tree frogs, and who knew what else serenaded them with *chirps, breek-breeks, woos,* and *zip-zeeps.*

About two-thirds of the way across the lake of ferns, the Seven saw Migmar pop-up from the foliage ahead. His back very straight, chest puffed up, and a very stern look upon his face, Migmar held up a hand.

"That's far enough, my friends," he said.

When the Seven, confused by the strange command, continued on a few paces, Migmar turned beet red. "I said STOP!" he yelled. "Stop you must now or face consequences!"

It might have been the comical, overly dramatic look of authority on Migmar's face or the fact that his best commanding voice sounded like someone who'd inhaled a helium balloon. But while the Seven did stop, they also burst into spontaneous laughter.

"Migmar, what are you talking about?" Tommy asked.

Migmar didn't answer at first, but from the ferns all around the Seven there came a strange sound, kind of like a collective gasp. Kat looked around the ferns. "We're not alone," she said. "Gnomes . . . lots of them."

"Um, it looks like they're goin' to attack us," said Jimmy.

"Autumn, get to safety," said Johnny.

"I don't know where safety is," she replied.

"Should I roast them?" Johnny whispered to Tommy.

"No," he replied, feeling pleased that they were looking to him for leadership. "No, not yet. I don't know how or why they mean to attack, but I still don't think they're a threat."

"Migmar," Tommy said. "What's this about? Why are your people surrounding us?"

Migmar's emerald eyes widened. "Regret you having to come in this fashion, I do," the little man replied. "Is the way of my people."

"But we mean you no harm," said Tommy.

"Should I roast them now?" whispered Johnny.

"No," Tommy muttered, holding out an arm to restrain Johnny.

"Is harm already," said Migmar gravely. "Traveled you on sacred Gnome land."

Tommy felt his temper slipping, not just because of the sudden, unexpected threat, but because his friends had trusted him, and he'd led them into a trap. "Look, Migmar," he said. Another gasp from the ferns. "If we did tread on your land, it was only to save your skin."

"Leave that, we must, to the court," Migmar replied.

"Court?" Tommy blurted out incredulously.

"Stand trial is the only way permitted by our laws."

"Trial? That's just crazy," said Tommy, his hand straying to the hilt of his sword. "You've seen us in action. I give the word, and Johnny will light up everything within fifty yards of us."

"Afraid, I was, it would come to this," Migmar said. He put one finger in the corner of his mouth and produced a strange, warbling whistle.

"Owww!" said Kat.

"Hey!" said Johnny.

Then Tommy felt it, too, a pinprick on his neck, followed by an unnerving, spreading cold. In seconds, he saw a field of stars and then a great blue wave.

Peculiar Justice

"WAKE YOU up!" came a high but terse voice.

Tommy felt the tip of something sharp prick the bottom of his feet. He awoke, seated in a little gray torch-lit room with a trio of armed Gnomes staring at him and brandishing some long, twin-sided axe-spear weapons. The forward Gnome poked Tommy again.

"Owww!" exclaimed Tommy. "Cut that out!" He tried to reach for his foot, but found his arms restrained at the shoulders and elbows.

"Tell us not what to do, trespasser," said the Gnome. He poked Tommy's foot again.

"That hurts!" said Tommy. He suddenly realized his boots were gone. "What . . . what have you done with my boots?"

"Trod upon sacred land, you did," said the Gnome. "Destroyed boots, we did."

"Look," said Tommy. "This is all a huge misunderstanding. We're on an important journey, but we diverted to save Migmar." The three Gnomes gasped at the mention of the name, but Tommy went on. "We had no intention of stepping on sacred land." Tommy used his legs to stand, pushing his back up against the wall behind him. As he rose, he found that his arm restraints were elastic . . . or at least they stretched somewhat.

"Escape not," said the Gnome with a laugh.

Tommy stretched forward and heard a chorus of groans from either side of him.

"AH! Stop!"

"Please!" said Kat. "You're breaking my arms!"

Tommy realized with a shock that his restraints were tied into a complex system of wheels, switches, and pulleys. If he pulled away from the wall, it tightened the restraints and bonds of the others who were also captive. Tommy quickly let himself slide back down against the wall.

"Wha-what's going on?" Jett asked, just waking on the other side of the square room. "Why am I . . . oh, those little boogers drugged me. I'm gonna—" He started to stand.

"Jett, WAIT!" Tommy yelled. "Don't pull away from the wall. We're all wired in. If you use your strength to get free, you'll kill us."

"Told you," said the Gnome.

Johnny had awakened shortly after Tommy and had seen about all he could stand. "I'll take care of this," he said, lifting his hands to loose a stream of flames. He stopped the process and stared. His hands were encased in grapefruit-sized orbs made of a smooth metallic blue material. *Like this is going to stop me?* he thought, resuming the process of bringing his fire. He was going to hit the Gnome soldiers with a few bursts at their feet, just to scare them, but when he released fire within the orbs, he screamed.

"Ahh!" Johnny banged the orbs on the floor. "Ah, take them off! It's squeezing, breaking my hands. Ahh, make it stop!"

"Make stop, you can only," said the Gnome, scratching at a reddish sideburn. "Constricts, sinter-stone does, when heated. Turn off, you must, your fire."

Johnny stopped the fire immediately. As the stone orbs cooled, they expanded back to their original size.

"Are you through?" asked the lead Gnome soldier. "Try to escape, you must not. Awaits your trial does."

Tommy's face reddened. "Yes, we're done," he said. "For now, guys, let's just do what they say."

The Gnomes went immediately to work in each corner of the room, detaching small t-shaped keys from their belts and pockets. Several clangs and clicks later, the entire shackle-pulley apparatus detached from the wall, yet still held tight to its prisoners. *Great,* Tommy thought. *It's portable.*

"Am Thorkber," said the lead Gnome. He nodded to the Gnomes at his side. "Is Gilbang," he said, motioning to the Gnome with bushy black eyebrows and a metal helmet that sat cockeyed on his head. "Is Sarabell," he said, pointing to the female Gnome with silver-blond hair in pigtails.

"Lingered, we have, too long," said Sarabell. "Waiting is the Barrister."

"Are correct, my wife," said Thorkber. He turned back to the Seven. "Try not anything on the way."

The Gnomes led the young lords up a narrow spiraling ramp with a low ceiling and out through an arched doorway. Silvery moonlight shone down upon a village bouncing with night activity. Gnomes ran hither and thither, some wearing purple ribbons around their waists chasing others wearing green. Others vaulted across the busy marketplace on flexible poles. And still others appeared to be swimming through the air.

"They climb the air like I do," said Kiri Lee, incredulous but smiling.

"Have hand chutes, do you?" asked Gilbang.

Kiri Lee looked closer at the seemingly flying Gnomes and saw that, indeed, they used devices to climb into the air. She watched a Gnome, already seven feet off the ground, toss a rumpled ball into the air with each hand. Each of these unraveled into a surprisingly large wind-catching chute. The Gnome was light enough to pull himself higher. Some climbed ten, fifteen, even twenty feet into the air.

Kiri Lee wished she could free herself from her bonds, but she had little hope. The network of cables around her wrists and ankles would tighten and potentially hurt her friends.

Kat found herself gasping at strings of multicolored lights strewn among the lower boughs of the massive trees that grew in the area. Colors sparkled in the eyes and on the faces of Gnomes too numerous to count.

The scene reminded Tommy of the boardwalk of Ocean City at night . . . only with little people. Gnomes sang and danced, ate and drank, bought and sold. The marketplace was abuzz with Gnomes haggling cheerfully over prices or trades.

"Oh!" said Autumn. "Look at that!"

The group stopped, even their Gnome captors. Autumn pointed high. One of the trees had been fitted with an ingenious metal collar around its trunk like a man might wear a belt. But this collar was rotating slowly up and down the trunk as if on grooves. Ornately crafted spokes protruded from all different sides of the collar. Suspended beneath each spoke were two or three swings. Gnome children swung freely, back and forth, 'round and 'round, and up and down as the collar spun, rose, and fell.

"Cool," said Jett, in spite of their situation.

"Do yu suppose they'll let us ride it?" asked Jimmy. But he stopped laughing and frowned in concentration. "No, no, no," he said, looking up at the kids on the high swings.

"Oh no!" exclaimed Kiri Lee. "Let me go, right now!"

While Thorkber and the other Gnomes showed no sign of loosening their bonds, they all looked up at the swing. There a Gnome child, a little girl with red pigtails, was losing her grip on the swing. She slid from her seat and held on to the outer chain with just one tiny hand.

"Let me go!" Kiri Lee yelled again. "I can save her!"

"Save her from what?" asked Sarabell.

Suddenly the little Gnome lost her grip completely and came free of the swing. She plummeted and hit the ground near the tree's roots with a horrible thud.

"No!" Kiri Lee fell to her knees and wept.

"Wait, Kiri Lee," said Jimmy. "She . . . she's all right."

They all looked on. The little Gnome redhead popped up from the grass near the tree's roots. She wobbled a bit, giggled, and bounced back toward the tree swing.

"How did she survive that fall?" asked Kiri Lee.

"What that?" asked Thorkber, grinning. "Made of tougher stuff than that, we Gnomes. Dive off a cliff, maybe would hurt. Done it, I have, and survived. Come, Sarabell, demonstrate."

Sarabell handed her restraint cords to Gilbang. She waddled over to the edge of the woods, found a suitable dead branch, and then returned. So thick was the branch it looked more like a small fallen tree. Jett was amazed the Gnome maiden could carry it with such ease.

She walked up and presented the branch to her husband. Thorkber looked at it approvingly.

"Whale away, my flower," Thorkber said.

Sarabell swept back the branch, swung it high in the air, and brought it crashing down on Thorkber's head. The branch cracked in half, but the only impact the blow had on Thorkber was to slide his helmet a little off-center.

"That would've knocked me out cold," said Johnny.

Tommy whistled.

"Struck me well, she did," said Thorkber.

"Never well enough," said Sarabell, affectionately picking twigs out of her husband's hair. "Won the Thrashing, last year, he did."

"Thrashing?" asked Tommy.

"Test of Gnome toughness and valor, it is," said Gilbang. "Beat Strubthak the Old, he did."

Thorkber laughed deeply, which sounded strange given his high Gnomish voice. "Talk of this no more," said Thorkber. He took back his restraint cords and motioned for all to follow.

The Gnome village was long and narrow, but with all the merry Gnomes running about and all the warm lights, it felt cheery rather than confined. Their dwelling places, shops, and taverns had all been carved into the massive flaring trunks of the living trees . . . without doing any noticeable harm to the trees themselves. Tommy noticed that the trees were all practically bursting with foliage and bloom.

"It's beautiful here," said Kat. Tommy nodded.

"Thorkber," said Kiri Lee. "Why are all the young Gnomes up so late at night?"

Sarabell giggled. Thorkber said, "Know you not the ways of Gnomes? Moonchildren, we are. Sleep, we do, by day."

"Oh, nocturnal," said Kiri Lee. "That explains a lot."

As they passed out of the village proper, the road narrowed more, and the trees even seemed to lean in. But still, Tommy thought it was more of a cozy feeling. Up ahead, the road appeared to end at an impossibly thick, barrel-shaped tree trunk.

"The Justice Tree," explained Thorkber. "Hope, I do, that things go well for you."

Tommy hoped so, too . . . though, honestly, he couldn't imagine that the Gnomes would do anything serious to him or the other Elves. *We're the Seven Elven Lords of Berinfell,* he thought. *If the Gnomes so much as delay our mission, it could make our two races enemies for a long time.*

Kat read his thoughts and projected back her own. *"They might not even know."*

Know what? he asked in reply. *That we're Elves? What else would we be?*

"I don't know, but our ears aren't right. Maybe they've seen humans."

But they've seen our powers, some of them, Tommy persisted. *They must know we're Elves.*

"Maybe . . . but that brings up a different possibility. What if Gnomes don't like Elves?"

You're not making me feel any better about this, thought Tommy. *Get out of my head.*

"Leave you, we must, in the hands of the Leaf Guard," said Thorkber as they came to the wide entrance at the base of the tree. Gnome soldiers stood on either side of the spade-shaped opening. More guards stood beside them, side-by-side, seemingly around the tree's perimeter. The Gnomes of the Leaf Guard were heavily armored with breastplates for chest protection and thick iron pauldrons to cover their shoulders. Each piece had been forged of some strange metal that was black here and blue there, gray in other places, and had been cunningly engraved to look like tree branches with wide leaves. The Leaf Guard obviously believed in being battle ready at all times—including weapons. Some held the long poleaxes like Thorkber's. Others had crossbows. Many had thwack hammers thicker than a man's arm.

Whoa, thought Tommy. *I'd hate to get smacked in the head with one of those.*

The Gnome soldiers bowed once and stomped one foot, apparently a more formal military greeting, and then received the restraint lines from Thorkber, Sarabell, and Gilbang. Then, waving to the Elves, Thorkber muttered, "Hope we see you again, I say." The three Gnomes strode away, giggling sinisterly.

"That's not funny," said Jett. "If we ever get out of this gadget, I'm gonna—"

He stopped in midsentence as Kat's unspoken but urgent plea entered his mind.

Four of the Leaf Guard escorted the Elves into the Justice Tree. Their path forked, curling around the wide section of the inner tree. The torches ended, and they plunged into darkness.

"What's going on?" asked Jimmy.

"Silence, trespassers!" came a peculiar voice from somewhere up ahead.

Without another word, they walked slowly for about thirty paces. Certainly, the Justice Tree seemed colossal from the outside, but Tommy wondered just how deep the tree could go inside. Up ahead there appeared a shimmering green glow as if a small pool of emerald green water was lit from within and shone upon a dark wall.

"A few more steps," came a gruff voice at their side, one of the guards. "Stop you here."

They obeyed the bodiless command, felt a slight tug on their restraints, and heard a series of clicks and snaps. Suddenly, in the middle of the green glow, there appeared a small dark figure. "Arise, Moonchildren!" cried the figure, raising his arms high.

There was a massive shuffling of feet. Lights, dozens of small lights, appeared on either side of the Elves. One after the other, blood-red candles were revealed. In their flickering light, Gnome faces materialized. Stern faces . . . even frightening, and so very many. Three, four rows deep . . . a small army of Gnomes.

The green light intensified at the feet of the Gnome up ahead. He stood on a raised platform and stared down at the Elves ominously. Like a Victorian Englishman, this Gnome wore a gray wig and a great-coat with a loose chain dangling from each of four pockets. The sum of his appearance reminded Tommy of Marley's ghost from Dickens's *A Christmas Carol.* Not a very comforting image.

The Gnome lowered his hands and pointed at the Elves. "Come, you have, to the Justice Tree!" he said. "Stand accused, you do, of a most heinous deed: trespassing upon sacred Gnome land."

A wave of hissing crashed down on them from the Gnomes all around them. Each of the young lords jumped. Startling and disconcerting, the hissing went on until the leader motioned with his hands. "Lord Barrister Gnome am I," proclaimed the Gnome. "Hear, I will, your testimony and defense. Decide, we will, your judgment, your fate."

"Fate?" Johnny echoed. "Hold on a minute here." He struggled against his restraints, even kindling flame within the orbs. But stopped as the orbs constricted.

"Barrister," muttered Jimmy. "So this wee fellow is a barrister, then?"

"What's that?" asked Autumn.

"In the UK," Jimmy explained, "a barrister's like what yu'd call a lawyer."

"Seems more like a judge to me," said Autumn.

"Judge he is," said one of the Gnome soldiers who overheard. "The highest judge in our land, but more as well. Chief Accuser, he is also, and . . . should your testimony merit it . . . Chief Protector."

"Do you smell something?" asked Kat. "Jett, did you—?"

"Not me," said Jett. "Why are you askin' me anyway?"

"Answer, you must, the charges!" declared the Barrister.

"Not guilty!" Tommy blurted out. "At least not on purpose. We had no idea the land was sacred to the Gnomes." More hisses cascaded down from the spectators.

"Suffer not, we Gnomes, trespassing on our land. Is ignorance your only excuse?"

"Be careful, Tommy," Jett urged. "He's trying to catch you in something."

"Tommy!" Kat's thoughts entered his mind. *"Does the Barrister seem familiar to you?"*

Not now, Kat, Tommy fired his thought back. *I'm kind of on the spot here.*

"Lord Barrister," Tommy addressed the Gnome. "We wouldn't

have come onto your land at all, but we heard Migmar screaming for help. I mean, he was screaming his head off. What were we supposed to do?"

More hisses—louder and mixed with angry muttering.

"Silence!" cried the Barrister. He lowered his brow and glared at Tommy. "Behold! Am Migmar, Lord Barrister Migmar!"

"I knew it," said Kat.

"Screaming," Migmar went on, "not hardly."

"Awww, come on, man," Jett interrupted. "You were screaming bloody murder. Hadn't been for us, you'd a' been a midnight snack for that forest dragon."

"Jett!" Tommy muttered over the new chorus of hissing. "That kind of talk is not helping."

"What is that smell?" demanded Autumn. "Johnny?"

"Wasn't me!"

"Dare you insult the Ruler of all Gnomedom?" asked Barrister Migmar.

Oh, great, thought Tommy. *He's a king, too.*

"Well?"

The hissing intensified. Tommy sensed movement on either side. The Gnomes were descending from their seats, coming down onto the floor . . . coming closer.

"We were on an important mission," Tommy said at last, "near this area of the Thousand-League Forest."

"Mission?" asked Barrister Migmar. Then he paused, and an odd look came over his face. There was a sound like a sudden, quick buzz. "Speak you more of this mission."

"In truth? We are trying to find a Keystone."

The flowing, angry hiss turned to a gasp.

"Said you nothing before of this Keystone," said Migmar. "Only the Elves—"

"We are Elves!" said Tommy.

"Take us for fools?" asked Migmar. "Dressed you are as Elves, but have you left your ears at home?" Harsh laughs fell like poison rain from the surrounding Gnomes.

"And not just Elves," said Tommy, undeterred. "But the Seven Elven Lords of Berinfell."

"Ridiculous!" said Migmar, and the hisses rose again. "Know, we all do, that the Spider King murdered the Lords of Berinfell."

"Our parents," said Tommy, wincing at the unpleasant odor now seemingly all around him. "The Spider King killed our parents. We were taken by the Drefids as babies."

"Kill, the Drefids do, everything they touch."

"No," said Tommy. "Even the Spider King was afraid of the curse. . . . The Berinfell Prophecies tell of three generations of horror for anyone who kills a pureblood in the line of lords before he or she reaches the Age of Reckoning. The Drefids knew the curse and took us into another world."

"Another world?" Migmar crossed his arms. "Heard, we have, enough. No Elves are you."

"I am Felheart Silvertree!" yelled Tommy. "Son of Velaril and Tarin Silvertree."

The name Silvertree gave Barrister Migmar pause, and barely a hiss came from the still-closing crowd.

"Know, we do, Silvertree," he said slowly. "Speaks, history does, of that name often. Know not what you are, but unconvinced that you be Elves."

"But I'm blue!" Kat blurted out. "You've seen our powers. What else can we do to prove it to you?"

Barrister Migmar motioned with his left hand as if he was drawing a capital *Y* in the air. From the darkness, drums began to pound—*boom, boom, boom.* Drums so low and deep that the young lords felt the vibrations in their armor, their bones, and especially through their bare feet on the smooth wood floor.

For a moment it seemed that a living, walking red flame had appeared, approaching the Seven from the far left of the Barrister's platform. Another approached from the far right. Kiri Lee spun around and beheld a third approaching from behind.

The drums continued their slow, sonorous heartbeat. As the walking flames grew close, it became clear by their stature that they were

Gnomes . . . Gnomes wearing red robes and hoods so that no one could see their faces. And each one held a white candle in one palm and a long, silvery tube clasped reverently in the other.

Migmar held up his hands. The drums stopped. The figures in red halted and turned to the Elves. Kat tried to read their minds, but her own fears created such an agitated jumble of thoughts that she could not focus. She could not, for long, endure the eyeless stare of the hooded Gnomes. She turned away and closed her eyes, sending a thought to Tommy, *"Is this really happening?"*

"Come forth, the Breath Thieves have. Bear, they do, darts filled with a poison so potent fell a Gwar champion, it would, in three heartbeats. Sentenced, you are, to die . . . the fair and just penalty for trespassing in our most hallowed grounds."

"Fair?" exclaimed Tommy, yanking at his restraints. "This is insane! You can't just kill us because we walked in your backyard! We were saving YOUR life!"

"Preach it, Tommy!" said Jett. "We are the Seven Elven Lords of Berinfell! You kill us, the Spider King wins. And even if he doesn't, you'll have war with the Elves forever."

"Threatening us, you are?" asked Migmar. "Fear, we do not, the Spider King or the Elves. Commands, our law, that you must die. Accept, we must, the consequences for our actions."

Another Gnome appeared on the platform next to Migmar. He bowed, stomped his foot, and removed a rolled parchment from a fold in his robe. He gave it to Migmar and whispered to the Barrister as he read.

The Gnome leader fell quiet for a moment and then said, "Have a provision, we do, in our law: one life for one life. Saved, you did, my life. Owe, we do, one life of yours. Choose, you may, one of your number to live and go free. A moment I give you to confer."

As best they could given the restraints, the Seven huddled together. "This . . . this is madness," said Tommy.

"We've got to do something," said Johnny.

"Fight," said Jimmy. "That's what we've got to do. Break those things on yur hands, and fry those psychotic midgets."

"I should have fried them before," Johnny muttered.

"No, I don't think so," said Tommy. "I mean, now, it seems like that would have been the smart thing to do, but I just felt like it was wrong . . . horribly wrong. I still feel that way."

"Too late now," said Johnny. "I can't break 'em. I've tried."

Kiri Lee pulled a foot of slack from her restraints and stepped forward. "What if . . . what if Jett used his strength to bang Johnny's hands together? Do you think those stone balls would shatter?"

"What if my hands shatter?" asked Johnny, but he wasn't laughing.

"I'm game," said Jett. "Let me try. Crowd in as close as you can."

Their huddle shrank until their faces nearly touched. Johnny held his orb-encased fists as far out as he could. "I'm ready, I think."

Jett grasped the two orbs, looked Johnny in the eye, and then slammed them together. Not only did the orbs not shatter, but there was no discernible mark on either one. But Johnny fell to one knee and nearly passed out from the intense pain. Jett wrung his hands, trying to ease the throbbing. "Okay, bad idea."

"Decide, you must," said Migmar. The undercurrent of hissing continued. The red-robed Breath Thieves stood just yards away. "A life for a life."

"Say what you want about these Gnomes," said Jett, "but they've got an answer for every one of our gifts. How are we supposed to fight the Spider King? We can't even beat a bunch of little—"

"Maybe we're not supposed to beat them," said Tommy.

"They're going to kill us," said Jett.

"Not all of us," said Johnny. "He said one of us can go free. I think it should be Autumn."

"Me?" Autumn's face seemed to knot up. "No way. All I can do is run. It should be you, Johnny. You can do the most against the Spider King."

"Hold up," said Jett. "Yeah, he's got fire, but I can hardly be killed."

"Tommy's our leader," said Kat. "It should be him."

"I think Tommy, too," said Jimmy, and then he muttered, "Certainly shouldn't be me."

"Delay, you must, no longer!" Migmar commanded.

Tommy shook his head. He remembered Grimwarden's many lessons. The Guardmaster himself had chosen Tommy as the leader of their young group. It was in his blood, Grimwarden had said. *Why don't I feel like a leader?* Tommy wondered. *Everything's coming apart, and I haven't any idea what to do.*

"*Do not be afraid,*" a voice spoke in Tommy's mind. "*I am with you.*"

Tommy smiled and thought, *Thank you, Kat. I needed that.* He looked up at his blue-skinned friend. She did not return his gaze. Then he turned to his friends once more. "Listen to us!" he said above the others. "Just a few months ago our biggest fear was having to read a part in a play to the whole class, or maybe that a pimple might show up in the middle of our forehead. Now, Barrister Migmar is telling us we need to decide which one of us lives or dies?"

Kat giggled nervously at the irony.

"We're scared," Tommy went on, fixing his eyes on Jett for a moment. "ALL of us. I'm terrified. But we can't forget what Grimwarden and Goldarrow taught us. We're all part of one body, none of us better than the other."

"It should not be any one of us," Kiri Lee whispered.

Jett's jaw moved and his nostrils flared. He nodded.

Autumn and Johnny stared at each other. She held out her hand. Johnny took it.

Jimmy couldn't help it. Pride swelled within him like Craignish Loch after a flooding rain and a high tide. All his life, all he'd ever wanted was a family. A safe place where everyone else thought well of you and looked after you. And now, maybe a million miles away, in a world he'd never thought existed, here he was with a jock, a beauty queen, a bully, a know-it-all, a goth, and a dweeb . . . and they, they were his family. No, Jimmy couldn't help it. Tears rolling down his face, he smiled and practically burst out, "Live together?"

"Die together," said Tommy.

"Die together," Jett repeated.

"Die together," said Kat. And so each one replied.

Clasping hands as best they could in their manacle-restraints, they turned and faced Barrister Migmar.

"Lord Barrister," said Tommy. "We don't agree with your law or the penalty for breaking it." Hisses erupted. "But . . . BUT this is your land and your court. We are in no position to change your laws or customs. But likewise, we are in no position to decide who lives and dies. Only Ellos, our mighty God, has a right to decide our fate. We will not choose."

"Decided, you are, that all should die?" asked Migmar.

Tommy felt a squeeze from Kat's hand on his left and Jimmy's hand on his right. "Yes," said Tommy. "We are decided."

Migmar raised a bushy eyebrow and did not at first respond. Thoughts creased his forehead, and he worked the muscles in his jaw. The three red-robed executioners inclined their hooded heads toward their leader, waiting, it seemed, for instructions. The hissing vanished, replaced by hushed but urgent conversation.

"Very well," said the Barrister. "Made, you have, your choice. Believe, I do, that the decision was nobly made, much in keeping with Elvenkind. Know you, however, that Ellos grants the power of life or death to rulers and authorities . . . such am I." He paused long enough to look at each of the young lords in turn. "Give you, I will, one final question . . . one final chance. Answer well, you must."

"If we do?" asked Tommy.

"Live, you will, and be free," said Migmar. "Satisfied, we will be, that you are the Seven Lords of Berinfell."

"And if we get the answer wrong?"

"Know, you do, already your fate," replied the Gnome. "Decide, you must, who will answer."

"Tommy!" came six Elven voices.

Tommy turned around and laughed. "Thanks a lot!"

"You studied more than any of us," said Jimmy.

Tommy shook his head. He had studied more than the others. But he still hadn't studied enough. "I'll answer the question," he said. "I'll try."

The other lords stood beside their leader, a close family of Elves.

Tommy became aware of the other Gnomes closing in around them, with their candles, like a slow-moving whirlpool of stars. The red-robed executioners raised their silver tubes, fixing their aim.

"Tommy, if you need help"—Kat's thoughts tiptoed into Tommy's mind—*"not that I know half the lore you do."*

No, Kat, he thought back to her. *No, I've got to do this right.*

"Know, you must, this answer," declared Barrister Migmar, "if you be lord-born. Come, it does, from Elven antiquity. A worthy question for such an occasion as this." He paused once more and then delivered the question. "When was the Dread War of 6016?"

Tommy felt like he'd been kicked in the stomach with a steel-toed boot. He'd studied a lot of the battles, especially wars in which Grimwarden had served. He had learned tons about war tactics, flanking, feints, and such. But he hadn't spent a lot of time memorizing dates. He could feel the weight of hundreds of eyes pressing down on him, but none weightier than those of his friends. Once again, he'd let them down.

Even in social studies back on Earth, he'd had trouble mem—*Wait a minute!*

Could it . . . could it? No way. But what choice do I have? Tommy looked up at the Barrister and said, "The answer is . . . 6016."

Such a roar whooshed up all around Tommy that at first he thought the red-robed Breath Thieves had hit him with a poison dart, that he was hearing his heart exploding, blood pressure thrashing in his ears. Bright light nearly blinded him, and he raised his arms to shield his eyes. He'd always heard that people see a bright light when they die. *My hands are free! The shackles and cords are gone.*

26

The Verdict

WHEN TOMMY realized he was, in fact, still very much alive, he looked around. He was still inside the Justice Tree, only now huge braziers burned with bright-white fire. Torches and hearty fireplaces were kindled all around the room. Gnomes were bouncing here, there, and everywhere, singing, shouting, couples dancing . . . celebrating. All the Gnomes who had held the red candles were now using those candles to light the fuse on strange fireworks that launched right out of their palms, flew high toward the roof of the chamber, and then exploded in dozens of curlicue streamers. Tommy nearly had a heart attack when he saw that the red-robed executioners were still aiming their silver tubes. "NO!" Tommy yelled as they fired. But rather than being poisoned, Tommy found himself surrounded by a whirling, snap-crackling cloud of glittery confetti.

Migmar leaped from his platform right at Tommy's face. Tommy caught him with ease, but the Gnome suddenly kissed him on both cheeks. "Congratulations, honorary Moonchild!" Migmar cried. "You and your friends did it!" The Gnome leaped down and danced a peculiar hopping, skipping, spinning dance at Tommy's feet.

Suddenly Tommy felt himself being lifted up in the air and spun around. "YEAH, boyee!" Jett yelled as his bonds were loosed. "We're in, baby! You were SO right!"

"Bring in the FOOD!" yelled Migmar. "Forget NOT the dragon-root!"

Arms wrapped around Tommy from behind. "Oh, Tommy, isn't it wonderful?"

It was Kat . . . hugging him. "Um . . . I . . . uh . . . yes, yes, it is wonderful." He hated to unhook from her hug, but he couldn't take it anymore. "Kat, what in the world is going on? I thought we were all just about to be killed!"

"It was a test, Tommy!" Kat said, her eyes bright and glistening, warm purple appearing on her cheeks. "The whole thing."

"A test?" Part of what Kat said, part of the circus going on around him—just a part began to sink in. Just not enough to totally let down his guard. "A test of what?"

"Of us," she replied. "Oh, Migmar, you tell him."

"Tell him, I will," the Gnome replied. "Sit him down, we shall, at my table. Explain all, I will."

"Eat, drink!" said Migmar, stuffing his face with some kind of puffy purple fruit.

"But what about—?"

"Food first," said Migmar. "Always food first."

Hesitantly, Tommy picked up a triangular, bread-looking thing. It was heavy, like a pastry filled with cream cheese. Tommy took a nibble. The flavors hit his tongue like a marching band. It was not salty, not sweet, not tangy, sour, or spicy. It was something brand new, a taste like cold air spraying in all directions in his mouth.

"OH MY . . . AWWW, MANNN, OH, THIS IS GOOD!" Tommy turned and saw Jett, both hands full of exotic chips of all different shades of red. He seemed enraptured, closing his eyes and swaying his head to music no one else could hear.

"How odd that he should take such a liking to gickers?" asked Migmar. "And without rosco sauce, too."

"Gickers?" Tommy echoed. Certainly, Jett seemed to be enjoying them.

"Harvest, we do, from gorc trees," Migmar explained. "It's a fungus that grows where glomper frogs have been nesting."

"Oh," said Tommy. "That . . . um . . . doesn't sound very good."

"Not without rosco sauce," Migmar replied.

Tommy was about to ask about the sauce but then thought better of it. After twenty minutes of relentless eating, Migmar leaned back in his chair. He munched on a twisted orange dragonroot and said, "Gather your Elvenkin."

Tommy called them over.

"Tell you, now, I will of why we put you through such an ordeal," said Migmar. "Trespass, you had. Trod, you had, upon sacred land. But you saved my life. Owed a debt to you, I did." He looked up suddenly. "Ah, Thorkber, Sarabell, Gilbang, come sit down and join us."

"How much dragonroot have you had?" asked Thorkber warily.

"Not much," said Migmar. "Just one sprig."

"Uh-huh," Thorkber said as he sat down next to Johnny and Autumn.

"Explaining 'The Moonbeam', I was, to the Elves," said Migmar. "The powers of highborn Elves, you seemed to have. Firehand, air walking, strength of giants, and more. But still, sworn by your ancestors, the original Elves of Berinfell, we are, to test any who come searching for the Keystone."

"You know about the Keystone?" asked Autumn.

"Yes," said Migmar. "It is well known to us. Helped design and build the Terradym Fortress, our ancestors did, where the Keystone now lies."

"You know where the fortress is?" asked Tommy, nearly shooting out of his seat.

"Of course," said Migmar. "In the region of Needlemire, north and west of here. But simply tell you where it is, we could not. Needed to be sure, we did, that you are lordly Elves, not treasure hunters. 'The Moonbeam' is our test, the ceremony of life and death. By refusing to select one above the other and by appealing to Ellos the Maker as sole giver and taker of life, passed the test, you did." Migmar nibbled another inch from the orange dragonroot and leaned back even farther in his chair.

The Seven pondered this new revelation. The Berinfell Prophecies were all true. They had to be. And the creepy, weird thing about it was that their Elven ancestors, thousands of years earlier, had known so much, long before it happened.

"What was that?" Kiri Lee whispered. She'd heard a peculiar sound. They'd all heard it.

"Oh no!" said Thorkber. "I'm leaving."

"What?" asked Migmar.

"You know what." Holding his nose and muttering indignantly, Thorkber hurried away from Migmar's table.

Sarabell leaned over and whispered to Autumn, "Dragonroot is too spicy for Migmar. It makes him poof."

"Poof?" Autumn had barely uttered the word when she took a whiff of air and realized all too clearly what Sarabell was talking about. She spun around in her chair and glared at Migmar.

"Sorry," he muttered, turning red from ear to ear. He was grateful when Jett broke the silence.

"You called us honorary Moonchildren," Jett said. "What's that mean?"

"With that title," said Migmar, "Gnomes the world over will call you friend and give you leave to travel freely in their territory."

"How will they know we're honorary Moonchildren?" asked Kat. "Do we get a necklace or something?"

"No," said Migmar. "Gnomes care little for jewelry. You will have a tattoo."

"Uh-uh," said Jett. "Not me. I hate needles."

"Needles?" Migmar echoed. "Oh, like the Gwar who cut their designs into their flesh, you must mean. Oh no. We are not that way. Ink, our tattoos are . . . ink of a kind that does not come off, not unless we want it to, that is. But more, there is. As a friend of Gnomes, your friends are our friends, your enemies are our enemies. In plenty and in want, your kindred, we Gnome will be. Children of the Sun and Children of the Moon, together, as Ellos the Maker would have it. Ah! And speaking of plenty, arrived have the desserts!"

"Desserts?" said Johnny. "I'm totally full."

"Not me," said Migmar. He stood and patted his stomach. Then he frowned. "Oh, dear. Upset, my stomach is."

"Uh-oh," whispered Jimmy to the others, seeing what the immediate future held. "I think we might want to move to another table."

27

Death in the Abyss

"TAKE YOU, Migmar can, no farther," Migmar said, folding his hands nervously. The Seven shared a few glances, uneasy with the sudden news given the sun's swift descent toward the eastern horizon. That and this part of the forest seemed particularly unwelcoming.

"You mean as far as you *wish* to take us," corrected Kat.

The Gnome stared at her wide-eyed. "Wish to, yes. That's it." The Gnome pointed. "Beyond that thicket, cave there is; only entrance to forgotten fortress, hidden Elven stronghold. Burcherond, called by us."

"Burcherond?" echoed Kiri Lee. "It almost sounds French. What's it mean?"

Migmar hesitated, glancing left to the path they had trod. "Means painful building."

"Just where I wanted to go," muttered Johnny.

"Nah, man, don't think that way," said Jett.

"Thank you, Migmar," said Tommy as he placed his hand on the kind soul's shoulder. "You've already helped us so much." Truth be told, the little Gnome had done far more than Tommy ever could have hoped. Had it not been for him and his community, the Seven might still be wandering in the Thousand-League Forest alone. And what's more, nowhere close to finding the Keystone. "We are grateful for all you have done, and will remember you fondly when the thrones of Berinfell are restored."

"Oh, a grand day indeed," he grinned. "And fine party, I presume."

"The finest," said Kat, leaning down and giving him a kiss on the cheek, to which the Barrister Gnome blushed and stepped backward. The strange odor they had grown accustomed to filled the air . . . apparently a nervous tick, as well.

"Going, am I," he bowed. "Come you back anytime."

"And have a safe journey," said Tommy.

But as the Gnome was about to vanish into the wood, Kat felt a strange pit form in the bottom of her stomach. She glanced at Tommy. "Did he say *why* he wasn't going to take us into the fortress?"

"No. Maybe he's afraid of the dark."

Kat thought for a moment. "Afraid of something," she repeated. "Migmar! Wait!" Kat took off running after the little man.

Tommy nodded to Autumn, who was off in a flash. Suddenly Migmar reappeared on the path, pushed behind from Autumn. Kat returned and drew close to the Gnome. "What are you so afraid of?"

Migmar shook his head.

"What's he thinking?" asked Tommy.

"Migmar, tell us," asked Kat again. But the little Gnome only shut his eyes, twisting his head back and forth.

"Kat?" asked Tommy once more.

"I can't tell," she replied over her shoulder. "Something about a *keeper*."

Migmar burst out then. "The Keeper of the Cistern!"

"Keeper of the what?" asked Tommy.

"No! Don't make Migmar go!" Migmar turned on Autumn and forced his way past her. "Let me go home! Just let Migmar go back home!" And with that he disappeared into the tall trees, his whimpering swallowed whole by the thickness of the forest.

"Well, now I'm freaked out just a little," said Kiri Lee, turning to look at the cave entrance.

"Don't be silly," said Jimmy. "Our people have been living underground for the past eight hundred years." He pushed up his sleeves and withdrew a torch from Jett's backpack. "What's a cave to us? I'll go first."

"You really should know—"

"What I'm doin', Tommy? What's t'know?" He winked at Kiri Lee, then looked ahead to the cave entrance, gaping wide like the black mouth of a starving beast. "Care to do the honors, Johnny?"

Johnny looked to Tommy and then back to Jimmy. A quick wave of his hand and Jimmy's torch sprang to life.

As Jimmy walked into the entrance of the cave, Kat leaned over to Tommy and whispered, "One day that kind of attitude might get us in trouble."

"Yeah." Tommy ran a hand through his hair. "Like tonight."

"See anything?" Johnny ased, holding a flickering flame in each palm. He remained in the back to illuminate their path while Jimmy strode in the front of the line carrying a torch. The tunnel did not deviate from its straight and flat course, interrupted only occasionally by a pile of rocks long-since relieved of their status in the arched ceiling. The smell of mildew and animal musk filled their nostrils, making it obvious that it was traveled far more often by roaming beasts than Elfkind.

"This place," said Kat, "I don't know how to explain it, but it feels . . ."

"Creepy?" said Johnny. "Way creepier than the tunnels at Whitehall."

"That's because we always knew Grimwarden would come rescue us," said Autumn. She didn't need to point out that there would be no such salvation in this place.

"Uh-huh," said Johnny, a slight flicker washing across the walls as his hands trembled. "Do you think this place is . . . haunted?"

"Don't be silly, Johnny," said Autumn. "There is no such thing as—"

"I dunno." Jimmy turned around. "An ancient Elven fortress seems like a good place fer ghosts to me."

"And what about the cistern keeper?" asked Jett. "The way Migmar talked about that, seemed like he'd seen a ghost once or twice before."

"All of you, stop it," Tommy said a little louder than he meant to, his voice echoing down the corridor. Something fluttered deep in the distance.

"What was that?" Kiri Lee jumped.

"Probably just a bat," Jimmy said.

Tommy looked around. "Seriously now. Everyone take a deep breath. We are here to retrieve the Keystone. Our kind friend Migmar is clearly spooked by old legends, and we all know ghosts aren't real."

"But spirits are," said Johnny.

"Johnny! Please!" Tommy was exasperated.

Autumn gave Johnny the stink look.

"Well, they are!" he mouthed to her.

Tommy allowed everyone to settle down for a moment. "Let's just stay quiet and keep moving. Come on."

After nearly twenty minutes of walking underground, the tunnel ceiling disappeared and before them lay a vast expanse of black. Subtle footfalls echoed into near oblivion as the sound traveled out and away, returning seconds later, amplified as it expanded higher into the space before them. The small firelight that had guided them this far was now useless.

"Johnny?" asked Tommy.

"No problem." Johnny shot one hand skyward, and a short stream of fire leaped into the air, arched, and started a slow, floating descent. A thousand small creatures darted away from the light. The Seven marveled at the sight. Across a vast, bottomless abyss, spanned only by a narrow wooden bridge, sat an immense stone fortress, carved out of the very subterranean rock around them. Blackened windows, voids in the gray stone, stared out coldly to the Seven. Tier upon tier of rampart sat atop the next, layers of crenellations ending one embattlement and beginning another. The stronghold sprawled outward and upward until it became one with the solid, uncut rock of the cavern.

"Burcherond, I take it," Kiri Lee piped up. "And the Keystone is in there?"

"Only one way to find out," Jimmy answered, now making for the bridge.

Tommy reached out and grabbed Jimmy by the arm. "Wait."

Jimmy looked back.

"Seriously, mannn," said Jett. "That thing wasn't built yesterday."

"Don't yu worry now, Jett," Jimmy answered. "If there's one thing I know after livin' in a land of castles, it's stone."

Tommy shook his head. "Jimmy, just hold up a minute."

Jimmy didn't reply. He just glared back at Tommy. Tommy couldn't tell if Jimmy's eyes just looked cold from the fading light, or because of something else.

"We need another blast," Jett looked to Johnny.

"Now that we know the layout," Johnny looked around, "I'll put one there," he popped off a larger burst, "and there," and another, both slamming into their ceiling-bound targets with a flash of light and heat. Ample light came down from the steady glow of flames dancing upon red-hot stalactites.

Jimmy strode forward and placed his foot onto the bridge. Bits of rock rained into the endless dark below. He took another step and proceeded far out onto the middle. "Well? What are yu waiting for?"

"You think it's safe for us?" Kiri Lee asked Tommy.

"I'm not sure," he replied, eyeing Jimmy. "Let me go next." Tommy trod out onto the bridge and looked down at the stone. *Are those cracks?* In the weak light, he couldn't tell. He did his best to keep his fear of heights at bay, looking at the rails of the bridge but not into the crevasse below.

Jimmy was nearly to the other side when Tommy motioned back to Kat. "Seems safe!" he called.

"I don't know," she said. "Every step you guys take, dust and stuff falls from the bottom of the bridge."

Kiri Lee sidled in front of her. "Then I'll go."

"Hey—I"

But Kiri Lee was already out and walking, doing her best not to aggravate the ornery stone underfoot. *But it wouldn't matter to you if it broke, Miss I-Can-Walk-On-Air, would it?* Kat puffed out her cheeks and went next.

"I'll follow you guys," Autumn said to Jett and Johnny.

But Jett would have none of it. "Ladies first," he said, bowing with his arm extended.

"Real suave," Johnny jested.

As Jimmy set foot on the far side's landing, he turned around to watch the progress of the others. It was in that brief moment that a shudder rippled through the bridge, a grinding stone-against-stone sound.

"What was that?" Kat yelped.

"The bridge!" Jimmy cried out.

"No one move," said Tommy. "Hold absolutely still."

The momentary pause silenced the bridge. But only for a moment. Stone moved again. Everyone on the bridge felt it.

Jett leaned over the rail and looked down. In that very second a hunk of gray stone released from the bottom of the bridge. Jett watched it fall until it was swallowed up by the deep hole, and then he listened. And listened. He never heard the stone hit bottom.

Johnny felt another shiver beneath his feet. "Guys?" And that's when everyone heard Jimmy yell, *"RUN!"*

The collapse begun, the bridge began to disintegrate right out from underneath them, one stone at a time.

"Run! Run! Run!" Jimmy echoed.

The girls screamed as they strode forward, legs pumping, arms flailing. Kiri Lee took to the air to give the others room—and she was too scared to bind her fate to a bridge that she trusted not nearly as much as open air, even air over an abyss. The bridge bucked, loosing itself of stone like an avalanche. Foundations cracked underfoot, shards of stone shooting out in all directions.

The lords tried desperately to keep their feet underneath them, managing by some miracle to keep from falling off. But even so, would there be any bridge connected to the far side in the next few breaths?

Tommy leaped the final three steps, colliding with Jimmy and knocking him over. Kat was a second behind, and Kiri Lee touched down after her. The four turned around to see Autumn, Johnny, and Jett leaping over gaps that appeared in front of them.

"Come on!" they yelled. "Run!"

Autumn kicked it into high gear, pulling Johnny, who pulled Jett. Autumn fell down the slope of the bridge, and Johnny tumbled after, screaming for Jett. Their hands had separated, and Jett had fallen to a knee behind them.

"No!" Jimmy cried out.

What was left of the bridge beneath Jett gave way, and he fell.

"NO!" Tommy yelled.

"Gotcha!" Kiri Lee cried out, and then she groaned, jarred by Jett's momentum. She stood on an invisible island of air and had both hands wrapped around Jett's wrist. "You are heavy," she said, grinning.

"It's all muscle, baby," he said back.

But Kiri Lee didn't laugh. "We're sinking!"

"C'mon, Kiri Lee, climb!" yelled Tommy.

"I know!" Kiri Lee shouted, now pulling up on Jett and back-pedaling, churning her legs in reverse as if on some aerobic bicycle. "Hold on!"

"I am!"

Kiri Lee worked her legs as hard as she could, ascending ever so slowly and watching the last chunks of the bridge fall away below them. The five other teens watched in stunned amazement as Kiri Lee defied gravity not only herself, but hauling Jett with her, both of them hanging over a bottomless pit.

"Hey!" Jett called, working his legs. "I feel something . . . under my feet! Feels like wet sand . . . like I can almost climb it!"

"Kiri Lee's gift," Tommy muttered. "It's maturing." Tommy snapped from his thoughts. "Give him more of your power, Kiri Lee!"

"I'm trying," she cried back. "But I'm not sure how!"

Tommy spun on his heels. "Autumn, zip around here, find a rope, a branch—"

"Where?"

"I don't know, just look!"

Autumn flashed away, grabbing Jimmy's torch right out of his hand. Tommy and the others urged Kiri Lee and Jett on.

For a moment they were climbing, still about twelve feet from the landing, but getting closer. "Come on!" the lords yelled.

But Jett's pedaling with his feet put an awful strain on Kiri Lee. "Ah! You're slipping!" she cried. "Stop moving your legs!"

"But I almost had it," Jett yelled. "I think if I keep trying—"

"If you keep trying, I'll drop you," she said. "The sweat . . . your arm is slipping through my hands."

The moment Jett stopped struggling, the pair began to sink more rapidly. "Ah! This isn't good!" yelled Jett.

Autumn suddenly appeared. "I can't find anything!" And then she saw Kiri Lee straining to hold Jett, but the two of them falling in slow motion. "Oh no!"

"Tommy, hold me arm!" yelled Jimmy. He stepped to the edge of the crevasse and held out his arm for Tommy. Tommy did just that, and using his weight as a counterbalance, he let Jimmy lean out.

"Uhnnn!" Jimmy grunted. "Ah, they're just too far . . . out 'a me reach!"

"There's gotta be something around here!" Johnny growled, the flames flaring in his hands. In his rush to find some object or piece of debris to help his friends reach out to Kiri Lee, Johnny caught the toe of his boot on a jag of rock and tripped. He fell hard, but there was a sudden burst of light, and Johnny never hit the ground.

Flames bursting from his palms kept the young lord seven inches from the floor. Johnny surprised himself by bringing forth more fire, using the powerful streams to push himself to his feet.

"No!" Kiri Lee shrieked. "I—I can't!"

Johnny turned and took in a nightmarish scene. Tommy and Jimmy were still trying to stretch out, but even with Kat helping anchor them it was no use. Kiri Lee looked exhausted, desperate, terrified. Jett dangled beneath her, helpless. He was staring at Johnny and muttering something, maybe a prayer.

That was when Kiri Lee let go.

She hadn't meant to, but finally her strength gave out. "NOO!" she cried, flailing at the air, but Jett was gone.

Johnny, rather than panicking, felt an odd prickle on the bottoms of his feet. It matched the tickling of an idea in the back of his mind. He looked over at Tommy, but caught Jimmy's eye instead.

"Do it," said Jimmy.

That was all Johnny needed. In a blur of motion that would have made Autumn proud, Johnny raced forward and dove over the edge.

Everything had happened so fast. In a matter of seconds two of their number were gone. So utterly spent was Kiri Lee that she fell out of the air into Tommy's arms and lost consciousness. Jimmy stood at the edge of the chasm and looked down.

"Why did he do it?" whispered Autumn. "Why?"

"Wait," said Jimmy. "Yur brother—Johnny—knows what he's doing."

A flash! Followed a second later by a tremendous *boom!*

"What . . . ?" Kiri Lee awoke with a start just as a brilliant flare of pure white light exploded from the abyss.

The four teens joined Jimmy near the ledge and looked. Trembling upward at a slow, lumbering pace came Johnny with enormous furrows of white-hot fire rocketing from his hands and feet. And clinging to Johnny like an enormous backpack was Jett. He grinned up at his friends and yelled, "This guy has rocket feet!"

The pair gained speed until finally Johnny cut his afterburners, and the two sailed in a gentle arc through the air and landed on the stone.

The two were surrounded by exuberant cheers and smothered in hugs. And for once in his life, Johnny felt like a *somebody*.

Like a hero.

Keeper of the Cistern

JUST AS the echoes of the Seven's celebration faded, the flaming stalactites burnt out leaving them in darkness once more.

"Got any flame left?" asked Tommy, hearing *tip-taps* of tiny creatures scurrying once more.

"On it." A *whoosh* accompanied a dazzling light.

Tommy looked back at the chasm and the remnants of the bridge.
"Looks like we've burned our bridge," he said. "I guess Johnny could
fly us over one at a time. Mannn, that is the coolest thing ever."

Jimmy stepped into a brightened patch in front of the others. He
stuttered a bit as he spoke, "I just . . . just wanted t' say I'm sorry. I
should 'a been more careful, like yu said."

"Mannn, don't sweat it," said Jett, grabbing Jimmy's shoulder.

Kat was still a bit angry, but if Jett could forgive him, well . . . she
thought she should, too. "Ah, Jimmy," she said, "you couldn't have
known."

"But I should 'a known, shouldn't I?" Jimmy asked.

"Maybe you learned a hard lesson," said Tommy. "For all of us.
This place is no joke. We've not even entered the fortress and almost
got a couple of us killed. We ALL need to be more careful . . . and we
need to work together. To remember our gifts." Nods all around. "Now,
Johnny, kindle our torch. It's time to enter Burcherond."

The team entered a low-arched corridor that appeared to lead
into the heart of the fortress. No windows or doors, no fixtures or
carpeting. Just a long hallway. Soon the light from Johnny's hands fell
on something none of them were expecting.

"A dead end," said Jimmy.

Jett scratched his head. "I don't get it."

"Neither do I," Tommy said. The Seven stood in a circular room with not even the faintest hint of a handle or hinge or crack. "Maybe we missed something back at the entrance."

As Johnny held the lit torch, the others searched the perimeter of the room by feeling the wall with their hands, finding nothing unusual until Kat whispered, "Guys, look at this!" She probed a dime-shaped dimple with her index finger and the back of the hole pressed inward. "Whoa!" Then a *click* from somewhere inside the wall, followed by grinding.

"A secret passage!" Johnny exclaimed, standing in the middle of the room. But as he looked around, nothing appeared. No door. No hatch. And still the grinding continued.

"I don't have a good feeling about this," said Autumn, spinning around slowly.

"Oh no!" said Jimmy, lunging for the opening to the room.

Thud!

Jimmy hadn't been fast enough. A solid rock wall slammed shut, closing off the corridor to the outside and sealing the Seven in the circular room.

"Oh great!" Jimmy complained. *Why did I not see that one coming?* Jimmy wondered to himself. *The bridge fallin', too. Doesn't seem like me gifts are growin' like they should. Somethin's wrong.* But Jimmy had no more time to worry about his gifts.

Bits of dust and stone dribbled down on the Seven as the ceiling began to give way, descending ever so slowly from its lofty place.

"It's a trap!" screamed Autumn, watching the rock inch its way toward her.

"Don't panic!" Tommy tried to calm them. "We'll figure a way out!"

The ceiling dropped lower, now just above their heads.

"My gift is no good here!" yelled Kiri Lee.

"Do something!" Autumn pulled on Johnny's arm. "*Johnny!*"

"I can't!" he hollered back, trying not to burn her with the flames in his hands.

"But I can," said Jett. The other six turned to watch as Jett planted his feet and placed his palms against the ceiling, now at shoulder height. Jett closed his eyes, and every vein in his neck began to bulge. He groaned, the ceiling slowing only slightly.

"Everybody else, on your backs," commanded Tommy. "Use your legs to press the stone up!"

"Ahgk, that's a little better," groaned Jett.

"It's not working!" Kat yelled. "Try harder!"

Jett clenched his teeth. "*I—am!*" Jett opened his eyes. They were giving it everything they had, and still the ceiling pressed down. They would die if he didn't stop this thing. Crushed to death. *Had they really come all this way to die here? Now? So close?*

It was then that Jett realized he truly held the futures of his friends in his hands. He thought of the Elves in Nightwish. He even thought of his parents back on Earth. And it was then something else came to mind. Jett closed his eyes and saw an image of his mother kneeling beside her bed as she did every night. Praying. *What a pointless ritual,* he had once thought. But ever since Grimwarden had begun to train them in the way of Vexbane, talking to Ellos, talking to God, didn't seem so strange. And right now it seemed like the only option. "*God,*" he grunted, "*if you're . . . there—I need—you.*" It was all he could do to keep the ceiling from folding him into the floor. "*Need . . . strength.*"

Jett felt a strange sensation course through his spine right then . . . like someone had plugged him into a wall socket. The burn in his muscles drained away, replaced with a flourishing reservoir of power—utter, raw power. A memory flickered back at that moment . . . of carrying half the Clifton Tigers football team across the goal line. That seemed so long ago, and now, Jett knew, he was much, much stronger.

"For Ellos!" he yelled, expending his might.

"You're doing it," the others started to whisper. Then louder, "Jett, you're doing it!"

Jett bared his teeth, yelling back in defiance. The ceiling, for the first time, had stopped. Sweat poured down his temples, his arms and legs trembling. He got off one knee and drove his right foot into the ground. Then pressed up. With the sound of gears being torqued in a direction they were never meant to go, the ceiling started upward. Farther above them, the Seven could hear the sounds of rope snapping, bars bending. Metal objects clanked together and dropped out of place. A strained, grinding sound shook the entire room, and soon Jett was on both feet and roaring like a giant as the ceiling ascended higher and higher.

Just when the ceiling was about out of reach, Jett snapped his body tight like a pillar of stone and thrust the ceiling upward so hard that it smashed into the framework above; but more, it went *through* it. Debris fell down all around the Seven as they covered their heads. Johnny's flames went out, and all went dark. Parts of the mechanism above littered the floor, and a few of the Seven coughed as dust filled the space. Then all was quiet.

The others peeked out from under their hands and gazed up. Above them was open space, filled with a soft glow from something in the distance.

Autumn gave Jett a hug. "You did it, Jett. Thank you." The others gathered around to thank him, too.

"Now let's get out of here," Tommy said, looking up. "Kiri Lee, care to take a look around?"

"Gladly," she smiled and took to the air. Four steps later and she was out of the hole, standing on the upper edge of the room.

"What do you see?" asked Tommy.

"Better see for yourself." She disappeared, and a moment later a thin rope dropped onto the floor in a coil. "Tommy, do your thing."

"Seems like someone knew we'd be coming," replied Tommy. He removed his bow, tied one end of the rope around the shaft, and triple looped it creating a cinching hitch—a trick he'd learned from Grimwarden. Then he nocked the arrow and let it fly, driving it deep into the rock ceiling somewhere above. With a few strong tugs to make sure it would hold his weight, he looked to Kat. "After you."

The remaining lords followed until they were all standing above the circular room. One by one they turned to see what Kiri Lee had found: a luminous shaft of silvery light at the far end of a wide chamber. It was moonlight, pouring down from an unseen opening far above and illuminating an ornate, stone well that stood about waist high. The Seven walked through the mechanical ruins of the now-destroyed ceiling trap and neared the shimmering pool of water.

"What is it?" Johnny asked.

"The cistern Migmar was talkin' about," Jimmy replied.

"I don't even know what a cistern is," added Tommy.

"It's an old word for a water hold, or a well of sorts," explained Jimmy.

Kat held up her hand. "Wait. The Keeper of the Cistern." She thumbed behind them. "Migmar warned us of the Keeper of the Cistern."

"Right," said Jimmy. "That's why I said *the* cistern. Bad news."

"And the Keystone?" added Kiri Lee. "How will we know it?"

"When we see it," said Tommy. "If the cistern is worth guarding, perhaps it's in there."

"Well, only one way to find out." Jimmy walked forward, taking the lead once again.

"Careful, Jimmy," called Kat. The words had no sooner left her mouth than Jimmy stopped and jumped back.

Everyone froze. "What is it?"

"Listen," Jimmy said, trembling ever so slightly. As if on command, the sound he'd heard a moment before in his mind's eye now blared out at them. A blood-curdling howl pealed through the air, making the hair on the backs of their necks stand up.

When at last the haunting wail subsided, the Seven stood deathly still. "Not cool," was all Jett could think to say.

"Hold yur ground," Jimmy warned, his powers returning. "There be a great beast comin'."

Wandering into the moonlight, a massive wolfish hound appeared between the Seven and the cistern beyond. Standing nearly ten feet tall at its shoulders, the creature arched its back and blocked most of the moonlight from view. Johnny responded by lighting up the room with a fireball to the ceiling.

Saliva dripped from its jaws, and the thing's breaths were so deep and heavy, the Seven could feel them across the room. Pale eyes glistening with mucus, the creature looked upward and winced at the bright light. True in form to a wolf—only enormous—the beast was mangy with thick hackles of black and gray hair standing on its back. It growled at the flames now licking the rock over its head, and then leveled its yellowish gaze on the Seven.

"It's got fur," Johnny whispered. "That means it'll burn."

"Not yet," said Tommy.

"Maybe it just wants to make sure we are of noble blood," Kat said, remembering the scarlet raptor. "You know, to trust us with its secret."

"But how's it going to test our blood?" asked Jett. "By eating us?"

It was then Jimmy dove at all of them, shoving them to the side. "*Get down!*" They all tumbled into a heap on the ground to the right just as the wolfhound snapped its fangs in the air where the bulk of them had stood.

"Move! Move! Move!" Tommy ordered. The beast turned its head to find the lords struggling to their feet. It snarled and lunged again. But this time Johnny blasted it in the snout with a shot from his hands. Stunned, the beast shut its mouth and flinched, jumping back. It shook its head frantically, pawing at its face. By the time the flames were extinguished and it could see again, the Seven had scattered.

Tommy started giving orders. "Kat, you get to the cistern and see if you can pick up anything from those rocks. Johnny, that over-grown dog gets near anyone and you blast him good, but don't kill it just yet; not sure if it's friend or foe. Jimmy, give him a heads-up. Autumn and Kiri Lee, use your speed, use the air, keep it distracted. Jett, come with me."

The Seven split up just as Tommy had ordered. Autumn began giving the wolf the worst run-around it had ever experienced, and Kiri Lee simply leaped up over its snout, walked right over its back, and down the other side. Jimmy gave instructions moments before the beast made a move, and Johnny kept it from seeing the other three lords making for the cistern, firing fire blasts in front of its head.

Tommy and Jett caught up with Kat, who now stared into the pool of water. Even with all the commotion, the water looked as smooth as glass. The moonlight streaming down from above cast a dazzling light on Kat's face as she examined the pool. Her bluish skin glistened like a map of stars. Tommy was awestruck. *She is absolutely beautiful,* he thought.

At that moment, Kiri Lee yelled, "Here, boy, catch me if you can!"

Kat had been trying hard to pick up something from the cistern, but she'd heard the ending of Tommy's thoughts instead. Only when Kat looked at Tommy, he was looking at Kiri Lee. *I should have known,* Kat thought. *Everyone always goes for the pretty girl.*

"Kat? Anything?" Tommy asked.

She shook her head. "No. Nothing helpful anyway."

Tommy and Jett looked at each other, then back to the commotion around the wolf; so far, the others were keeping the beastie quite entertained.

"I'm going to try something," she said. "Here goes nothing." Then she slowly submerged her hand into the pool. The water was extremely cold, tingles shooting up the nerves in the bottom of her wrist. Her fingers grew numb within seconds. She closed her eyes, lowering her head. And then it came.

Sing me your song.

Kat's eyes shot open, and she went to pull her hand from the water. But it wouldn't budge.

"Kat?" asked Tommy. "What is it?" Jett also eyed her, worried.

"It's stuck," she yelled, trying to pull her hand free. But it remained submerged, as if the water in the cistern had frozen solid around her wrist. The cold was creeping up her forearm now, her hand devoid of feeling.

"Here, let me help," said Jett, tugging on her forearm. But to his amazement her hand wouldn't budge. Not an inch.

"We will get you out of this, Kat," said Tommy. He placed his arm around her shoulder. "You heard something, didn't you?" Kat glanced at him. "What did you hear?"

For a split second, Kat forgot all her problems. "I—uh—" She was shivering.

"What was it, Kat?" asked Jett.

She looked to him. "I'm not sure. It was absurd. Probably just—"

"Kat!" prodded Tommy.

"'*Sing me your song.*'"

"Uh," Jett stuttered. "My song?"

"No, the pool. It said, '*Sing me your song*'."

"Oh." Jett looked at Tommy.

Tommy shrugged his shoulders. "Beats me."

Tommy suddenly noticed Kat's lips turning purple. "We've got to figure this one out fast, Jett."

"Yeah." Jett turned around and looked at the others. The wolf seemed to be tiring of the circus, and then caught sight of the three Elves standing by the cistern.

"He's going for the well!" Jimmy yelled.

Johnny looked to Tommy, Kat, and Jett and saw the threat. He clapped his hands and arms together and began releasing fire. Then he opened his arms like the jaws of a gator spreading a wall of fire on the ground between the wolf and the cistern. The beast yelped and jumped back. Kiri Lee ran through the air just above its head to distract it.

Tommy watched as Kiri Lee walked through the air. "That's it!"

"What?" said Kat, her teeth now chattering.

"Kiri Lee! Her music!"

"Of course," said Jett.

"Kiri Lee!" cried Tommy. "Come quick!"

She turned in midair to look at them, took a few steps over the wall of fire, and descended to the cistern. "What is it?"

Kat looked up, her body was shaking. "S-s-sing your s-s-s-song."

"My song?"

"You must have a song in you," said Jett. "You're the musical one. Isn't there something in that pretty head of yours?"

"Well, yes, but—" *He thinks I'm pretty?*

"*NOW!* Kiri Lee," urged Tommy.

"All right!" Kiri Lee stood next to Kat and shut her eyes, searching the recesses of her mind. She began journeying to the hidden places of her heart where she knew the songs dwelled. And not just any song . . . *the* song. The one she had first heard at the Medici Fountain in Paris, and then so many times after. The song taught to her by the Great Composer.

Kiri Lee relaxed her mind and slowly shut out all the other noises around her. The howling of the wolf . . . the *whoosh* of fire . . . the machine gun of Autumn's feet on the stone floor—it all faded. And soon Kiri Lee was left alone, floating through the inner world of her heart. Traveling. Looking. Dark, ominous clouds rolled in over her, glowing occasionally from sudden flashes of lightning within. This was it. The song had arrived.

Kiri Lee opened her mouth. At first, silence. But then, a sound. Faint. But rising like a clarion call, the whisper became a note and the note became a sword, driving deep into the subconscious, dividing—

"N-n-n-not to me!"

Kiri Lee snapped out of her trancelike state. "What?"

"Don't s-s-s-sing it to m-m-me," Kat shook her head, her face nearly purple. "S-s-s-sing it to *it*."

"It?"

"It?" asked Tommy and Jett, as perplexed as Kiri Lee was.

"S-sing to the wolf!" said Kat, as all at once her knees gave way to the extreme cold. Jett was behind her in an instant, hands under her shoulders.

Kiri Lee looked back at the wolf, now running in circles and growing more aggressive in its attacks. "Here goes nothing." She closed her eyes again, the song ready and waiting. She took a deep breath and out came the song, only this time more confident . . . more meaningful. There were no words exactly, more tones strung out by vowels and consonants . . . but a song nonetheless. And it was both beautiful and haunting. Dark, and yet somehow sweet and lofty.

And it was then that Jimmy first noticed a shift in the wolf's stance. "Guys, look!" Everyone turned and eyed the massive animal as its ears perked up and its attention turned toward Kiri Lee.

"Johnny!" said Tommy.

"I'm ready!" he replied. "Just give the word, Jimmy!"

But Jimmy shook his head. "Nope. He's just going to walk toward her. Curious, I think." Johnny put flames in his own hands nevertheless, ready should things go wrong.

Kiri Lee continued to sing, the melody working its wonders, mesmerizing even the lords with its beauty. Astonishingly, the wolfhound approached the diminishing wall of fire and stepped over it, moving slowly toward the cistern and the lords gathered near.

"I don't like this," said Jett. "Johnny!"

"No, wait!" demanded Kat. "Look!" The others gazed up at the wolf as it approached, its head lowered, its hackles flattened down. No, it was moving toward the song. Listening. It tilted its head.

"Whatever you do"—Tommy whispered to Kiri Lee—"don't stop." She nodded slowly and kept up the momentum of the melody. The rest of the lords followed after the wolf and watched, hoping for the best. Tommy and Kiri Lee both stepped aside as the large animal drew close and placed its head directly over the cistern. Jett tensed, but Kat held up her free hand, warding off his concern. As if completely disengaged from anything else that was going on around it, the wolf placed the tip of its snout in the pool and began to drink. Jett, Tommy, and the others who neared peered into the pool as the water receded. It slipped past Kat's hand until she was free, at which point Jett pulled her away. But she refused and struggled out of his grip, pressing back toward the cistern. All Seven now stood around the well, watching the wolf drink its fill. And then the unimaginable happened.

There, seated on a stone pillar in the middle of the cistern two feet down, was an unusual geometric object about the size of a basketball. Hewn from what looked to be a single piece of quartz, the pale white sculpture shimmered in the moonlight as the wolf pulled its head away and then looked down at the Seven.

"I could be wrong," said Tommy. "But I think our friend here just handed us the Keystone."

To which Johnny looked up at the beast and said, "Sorry about the whole fire thing."

29

Lyrics of Light

UNSURE IF the absence of her song would cause the giant wolf to return to its mad ravings, Tommy motioned for Kiri Lee to keep singing as he leaned into the cistern and grabbed the Keystone. He kept one eye on the wolf's snout as he wrapped his arms around the sculpture. But the mass turned out to be far heavier than he had first believed. That or it was attached to the pillar somehow.

"No way," Tommy shook his head. "Give it a shot, Jett."

Jett passed Kat—who felt all the better for Jett's healing touch— off to Jimmy, and then moved in to the cistern. He, too, cast the wolf a passing glance and then tried the object. But it wouldn't budge.

"So we've risked our life to find the Keystone, but we can't take it with us," said Johnny. "Great."

"So now what?" asked Jimmy.

"Here, let me touch it," Kat said, reaching out her hand.

"Hold on, Kat," Tommy stepped in. "You've touched enough today."

"So what do you think we're supposed to do with it?" Jett asked. The stone resembled a basketball with a flat bottom. Along the roundish upper section were seven flat panels—one on top and six directly underneath it, like a geodesic dome. The panels were flat, recessed about half-an-inch deep, and had circular boundaries. Within each circle were strange symbols etched seemingly at random. Everyone gathered close, eyeing the dazzling quartz as it glittered in the firelight.

"Can you interpret the lettering?" Jimmy asked Kat.

"Well, I thought it might be First Voice." Her months of studying the ancient Elven language in Whitehall came rushing back to her. *Imagine actually using what I learned in school.* She pointed to several spots on the Keystone. "See how these symbols are, with the dots over them? And here the swirl beneath these others, that looks like First Voice, but the rest . . . I just don't recognize."

"Some sort of code?" Autumn offered.

"I guess," said Kat. She looked at Tommy. "Maybe, if I touch it, maybe I could pick something up."

"No!" burst out Tommy. Then he shrank back. "I mean, no. What if—?"

"What if something happens?" she answered. How many times had she wondered the same thing? But now, in this very moment, new wisdom came to her. "Something is always going to happen, Tommy. It's part of being on a journey. But that's why we have each other." She paused. *"That's why I have you."*

Hearing the final thought, meant for him alone, Tommy blushed.

It was then that Kiri Lee abruptly stopped singing.

"Why'd you stop?" asked Johnny.

"It looks content," she replied. "Peaceful."

"That thing could turn on us and—"

"He won't," said Jimmy. "He's just going to sit there."

"Well?" asked Kat.

Reluctantly, Tommy relented. "Go ahead."

Kat bent over the cistern and reached down. Her fingers just inches away, she gasped.

"Kat, what is it?"

"No, I'm okay. These symbols on the Keystone, I recognize them. I used to draw them, more like doodles, really."

Kiri Lee looked strangely at Kat. "You doodle in First Voice?"

"Not exactly. It started back home—er, in California, when my powers first began to develop. I couldn't get these symbols out of my head. Now I know it's not just the ones on the Keystone that matter. When I bent over to look more closely, my medallion hung down from the top of my tunic."

She held hers aloft, and simultaneously the other six withdrew their own medallions, their tribes' seals, first given to them in the lordship ceremony.

"Is it the same?" Jett asked, scrutinizing his medallion.

"Not the same," said Kat, slipping the chain over her neck. "But unless my memory is completely messed up . . ." She leaned over the cistern wall once more and held her medallion up to the Keystone. "Here," she said, and there was an audible click. "It fits!"

Everyone held their breath. But nothing happened.

"Weird," said Johnny. "I thought it might do something cool."

"Maybe it's broken," said Jimmy.

"Or maybe we all have to put our medallions in," said Jett. "Here." He took his off and leaned over the side. He worked around the well until he spied what he thought was a perfect fit. "Booya!"

"The rest of you," Tommy prompted. "Come on."

One by one, the rest placed their medallions into the Keystone, until the only place left was the panel on top. Tommy held his medallion over it. "You might want to stand back, gang. I'm not sure what's going to happen."

Ever so slowly, each lord moved back, their eyes never leaving the stone. Tommy tried to steady his hand as he lowered his medallion into the remaining recess. Then—*clink*. He winced.

Everyone stood, wondering. Waiting. Even the wolfhound seemed alert. An echo from a distant drip of water. The flickering of the dying flames behind them. And all the while the Keystone was still. No sound. No flashing lights. It was just a rock with seven medallions filling seven recessed panels.

"Well," said Jimmy. "I didn' see that comin'."

The others nodded. Kat glared down at the Keystone.

"Is it First Voice?" asked Autumn. "Can you read it?"

"It certainly looks like First Voice," said Kat.

"It does," Kiri Lee agreed. "But nothing makes sense."

"It's almost like the symbols are at a different angle, or backward," said Kat.

The wolfhound emitted a growling sort of squeal and backed up a few steps.

Johnny's illuminating fires snuffed out and again they stood in darkness.

"Um, this is definitely not cool," said Kat, backing away. The rest took a few steps back, too, as a faint hum came from the well.

Tommy looked to his right. "Jimmy?"

"Don't worry, we'll be fine."

"What did you see?" Tommy asked.

Jimmy hesitated. "Well, nothin' actually. But I have a feelin' we'll be fine."

Great, Tommy thought.

The hum grew louder until finally the Seven noticed a subtle glow coming from inside the cistern. The big wolf let out a small whine. "If he's afraid, I'm afraid," said Kiri Lee.

Then, as if someone flipped a switch, blasts of emerald light shot out of the cistern. The Seven shielded their eyes. Even the wolf winced and pulled back.

"Oh my goodness!" Autumn finally remarked. "Look!" She pointed to the ceiling. To the walls.

"It's—it's magnificent!" said Kiri Lee.

All around them were glowing Elven characters inscribed in electric green. They stretched out across the domed room in every direction, appearing like a nighttime sky full of stars . . . only, to the trained eye, these were no mere constellations; these were words. Written by the ancients. Hidden for countless ages. The team spun around slowly, taking it all in. The wolf strained its head up to see as well.

"What does it mean?" Tommy looked to Kat, then Kiri Lee.

"I'm working it through right now," Kat replied. "It's in First Voice."

"It's poetry," said Kiri Lee. Kat wrinkled her nose.

"Poetry?" the others repeated.

"How about . . . song lyrics," replied Kat.

"Nice, Kat," said Jimmy.

"The Rainsong!" Tommy exclaimed.

"So the prophecies"—Jett shook his head, still mesmerized by the inscriptions painted on the walls—"they're real after all?"

"Seem to be," said Kiri Lee. "In fact, judging by the syllables in First Voice, they fit that crazy melody that's been drifting through my head all this time. Like . . . perfectly."

"Then what does it say?" Jimmy asked.

"Yeah, can you sing it?" Tommy drew close to Kiri Lee.

"I can try. I'm putting it in English so everyone can understand. It won't rhyme."

Kiri Lee closed her eyes yet again, willing the melody to come forth. She found it more easily this time, having only held it in her mind's eye moments before. But this time, rather than a solitary silvery thread of notes streaming together, she opened her eyes and scanned the domed room, searching for a beginning. And then she began to sing.

> "Beneath the burning firmament of heaven
> Live the Children of the Light.
> Blood of kings, strength of queens,
> Sons and daughters, each we stand.
> Let every crooked road be straight.
> Let injustice suffer our wrath.
> By the hand of the justice bane,
> We dispatch the ruthless, wicked, and foul.
> See now, comes the dawn in darkness.
> Hear now, the song of the Chosen.
> We lift our voices as one Body,
> Righting ancient evil with our union.
> Let the captive be set free—
> The chains of slaves be broken at last.
> We shall cross ancient borders to defeat our enemies,
> And wake those who have slept for too long.
> The Lords of Berinfell take up their thrones,
> And the Mighty of Allyra, their mantel awaits.
> For Ellos empowers those who draw near,
> Holding hands as one, their destinies intertwined."

The song itself seemed alive, each Elvish script character brightening as Kiri Lee sang it. The presence of the song filled the hall with energy, the lords getting goose bumps as the presumed meaning of the lyrics washed over each one. Their people would not be subject to tyranny anymore. No more slavery. No more injustice. They would be free of the Spider King and his dominion. Without even realizing it, the Seven found themselves weeping.

Kiri Lee's voice, the melody, the words, the images—striking in their beauty.

It meant hope.

Kiri Lee sang the song a few more times until each lord had memorized the lyrics. When she let the last note fade, so too did the images. And once again the Seven stood in darkness. Darkness, no longer frightening, but like an enveloping safety. Like being held.

The massive wolf gave out a low growl and then a bark, startling everyone.

"Johnny!" Tommy yelled.

A blast of fire raced to the ceiling and stuck there, casting a bright light over everything. But surprisingly the wolf was still in place, staring at the high ceiling.

"We need to get out of here," said Jimmy. "Right now."

The wolfhound barked again, then lowered its body flat to the ground.

"What's going to happen?" Tommy asked.

"The roof's about to cave in."

Then they all heard it, a rumble, followed by a sharp crack. "Look!" Tommy yelled, pointing to the opening in the high ceiling where the moonlight still shone down. A silvery crack had appeared. Suddenly a piece of stone dislodged and fell.

The Seven dove in all directions. The heavy piece of rock plummeted, shattering the cistern and burying the Keystone under rubble.

"Lords!" called Tommy. "We need to leave and right now!"

"Bottomless pit behind us," said Jett. "Dead end up ahead. How do we get out of here?"

WOOF! They all turned to the wolfhound, still squat on the floor. It stared at them, its expression completely different from that of the ferocious beast they'd first encountered. It pawed the ground and whined.

"I think it knows we need to get out of here, too," said Johnny.

"But this is a giant wolf-dog thing, Johnny," said Autumn. "How could it—"

Wooooo, WOOF! More pawing. More whines.

"Ohhh," said Jimmy, his eyes fixed as if watching something on TV no one else could see. Jimmy suddenly ran at the wolfhound.

"Jimmy!" Kiri Lee cried, but it was too late.

Jimmy leaped up on the beast's foreleg and clambered up onto its shoulders. "C'mon!" he yelled. "He's our way out!"

"It's a he?" asked Autumn.

"I don't know," Jimmy retorted. "We can check later. Just get on!"

More cracks. More debris fell. The Seven said nothing more and climbed aboard the wolfhound express.

WOOF! WOOF, WOOOO! The beast rose up and took off like a shot into the darkness-shrouded corner far behind and to the left of where the cistern stood. The Elves clutched armfuls of fur as the beast gained speed and emerged into a curving gray-lit passage. The wolfhound had plainly traversed these corridors often for, without hesitation, it raced over obstacles and around blind turns.

Stone, timber, and other debris began to rain down on them. But the wolf was equal to the task. A huge plank fell in their path. The wolf darted left and leaped over the fallen wood. It came down on all fours and slid sideways to the brink of a dreadful-looking black hole in the floor. *Grrrrrr, ROOF!* The beast's claws found purchase, and with the Seven still holding on for dear life, the wolfhound sped away from the potential fall. It was a perilous journey, stretching the lords' collective nerve to its breaking point. By the time the wolf emerged under the stars on the backside of the fortress, the lords were barely conscious, barely holding on.

When the wolfhound entered the woods some two hundred yards away, the colossal mountain that hid the Burcherond collapsed. ✖

30

Return to Nightwish

JIMMY WAS alone on the back of the giant wolfhound. How long he'd been on its back and how far they'd come through the deep woods, he had no idea. But at last the creature came to a stop in a clearing where a small fire burned.

Woof, WOOF, WA-OOOOO! The creature howled.

Glistening eyes appeared all around the clearing. To Jimmy's horror, gigantic wolves emerged from the woods and closed on their position. It seemed the whole world shook with their growls. Jimmy frantically tried to climb off the creature's back, but the beast caught the back of his tunic in its jaws and flung Jimmy into the center next to the fire.

When Jimmy looked up, he looked into a massive grin of white teeth. The jaws opened and . . . AHHHHHhhhhhhhh!

There came a beautiful, melodic voice . . . like an angel: "Jimmy, wake up!"

Jimmy opened his eyes and found himself face-to-face with a gigantic wolf. He screamed as the beast opened its jaws and . . . felt himself knocked backward by a rough, wet tongue the size of a diving board.

Kiri Lee was at his side in an instant. "Jimmy, are you okay? You were having a bad dream. I called to you."

"Wha-whaa?" Jimmy's eyes finally focused, and he stared at Kiri Lee. "Yu're the angel," he said.

The other lords gathered around. "I think he's delirious," said Jett. The others laughed mightily.

Jimmy finally cleared the cobwebs. "Yu would be, too, if yu woke up next t' that, that, thing there! I thought it was gonna eat me."

"What, Bear?" said Autumn. "C'mon, he was just being playful."

She nuzzled the giant wolf under its chin. "Weren't you, ya big fuzzy, wuzzle, fuzzer bear!"

Jimmy looked on in disbelief and then back to the other lords. "Yu named it Bear? It's a giant wolf!"

"Well," said Tommy, "Autumn named him."

"I wanted to name him Sam," said Johnny. "After our dog that disappeared back home."

"But I said no," said Autumn. "Sam will find us. He'll come home. He always does."

"So Autumn was snuggling with him," said Jett, "just like now, and she kept calling him her big fuzzy bear, so . . ."

"So," said Tommy. "So the wolf's name is Bear."

Jimmy stood up and rubbed his side. "So where are we, then?"

"Near the Spine," said Tommy. "And the Spine will lead us back toward Whitehall, and Jett and I can piece together the way to Nightwish from there. You about ready to ride?"

Jimmy looked at Bear. "If I have to."

Had it not been for Bear, the trip back to Nightwish would have taken far longer than six days—if they ever got there at all. But at long last, the Seven Elven Lords of Berinfell began to recognize some of the environment.

"These are the big trees," said Autumn, the only Elf riding Bear as the others chose to walk for a while.

"You're right," said Tommy. "Grimwarden called them Silver Mattisbough. The entrance to Nightwish was somewhere in the middle of them."

Something snapped in the forest.

Bear's entire body tensed, the hackles on his back standing up. Autumn leaped down just as Bear rumbled out a low growl. The Seven took his warning and prepared to strike, senses alert. In the clearing they were exposed, the closest cover more than fifty yards away. The afternoon sun illuminated them, easy targets.

"Maybe it's just a wee squirrel or something," Jimmy offered up in a whisper. "Bah, I can't see what's going to happen."

But Tommy shook his head. "That was no squirrel," he said. "Bear doesn't think so, either."

"Wait," Jimmy said, holding a hand to his forehead. "There!" He pointed to a spot among the trees at the two o'clock position. The others looked, waiting for whatever Jimmy saw to catch up with present time. And then a lone Elf emerged from the woods, bow at the ready. He stood motionless for three beats and then raised a hand. And with it, more than one-hundred Elves emerged from the forest in a circle around the Seven and Bear.

"We are sorry, m'lords." The lead Elf crossed his wrists and bowed, the rest of the group following his lead. "But we had to be sure. Endurance and Victory."

"Endurance and Victory," Tommy said, stepping forward.

Kat reached up and patted the wolf on the shoulder. "It's all right, Bear. They're friends." He seemed to ease at her touch, but still took his protection of his new friends very seriously.

The lead Elf stood at Tommy's command and introduced himself. "I am Mathinil, flet soldier of the Third Order, Commander of the Twelfth, ordered by Guardmaster Travin."

"Guardmaster?" Kat inquired. "But Grimwarden is—"

"Thank you, Mathinil," answered Tommy. "We are grateful for your service. I am Lord Vel—"

"We know, sire. We have been expecting you." Mathinil stood aside and gestured with his hand into the woods from which he had emerged. "If you please."

The words *we have been expecting you* did not settle well with Tommy, or any of the others for that matter. They were each aware of the elders' plot to thrust them into battle. With Grimwarden, Goldarrow, and Alwynn gone, they feared the powers that now controlled the Elven survivors of Berinfell. And the fact that the elders had replaced Travin as the new Guardmaster confirmed Grimwarden's death. Travin had been loyal to Grimwarden . . . but would his loyalties still be true given the circumstances?

The Seven walked into the shade of the forest. They'd made it back to Nightwish, but they did not know what to expect. Bear followed them in, wary of the flet soldiers who filled in behind him. They walked for no more than a minute before Mathinil stopped beside a cluster of large boulders, the leader indicating a small cave behind a latticework of brush.

"You are fond of this creature?" asked Mathinil.

"Very much so," said Autumn.

"Yeah, we are," said Jett.

"Well, not all of us," mumbled Jimmy.

"I see," said Mathinil, clearly troubled. "I . . . I, uh, don't think it wise to bring it inside. The tunnels are cramped and there are children about. But you are the lords. We will do as you wish."

"No, that's okay," said Tommy. "You're probably right. But please see to it that he is watered and fed."

"As you command," said Mathinil.

Woof, WOOF! Bear turned toward Jimmy, shot out his tongue, and knocked the Elf off his feet. Then Bear turned, leaped over the flet soldiers, and disappeared into the woods.

"Oh, Bear!" Autumn yelled. "Oh, come back!"

Bear did not return. "We'll see him again," said Johnny. "I know we will."

"I hope not," said Jimmy, wiping gobs of wolf saliva off his face.

The long tunnel wound its way deep underground, intersecting others, growing larger and larger as it went. Finally it spit the entourage out into the northernmost section of Nightwish Caverns, standing on a ledge overlooking the entire city.

Like before, the incredible blue light filled the room, shining from the luminous rocks used to contain dremask. But unlike before, shafts of daylight mixed with the otherworldly hue: radiant beams of sunshine let in through large holes delved through the sandstone above.

But more shocking was the state of the Elven underworld. Where before the Elves went about their daily tasks, trapped in the dark routines of the subterranean, everywhere they looked their people were mobilizing for war. Whatever preparations had been stock-piled over the last eight centuries, they were being readied now. Weapons and armor were assembled and organized in various sec-tions of the city: sword blades, spear points, arrowheads, and axe blades fresh from the forge fires were taken to carpenters who affixed handles and arrow shafts; cured leather as hard as rock was pulled from the tanneries and passed off to metalworkers who bound the plates with chain mail; long bows and short bows were sanded to a stonelike luster before being married to the high-tensile bowstrings that the Elves had perfected over thousands of years of use. Helmets were buffed, daggers were sharpened, and sword weights were tested. The Elves took great care and accepted nothing but the highest quality.

Hearth fires spewed out dark smoke, laden with the scents of meat, vegetables, and spices. Vats of an Elven drink called lychestine were being emptied into canteens, as were the fresh pools fed by the under-water aquifers. Dates, apples, and berries plundered from the forest above—now with renewed confidence, despite the previous week's reported attack on Whitehall—were packed along with the wrapped meats and canteens into backpacks, ready to accompany the growing army that could been seen swelling in the streets.

And with all the sights and sounds of life also came the forebod-ing feeling that things were accelerating out of control. Tommy felt a knot tighten in his stomach, growing worse when Mathinil produced a horn from his belt and gave a single long blast.

The entire city below came to an abrupt stop and looked to where the new arrivals stood.

"Elves of Nightwish"—Mathinil's voice boomed out over the cav-ern as he raised a hand to indicate his company—"our lords have returned!"

Memories of their first arrival in Nightwish flooded back as the city streets erupted in adoration of the Seven Lords. The people pumped whatever was in their hands in the air—swords, spears, bows . . . fists if nothing else. Children ran through the streets with flags, women fluttering blankets from second- and third-story windows. But it was not the same. It would never be the same. While the cheering persisted, Mathinil turned and led the Seven down a wide staircase that hugged the cavern wall. They crossed the river and descended into the city streets among throngs of ardent followers. And with every step the lords took toward the Great Hall, their anxiety mounted, unsure of what reception might await them within.

They all waved, despite their inward feelings, realizing their outward appearance must have looked more befitting of trained warriors, what with months of Vexbane training behind them. Their stature and resolve alone were a far cry from the seven middle-school students who first floated into this hall, wide-eyed and speechless.

The lords tousled the hair of children and smiled at doting mothers. The men of the city offered forearms for the shaking, or dipped their heads out of reverence for their superiors in both royalty and now fighting skills. And all the while the Great Hall grew larger, now looming high overhead. What waited within was anyone's guess; the Seven were prepared for a fight. Going to war against the Spider King was hard enough, but marching on Vesper Crag without the map would be near impossible, and with Manaelkin in place of Grimwarden or Goldarrow? A death wish.

Mathinil took them inside the passage of the Great Hall and shut out the boisterous world behind them with the closing of the massive wooden doors. Then he disappeared into the council room, giving a quick, "I'll be right back, m'lords."

Tommy looked to the others, alone in the anteroom.

"I don't like it," Kat said, her face fixed on the council room door.

Suddenly there were loud shouts from within. Shouts and the banging of a gavel. "Manaelkin, no doubt," grumbled Tommy. The others nodded. "But we have a job to do, and I for one am not going to let some two-faced coward dictate—"

"If you please, m'lords," came Mathinil's voice from the opened door. "The council will see you now."

The Seven shared a secret glance. "Here goes," said Tommy, taking a step forward. What he saw took his breath away.

"Good of you to join us, Lord Felheart," boomed a familiar voice. *Grimwarden!* And beside him sat Elder Alwynn and Elle Goldarrow, all rising to their feet to welcome the Seven.

Tommy stammered for a moment before finally managing the words, "You're—you're alive! I can't believe it!" The lords filed into the room and spread out around the central table, trying both to ascertain the strangeness of the scene as well as Grimwarden's, Goldarrow's, and Alwynn's presence. "We thought you were—"

"Dead?" interrupted Alwynn. "We would have been, had it not been for Grimwarden here." He patted the battle chief on the shoulder. "In any event, we're glad you have returned."

"We are, too!" exclaimed Kat, tears bursting and running down her cheeks. She strode around the chair backs and embraced Grimwarden, who didn't quite know how to receive the gesture at first, but eventually relented and hugged her back.

When the others had finished greeting their favorite teachers and politician, Grimwarden indicated the high-backed chairs and they all took their seats, all but Grimwarden. He drew his rychesword and bellowed, *"Vex lethdoloc vitica anis. Wy feithrill e' Ellos abysscrahl nyas!"*

"We are not Wisps," said Kat.

"Yes," said Grimwarden. "I know that . . . now for certain. But we cannot afford to be burned again."

"But where are the others? Where is the council?" Tommy sat up, noticing the empty chairs.

"We may have time to discuss our escape from Whitehall and your expeditions at a later date," Grimwarden said. "But for now, I shall answer your question as simply as possible, Lord Felheart. Alwynn here is the last of the elders. All of them, including Manaelkin, were killed during the surprise assault on Whitehall."

"I proposed to the others that I run back to see how you fared," Autumn put in. "But when I arrived, I found Whitehall destroyed by the hands of Gwar and Warspiders." Her memories resurfaced, the images filling her mind. "We thought you'd all been killed."

"It was a horrific sight," said Alwynn. "I wish you had not seen it."

"So let me get this straight"—Jett said, leaning forward—"*all* the elders but Alwynn here are dead? Gone?"

"I am afraid so," said Grimwarden.

"Afraid so?" Jimmy nearly exploded out of his seat. "But that's perfect! No more opposition, no one to try and thwart our plans, we answer only to—"

But Grimwarden's glare stopped him cold. "The elders may have differed in their views, but they were still our brothers. And I mourn their loss, as well as the light of their collective wisdom being snuffed out too soon. We now care for widows and fatherless children who grieve. We dare not rejoice."

Jimmy suddenly felt quite ashamed. As did the rest of them. Grimwarden, of course, was right. And once again he proved his position by choosing compassion when he could have chosen righteous indignation.

"Forgive me," Jimmy said, lowering his head.

"Forgive us all," Tommy added, recognizing the community of thought.

"It is forgiven," said Alwynn. "For now, we"—he motioned to himself, Goldarrow, and Grimwarden—"will serve as your elder council until more members can be selected."

"I'm down with that!" said Jett.

Alwynn was puzzled. "What's down?"

"Nevermind," Goldarrow said to the elder, waving it off. "We must turn to the matters at hand, m'lords."

"Vesper Crag?" asked Jimmy.

The three elders at the table nodded, and the Seven felt a cool shiver go up their spines. The time had come at last.

"Preceding our attack, there are still two vital components missing, I fear," said Grimwarden.

Goldarrow addressed the Seven. "Neither Nelly nor Regis has returned with the map." The Seven shared a worried look.

Tommy spoke up. "Do you still think the map is necessary?"

Grimwarden nodded. "Essential, Lord Felheart. Without it, we would rely on brute force alone. An attack of that nature would invite utter failure given we are the aggressors on foreign territory, not defenders."

"What's the other bad news?" asked Johnny.

"Unless you have news we don't know of, we still don't know where the Keystone is."

"WE FOUND IT!" the Seven belted in one voice. The elders jerked back in their seats with surprise. The three of them were like little children.

"You did indeed?" Goldarrow leaned forward. "What, what is it?"

"Do you have it with you?" Grimwarden inquired, his hands nearly twitching.

"Sadly, no," said Tommy. "It was lost in a cave-in."

"Cave-in?" Goldarrow was horrified.

"We barely escaped," said Autumn. "If it weren't for Bear . . ."

"Bear?" asked Goldarrow.

"Actually, he's a wolf," said Jett.

"A giant one," added Jimmy.

Grimwarden waved his hand before his face as if clearing a plume of smoke. "So, then, the Keystone is destroyed?"

"Yes," said Tommy.

"But, Lord Felheart," Alwynn pointed to him. "You seem far from concerned."

"Well, we took from it what we needed."

Grimwarden clapped his hands. "Good lad!" He thought better of his outburst. "Well done, I mean. Resourceful, just as I taught you, young lord."

"Indeed," said Tommy.

"And?" Goldarrow pressed him further.

Tommy and the others went on to explain their introduction to the Gnomes, the subterranean fortress, and all the events surrounding the cistern, the Keystone, the Rainsong, Bear, and their narrow escape. Grimwarden was beaming with pride as he heard the account of the Seven working together and, against all odds, succeeding in their quest. His training had served them well. They all knew it.

"I wish I could have seen it," Goldarrow said wistfully.

"As do I," said Alwynn. Grimwarden nodded in assent.

"So the lyrics," said Goldarrow. "You have them?"

"Yes," said Kiri Lee. "I will require some parchment, a quill, and some ink right away."

"Yes, immediately." Grimwarden looked to Alwynn, but the high cleric was already at the door to the chamber telling a flet soldier to fetch paper, quill, and ink.

"We all know the Rainsong," Kiri Lee indicated the other lords. "But I will need to teach them the melody."

"Especially me," said Jimmy. "I canna' sing worth dirt."

Kiri Lee smiled kindly at him and then turned back to the elders. "According to the prophecies, the Rainsong has great power."

"The Rainsong," Alwynn nodded. "Oh, yes. Quite!" And rubbed his hands nervously. "May we—may we hear it now?"

"Here?" said Kiri Lee, looking around. "Well, I don't see why not. If it's okay with everyone else."

"Indeed!" said Goldarrow. She glanced at Grimwarden.

"Of course!"

"Very well." Kiri Lee cleared her throat. She closed her eyes, bringing the melody to the surface of her thoughts, and then drenched the lyrics, line by line, in the rich deluge of the song. When she opened her mouth, it was auditory color that everyone saw. Felt. Touched. It was as if she were painting with her words. Entranced by the sweetness of the tone, no one noticed the lights flickering, nor the subtle tremor in the ground, nor the smell of rain in the air.

Grimwarden could not remember the last time anything had moved him as much as this song. There was power in the Rainsong, perhaps enough even to defeat the Spider King once and for all.

31

Battle of the Heart

FOLLOWING KIRI Lee's moving performance of the Rainsong from the day before, the Seven young lords and the elders engaged in a lengthy and, at points, heated argument. While the map of Vesper Crag's inner-workings still eluded them, the manifestation of the Rainsong, as well as its apparent power, seemed to prompt the most impatient to war . . . especially Jimmy.

"But we have it! Yu feel the power in it, just as I do." Jimmy had his fist on the table. "I can't believe that yu would prefer we wait for a trivial, and even mundane, piece of reconnaissance when compared to the supernatural power of the Rainsong!"

"Trivial?" Grimwarden sat up. "Lord Thorwin, I have never said anything of the sort. I respect the power of the Rainsong, just as I respect the power of the prophecies. I would caution you of accusing me of anything less. However, I will say that in all battles, there are both elements supernatural AND natural. To be victorious, we are to be prepared on both fronts."

"I must agree with Guardmaster Grimwarden," added Elle. "Wars are won with as many allies as might be found. There is nothing unspiritual about waiting for the map, just as there is nothing natural about using the Rainsong."

"So you would have us wait?" Tommy suggested.

"Wait?" Grimwarden drummed his fingers on the table. "Yes, I would have it so, at least for a time. But ultimately, these orders are not mine to give. They are yours. Yes, Jimmy, even yours. For we"—he motioned to Alwynn and Elle—"are your advisors, not your dictators. We believe Ellos brought you back to us, and you are the fulfillment of the prophecies. I have done my best to train you in all the ways of war and discipline. Now the best we can do is advise you."

Jimmy began to argue more, but Tommy raised a hand toward him. "We thank you for your counsel," he said, trying to sound lordly. Then, glancing at Jimmy, he went on to say, "While we are not old in years, we are passionate." He gave a quiet laugh. "On Earth, we'd have said we're stoked. I guess we feel like we're ready now for what we've been called to do. And we intend to use the gift of our youth in battle. But while we are young, we lack the wisdom of years, and so . . . we look to you for it."

One week later Tommy stepped down from the table and cornered a runner. "Any word from Nelly or Regis?"

"Nay!" The Elf was red-faced and gasping for air. "May I assist you in any other matter?"

"No, nothing." Tommy ran a hand through his hair. "Thank you."

"Endurance and Victory."

"Endurance and Victory," Tommy replied, turning back to the main table in the center of the room. He stared at the wooden pawns scattered across it. Grimwarden stood beside him.

"Patience, my young lord. It will come."

"But we march for Vesper Crag at dawn! Was it not you a week ago saying we shouldn't attack without it?" Tommy smiled, half genuinely, half out of mounting frustration. "You confuse me sometimes."

"I did advise you to wait, but only for a time." Grimwarden stared at the table a moment and then continued. "I believe Nelly and Regis will return with the map. And if you still wish to honor my counsel, we will march at first light tomorrow."

Tommy shook his head, laughing nervously. "Thanks for clarifying."

Grimwarden looked up, catching a signal from Alwynn across the hall. "Ah, they are here."

"Who are here?" Tommy asked.

"Come and see," said Grimwarden cryptically. "We should get Kat, too. Given your shared love of heights, I think you will find this . . . rather exhilarating."

Grimwarden led Tommy and Kat down a well-lit corridor on the eastern side of Nightwish. The hall was narrow and made more difficult to navigate due to the barrels clumped in twos and threes on either side.

"I've never been this way," said Tommy.

"No," said Grimwarden. "Not likely. This is an access route to one of our storage halls. Elle tells me you would call them warehouses. Strange name, as if you don't know where to find them. But, anyway, this particular warehouse is special and newly outfitted for a different kind of cargo."

"You can say the Elven alphabet in your mind all you want, Guardmaster," Kat said, grinning. "But you're going to let some thought slip, and I'll figure out what you're hiding."

Grimwarden laughed. "I am a lifelong military strategist and tactician. The day I can't hide—"

"Birds!" Kat shouted. "You've got more of the scarlet raptors! Oh, my goodness!" Kat ran ahead.

Grimwarden was dumbfounded. "But I . . . I didn't think it . . . not anything so obvious!"

"She's good," said Tommy.

Grimwarden harrumphed and increased his pace after Kat. He led Tommy to a vast, high-ceilinged chamber where brilliant sunlight poured in from dozens of newly delved porthole-size windows. Light also shone in from a wide gate cut into the rock wall at the far end, but Tommy was more captivated by the occupants of the huge chamber.

"They . . . they're beautiful," mouthed Tommy. "And fierce." Both Tommy and Kat stood marveling at the scarlet raptors, more than one hundred count. They stood in a straight line, all very still or quietly preening their wings. And each one bore an Elven rider. As Tommy gawked, the foremost rider deftly kicked up his legs and slid off his flying mount. He removed a leather helmet as he approached, and silver-blond hair spilled out onto his noticeably broad shoulders. His skin was dark like chocolate, and his violet eyes shone out brightly from beneath his silver brow.

The newcomer knelt, but his keen eyes never left Tommy and Kat.

"Lord Felheart and Lord Alreenia," said Grimwarden with a sweep of his hand. "I'd like you to meet Ethon Beleron of the tribe Nightwing. He is First Raptor Ward of the Old Ones. By Alwynn's request, the Old Ones have agreed to let us borrow some of their rare wild scarlet raptors. Ethon here has spent the better part of the past two weeks training flet soldiers to fly."

"M'lords," said Ethon. "It is the greatest pleasure of my life to meet you."

"You're an Old One?" Kat blurted out. She couldn't believe it. This guy looked maybe twenty-five, thirty tops.

Ethon stood and drew nearer. "I see your quandary," he said. "The Old Ones are an ancient council. I'm merely an apprentice."

This time Tommy blurted out, "You train to get old?"

Ethon laughed politely and glanced at Grimwarden. Then he said, "Not exactly. Time has a way of taking care of that. No, I train in First Voice, Vexbane, and, of course, raptor flight."

"Ethon has our flet soldiers flying with great skill," said Grimwarden.

"It is not all that hard," said Ethon humbly. "The raptors are incredibly intelligent, and they will bear a rider more safely than any land steed. Sometimes it's almost as if they know what you're thinking."

"Yes," said Grimwarden lustily. "They give us a decided advantage. Imagine, archers borne on the wind! And with whatever layadine we have left, we will be able to knock out their Warspiders like never before. Praise Ellos! We shall own the skies!"

"You are of the Nightwing tribe?" Kat asked.

"Yes," Ethon replied. "A distant cousin of Lord Hamandar, actually. I should very much like to meet him as well."

"And you will, later," Grimwarden said. "Jett is getting fitted for new armor. Seems the lad is growing. Now, Ethon, if you'll excuse us. Lord Felheart and I have some matters to attend to."

"Of course," he said with a bow.

"What about Kat?" Tommy asked.

"What about Kat?" Grimwarden repeated. "She is free to do as she wishes for now. Perhaps Ethon could give her a quick flying lesson."

"I would be happy to," he said.

"Really?" Kat replied. "I would love to fly."

"Excellent!" said Ethon. He turned to Grimwarden. "Wasn't there another? In your last dispatch, you said one of the Seven was particularly interested in flying?"

"Yes, right," said Grimwarden. "Lord Lothriel. Yes, very anxious to fly."

"Kiri Lee?" quipped Kat. "She already flies, practically."

Ethon looked at her strangely. "Fear not, Lord Alreenia, I have taught larger classes than two."

Tommy didn't need to be able to read minds to see that Kat was disappointed. *But why?* He thought he might know, but he was careful not to crystallize those thoughts, not with Kat nearby. But it bothered him.

"Come, Lord Felheart," said Grimwarden. "To the armory we must go."

"Call me Kat," Tommy heard her say as he and Grimwarden departed the raptor hangar. As they traversed Nightwish to the armory, Tommy found himself thinking more about Kat than the upcoming war.

"Let's review what we have thus far," Elle said later that evening from the other side of the map table. At her voice, about forty Elves gathered around the Seven, Grimwarden, and Alwynn. Before them was a map of Vesper Crag . . . not the one they had hoped for, but a bird's-eye view of what they knew about the eastern-most border of the region. To the right side of the map was Vesper Crag, a black dot on the peak of a mountain in a long range that ran north and south. To the left of that were the Lightning Fields, with the Dark Veil directly north, and the Southern Forest at the bottom, where the Seven had returned from Dalhousie Castle. Farther west lay a chain of foothills that gave way to the beginnings of the Thousand-League Forest. And in their heart, the ruins of Berinfell. Nightwish lay slightly north and west of Berinfell, and discovered as it was, Nightwish would remain the headquarters of the operation.

As Elle began to outline their strategies—plans that had been discussed, refined, analyzed, and discussed again—Jimmy felt a hand on his shoulder. He turned to see Grimwarden looking at him. Then he whispered in Jimmy's ear, "May I speak with you?"

Jimmy looked at him, to Elle and the briefing, and then back. "Now?"

"Aye. Now."

Jimmy blinked a few times and nodded. He followed Grimwarden from the Great Hall and slipped into a side anteroom. Grimwarden closed the door and indicated a bench along the wall. Both sat.

"Thank you for entertaining my request."

"Um, sure. Everything okay?"

"It will be." Grimwarden collected his thoughts. Jimmy felt a knot tighten in his stomach.

This can't be good.

"Lord Thorwin, I have had the privilege of watching you grow in these last few months. And I must tell you, it has been an honor I compare with little else. I hold you in the utmost respect, caring for your life and success more than my own."

Jimmy was visibly moved by Grimwarden's words, a small shudder streaking up his spine. "Why, thank yu, Guardmaster Grimwarden."

"But it is for this high regard that I must address something I've noticed."

Jimmy fidgeted with his hands.

"Back in Whitehall, you were always the first to volunteer for virtually anything I asked. You were the first to test a new weapon, a new skill, or venture into a challenge . . . seemingly without regard for your own well-being. And while this is a virtue shared by those who line the Hero's Hall, I do not believe it has the same root in you as it does in them."

"I'm . . . not sure I understand."

"Jimmy, why did you volunteer to be the first into a cave that Migmar warned you was occupied by the Keeper of the Cistern?"

"What? Who told yu that?"

"And why were you the first to run across a bridge before you had some knowledge of its safety?"

"Did Tommy tell yu this? Oh, when I get—"

"Answer the questions." Grimwarden's voice was as commanding as his expression. Jimmy stopped fidgeting. He looked down.

"I—I don't really know."

"No?" Grimwarden put a hand on Jimmy's shoulder. "I think you do."

Jimmy thought for a moment. A moment that felt longer the more he put off talking about it. Then finally a tear slipped down his cheek.

Grimwarden didn't say anything. He merely sat in silence. Waiting for more.

"The others in there"—Jimmy whispered, waving his hand—"they all have families. Adopted, yeah, but by parents who love them. Poor Kiri Lee told me that her parents must be dead—killed by Wisps, but at least she knew they adored her and gave up everythin' for her. Even Kat knows her parents love her. She told me herself. But mine—" Tears rolled over the rims of his eyelids like a dam bursting. He tried to speak the words, but he broke out sobbing. He couldn't say it. The words were caught in his throat like rocks. He wanted to throw up. He wanted to run. But Grimwarden's granite hand on his shoulder was a steadying force that wouldn't let him move. Jimmy knew that was no option here. "My parents . . . they hate me."

The words rang in his head like hammer strokes. "Sure, they pretended t' love me, but that went away fast, didn't it? Soon as me brother come along—pity that—it was out with Jimmy lad." He kicked at the bench leg with his heel and stared at the silvery dremask torch burning alone on the wall. "All I ever wanted was someone t' love me fer real, yu know? Someone t' matter t'. Is that so bad?"

He wiped the snot from his nose, and his chest heaved to take in a quick breath. "I wanted a father t' tell me I was strong enough, fast enough, good enough. And a mother t' tell me everythin' was gonna be okay." He felt so ashamed. Like he should be stronger than all of this. *Grow up,* he had told himself every night he cried himself to sleep. But years of pent-up pain—from his time at the orphanage and with the Grishams—delivered their load on him now. And in front of the last person he thought he'd ever tell any of this stuff.

Grimwarden remained quiet, letting the full weight of Jimmy's heart come to the surface. The heavy weeping eventually gave way to Jimmy taking deep breaths, trying his best to calm down.

"Why do I always race in?" He smeared away hot tears with his forearm, his will hardening right before Grimwarden's eyes. "I have nothing to lose. And, I suppose, I don't care if I die."

It was the first time Grimwarden had spoken in nearly five minutes. And when he did, his tone was low, nonthreatening, but not soft. "Your burden is heavy," he said. "You are weary of bearing it, but stricken with fear that, should you let it go, it will happen again. You will be betrayed. Love will be snatched from your grasp, and you will finally know beyond any hope that your life . . . means nothing."

With the revelation came another terrible wave of grief, one so strong, Jimmy thought he might collapse.

Grimwarden spoke again. "Such is the poison you have been fed for so long, Jimmy. A vile and perilous poison you have even fed to yourself. But no more." Grimwarden took Jimmy's shoulders and held his eyes with his own. "No more."

Jimmy fell forward, crying out in agony. Grimwarden wrapped two strong arms around the young lord and pulled him right into his chest. Jimmy's body shook and heaved. It was too much now, too much to hold back. Too much to cover up. He was tired of it. So very tired. And yet . . . it felt good to let go.

There in Grimwarden's arms, for the first time in as long as he could remember, he felt . . . *loved.* Though Grimwarden said not a word, his embrace spoke loudly. *You are valuable to me.* And with the knowledge came an even deeper revelation. The same thought, but from a new source. A stronger source. A more meaningful source.

You are valuable to me.

Jimmy felt the words rise up from somewhere deep within him, like a glowing ember in the bottom of an ash heap. And the words came again.

You are valuable to me.

The pain suddenly ebbed. It was not Grimwarden. And it was not even himself. Another voice was speaking. Jimmy stopped crying. He took a deep breath. And all at once he knew. *Ellos.*

"I am valuable to him," Jimmy said ever so softly. He could feel Grimwarden nodding above him.

"Yes," he replied. "And that's all he's been waiting to tell you."

Surprised he had any more tears to cry, Jimmy began again. But this time, they were not sorrowful. There was no regret. No shame.

He saw the faces of his adopted mother and father back in Ardfern flash in front of his mind's eye. To his utter astonishment, there was no animosity there. The absolute, unblemished love he felt in this moment—embraced in the natural by Grimwarden, adored in the unseen by Ellos—left no room for what he had been holding on to for so long: *bitterness.*

The words Jimmy had spoken in anger and hatred just moments before, words for everyone who had hurt him, now seemed so small in comparison with what Jimmy said next. "I . . . forgive . . . you."

Chains of the past were ripped away, shackles broken for good. What had held him captive before would no longer hold him again. And in its place there would be love, acceptance, value, and meaning. All at once, Jimmy had something to live for . . . something greater than himself. His heart swelled with power and hope . . . and freedom.

"Remember what I'm about to tell you," Grimwarden said. "He who lives for nothing costs the lives of many. But he who lives for something greater than himself preserves all those he loves."

Jimmy nodded. "Thank you, Grimwarden."

But he shook his head. "No, thank you. Because I know you love me. Today I counsel a warrior greater than myself, one whose legacy will preserve me, and those after us."

32

Attack on Vesper Crag

DAWN HAD come far too early for some, and not soon enough for others. For Tommy's part, he barely slept. He'd paced the length of his bedchamber too many times to count, mulling over the battle plans in his mind a hundred times, front to back, and then back again. Guardmaster Travin will lead the siege, taking the forward infantry and engines right to the walls of Vesper Crag. That would elicit a powerful response from the Spider King, no doubt releasing a swarm of Warspiders. Ethon Beleron and Kiri Lee, who took to raptor flight with great passion and skill, would lead the air strikes against the spiders. If the Spider King showed himself, Kiri Lee would rejoin the other lords, and together they would engage him and, hopefully, defeat him. If he didn't show, the other lords would board raptors and join Kiri Lee to infiltrate the Spider King's lair. The moment the lords had left, Grimwarden, Goldarrow, and a team of seasoned flet soldiers would rescue the slaves. Of course, so much of the plan still depended on the map. "Ellos"—Tommy whispered as he gave up on sleep and left his chamber—"let them bring it back."

Tommy eventually made his way down to the dinning area where every available kitchen hand was busy with the finishing touches for the soldiers' rations . . . thousands of them. It had to be at least three in the morning, and yet they still worked on. *No doubt Mumthers is behind this.* She always had to have things *just so.*

Tommy dodged behind a pair of women carrying a long pole between them laden with salted gessette haunches, then ducked into the kitchen. It must have been a hundred degrees, Tommy figured, more kettles and stove fires than he had ever seen in his life. And there was Mumthers, dishing out bowls of stew to . . . Jett and Kat?

"Ah! My good Tommy!" She took the fat of Tommy's cheek between her thumb and forefinger and gave it a good squeeze. Finally, the words he knew would come. "Come here, lad. You look peaked. Join the others. And have a bowl."

"Couldn't sleep?" Jett looked up from his stew, a trail dribbling down his chin.

"No," Tommy said.

"We couldn't, either," said Kat. The three shared a laugh, and Tommy dug in, grateful for something to get his mind off what he knew awaited.

Before long, Johnny stumbled into the kitchen, accidently knocking into a woman carrying a full set of pots. He apologized, then made his way into Mumthers's care. Within the hour, the rest of the Seven had joined them at the table. Despite the ordered chaos that threaded around them, the lords enjoyed one another's company as much as they enjoyed Mumthers's food. For the briefest of moments, they were back in Whitehall, sitting at the board, sharing in their newfound camaraderie. And Mumthers never let their bowls show the bottom, sure to make this meal their finest.

As the sun warmed the western sky, the war horn blast filled Nightwish and summoned the Elves to begin the long march out of the caverns. Like a sleeping giant now awakened, the entire might of the Elven army stepped in line. Where once they had burrowed like mice, now they stood like conquerors. In the lead were six of the Elf Lords of Berinfell accompanied by none other than Guardmaster Grimwarden, Elle Goldarrow, and Elder Alwynn. Kiri Lee would join them later. Each of them wore an array of battle dress: black tunics tucked into loose-fitting breeches, their torsos clad in hinged armor fashioned of hardened leather, heads adorned with the gold-winged helmets of Berinfell. On their feet they wore war boots, laced up past their calves. Majestic purple cloaks slung over the shoulders hid a variety of perilous weapons: rycheswords, siege axes, hammers, polearms, maces, daggers, and bows. Most carried a shield bound to the forearm or slung over the back. And boldly displayed on their leather breastplates, each of the lords bore their tribe's medallion. It would herald to the enemy that the Lords of Berinfell lived!

Behind them came the entire host of Sentinels and Dreadnaughts, followed by the flet soldiers: longbow archers, spearmen, and men at arms. More than eight centuries of living underground had stripped them of their cavalry, but the Elves had another card to play. Sometimes airborne and sometimes resting in specially designed carts, the scarlet raptors came forward as well.

Up into the morning light the line went, shedding the subterranean haunt like an old skin. The line continued well into the morning. Hundreds, and then thousands, and then tens of thousands spilled into the forest. A haze filled the air, stretching due east as the line marched toward one locale: Vesper Crag.

Unlike the enemy's attack eight hundred years before, the Elves had no need of surprise. In fact, their victory depended in part on the enemy extending himself beyond his walls.

The march eastward took three days. If the Spider King knew of their coming, he did not react. They met no challenge, not even a single Gwar.

"The Lightning Fields," Grimwarden noted with a pointed finger. The Elf Lords beside him looked out into the valley, remembering the scene from when they had first arrived in Allyra. Their long trek north to the Dark Veil had taken them right through here, right beneath the watchful gaze of Vesper Crag. The sky was eternally dark, casting the sun behind a dismal, overcast blanket. And from the heavy clouds came any number of lightning bolts, reaching from above and blasting into the barren landscape beneath. Rocks shattered, craters were gouged out, while lava flows meandered like silent killers, streaming down from the mountains above and then disappearing into unseen fissures.

"Think I'll opt for a summer home here," said Jimmy, smirking. But few smiles met his attempt at humor.

Every battle plan had a transition from paper to reality. And the Elf Lords had just experienced that transition.

"This is really happening, isn't it?" asked Autumn.

"It is," said Goldarrow. She turned to her. "Are you all right?"

She stood a little taller. "Indeed."

"Don't worry, Autumn. I've got you covered. Bring it on," said Johnny, hand on the pommel of his sword.

And bring it they did. Grimwarden looked to Tommy, and the leader of the Elf Lords lifted his fist, summoning a great beast to life. From where they stood, a virtual sea of Elves surged forward and wrapped around them, spreading out to the northern and southern flanks. Tommy spoke no word but thrust his fist forward, and Travin's forces charged across the Lightning Fields.

Speed was key to this phase, getting as many Elves across these dangerous plains as rapidly as possible. Blasts of lightning took six from the front lines alone and continued to strike with devastating power. Some Elves were merely stunned by nearby strikes. But they recovered quickly, filling in the gaps and surging forward, their eyes on one prize: the defeat of the Spider King.

The main fortress of Vesper Crag thrust upward out of a dark and gangly mountain, its side split open like an overripe fruit. Turrets and bastions, keeps and gatehouses grew out of this gash at odd angles. More dark architecture punctured the surface of the mountain's western face and southern flank as well. Surrounding it all and even the entire base of the mountain was an immense—and as Grimwarden described it—unconquerable wall.

Just beyond the northern section of wall, at the granite feet of the low jagged mountains, a wide red gash yawned open. Fresh molten lava vomited out from the crevasse, bathing rock and plain in blistering red. Lightning flashed there, too, blasting down from clouds burgeoning with ash. As the flet soldiers picked their way through the Lightning Fields and edged closer to the base of the mountain, Elven craftsmen busied themselves behind the line with the construction of the cannons and catapults. The cannons had been converted from shooting layadine —the substance which Manaelkin had all but hastily used up during the invasion of Nightwish—to shooting small exploding balls of iron. Still effective, but not nearly as deadly a weapon as layadine. The parts for the catapults had been freshly hewn from trees in the Thousand-League Forest based on plans the architects had drawn up long before. Tommy and the others watched with fascination as the engineers pieced them together with practiced hands and perfect accuracy. Boulders the size of a crouching man were piled up beside each of thirty catapults, while the casks of smaller black-powder-filled balls were stacked in crates beside the twenty cannons.

"I'm getting nervous about the map," Tommy said to Grimwarden as his eyes searched the progress before them, hoping he might see Regis or Nelly pop-up somewhere in the throng.

"It will come," Grimwarden said confidently.

Tommy eyed him. "Yeah, but what if it comes too late to be of any use?" He pointed to the war host they had assembled. "The attack's begun."

Grimwarden turned to Tommy. "Do you trust me?"

Tommy fumbled. Of course he did. But this wasn't some test in Whitehall. Those were lives down there. Real lives that Tommy held in his hands. And it seemed to him that, despite their sizable appearance, they were marching to their deaths. Seeing Vesper Crag, he very much doubted any of their plans would succeed. Even with the map.

"Do you trust me?"

"I do," Tommy said.

"Then let us proceed. And let us together trust that the map will come in time."

"Lord Felheart!" came a voice. A flet soldier charged up the hill. "M'lord," he said and bowed.

"Yes, flet soldier?" answered Tommy.

"I bear word from Guardmaster Travin. The enemy has loosed his Warspiders."

"You see?" said Grimwarden.

Tommy looked to Kat and grinned. The enemy would never see this one coming. Turning back to the flet soldier he said, "Very good." He said a silent prayer for Kiri Lee. Kat looked away. "Return to Travin and tell him the aerial assault will begin immediately. In fact, the raptors will likely fly over your head before you get to him!"

"Endurance and Victory." The flet soldier crossed his forearms, bowed, and was gone.

Tommy turned to the west. Fifty yards back, Ethon Beleron and Kiri Lee stared back. Tommy held up both tightly closed fists and then sprang them open, his fingers wide. The scarlet raptors climbed into the air together, hovering for a moment like a red flag before shrieking into the sky. Each one held large rocks or thick pieces of lumber in its talons. And each one bore an Elven archer. Tommy grinned, seeing the holsters stuffed with arrows.

"I know Goldarrow has already told you so," said Grimwarden. "But your idea to caulk each arrowhead with layadine was brilliant. It is the one way we can spread our sparse reserves."

Tommy remembered the battle at Dalhousie in Scotland. It was then that the idea had first struck him. He even had some layadine arrows in his own quiver.

Now overhead, the raptors swept east like a storm. Tommy spotted Kiri Lee and Ethon on the lead raptors. They waved as the birds of prey climbed. Tommy could hardly believe it: the Elven air force was led by the musician girl from Paris.

The raptors screeched again as they flew over the Lightning Fields and its violent and random bolts of electricity.

The birds dipped and swerved, trying to anticipate the next bolt by watching the red-glowing buildup of electricity in the clouds. But more than one raptor succumbed to a stray white bolt that leaped sideways, connecting with the bird and then continuing on its path to the ground. The result was horrifying.

As fast as they were, it seemed as if it took the raptors an eternity to make it over Vesper Crag.

33

Death from Above

KIRI LEE'S raptor circled over Vesper Crag, empowering her with a bird's-eye view of the enemy's stronghold. The giant bird was named Serion, and he had been as easy to ride as a well-trained horse. Still, she was nervous. But with each passing minute, she had eased her death grip on the raptor's feathers and soon felt sure enough of her abilities to free her bow from his back.

Unlike those on the ground, Kiri Lee was witnessing the full power of the Spider King's minions organizing far below. Like busy ants, Gwar swarmed the fortress, setting up defenses, and distributing weaponry. It would be but moments before the wrath of the enemy rained down upon those gathered in the Lightning Fields. *Ah, if only Kat could pick up my thoughts out here!* Kiri Lee lamented. *But the distance for now is too great.*

Just then, Kiri Lee noticed a large defense just out of sight of the ground flet that was hidden behind the castle's walls. It would make a perfect first target.

She urged her raptor into a steep dive. *Perhaps a little too steep,* Kiri Lee thought. She nearly lost her bow, but managed to keep both herself and her ride on target. The great bird dove toward the turret, but it was coming up very fast. The raptor shrieked, and the surprised Gwar looked up. They were about to be dashed on the fortress ramparts. A quick stab with her heel, and the raptor released his boulder. Kiri Lee dug her legs into the bird's neck. Serion spread his wings and stopped his descent, swooping in such a deep curve that Kiri Lee was sure her stomach had been relocated to her knees. She felt the blood rush from her head and did her best not to black out. She glanced behind her left heel, fifty feet below, as the boulder crashed into the catapult. Shrapnel from the structure and Gwar bodies exploded over the fortress, the turret rupturing with a sound that could be heard for miles.

Kiri Lee gave out a cheer before almost losing her balance, startling herself back into a death grip on her raptor. This would take some getting used to, and quick.

Tommy and the others watched as the raptors rained down terror from above. He thought they resembled little sparrows defending their nests against an invading crow, diving and recovering, each swoop down bringing added pain. But these were not mere songbirds pecking at the head of a nuisance. They carried hundreds of pounds of rock that when dropped buried deep into the siege engines of the enemy.

The entire Elven war host watched as each boulder careened into the sprawling fortress, and the Spider King's vast network of tower defenses was blown to pieces.

But it wasn't long before the retaliation began.

Massive crossbows rigged with bolts the size of small trees took aim at the raptors that buzzed overhead. The *slap* of bowstrings filled the space over the fortress, followed by the shrieks of Elves and raptors as they plunged to their deaths on the side of the Crag. The precise aim with which the enemy took on the flying targets was staggering, as one by one the raptors started to vanish from the sky.

Tommy noticed that the number of giant birds had thinned somewhat, but he lost focus when the first boulder came hurtling at the flet soldiers gathered at Vesper Crag's base. At first Tommy thought some wounded raptor had inadvertently released his projectile on the Elves. But the stone was arching through the air, fired from one of the remaining catapults behind the enemy line. It crashed into the right flank, crushing five flet soldiers beneath it. Travin could do nothing but keep his soldiers at their posts, firing cannons and catapults at the walls and those who stood atop them.

More and more boulders were flung over the wall by the Spider King's forces, suspended in midair for the briefest of moments before slamming down into the flet soldiers. Some of the stones landed in the lava flows, producing explosive spatters of molten rock that showered the army in a lethal wash of red and orange. Flet soldiers screamed out in terror as the hot lava ate through their armor. They tried to bat it away, brushing it from their chain mail, but it was no use. The lava clung to them like cement, burning deep into their flesh.

"We've got to make them stop!" Kat screamed, looking away.

"We will, Kat," Tommy said, looking to the front lines. "Our soldiers are gaining some ground on the walls! Look!"

The moment any space cleared on the high parapets, Travin signaled and tall ladders were thrown up. The Elves, who could climb a tree in seconds, raced up the ladders in no time. But the defenses were swift to respond. Warspiders.

The Warspiders crept out of unseen ports in the sides of the mountain. They poured out and clambered up the walls and over, devastating the Elves on the ladders. Thick strands of web sailed out over the Elves at the foot of the walls as well, snaring them long enough for other spiders to slay them.

Far above the battle, Kiri Lee saw a small flash of yellow light from the command hill where the other lords and Grimwarden were directing the battle plans. She turned and motioned to Ethon on the nearest raptor. The two leaders split and flew at the walls, circling in from opposite directions. Not nearly as skilled with a bow as Tommy, Kiri Lee hoped she wouldn't have to be. She nocked a layadine arrow and used her legs to guide the raptor in low. She spotted a massive Warspider hanging its bulbous abdomen over the wall and spraying gobs of thick webbing on the Elves below. Kiri Lee took aim and loosed her arrow. The shaft went off-center but still plunged deep into the spider's thick hide. In moments, the Warspider screeched and shuddered.

The other Elven archers released their first volleys as well, crippling the first wave of spiders. The problem became immediately apparent: it was only the Spider King's first wave of Warspiders. Waves two and three flooded out of the mountain and clambered over the living and the dead. Kiri Lee, Ethon, and the other archers made run after run until their layadine arrows were spent. But still the Warspiders came on. It seemed Travin's assault team might never get lasting purchase atop the walls.

Kiri Lee looked to Ethon and gave a different signal. Raptor to raptor the signal made its rounds. Each of the airborne flet soldiers produced a small flint stone kit, able to produce a spark with one hand. A few flicks of the tool set one end of a long powder-laden wick aflame, the small orange tongue of fire whipping violently in the wind. Each flet soldier released the wick from a clasp in their belts, the cord now dangling free far below them. The fuse now burned upward toward the oblong tube of metal harnessed on the side of the raptor: a bomb.

As fuses burned low, the birds raced on, closing the gap between them and the wall with incredible speed. Kiri Lee worried the bombs might bounce off the wall and roll back into the advancing army or explode prematurely while still held by the birds. Either way, the results would be catastrophic; she knew here, as in her music, timing was everything.

The wall was coming up quickly now. Too quickly. She glanced down to her right; on hers the wick was burning as planned, but perhaps too slow. She had given the order too late. The bird needed to slow down. But when she looked to the wick on her left, her stomach knotted. She tried to speak, but her throat closed up. Finally, "LET GO!"

Three of the birds skimmed across the top of the army, not thirty feet above. The men cheered as the two bombs were lit, all eyes on Kiri Lee as she waited to give the order. The gap between them closed, and soon the birds angled up against the base of the mountain.

But it was Tommy who first noticed something didn't seem right. Kiri Lee was waving frantically to the bird on her left.

"Oh no," he heard Jimmy say.

Tommy looked to him, then back to the three birds in flight.

Something was definitely—

A bright flash followed by a fiery explosion lit up the dim sky like the Fourth of July. Tommy winced, half at the eye-shattering light, half in stupefied horror. The raptor to the left was gone. Obliterated. The shockwave of the explosion shot the two remaining raptors sideways, dropping them out of the air. And with them sank the second bomb, now free from the raptor's talons.

Kiri Lee's bird flapped incessantly, trying in vain to recover the freedom of flight. Broken wings and blind eyes made it impossible. Kiri Lee was still holding on, as far as Tommy could tell, but when the bird disappeared behind the enemy wall, he feared the worst. The second raptor managed a few more flaps before succumbing to a bolt through the chest, its rider knocked off and crashing into the fortress below.

It was the next bomb that captured everyone's attention next. It landed not at the base of the wall as intended, but right in the ramparts, cradled between the crenulated wall and the wooden railing. The Elf Lords watched as dozens of Gwar attempted to dislodge the object or tried to snuff the wick out. But it was too late.

The explosion was far greater than the first. A muffled *wumph!* came just before a deafening *boom!* that blew the top half of the wall sky high. Rock, wood, and fire exploded from the fortress, raining down on those below. Gwar were flung through the air as if they were rag dolls, flipping lifelessly to a crude end, dashed on the mountainside.

"We have to get in there!" Tommy took a few steps forward. Grimwarden caught his arm.

"No you don't," said Grimwarden, his hand over his eyes.

"But Kiri Lee!" Jett exclaimed.

What Grimwarden said next was spoken as a warrior. "*If* she is still alive, our men will find her." He looked to Jett. "And *you* can heal her. But right now, we wait."

"WAIT?!" Tommy was nearly jumping out of his skin. "Our men are dying out there, Kiri Lee is trapped on the inside, and you want us to wait?"

"Tommy, such emotions are to be expected. But if they rule you, they will destroy you. Whatever planning we have done will be lost, and the enemy has the advantage."

"Planning? So far, our plans have gotten people killed! How bad do things have to get before you'll let us go wreak some havoc?"

Tommy had not seen enough of war to know just how much worse things could get. The lord's attention was drawn back to Vesper Crag as the raptors began shrieking. Rising from behind the mountain came a dark cloud, accompanied by a low drone.

The Spider King stood on the Black Balcony, commanding his forces through his generals, his generals through their runners. So confident was he in his own plan that a menacing red light flashed behind him, ensuring that his enemies knew where he was and that he was in command of all that transpired. Most everything was going according to plan, save for the infernal birds, and he tired of such uncertainties. They could be easily crushed, but it meant releasing his newest creation prematurely. No matter. Winning was winning, even if it wasn't as methodically as he desired.

Without ever saying a word, the Spider King lifted two fingers on his right hand. He felt ten pairs of eyes follow the command, and immediately orders were barked behind him. The communication would be swift and efficient. It always was. Those who couldn't or wouldn't comply with his procedures were simply executed. It made for a tight chain of command.

When the air began to stir above and behind him, his heart quickened. He longed to see his new inventions at work. *What havoc they will wreak,* he thought.

"What—what is that?" Autumn asked, squinting.

"I . . . I cannot be certain," Grimwarden whispered. "If it is of the

Spider King's design, we can only be sure that it is meant for our demise."

"Jimmy?" Kat turned to him, tugging on his elbow. "What is it?"

Jimmy wasn't staring. In fact, his eyes were shut tight. "It's, it's a swarm."

"Of what?" Tommy demanded.

"Warspiders with wings," Jimmy said, his words shaking with his own disbelief. "No . . . not spiders. Huge eyes, long bodies, claws—they're dragonflies! Call the raptors back. They're about to be shredded!"

Grimwarden jostled Tommy, and the two of them raced across the hill trying to signal the raptor riders, but they were too late.

Ridden by Gwar soldiers, these Warflies, as the Spider King dubbed them, darted high above Vesper Crag and then dove swiftly at their outnumbered prey.

As big as the raptors that the flet soldiers rode, the Warflies engaged them in midair, their distinct advantage being they could hover when the raptors could only move forward. The Warflies swooped, dipped, and ducked around the free-flying birds of prey, the Gwar on top swinging long-handled battleaxes and swords especially made for this form of combat. The birds suffered the most, losing legs, wings, dozens knocked senseless. Raptors were tumbling from the sky. Some flet soldiers managed a lucky blow on a Gwar, but in all, the Warflies were simply more maneuverable than the raptors.

But when one heedless Gwar steered his ride into the path of an oncoming bird, the result was staggering. The raptor ripped into the insect flesh with its talons, squeezing the life out of the creature. At the same time, its beak went to work on the two Gwar clinging to the bug's back; a few quick pecks and the warriors were headless, one also wrested of his arm. And with a massive beat of its wings, the bird thrust the carcasses away and dove to regain its speed.

Tommy and the others let up a whoop, rejoicing over the kill. But it was paled by far many more losses. Too many. Grimwarden could sense the group's mounting frustration. It was not uncommon to see in over-eager young warriors; he hoped they would hold to his counsel. It was, after all, out of centuries of doing battle. He took a deep breath, watching the six of them out of the corner of his eye. It was one thing to accept counsel in planning, but quite another in the midst of battle where passions ran high. *Hold.*

Kat looked over at him. He'd forgotten she was a thought-reader. But a simple smile and a slight bow of her head put him at ease.

Thank you, he said.

"No, . . . *thank you, Grimwarden. Sir,"* she added out of respect. She smiled at seeing the look of surprise on his face.

At the base of the fortress's walls, more and more ladders went up. Flet soldiers made ready their grappling hooks as well, focusing on the gaping hole in the middle of the wall. The iron hooks sailed through the air, striking true numerous times. The flet soldiers made quick work of scaling the wall, and those archers in the turrets did their best to cover the advance from above. Flet soldiers began pouring over the wall.

The lords thrilled to see such progress being made. And it was only increased as the catapults and cannons delivered their first volley. A round of more than forty projectiles crossed the Lightning Fields and slammed into the upper fortress. More than one tower was demolished, and Tommy hoped it was not one with flet soldiers atop.

Upon seeing the catapults, the Gwar on the Warflies regrouped and changed their point of attack from the raptors to the projectile weapons. The ground trembled as the deafening hum of the dragonflies whizzed overhead. More than one cannon managed a direct hit, but the sheer mass of overgrown dragonflies was simply too much to manage. But where the raptors had a great deal of destructive power in their talons and beaks, the Warflies had only maneuverability, relying on their riders to do the dirty work.

Gwar slipped off their mounts and went to work on the heavily defended catapults and cannons. An axe blow to the cannon barrel or a slicing of the catapult tension line rendered the weapon useless. Still the cannons blasted away, trying to pick the Warflies off at point-blank range. The air filled with a haze of smoke and the smell of sulfur.

But as much progress as the Elves made, the enemy always had an answer.

Tommy watched the hole in the wall and other elevations teaming with Elves, hundreds of lines with flet soldiers ascending to the ramparts engaging with the enemy. And from where Tommy stood, they were winning. Even though the raptors had been nearly destroyed by the Warflies, they had done their job thinning out the Warspiders and breeching the wall. For a fleeting moment, Tommy dared to hope the Elves might overpower the Spider King's forces early. But a word from Jimmy changed everything.

"Spiders," he said.

"What?" asked Tommy. "We know about the Warspiders."

"Not these," said Jimmy. "Guardmaster Grimwarden, remember the spiders that hit us in the trees?"

Grimwarden became alarmed. "You mean the small ones—they nearly overwhelmed us."

"The Spider King is about t' unleash a great, massive lot a' them."

"How many?" Grimwarden demanded.

"I dunno," Jimmy replied. "But it looks like millions."

Less than a minute later, Tommy yelled, "Look!" A black mass appeared and approached the Elves on the ramparts, like a black fog creeping, it seemed. Tommy had heard Jimmy's warning. His mind told him what he must be seeing, but he still couldn't believe it. Like some malignant thing it spread toward the Elves . . . and engulfed them.

The Phantom Army

EERIE PURPLE and bright white lightning flashed, striking the foothills of Vesper Crag and flickering in the Guardmaster's eyes. "How deep are the bowels of Vesper Crag that he can breed such a teeming, murderous brood? Our front lines are failing."

"Now?" Tommy asked, speaking over the thunder.

"Nay, lord," said the Guardmaster. "I do not want to reveal our full strength too quickly. You will go in, only if we cannot stem this onslaught any other way."

Tommy rushed over to the other lords. "Get ready!" he commanded.

"No joke," said Jett, shifting his weight from one foot to the other rapidly. "He's ready to send us in?" He felt like his coach was keeping him on the sidelines when he knew he could win the game with Jett.

"Trust Grimwarden," Kat's thoughts spoke into his mind. *"No one knows battle tactics like he does. No one."*

I know, Jett thought back. *I know in my head, but my gut's just wrenching.*

"I should run out there," argued Johnny, ". . . lay down a suppressing wall of fire . . . like Grimwarden showed me back at Whitehall. Then have Autumn race through them with her axes."

"Well, that sounds right good," said Jimmy. "And I can cover yu, let yu know what they're doin' 'fore they do it . . . so long as I see it in me head."

"Okay, okay," said Tommy, holding out both arms and pressing his hands downward. "Just wait here for now." He jogged back to Grimwarden, who was deep in conversation with a field commander.

"Won't work, Vanagin," he was saying. "They're bludgeoning us

317

with a force of sheer numbers. We've got to divide that mass of spiders!"

"Sir, we've tried three times," said Vanagin. "Since we have no more layadine powder, they crawl over us like we were no more than a mild hill!"

"You must be a hill with teeth!" growled Grimwarden. "Take a brigade of spearmen. Do not charge the center. Aim for their left third. Have twin squads of axemen follow you and chop their legs out from under them!"

"Yes, sir!" said Vanagin. He raced to the edge of the hill, leaped upon his black rangesteed, and was gone.

"Do you think it will work?" asked Tommy.

"It had better," muttered Grimwarden. "Are the lords prepared?"

"Yes."

"Good, good," said the Elven military leader. "Now we watch . . . and pray."

The mass of spiders had slowed, moving in a slow arc mirroring the shape of the outer walls of the Spider King's fortress. But they had swept away hundreds of flet soldiers. And even as their speed slowed, they engaged a large force of Elves led by a pair of seasoned Dreadnaughts. Their Vexbane attack seemingly frustrated the first rank of spiders. Warspiders' jaws snapped at air where once an Elf had stood as the Dreadnaughts leaped from spider to spider. With each landing, they drove a razor-sharp longsword between the Warspider's torso and braincase, killing the creature instantly. But like a black flood, the Warspiders drove on. Spiders crawled over spiders crawling over spiders. Soon there was no place for the Dreadnaughts to safely land. More and more spiders piled on, and the Elves began to go under.

"No!" barked Grimwarden. "Not that way."

Tommy looked at his commander. "You want to go out there, too, don't you?"

Grimwarden turned. Fire burned in his eyes. His clenched jaws flared. "With every fiber of my being," he said. "Far easier is it to lay one's own life on the line . . . than to command others to do so."

Tommy thought about how terrible a responsibility that would be. Then it hit him: *I'm the leader of the lords. I share that responsibility now.*

"Look, there goes Vanagin's team!"

"Come on!" Grimwarden shouted. "Cut them in half!"

At first it seemed the Elves would do exactly that. Vanagin led with spearmen, just as Grimwarden suggested. Their spears parallel to the ground, they charged at the Warspiders, daring them to joust. The mass of clicking, gnashing creatures swerved toward the Elves, inexplicably moving as one sentient organism like a flock of birds. At the last moment, the Elves stopped hard and drove the dull ends of their spears into the ground. As the spiders drew within a few yards, the Elves raised sharp ends of their spears impaling the spiders. Supporting flet soldiers joined the spearmen skewering more spiders. But some spiders managed to climb over the dead and leaped at the spearmen. Axe-wielding soldiers—while not trained as extensively in Vexbane as the Sentinels and Dreadnaughts—possessed their own style of acrobatic combat techniques and vaulted to meet the spiders in the air, cleaving several limbs with each swing. The axemen landed as sure-footed as cats and swiftly swiped at the next in line.

But the Warspiders were not the mindless arachnids one might daunt with a footstep and crush beneath a heel. They recognized their original rush was no longer effective. Oncoming Warspiders stopped their reckless charge and engaged the Elves while the spiders behind them turned and aimed their spinnerets skyward, spraying at first a fine mist of webbing over the throng of Elves. The mist turned to threads, and threads to streams. Many of the Elves found themselves immobilized. Chopping furiously at the webs with sword and axe, the Elves were easy prey for the next rank of spiders.

Vanagin's team had been overrun.

Grimwarden watched as the spiders united and flowed toward Vesper Crag's walls where Elves and Gwar battled among the siege engines and catapults. He crossed his arms and closed his eyes. Little help could be counted on from the dwindling number of raptors who streaked in and out of the heavy mantle of clouds while trying to elude the Warflies. *We needed that map!* Frustrated, Grimwarden quickly considered various strategies.

"Sir?" Tommy looked to Grimwarden. "Sir, do we go in now?"

Grimwarden did not answer and he did not look at Tommy. Instead, the Guardmaster opened his eyes and drew his rychesword and ran his fingers over the Words of Ellos inscribed on the blade. It helped him think . . . and pray. *I cannot let this continue,* Grimwarden continued his internal debate, *but to send the lords in so soon? The Spider King knows what the Seven are capable of. His Drefids will be lurking . . . and Wisps, too. Ellos, grant me wisdom. I do not want to fail . . . again.* Grimwarden's face was unbelievably taut. "We can delay no longer," Grimwarden muttered. "You must lead your te—"

"LOOK, LOOK!" Jett ran over, smacked Tommy on his shoulder, and nearly knocked him off the hill. "Something's happening to the Warspiders." Johnny, Autumn, and the others watched, too.

The black mass of spiders had been coursing toward the Elven back lines at the walls of Vesper Crag. Just as the flet soldiers were about to find themselves caught between a smothering blanket of spiders and the teeth of the Spider King's defenses, something started happening to the Warspiders. It looked as if a great chasm had opened up in front of their advance, and the spiders were pouring in.

"Dear Ellos!" Grimwarden exulted. "Has the Almighty opened the jaws of Allyra to swallow the enemy?"

"I . . . I don't think so," Tommy muttered, and he swayed where he stood.

"Tommy?" Kat whispered. She was at his side in a heartbeat. "Tommy, what's wrong?"

Tommy stared across the field of battle, the sensation disorienting and awkward at first. He felt as if his eyes had detached from his head and flew of their own accord through the carnage, through the battle, and over the flank of the spider throng. Suddenly he could see as if he were standing next to them. "The spiders aren't falling into anything! There's no sinkhole opening up or anything like that."

"What then?" asked Grimwarden, straining to see.

"I . . . I'm not sure," Tommy replied. "It looks like they're tripping all over each other, running like mad things, and then suddenly they stumble—collapse—as if, as if someone is cutting their legs out from under them—like Vanagin's team was trying to do!"

"Travin, you sly fox!" Grimwarden growled. "You've set a trap for them."

"But I don't see anyone," said Tommy. "Travin's teams are still busy with the Gwar . . . and a fistful of Drefids. What's going on? Who's doing th—I can't—NO WAY!"

"Tommy, if yu don't quit that," Jimmy growled. "What are you seeing? My foresight shows only more and more spiders going down."

"It's the Gnomes!"

"AHA! Really?" Autumn laughed with joy. "Really? Do you see Migmar?"

"No, that's just it," said Tommy. "I don't really see them."

"Uh, explain that," said Jett.

"Remember?" asked Tommy excitedly. "Remember when Kiri Lee first brought Migmar down out of that tree? He was covered in some kind of camouflage. It made him blend in with everything around him. But I saw a Gnome appear"—his voice grew low—"when a spider killed him, I could see him. I see more Gnomes now."

"Whatever it is that makes them invisible," Kat said, "they must control it mentally."

"There must be hundreds of Gnomes out there," said Johnny. "Even I can see they are doing a number on those spiders."

Tommy watched as wave after wave of Warspiders collapsed and tumbled upon each other. Hundreds of Gnomes had to be scurrying beneath the spiders, hacking away at their legs. Tommy laughed. He remembered all too well the ingenious contraptions and devices the Gnomes had created. Who knew what battle gadgets they had?

But even as he surveyed the battle, he realized that the Gnomes must be running about on top of the spiders as well. Here and there, a Warspider would rear up and claw at its eyes. And then its eyes would burst, one by one, spraying a fine yellow mist into the air.

"Guys," said Tommy, "I wish you could see this. It's a good thing we didn't try to fight the Gnomes. They are fierce little guys."

"Ellos has answered our prayers," said Kat, surprising herself. "I mean, the Earth didn't swallow up the Warspiders, but—"

"The Gnomes did," said Johnny.

From the north, a piercing howl rose above the clamor.

Jett bounded up the hill toward Grimwarden. "You guys hear that?"

"Near froze my blood," said Jimmy. "Please tell me the Spider King doesn' have some kind of mutated giant. . . ." His voice trailed off for a moment. "Oh no."

"What?" asked Autumn. They all stared at Jimmy.

He didn't answer, but Tommy did. "It's Bear! It's Bear! Look!"

"Wha—really? I don't see him," said Jett.

"He just ran behind those trees—no, wait!"

Then, though not as clearly as Tommy, they all saw Bear. He was running circles around a patch of black trees. But Tommy saw something the rest could not. "The trees have eyes!" he yelled. "They're Cragons!"

Bear howled again and ran south across the battlefield. The lords watched as the Cragons suddenly fell over in a heap.

"Did Bear do that?" asked Jett.

"I don't think . . . I don't really know," said Tommy.

"I never cared too much for that grand big wolf," said Jimmy. "But if he can take down Cragons five at a time—"

"The Gnomes are helping with the Warspiders," said Johnny. "And Bear comes back to do a number on some Cragons . . . it's almost too good to be true."

Autumn shook her head. "Guardmaster Grimwarden, sir, have you ever seen anything like it?"

"Ellos answer prayers?" he clarified. "Yes, I have seen him answer prayers . . . many times, and often in the strangest ways . . . ways both unlooked for and impossible to predict. But, no, I have never seen anything like this before. The Elves and Gnomes have not fought side by side in thousands of years . . . since the First Days, when Allyra was young, and the First Lords claimed their birthright."

"Passed much time has," said a high voice behind them. "Generations of time, in my reckoning, misused by both races, it has." And slowly Migmar melted into existence beside Grimwarden. He bowed to the Guardmaster and dropped a quick knee in the direction of the lords. "If not for wayward rascals"—he thumbed toward the lords— "separation, much longer, I presume."

Migmar turned to Tommy. "Survived you the Terradym Fortress. Very good. When all is done, you tell Migmar all your stories." The Gnome sovereign took out a sprig of dragonroot, chomped off a bite, and passed gas like a bass saxophone.

A look ricocheted between the lords. "Uh, Grimwarden," said Tommy. "Meet Migmar, Barrister King of the Gnomes."

Migmar nodded to Grimwarden. "Pleased am I to meet you at last."

Grimwarden crossed his wrists and bowed. "Sovereign of Gnomes, you and your people are a blessing beyond estimation."

Tommy looked closely, saw tears in the Guardmaster's eyes. *Wow,* he thought. *He's getting emotional.*

Kat's thought popped into his mind. *"I don't think that's why his eyes are watering."*

"Be a bigger blessing yet, Guardmaster," said Migmar. "My army, two-thousand strong, you command," he said. "You see only some advantages, we have. Devices, we have. Observe perhaps the Keeper and the Cragons?"

"Keeper?" echoed Tommy. "You mean Bear? The big wolf? Migmar, you brought him here?"

"Taught him new tricks, we Gnomes have, ha!" Migmar chomped another bite of Dragon root. "Made him friendly, you did."

"Migmar," said Tommy. "What else can your soldiers do?"

"Scale walls and diminish defenses, if you wish. Harder there, Gwar have keen sight. See us plainly, they can't, but see our movements, they do. The Drefids, chief trouble for us. Their black eyes see everything, even shadow world."

"We will need your aid behind the walls," said Grimwarden. "But not yet. We wait for more aid . . . a map from our kinsmen venturing far from here. From this map we will know the fortress's weakest points.

From it we will learn how to enter with least resistance. We seek to free the slaves in the bowels of Vesper Crag . . . and empty its throne of the Spider King once and for all."

"Little we know of Spider King. If foolish, you say, to infiltrate fortress without more guidance, we wait. Then what for Migmar and his Gnomes?"

"Your army has rescued our forces fighting at the wall," said Grimwarden. "You have slowed the mass of Warspiders and kept them from assailing our siege force from behind. If I may command that which is yours by right, then I ask that you continue to protect our flank from the Warspiders, Cragons, . . . and whatever else may come."

"As you ask." Migmar bowed, and as he did so there came a sound like the quack of a duck.

Jimmy started to laugh, turned away, and quickly walked in the other direction. Kat held her breath.

"Before Migmar returns to front lines with my people, something I must know," said Migmar, and even as he spoke, his boots and legs blurred, melding with the grassy hill and stone beneath. "Master Grimwarden, by your side, fight, we will. Your enemy, our enemy. But mark time, we cannot, with lives of our soldiers . . . nor, reckoning, can you. Laid siege, you have, upon the Spider King, have you not? Conquer, you intend to. Do not your kindred return with map? What then?"

"By Ellos's hand, we will conquer," said Grimwarden. "With or without the map. When the time comes, I will release the doom of the Spider King, his curse. I will unleash the Seven Lords of Berinfell, the finders of the Keystone and bearers of the Rainsong, to do what they may."

Migmar looked quizzically at the six lords gathered there, seemingly weighing them with his eyes. Tommy wondered what he was thinking. Did Migmar see the awkward teen warriors who were so easily drugged and captured by the Gnomes? Or did he see the true Lords of Berinfell who passed all the trials and tests of the Terradym fortress? Tommy almost asked Kat to relay the Gnome's thoughts. *But then,* Tommy thought, *I might not want to know.*

Migmar bowed. "As you say, Master Grimwarden." By now, he was just a face and a head sitting atop a wavering mirage of a body. Seconds later, Migmar had vanished altogether. "Go now Migmar," came his disembodied voice, "and spiders cut to pieces! Oh! But hate, I do, smell when abdomens burst!"

"It can't be much worse—," Johnny started to say, but in a flash Autumn covered his mouth with her hand.

"Migmar?" Tommy called. "Migmar?" But the Gnome was gone.

"Those little people are certainly a force to be reckoned with," said Jett. "Lights out."

"Actually," the Guardmaster replied wryly. "Actually, I was thinking of those who face just Migmar. Bah, it is good to breathe clean air again."

Kat, Jett, Johnny, and Autumn laughed . . . but not Tommy. He shared Migmar's concerns: Do not your kindred return with map? What then?

Jimmy hadn't laughed, either. *How long had it been since Kiri Lee fell behind enemy lines? Is she okay?* Of all the futures he wished he could see, it was hers. But he could not; his powers were not maturing as fast as the other lords'. So Jimmy decided to try something else. *Dear Ellos . . .*

Ashfall

A HARSH red light shone forth from the highest tower of Vesper Crag, and a dark figure stood out upon its balcony. All the lords and Grimwarden could see was that the figure raised his arms high, parting the blazing red light, creating shadowy phantoms in its otherwise unbroken streams.

But Tommy could see farther. Once more his vision crossed the vast battlefield, passed over the hissing mad Warspiders and the Gnomes who harassed them. Above the heads of the Elven flet soldiers and their catapults and siege engines. Up and over the main walls of Vesper Crag and the Gwar defending it. Climbing the high passes and twisting trails up the jagged mountain to the high tower itself. And there, Tommy beheld him.

Tall and broad, muscular but less pure bulk than the average Gwar, the Spider King lowered his arms and smiled. The canine teeth of his lower jaw were stark white and protruded in a hideous grin. But it was the Spider King's eyes that chilled the marrow in Tommy's bones.

Tommy had come face-to-face with many Gwar. He'd looked into their eyes and held his ground. But these eyes, these terrible eyes, were different. The shape was half-moon, but they had an odd slant, a kind of unnerving clever tilt. The vertical sickle-shaped pupils looked like smears of blood on his black irises . . . reminding Tommy of the hourglass of the black widow. And somehow, though perfectly impossible from that great distance, Tommy felt like the Spider King was looking directly at him.

Tommy shivered. Then he ducked.

An explosion rocked Vesper Crag. For a moment, all fighting stopped. A mile north of the battlefield, a bloody red crack in the ground vomited fiery destruction into the sky. Blast after blast shook the ground. Bright yellow and orange flames shot upward and, in slow motion, arced toward the battlefield. The first flaming chunks of debris knocked the Elves, Gwar, Drefids, and Warpiders out of their trances. One blazing piece slammed into the forward wall of Vesper Crag, exploding into dozens of smaller hunks. The wall sustained no damage, but Elves below could not move fast enough. Crushed, crippled, or burned, hundreds fell.

"Did you see that?" Jett exclaimed.

"What are those walls made of?" asked Johnny.

"Oh no," said Autumn. "Travin . . . no."

"Grimwarden! Sir!" yelled Jimmy urgently. He yanked at his commander's elbow. "Sir, we've got to do something. The Gnomes, the ashfall, Travin, and his men . . . I've seen it . . . they have to—"

"Have to what?" Grimwarden said sadly. "Leave the field of battle? We cannot. Travin will not. He will position his troops as best he can to keep them safe, but he must maintain pressure on the enemy. All our plans depend on it, and maybe Kiri Lee's life depends on it."

More thunderous explosions. A great cloud, shot through with bursts of fire, rose up from the now-gaping fiery mouth of the volcano. As the cloud ascended, it was absorbed into the stormy mantle that already hung there.

"But, Grimwarden, sir!" Jimmy persisted. "We've at least got to warn the Gnomes!"

"Warn them of what?" he asked. "They know about the volcano by now."

"Listen to him," Goldarrow whispered to her commander, but not loud enough that anyone else might hear.

"No, not that," said Jimmy. "I mean, it is that, but . . . well, just listen."

Jimmy explained what he'd seen in his vision. The other lords gasped. Grimwarden looked up at the volcanic cloud spreading above them. Jagged roots of lightning crawled across the sky.

"We've got to do something!" Kat cried out. "They'll be slaughtered."

"I'll go," said Autumn. "I'm the only one who can. I'll warn them. I'll get in and out in a minute."

"How will you warn them?" asked Goldarrow. "You cannot see them."

That silenced all discussion for a moment, but then Grimwarden said, "Our own soldiers knew what they were getting into. But the Gnomes came blindly to take up our cause. My heart is torn, Autumn. If you should not return—"

"I will," she argued. "I'm not the reckless little kid who got skewered in Scotland. I have twice the speed now. I have my axes. And I have Ellos!"

That was when Grimwarden did something no one expected. He leaned over and kissed Autumn on the top of her head. "Go," he said, "with my blessing."

"No!" Johnny protested. "Let me go with her! I—"

"You could never keep up," Grimwarden replied.

"But I can use my fire to—"

"Yes, you will use your fire, but not for this. To do so now would announce 'Here we are!' to the Spider King and every enemy on the battlefield."

They fell silent. Autumn drew her axes. She was a momentary blur, and she was gone.

Johnny felt as if his heart had torn free of his chest and gone with her.

As fast as the landscape went by Autumn, she saw it all, every detail. It was not like watching a movie but like watching a slideshow. First just rocky terrain. Then carnage: wrecked catapults and siege towers, broken bodies, fallen warriors. Finally she flashed up behind the teeming Warspiders, still locked in a struggle against thousands of foes they could not see.

Goldarrow's words came back to her. *How will you warn them? You cannot see them.* She had no plan, but she acted. Her eyes darting, scrutinizing the slides of vision, and analyzing every possible threat.

She sprinted around the Warspiders, between them, even over them. Her movements were not smooth, not graceful, but they were fast. And while she ran she yelled out her warning to the Gnomes.

Finding a clear patch of ground, Autumn stopped to breathe. Seconds later, the Warspiders found her. From all directions they came, but the moment they were upon their prey, their prey was gone. Not knowing if the Gnomes had heard her above the din of battle, Autumn continued yelling her warning.

Barely a minute gone, she'd made a lightning-quick circuit of the undulating mass of spiders. Halfway through her second revolution, she tripped. Even as she tumbled beneath a huge Warspider, she could not imagine what she'd tripped over. She hadn't seen anything.

A Gnome.

The Warspider backed up. Its massive fangs hung in the air above her. But Autumn yelled out, "Gnome, are you okay?!"

"No thanks to you!" came a disgruntled voice from nowhere. "You Elfkind? Ah, a second, please."

Autumn didn't have a second. The spider was upon her, the fangs crashing down.

And then there were no fangs. The Warspider shrieked, its fangs sheered off to bleeding stumps, and reared back to crush Autumn. But Autumn was not helpless. She sped out from beneath the spider. As it collapsed to the ground, Autumn's axes moved with swift and terrible speed. When she finished, there wasn't much left.

"On your bad side, surely I will not get, Elf," said the Gnome.

Breathing heavily, Autumn stood over the dead creature, now a bloody pulp. She wiped her face. That's when she felt it: a light sensation on her nose. Then on her cheek. She saw the flakes, falling like snow. "Gnome!" she yelled. "Tell your people my warning!"

"What warning, Elf?"

Autumn told him.

"Oh, dear," he replied, just as another Warspider advanced on their position.

"I've got to run!" cried Autumn. "Warn your people!"

"I will!" promised the Gnome.

A second silence fell over the battlefield. This one not spurred on by the shocking explosion, but rather by an eerie muffling of all sound. The ash had begun to fall. Tommy held out his hand and watched the gray flakes collect on his palm.

"Come on, Autumn," muttered Johnny. "Get out of there."

"She'll make it," said Kat, patting him on the shoulder.

"But what about Kiri Lee?" asked Jimmy.

"The volcano likely has bought her time," said Goldarrow.

"If she lives," said Jett. He still felt they should have gone in after her the moment she went down behind the wall. Forget the map. Forget the walls. Kiri Lee was one of their own.

"You lords are made of tougher stuff than that," said Grimwarden. "You may all meet your fate this day, but I very much doubt it will be from a fall. If anyone could survive plummeting from a height, it's Kiri Lee."

"Yeah," said Tommy, trying to sound cheerful. "I bet she floated down like a leaf."

"What was that?" asked Kat.

"Volcano's still rumbling," muttered Jett.

"No, I heard a kind of whistle," she said. "A warbly kind of whistle."

Jett shrugged.

The volcano continued to growl, though now its sound was dampened by the falling ash. Molten rock bubbled and gurgled, spilling over its edges and rolling across the ground in fiery globs. But more than the lava now, massive towering pillars of smoke and ash boiled into the sky. Whatever air current prevailed above, it seemed to be carrying all the ash over the battlefield. For now, it came down harder.

The Elves watched from their promontory. But Tommy was the only one who could see what the ash was doing. Of course, Jimmy had seen it, too, just minutes before it happened. Falling like a heavy snowstorm, the ash coated the battlefield in a blanket of gray. Tommy watched the Warspiders, wondering if the Gnomes had gotten the warning.

Clearly, some had not.

The ash began to adhere to the Gnomes revealing them, especially the ones out in the open or leaping from spider to spider. Before the Gnomes could drive the beasts mad, their hacking and stabbing coming from unseen hands. But now the battlefield was filled with little gray shadow-beings. Warspiders began to snap the Gnomes out of the air. Using their forelegs as spears, they skewered the miniature people as they fled. It soon became chaos. No longer invisible, the Gnomes raced in and out of spider legs beneath the creatures, seeking some path to safety. But, as far as Tommy could tell, very few were finding their way out of the death trap.

"The Gnomes are getting killed out there!" Tommy exclaimed. "Autumn must not have warned them in time!"

"I did so!" declared Autumn, appearing suddenly between Tommy and Grimwarden.

"AUTUMN!" Johnny picked her up and hugged her.

"Thanks, Johnny, but put me down."

Reluctantly, Johnny put her down. "Sorry. I'm just glad, that's all."

"Autumn, I can see the Gnomes," said Tommy. "Because of the ash. The Warspiders can see them now, too. The Gnomes are getting torn to shreds."

"Nooo," said Autumn. "I warned them. I really did. I even got a chance to talk to one of them. I . . . warned them."

Tommy stared at his feet. Death, death, and more death—that's all he'd seen since the battle began. And he had been able to do nothing to help. He was fed up with standing still. "Grimwarden, we've got to go help."

"We have helped," he replied, staring into the strange ashen twilight. "Against my better judgment, we sent Autumn to warn them."

"But it didn't help," said Tommy, earning him a swift stinging glance from Autumn. "Migmar's whole army could die. If we all go out there, we could save them."

"You would indeed save the Gnomes," said Grimwarden, eyes fixed ahead. "And you would strike a blow against the Spider King by annihilating an immense portion of his Warspiders. But . . . you would cost us all the war."

"You've said things like that before," said Jett. "I don't see how smashing those spiders to smithereens causes us to lose anything."

"Jett," replied the Guardmaster. "Do you not see how evenly matched we are . . . the Spider King's forces and our own? Back and forth, the battle wanes. His Gwar resistance opposes our flet soldiers. His Warflies oppose our raptors. His power over the volcano counters our legion of Gnomes. Move and countermove."

"But, sir," said Jimmy, his mind lingering on Kiri Lee. "The Spider King . . . he might be able to match everything we've thrown at him so far. But he doesn' have us."

"Are you certain, Jimmy?" asked Grimwarden, his voice like steel wrapped in velvet. "Has your foresight grown so long that you can see what the Spider King has hidden away in that fortress of his?"

"No," Jimmy said, lowering his head.

Grimwarden waited a tick. "Nor can I."

"But we're going to have to go in there," said Tommy. "Sooner or later, we'll have to face whatever he has in store for us. You trained us for that, right? What are we waiting for?"

"The map," said Grimwarden quietly. "With that map, we will enter Vesper Crag at our bidding, not his." He pointed to the tower where the red light shone.

Jett rubbed his temples. "But we left Nightwish," he said, "knowing that we didn't have the map. Now we're gonna just sit here?"

"This is war, Jett," said the Guardmaster. "We are in command. For now, we must give the orders and wait for our time to go forth. You do not see the Spider King down there chasing after Gnomes, do you? He bides his time. So must we. Nelly and Regis will return, and they will bring the map."

"But, sir," said Tommy. "They might get here too late. If they take even a few days on Earth, they'll come back long aft—"

"TOMMY!" Grimwarden spoke louder than he desired. He lowered his voice and said, "I'm speaking in faith. I know Ellos. The map will come or . . . or Ellos will provide something else." He was quiet a moment. "You have all the authority here, young lords," he said. "I command the military, but you command me. Do as you will, but remember . . . what authority you have is given to you."

Tommy and the other lords bounced their eyes between each other and Grimwarden. Clearly he had the end in mind, not the immediate. And doing so required more discipline—and perhaps more faith—than all of them put together. Perhaps that's why he is still alive . . . and had kept so many of his people alive as long as he had.

"I'm sorry, once again." Tommy dipped his head in respect. "We will wait."

"I do not expect you to master in hours what has taken me centuries." Grimwarden looked up. "When the time comes, I expect you to do your part. That's what you have been trained for, that's what you are gifted for. But for now, let me do my part."

"Uh, Tommy!" Jimmy said excitedly. "Look!"

"What?" asked Jett, staring into the whirling ash. "All I see is spiders. They're pushing south."

"Wait," said Jimmy.

Tommy extended his vision. The Warspiders were indeed moving south, mowing down Gnomes as they went. But as Tommy looked more closely, he saw that as many Gnomes fell beneath the mass of arachnids, others scrambled out from beneath the spiders and crept to the west. Still other Gnomes were behind the spiders now.

Above the rumble from the volcano and the sounds of the battle, and in spite of the muffling ash, there arose such a grating wail that the young lords covered their ears. Tommy squinted and got the surprise of his life. The Warspiders came to an impossibly abrupt halt. They shrieked and flailed, but they didn't seem to be able to move. The Gnomes, meanwhile, in even greater numbers than Tommy realized, had the Warspiders surrounded. And these little warriors were leaning backward, pulling hard on something Tommy could not see—pulling as if they were playing tug-of-war with the countrymen on the other side.

"Here it comes," said Jimmy, clamping his hands over his ears.

The other lords replied with a chorus of "What?" "Huh?" "Here what comes?"

KerrrracckKK!

If a giant had piled up a dozen dead trees the size of castle towers and then crushed them under his foot, it would not match the sound heard on the battlefield at that moment. When the young lords looked again, the mass of Warspiders was no more. It its place were dismembered spider parts and spider gore.

"The Gnomes!" cried Jimmy. "Those little ruddy-faced geniuses!"

"Unbelievable!" yelled Tommy.

"Believe it," said Migmar, or at least an ashen replica of Migmar, appearing at their side.

"Small warrior," said Grimwarden. "Tell me . . . how did you dispatch such a group of Warspiders?"

Migmar held up a strand of cord as thin as fishing line. It was black but glistened as if alive with silver light. "Cutting cord, it is," he explained. "Smelt vanadium and dremask, we do, to make alloy filament. Pull taut, it burns and cuts—very effective."

"Uh . . . yeah," said Jett. "Ouch."

Still looking back and forth from Migmar and the remnants of the spiders, Tommy said, "So all that time your army was hopping around between the spiders, fleeing for your lives . . ."

"String them up with cut cord, we were. Ha, tangled those web spinners in a Gnome web! Ha!"

Grimwarden took Migmar's hand, shook it—and the Gnome— vigorously, and said, "Praise Ellos for your ingenuity. You have bought us precious time."

"Tommy!"

Tommy spun around. A scout on a pale rangesteed rode up behind him. He was drenched with sweat and covered with muddy ash. Gasping for breath, he said, "By your leave, m'lord?"

"Huh?" Tommy felt clueless for a moment. Then he remembered his position. "Speak, please. What is it?"

"I am Celedain from the Berylinian Brigade to the south. We've been watching the passes up into the mountains, but there is heavy resistance—Warspiders, a legion of Gwar, and nearly constant bombardment by those airborne insects—"

"Warflies," said Grimwarden.

"Yes," Celedain said. "They are perilous, but we have kept our post, if barely. But something strange happened. There came fighting from the path!"

"What path?" asked Tommy.

"Why, the path to the portal," Celedain said. "There was intense fighting, much fire. Two Elves escaped it and are fleeing west—"

"Two Elves you say?" Grimwarden's eyes burned eagerly.

"Yes," he replied. "But my forces are engaged and cannot help them. These two, whoever they may be, are hemmed in."

"Nelly?" Autumn blurted out.

"Regis!" exclaimed Jimmy.

"How long ago did you leave them?" demanded Grimwarden.

"Some minutes," Celedain said. "I rode like the wind itself."

Tommy came alive. "I want two-hundred archers deployed at once."

"As I said, sir, we have no more archers. It was by Ellos's hand that I even escaped to bear the news."

"Grimwarden, what do we have left here?" asked Tommy.

Grimwarden shook his head. "No bowmen to move that quickly," he said. "They cover Travin at the wall. Wait! Flet Marshall Thorian's battle group remains—fifty archers, twice that number in spears."

"We've got to send them," said Tommy. He paused, looking questioningly at Grimwarden. "Don't we?"

"They are yours to command," Grimwarden replied.

Tommy did not blink. "They go south, then!"

"Yes!" Celedain exclaimed.

"I will see to it," said Goldarrow.

"Kinsmen, you speak of?" asked Migmar. "Carry the precious map, they do?"

Grimwarden's eyes narrowed. "By Ellos's name, I hope so."

"Ah," said Migmar, scratching thoughtfully at his sideburns. "I wonder . . ."

"What is it?" asked Tommy.

"Might we help?" asked Migmar.

"YES!" the Elves replied in unison.

Migmar spun on his heels and raced away.

Twenty minutes later, the volcano still fuming, the ash still falling heavily, Jimmy grabbed Tommy's shoulder and pointed to the south. "They're coming."

Tommy and the others looked to their right, hoping beyond hope that they might see the two faces they had long prayed for. But cresting the horizon came not two but dozens. More than a hundred easily . . . and all running as if their lives depended on it.

"Uh-oh," said Johnny. "That's not good."

"Is it them?" asked Jett.

"Two Elves, yes! But . . ." Tommy let his vision flow to them, trying to make out faces. "There are Gwar, too . . . a lot of Gwar."

"That's really not good," said Jimmy.

"Come on," Tommy was growing frustrated. "I can't make out their faces. But their clothes are Elven! It's gotta be them! And the enemy's gaining."

"Where are the Gnomes?" asked Jett. "Should we—"

"Look!" Tommy cried out, pointing.

They all did. Once more, the Gnomes had come to the aid of the Elves. But due to the incessant ashfall they had not the advantage of invisibility, and they had no more cut cord. It was hand-to-hand combat and they were little match for charging Gwar. Gnomes were tossed and kicked aside. They barely slowed the pursuers.

Tommy watched as two figures ran a serpentine path, dodging enemy darts and arc stones, fleeing for the small rise where the commanders stood. But in the dim light, Tommy still could not make out exactly who they were. One certainly moved like a lady warrior, lithe and swift. But the other . . . more like a man . . . *Who?* Tommy's heart quickened. *What had happened to Nelly and Regis?*

"I think it's time," said Grimwarden.

Tommy and the young lords looked to their mentors. "Time?" Tommy echoed. "For us?"

"Go," said Goldarrow.

SCHIIING! The young lords drew their weapons and charged off the hillock.

"I've got the first two enemy lines!" yelled Autumn, and then she was gone.

"I'll fry the next two!" Johnny exclaimed.

"Jimmy and I will pick off any that get through!" Tommy returned.

"What about me?" asked Jett. ". . . And Kat?"

"Bodyguards!" Tommy replied. "Get to the Elves and escort them back to the hill! Anything gets near you, crush it!"

"You can count on it!" exulted Jett. "You ready, Kit-Kat?"

Kat whirled her fighting knives like pinwheels as she ran. "I think so," she said.

Sliced, burned, shot through with arrows, and pummeled—the Gwar fell away, and Tommy led the young lords and the two Elves they'd rescued back to the hill.

They came immediately to Grimwarden and Goldarrow, and neither could read the look on Tommy's face. There was a kind of grim satisfaction there, a restrained joy. Without a word, the lords parted, and up came Regis, her dark hair matted to her face with sweat. Her clothes were torn, even bloodied, but her face was still strong, and she clutched a jagged Gwar sword.

She smiled bravely and handed Grimwarden a rolled parchment. "We . . . we got it," she said, and then she collapsed into his arms.

Goldarrow stood dumbstruck, staring at the dark-skinned Elf before her. "Charlie?" she said. "Charlie . . . is it . . . is it really you?"

"Yes, ma'am," he replied.

Goldarrow embraced him. "I don't know how," she said, her voice tremulous. "We thought . . . I mean, we assumed the Wisp . . . and . . ." she couldn't finish. "Oh, thank Ellos you survived." She hugged him and wondered why his grip was loose, tentative. Then she realized.

Goldarrow pulled away and scanned the hill. Autumn and Johnny stood side by side, blinking mutely.

Regis recovered enough to stand. She whispered, "Nelly . . . she didn't make it."

"We had to fight our way to the portal," said Mr. Charlie. "Drefids was waitin' on the other side. Nelly took down two of 'em, 'fore they slew her." Mr. Charlie shook his head. "I got there too late."

The volcano exploded once more; orange light bathed their hill and glimmered in their wet eyes.

"The portal goes to Canada," said Regis. "Northern Canada. The Spider King has assembled the greatest army I have ever witnessed in a vast forested region. Regardless, we made our way through the enemy camp, only to find Charlie there. He'd already made his way northward in the hopes of returning through the portal—"

"Which I discovered through a little pressure on a Drefid spy," Charlie interrupted, then gave a small gesture for Regis to continue.

"Charlie provided us a seaplane on one of the area lakes. We flew back to the Briarmans' home, where we found the map."

"Were our parents—um, the Briarmans, were they there?" asked Autumn.

"No one was in the house," said Regis, gaining energy as she spoke. "But it was the middle of the morning, a Tuesday. They were likely out working or shopping or some such."

Johnny and Autumn thought that was a possibility. Their Earth parents liked to hit the farmers' market during the week when it was less crowded. Their minds traveled from there, through town, to a little bookstore they knew was no longer there . . . and to a shopkeeper they would never see again.

Grimwarden gently unrolled the parchment. "It's more detailed than I thought it would be."

"Sir," said Regis. "If I may?"

"The lords are in command," said Grimwarden.

"Lords, with your leave?"

"Regis, I'm still just Jimmy," he said.

"Well, Master Jimmy," she said, giving him a weak smile. "To you and the other lords, I say this: I've spent a day and a night going over this map with Charlie and . . . and Nelly. I now know everything about Vesper Crag. I know where we should place our siege towers. I know where we should aim our catapults. I know where there are relatively unguarded entryways in the mountains. Once inside, I know how to get to the slave chambers. I can even tell you how to march right to the Spider King's private living quarters if you like."

Grimwarden, Goldarrow, Tommy, and the others were speechless.

"So in short, m'lords," Regis went on, "in Nelly's place and to honor her, I would like to advise you how to conquer Vesper Crag."

"I say AYE!" proclaimed Jimmy. "Um . . . sorry, mates. Tommy?"

Tommy looked at Jimmy kindly and said, "I yield to the military experience of Grimwarden and Goldarrow. Will you accept Flet Marshall Regis as Chief Battle Planner?"

"Tommy," said Regis, blushing, "I'm merely a Dreadnaught, not a Flet Marshall."

"You are now," said Tommy. "I promoted you." He paused and looked at Goldarrow. "I can do that, can't I?"

"Yes," she replied. "And I heartily accept Regis as battle commander."

"As do I," said Grimwarden, his voice swelling with military pride. "Nelly did not surrender her life for nothing. We will see to that."

36

The Enemy's Backyard

BRILLIANT, TOMMY thought as they crept through a mountain pass high above the battlements of Vesper Crag. He'd always thought of the Dreadnaughts as kind of wise beings, but Regis took the cake. Her plan was masterful. As soon as they'd all understood it in its intricacies, messengers had been dispatched to Travin and the other battle commanders. They'd had the siege engines spread along the northernmost section of the fortress's main wall—the worst possible place. The wall was lower there, but there were no fewer than a dozen access ramps leading up from the enemy armories behind; the Elves trying to gain access to the walls fought a near inexhaustible stream of Gwar soldiers. Instead, Regis had pointed out the sheer drop behind the wall just south of its midpoint. There were no access ramps for sixty yards on either side. Such a design meant it would be much more difficult for enemy reinforcements to defend. Flet soldiers saw the impact immediately, storming out of their siege towers onto the enemy walls. The real battle had begun at last.

Flet Marshall Regis hadn't known about the Gnomes, of course, so she hadn't planned for their phase of the battle. But Migmar was as good with maps as he was with gadgets. Examining the map, he, Thorkber, Sarabell, and the other Gnome military commanders had found drainage pipes through which warriors of their stature might gain access to the fortress. Once inside, the Gnomes would be near an area with water where they could wipe free the ash that hindered their camouflage. And once invisible, Migmar promised to wreak havoc on the enemy in the most inventive ways.

Meanwhile, Grimwarden, Goldarrow, and Charlie would lead a team through a lava tube into the Vesper Crag underground. Regis had plotted a winding course through a bewildering network of tunnels to the catacombs where the Spider King kept his slave population. There were few guard posts noted in that area on the map, but the slaves worked in and among the Warspider breeding chambers. *That can't be good*, thought Tommy. But he knew Grimwarden, Goldarrow, and Mr. Charlie too well to worry about their success.

That left an arduous climb for the young lords over the spiny mountains to an old mine shaft and then through the narrow pass between two peaks into Vesper Crag. It had been carved from the living rock as an escape route for the Gwar, but according to notations on the map, it had mainly been used as a trade road with the Taladrim in the far east. The young lords would take that route and descend into the enemy's stronghold. Kiri Lee's raptor had gone down near one of the fortress's oddly tilting towers. If, by Ellos's hand, Kiri Lee was still alive, the young lords would put her in as secure a location as possible. Then they would go after the Spider King himself. Regis had identified what she believed were the most likely places to find him: a watchtower near the wall, a strategy-plotting chamber, and, finally, the Black Balcony in the high tower where the red light shone. A masterful plan, indeed.

Now if only they could carry it out.

"No guards yet." Kat's thought entered Tommy's mind as the young lords marched along the shadowy pass. *"I'm surprised he would leave the back door open like this."*

It's okay with me, Tommy thought back. *Once we're discovered, we'll likely have more company than we'd ever want.*

"Jimmy?" Tommy whispered back over his shoulder. "Anything yet?"

"Nothin' at all," said Jimmy. "I'm gettin' no foresight at all right now."

That news did nothing to cheer Tommy or the others. Sheer walls of dark, reddish-orange stone rose up on either side of them. It was confining . . . smothering. *A trade-off,* Tommy thought. They had a secret way into the enemy fortress, but if the Spider King had any thought that they might come that way, he could bury them in this tight place.

Flickers of lightning flashed in the narrow space of sky above them, coming from somewhere over the Lightning Fields beyond.

"Tommy," Johnny whispered from behind. "Did you hear what Regis said about the Gwar armies and stuff . . . up in Canada?"

"Yeah," Tommy replied. "I did, and I don't much like it."

"What's he doing in Canada?" asked Autumn. "More slaves?"

"Nah," said Jett. "It's got to be more than that. Sounds like an invasion force to me."

"I was thinking the same," said Tommy.

"Well, that's stupid," said Jimmy. "We've got better weapons . . . guns, missiles. We've got nukes."

"The Spider King is a lot of things," said Kat. "But he's not stupid. He knows about Earth weapons."

At last they emerged from the narrow pass to find three ramps, each leading over a hundred-foot fall to an arched gate at different levels on a massive cylindrical building. "Get back!" Tommy whispered urgently. They fell back against the mountain wall, hidden in shadow. The clash between Elves and Gwar was still far away . . . more than a mile to the front wall, Tommy estimated. But the top two gates here still had Gwar guards posted.

Okay, we've got to get over there, thought Tommy to Kat, hoping she'd read his thoughts. *But we don't want to be seen yet.*

"Autumn," Kat thought back. *"She could race across, take out the sentries."*

Tommy nodded. She could. *But the bottom gate is unguarded. We'll go that way.* "Lords," he whispered. "Bottom ramp. Stay low."

Tommy went first, trying to keep the massive stone ramps between him and the guards above. His bow rattled against his overloaded quiver a little as he hit the ramp. Tommy pulled up, but there was no response from the Gwar. One at a time, the others followed. Autumn came last of all, just a blur.

They stood on either side of the arched gate and wondered what they'd find on the other side of the door. "I'm gettin' something," said Jimmy. "Ten guards, four at a table, four drinking by a big barrel, two are coming out. They'll kill you if—"

Tommy didn't hesitate a moment. "Jett," he said, "Autumn and Kat."

Jett Green, former star halfback for the Greenville Raiders, kicked open the door, crushing one Gwar against the inside wall. The other Gwar stood in shock for a half second too long. Jett planted a crushing punch to the bridge of his nose and finished the falling Gwar with a blow of his hammer.

Autumn raced past Jett, axes flying, and dispatched the Gwar at the table before they could stand up. Kat wasn't as fast as Autumn. No one was. But she was very strong. She threw herself into a slide and kicked the legs out from under one of the Gwar at the barrel, throwing a crushing chop into his throat to finish him. She put her dagger in the eye of another. And by that time, Jett had slammed one of the remaining two Gwar into the wall. Autumn took down the last one. In all, the battle lasted seven seconds.

"Stairs," said Johnny.

"Good," said Tommy, rushing over. "Jett, rear guard."

"Got it."

It was a steep downward-spiraling staircase, and before long, they found themselves in darkness. "A little light please, Johnny."

Johnny opened his palm and a lick of fire appeared. Two minutes of descent later, they emerged from the building into a courtyard at the base of the mountains. It was bordered on one side by other stone buildings and somewhat surrounded by dark trees. But the stone of the courtyard and even the limbs of the trees were strewn with carnage.

"Oh, my gosh!" gasped Kat.

Dead raptors and Warflies littered the area. But that was not all. Bodies of Elf and Gwar, badly disfigured or contorted, lay motionless in pools of their own blood. Tommy averted his eyes a moment, fearing for Kiri Lee. Then he steeled himself and said, "Spread out. The fighting is still far ahead, but stay low. Anyone could be watching from any of these towers."

The search was grim and grueling. The Warflies were huge. Some had scarlet raptors still in their clutches as they crashed to the ground.

Tommy recognized some of the other raptor riders among the dead.
Come to think of it, Tommy wasn't sure what happened to Ethon
Beleron, either. Aviator casualties were very high. Tommy had been a
part of the decision to let Kiri Lee lead the air attack. He wished he
hadn't. The young lords would be far weaker without her, and they
would have lost a dear friend.

"Here!" cried Jimmy. "I found her . . . ahhh, NO!"

The lords raced to his side. There between a thick tree trunk and
the base of a narrow turret, Kiri Lee lay facedown upon her raptor.
The massive creature was dead.

"She's breathing!" Jett said, his fingers at her neck.

"Turn her over," said Tommy, "GENTLY, and be careful of her
neck."

"Don't you think I know?" asked Jett. He lay her on her back and
cradled her head in his hands. She groaned softly.

"Kiri Lee," said Jimmy. "Kiri Lee, it's Jimmy. We've come t' help
yu."

But Kiri Lee did not respond. Her cheek and forehead were terribly bruised, with gashes and cuts—probably from crashing through
the tree's limbs.

"Look at her stomach," cried Autumn. Her tunic had come untucked
from her breeches in the fall, and they could see beneath the leather
armor that Kiri Lee's skin was an ugly dark blue with patches of purple
shot through with fingers of red.

"She's bleeding internally, I think," said Johnny. "I saw something
like this on a medical show. They pulled a guy out of a car wreck,
looked like that."

"What happened to the guy?" asked Autumn.

Johnny wouldn't answer.

"Awww, no," muttered Jimmy. "No, not Kiri Lee."

"Uh-UHG!" Jett went suddenly rigid. His face became taut, almost
stretched.

"Jett!" Tommy yelled.

The muscles rippled in Jett's bare arms; veins appeared and
throbbed. His neck flared and thickened.

"Look!" gasped Kat.

The bruising on Kiri Lee's forehead and cheeks faded from the ugly dark colors to lighter shades and then was gone. The gashes and cuts clotted and scabbed, and then melted away as the young lords watched.

"You're healing her," Johnny blurted out. "But so fast?"

But Jett didn't respond. He seemed in great pain, leaning back and gritting his teeth, but never letting go of Kiri Lee. The massive patch of discolored skin on her stomach rapidly returned to its normal tone.

"Kiri Lee?" tried Jimmy tentatively. "Kiri Lee?"

Her breathing rate increased. Her chest rose higher as she breathed more deeply, and then she opened her eyes. "Who are you?" she asked.

"Huh?" Jimmy frowned. "Jimmy."

Jett slumped backward, but Tommy was there to keep him from hitting the ground hard.

"Is Jett okay?" asked Kat.

"I think he's asleep," said Tommy. "He's snoring."

Kiri Lee surprised them all by sitting up. "What are you doing here? Oh no." She rubbed her head. "I remember, my raptor, my poor raptor." She brushed her hand through the creature's feathers and looked up to Jimmy. "Jimmy," she said. "I was falling . . . seemed like forever"—she turned to Kat—"and I heard you call my name."

"Well, it was Jett who healed yu," said Jimmy.

"I was hurt bad?" she asked.

He nodded.

A black blur swept down from above. There came a howling roar. Thick, grooved, and gnarled, a massive hand of branches closed around Kiri Lee's waist. She screamed and fought.

In a flash, Tommy put arrows into both of its wide yellow eyes. Autumn went to work with her axes at the Cragon's base, but another Cragon swept at her.

Rrrrwwwwaah!

Autumn rolled away and raced to safety. More trees around them began to move.

Kat ran to Jett. "Jett, wake up!" she yelled, shaking his shoulders. "Get up! We need to go!"

"What?" he mumbled. "C'mon, Ma . . ."

Then Kat screamed her thought to him: *"JETT GREEN, GET UP THIS INSTANT!"*

Jett's eyes snapped open, and he slowly stood up. "I'm tired," he said.

"No time!" Then Kat yelled to Tommy, "That building . . . the one with the black flags . . . that's got to be the stronghold."

"Got it!" he yelled back. "Go! We'll catch up!" Kat helped Jett get to cover.

The Cragons closed in, as one still held tight to Kiri Lee. Tommy nocked another arrow and pulled the bowstring back beyond his ear, so far he was afraid the bow might snap. Tommy released it. The arrow disappeared between the creature's already impaled eyes.

Rrrrww—its breath cut off, the creature released Kiri Lee and then fell backward. Twigs and leaves shot skyward with the impact, the ground shaking underfoot.

"Let's go!" Tommy yelled to her.

"What?" Kiri Lee exclaimed.

Autumn, Jimmy, and Johnny looked up. "Aren't we going to stay and fight?" asked Johnny.

"We're not," said Tommy. "But you are, Stove Top."

Tommy motioned for the others to follow, and he led them through a gauntlet of rooty feet and grasping long hands. "Across there," he said to Autumn, Jimmy, and Kiri Lee. "Kat and Jett are there beneath that arch. I'll be right there."

He kept walking but turned back for a moment. "We'll wait at the first cross tunnel," Tommy called back, but before he rounded the corner, he glared at his friend. "Burn 'em, Johnny," he said, "to ashes."

Johnny Briarman thought of his parents and his aunt on Earth, all they'd been through, and were going through. He thought of Nelly.

There were eleven Cragon trees advancing on Johnny. Eleven hulking beasts against one thirteen-year-old boy. But Johnny faced them. And fire was in his hands.

37

A Stirring Revolt

"I THINK we're getting closer," Grimwarden said, raising the torch higher. This narrow tunnel was completely dark. But as the three walked on, a soft red light began to emerge ahead. Along with the stifling heat and the acrid smell, a low pulsing sound resonated in their ears. Goldarrow thought that if she were here for any length of time, the sound would give her a headache. Before long, the tunnel spit them out into a massive cavern, even hotter than the tunnel, and cast in a lurid red light.

"Great Maker of Allyra," whispered Grimwarden. All three of them held short.

Before them stretched a vast network of paths, rising and falling like the veins of a living organism. Beneath them were countless honey-combed chambers, each pulsating, covered in thin weblike filaments. And tending to the innumerable beds were hundreds and hundreds of people. Maybe even thousands. Some not full grown. And not Elvish.

"Slaves," gasped Goldarrow. "And many are just children."

"Humans," said Charlie. "Jackpot!"

At first the presence of the three warriors went unnoticed. Whatever manner of inhumane conditioning had taken place over the years, the slaves did not even bother looking up, nor did the guards turn from their whipping, nor did the adolescent Warspiders take any notice. The slaves continued hauling crates full of glowing yellow orbs from one bed to another, carrying cages containing dozens of fist-sized spiders on their backs, and rolling barrels of what Grimwarden thought might be food. Spider food.

The slaves were all thin, but the children were particularly emaciated, their skin sallow and hanging. But all of them, adults and children alike, were riddled with long scars from untold whippings and beatings.

"I count ten guards," said Grimwarden. "Clearly most have been called to battle up top." He pointed to empty guard towers placed throughout the cavern. "Must be a skeleton crew."

"And from the looks of them Warspiders, there ain't no adults to worry about," said Charlie. "I count twenty-five no bigger than two or three feet in diameter."

"That is a most unusual dialect," Grimwarden whispered to Goldarrow.

"He likes it," Goldarrow explained. "Leave him be."

"As long as he can fight, I guess."

"Y'all ready?" asked Charlie.

"Aye," said Grimwarden. "I'll take the guards; Elle and Charlie, you have the overgrown arachnids. Try and assemble the slaves back here as quickly as possible. The last thing we want is for them to go running."

Grimwarden ran to the first honeycombed bay and ducked beside the supporting frame of the walkway that swept overhead. As soon as the first Gwar walked directly above him, Grimwarden pulled him off the walkway with a violent jerk. The Gwar sailed through the air, but before his body even hit the ground, Grimwarden had used the sword in his other hand to sever the guard's exposed throat.

"Girell?" came a voice above. "You fall asleep?"

The second Gwar was coming to investigate.

Goldarrow crept along the right flank while Charlie moved to the left. With any luck, they could each clear out ten to fifteen spiders and be done with it.

She waited in the shadows of a large-wheeled cart. It hurt to breathe in here. She wondered how any of the slaves had survived. Goldarrow could feel empathy rising in her chest, feeling for the slaves, especially the children. She watched them move around like—*what had Tommy once called those things?*—zombies. Waking dead. Mindless creatures of the night.

"We will free you," Goldarrow pledged in a whisper.

Then her thoughts turned to Grimwarden. *Where is the sign?*

Charlie watched as the second Gwar toppled off the walkway, a spray of broken spider eggs shooting up from under his fall. The remaining eight Gwar turned as one, running toward the scene along the curving ramparts. At the same time, all of the slaves in the enormous cavern started cheering, realizing something foul was happening against their captors; what exactly, Charlie was sure they had no idea. But any pain or suffering for the Gwar was something he was positive the slaves would exult in.

"Now!" Charlie barked across the room to Goldarrow, who emerged from behind the wagon, weapons blazing.

Charlie bounded across ridges of two separate spider beds before thrusting his sword into the thorax of an adolescent Warspider. The arachnid went into a fit, shuddered violently, then dropped dead.

The slaves were dropping their wheelbarrows and starting to clap for Charlie.

Two more Warspiders on Charlie's left looked up in time to see the thin part of Charlie's shield flash across their faces. The two spiders collided with one another before they fell dead.

Charlie was about to move on when he noticed something move under the webbed covering to his right.

"Come on, you overgrown ape!" Grimwarden roared as he charged down a narrow pathway. Polearm extended, the Gwar growled as he barreled up toward the Guardmaster. The Gwar lunged—a huge mistake—and Grimwarden ducked beneath the polearm. Then he rose up underneath the Gwar's chin with a fist, knocking him off his feet. The Gwar flipped head over heels, landing in a nest just below—only to be replaced by more Gwar and Warspiders, and now the enemy was even turning on one another.

"OLIN!" came Elle's rising voice from somewhere to his right.

"We've got to get out of here!" cried Charlie.

"Forget the enemy," commanded Grimwarden. "Get the slaves out of here!"

With the guards now preoccupied with what could only be described as a spider revolt, the three Elven leaders began calling out to all the slaves. Of course, the Elven newcomers certainly had the slaves' attention, what with slaying a few Gwar and Warspiders as they had. But now the leaders were waving frantically, yelling to the slaves.

"THIS WAY!"

The slaves started running, tossing aside their tools, helping one another, and giving more than one Warspider a passing blow. As the slaves continued to race to the front of the room, Grimwarden, Goldarrow, and Charlie pulled back, heading toward the exit. Hundreds and then thousands of young people followed behind them, cheering as they went.

But it was Charlie who noticed what else was happening in the room. No longer concerned with the escaping slaves, the rest of the Gwar busied themselves with trying to maintain control of the spider beds. But they failed miserably as the rebellion was far out of control. Millions of tiny spiders were roused, and within moments, it was all the Gwar could do to stay alive.

"Grimwarden!" Charlie yelled over the din of their escape as the three stood aside ushering the slaves into the exit tunnel. "We have a problem!"

Grimwarden looked back and saw the rising flood of baby spiders spreading after the slaves. Even if they did escape, the spiders would overtake them in the tunnel. It would be a lost cause. He turned to Charlie. "Have any of that tar root left on you?"

"Sure thing. An arc stone, too."

"How many?"

"Just one."

One is all we need. Grimwarden grinned, then looked to the ceiling of the tunnel just before it shot upward to form the roof of the cavern. "You thinking what I'm thinking?"

Charlie gave a quick nod, then went to work. While Grimwarden and Goldarrow helped the slaves file past them and into the tunnel, Charlie wrapped the remaining arc stone in tar root—three times as much as he used on the last stone. He left a small spot exposed for the ignition. It was nearly the size of a baseball when he was through.

"This is going to be close!" said Goldarrow, seeing how many slaves still needed to be evacuated.

"Come on!" Grimwarden shouted, spurring the slaves on. "FASTER!"

The wave of baby Warspiders was now almost even with the last few rows of slaves. "I wish Johnny was here," said Goldarrow. "Hey, Charlie! Where are you going?"

But Charlie didn't respond. He ran to the back of the line and started using the flat of his shield to smash the tiny little buggers, hundreds at a time.

"Oh, Ellos, help us!" cried Goldarrow. She and Grimwarden were shoving slaves now, the time growing short. They had seconds, not minutes. She looked back at Charlie. He was batting the spiders away like flies.

"That's the last of them!" Grimwarden yelled. "*CHARLIE!*"

Charlie acknowledged him with a nod, then turned and ran to meet them. He produced the prepared arc stone and struck it across the rim of his shield. The thing sparked to life. Charlie followed Grimwarden and Goldarrow into the tunnel, and underhanded the arc stone onto the ceiling. It stuck as expected, and again, Charlie counted to himself, gritting his teeth against the pain of the spider bites. He turned around to see a dark wave of arachnids climbing the walls, pouring into the corridor like a tidal wave. "*GET READY!*"

A flash of light.

A deafening blast of air.

Charlie catapulted forward, colliding into Grimwarden and Goldarrow, who also shot down the tunnel.

Rocks slammed into them, dust filled their lungs. Then darkness.

Grimwarden's ears were ringing. A good sign. At least he was alive. Other than an ache in his back and his head, he felt intact. No major bleeding. And surprisingly, no broken bones. He opened his eyes and tried to sit up. Rubble scrapped together all around him. Someone coughed to his right. "Goldarrow?"

Grimwarden crawled over to her and helped her up. "You all right?"

"If you can cure me of this infernal ringing in my ears, I think I'll be fine."

"Guess I may have used a little too much," came Charlie's voice from a heap of stones.

"Charlie!" cried Goldarrow. "You're alive!"

"Is that what this is called?" He grunted and pressed himself up, covered from head to foot in white dust.

The three of them laughed. But Charlie, facing back the way they had come, stopped laughing. He pointed a finger. "Look . . ."

Grimwarden and Goldarrow turned. With torches in hand, as well as weapons they'd picked up from somewhere farther down the hall, the slaves were returning to thank their rescuers. Only they weren't slaves anymore. Just people.

Lessons from the Past

EXPLOSIONS LIT the courtyard just as Tommy was shutting the door. The six young lords careened down a corridor the map said would bring them eventually to a great hall with a wide staircase up into a long corridor to another spiral staircase, and at last into the Spider King's center of military operations—his Plotting Chamber.

They stopped in the shadows at the first cross passage to wait for Johnny. It seemed that the battle outside was spilling over within the walls of Vesper Crag. To their left, Gwar and Drefids raced up the hall, recklessly slinging weapons and staring straight ahead. They didn't even notice the intruders as they ran by.

"Thanks for waiting," Johnny said, skidding to a halt beside his friends.

"You take care of those stinkin' trees?" Jett asked.

"Only ashes left," Johnny said.

"Good work," said Tommy. "Those explosions you, too?"

Johnny shook his head. "I wish," he said. "No, it's getting crazy out there. I think our flet soldiers have taken part of the wall, and the battle has come to this side. Soldiers running everywhere. I barely made it here. But the explosions? I dunno, I'm guessing the Gnomes had something to do with it."

"I'm really starting to love those guys," said Kat.

Another stream of Gwar soldiers stampeded by. The Seven pressed their backs against the wall. "We canna' stay here," said Jimmy.

"Right," Tommy replied. "Come on. We need to find that wide staircase."

"Then what?" asked Jett.

"We fight our way up," said Tommy.

"Thought you might say that." Jett cracked his knuckles.

After passing two similar cross passages, they saw a wide opening up ahead. The main stairs rose up from the center floor, dividing a vast hall with a high ceiling, great columns, and arches. The walls were overhung with black and red flags and tapestries depicting battles and events of the past.

"I didn't realize it would be so . . . so open like this," said Kat. "How are we going to get to those stairs without bringing every available enemy in Vesper Crag down on top of us?"

"C'mon," said Jett. "We're the Seven, right?"

Johnny couldn't help but grin. Jett's good-natured enthusiasm was contagious. They were the Seven Lords of Berinfell and that did mean something. If the only way was through that massive hall, then so be it.

"Together?" Johnny whispered and held out his hand.

Their hands joined his. "Together," they said.

"Head for the longer flags and tapestries. We can hide behind them," Tommy said.

The lords began to move when Jimmy whispered, "Wait!" He held his arm back to signal the other lords to flatten against the wall. "Not yet."

What looked like a battalion of Gwar soldiers, flanked by Drefids on their red Warspiders, marched down the wide stairs and across the central floor. Another explosion—this one close by—cast a flickering, bloody orange light on the entire hall. The hall turned to chaos, Gwar soldiers loping this way and that, some with weapons drawn, others carrying crates and barrels. A Warspider, frightened by the explosion, broke its tether. It killed one Gwar and stabbed another with its foreleg before they netted it and put it down.

"The war band is leaving the building," said Tommy. "We're not going to have a better time. Follow me, but be ready to fight."

Taking a breath as if for a deep, uncertain plunge, each of the Seven fled into the hall. Passing the lip of the passage out into that open air made them feel as if a great spotlight shone down on them. They raced from spot to spot, hiding wherever they could for a few seconds at a time and then sprinting. Then they came to a sticky point. They were hidden well for the moment behind a stack of crates. But if anyone came, or worse moved a crate, they would be caught. "Beneath the stairs," Tommy whispered. "But we'll need to knock that tapestry down to cover the opening. Kiri Lee, just before we duck under the stairs air walk and drop that tapestry.

"Kiri Lee?" Tommy turned to look at her, worried. *She's exhausted and not listening.* "The tapestry?"

"Oh," she said softly. "Yes, I'll get it."

"Okay," whispered Tommy. "We go . . . now."

The Seven slipped out from behind the crates and raced over to the stairs. Kiri Lee was the first into the hiding spot. Tommy ducked in. "Kiri Lee, you didn't knock down the tapestry."

"So tired," she said, slumping against the stone behind her.

Tommy left her there for a moment. "Jett," he said. "Toss Jimmy up there to knock that down."

"You got it," Jett replied, and in a moment their hiding place was covered.

Gulping air, they waited in the shadows. Tommy, using his telescopic sight, scanned the area they'd just traversed. Squads of eight Gwar soldiers ran back and forth across his field of view. But it was the same chaotic activity from before—just troops trying to account for the throes of battle, not enemy sentries changing their location, looking for spies.

Tommy could see through the pillars that there were enormous open windows on the west side. Lightning flashed, illuminating a surreal scene upon the outer walls: untold numbers of combatants teeming atop the parapets and rooftops, a thousand fires burning, arc stones rising and falling, and still more than a few raptors and Warflies wheeling about in dogfights. A reddish glow to the north told the story that the volcano continued to blaze. And the entire scene was through a veil of falling ash.

"Unbelievable," Tommy whispered.

"What?" asked Jett.

"The battle out there." Tommy paused. "I can see tens of thousands out there . . . so many."

"We weren't seen," asked Johnny, "by anyone?"

"No one's coming," Tommy said. "Jimmy, you getting anything?"

"Nothin'. I wish I could turn it on and off at will like Kat's thought reading or Johnny's fire."

"Ah, man, don't sweat it," whispered Jett. "It comes when you need it, like a life preserver."

"Ah, what an idiot," Tommy muttered under his breath.

"Hey," said Autumn. "He was just trying to help."

"No, not Jett. ME. I messed us up royally."

"What is it?" asked Kat. But she knew before she'd even finished the question.

"I've got us hidden under the stairs," Tommy muttered. "From here we can't see who or what's on the stairs."

"Oh," said Autumn. "That was pretty dumb."

"Thanks," said Tommy.

"But it's not a big deal," Autumn reassured him. "I'll be back in a flash. Just be ready."

"Autumn?" Johnny's question fell on empty space.

"We need to wait," Autumn said, appearing next to them once more. "Looks like a Warspider resupply out there right now."

The speedy Elf went out and back five times, and each time there was too much traffic on the stairs.

"It's got to clear up soon," said Jett. "This is killing me."

"We can't wait until it's totally clear," said Johnny. "It'll never be totally clear."

"Right," said Tommy. "But we don't want to charge out there into a brigade of Gwar, either."

"I hate waitin'," Jimmy agreed. "Don't you, Kiri Lee?"

"Sometimes it is necessary," she replied.

"Yeah . . . yeah . . . isn't that the truth?" It wasn't exactly the support from Kiri Lee he had been looking for.

"Okay," Tommy said, "Autumn, you be ready to try again. We need to stay sharp. Remember, we get up the stairs as fast as we can. Take out anything that crosses our path, and make sure not one of them sounds a horn or we're done."

"From there," said Jimmy, thinking aloud, "through the big arched opening and take a long, straight shot past six gates."

"Right," said Tommy. "Then we should see the spiral stairs."

"Okay, Tommy," Kat said. "We know, we know. Just let Autumn go."

Tommy shook his head. "Sorry, I just don't want to screw up again. Go ahead, Autumn."

This was it. All their hearts were racing, adrenaline pumping. The fact that they had even infiltrated the enemy's lair was cause enough for panic; but now that they were burrowing deeper into the stronghold, each one of them knew there was no going back from here.

Autumn darted out of their hiding spot and returned moments later. "Now!"

The young lords poured out and into the open once more, raced around the corner, up the stairs, and smacked into the back of a Gwar soldier. He was armored head to foot, but before he could turn around, Jimmy had clambered up his back and put a dagger in his neck to silence him. Jimmy did a backflip off the falling creature and landed on his feet.

But the Gwar had not been alone.

Tommy and Jett charged around the dead Gwar and came face-to-face with two Drefids. The creatures hesitated a moment, leering at the Elves who had the nerve to enter their inner sanctum. Tommy used the uncertain moment to nock an arrow. Jett swung a blow with his hammer that would have knocked a bull elephant unconscious. But the Drefids were swift. High in the air they leaped, extending their claws and shrieking. Jett's stroke missed entirely, and he fell off balance. One of the Drefids gashed Jett's shoulder, and bright red blood spilled down his leather plate armor.

Tommy fired an arrow straight up at the other Drefid, but the creature timed it perfectly and slashed the shaft out of the air. The Drefid landed behind Tommy, but when he drew back his claw to stab Tommy in the back, he felt two cold hands grab his head. But the hands did not stay cold.

A sudden flash of fire, a horrid smell of burnt hair, and Johnny let the Drefid fall away. Having seen his comrade's unpleasant death, the other Drefid leaped off the stairs and began to run. If he escaped, he'd surely reveal their location.

Tommy's first arrow hit the Drefid between the shoulder blades, sending the creature sprawling onto the marble floor. Tommy's next two arrows stilled the creature.

"Come on!" yelled Kat. The damage had been done. Enemy soldiers converged on the fallen Drefids, looked to the stairs, and began the chase.

The Seven fled under the high arch and into a long passage. "Johnny!" Tommy cried out. "Give us a little breathing room!"

Johnny stopped, spun around, and unleashed a powerful flame that adhered to the archway and created a raining curtain of liquid fire. For good measure, Johnny blasted forty yards of the floor behind them as well. He turned, but the others were well ahead. *Only one thing to do,* he thought. He hated to lose another pair of boots, but it couldn't be helped.

White fire burst from his feet, flash-melting the soles of the boots before launching them altogether off his feet. Johnny used the flame from his hands to balance himself vertically while he propelled himself forward with his feet.

He caught up in no time and found Jimmy warning the team of what to expect as they passed each of the upcoming passageways.

"Spiders coming from the left!" he yelled, and the young lords raced to the right side of the hall.

"Gwar on the right, JETT!"

Jett charged ahead and bludgeoned the unsuspecting Gwar as it took its first step into the hall.

Between Johnny's fire behind and Jimmy's foresight ahead, the Seven had gained time on any pursuit. At last, Tommy saw the entrance to the spiral stairs ahead. He led the team, three steps at a time, up the stairwell, then through an archway, turning into a chamber well lit with torches and a massive candle chandelier.

Johnny cut off his fire and warily followed his friends inside. It was a deep room, but not very wide. Maps made of some kind of leathered skin adorned the walls, recording graphically the advances and tactics of battles old and relatively new. Wide pillars held up the domed ceiling overhead. And littered beneath it were tables strewn with maps, carved pawns, and drawing tools. This had to be the Spider King's war room. There was only one problem.

"Where is he?" asked Jett, examining a map streaked with red.

"I don't know," said Tommy.

"I did not see this coming," said Jimmy.

"Where did Regis say we should check next?" asked Johnny.

"The throne room," said Tommy. "It's up one floor from—"

"I rarely spend time in the throne room," came a voice from somewhere in the back of the long room.

The young lords found themselves bunching up protectively. They'd never heard his voice, but they were sure it was him. Yet where was he? Was there a false panel in the back of the room? Weapons ready, they edged toward the voice.

"Thrones are for bloated despots who speak often, but rule little. I prefer this room," he went on, his voice clear and penetrating. "This is a place of action and reaction, where one can study the past and learn from it. Do you like it?"

"Jimmy," Tommy whispered. "Where is he? What's his move?"

"I-I'm not seeing things clearly," Jimmy replied. "Somethin' is messed up."

"Well, do you?" came the voice once more.

The young lords had almost reached the back wall. Tommy's eyes ricocheted from map to map. "No!" Tommy blurted out at last. "I don't like this room at all."

An abbreviated laugh. Still no sign of him. Just the voice. "Surely you comprehend the importance of learning from the past?"

"Jimmy!" Tommy whispered more urgently behind him. But to buy more time, he raised his voice: "The only past to learn from here is enslaving, conquering, and killing."

"And you've come to my realm then . . . for tea?"

"It's not workin' right," Jimmy whispered, stepping up beside Tommy. "I tell yu, it canna' be."

Kat spoke into Tommy's mind. *"I'm reading Jimmy's thoughts, and Jimmy's right. It's like thinking a nightmare that keeps changing. I don't know—"*

"All out of tea," said the Spider King, his voice louder or thicker somehow. "But I feel I should give you something in return for the gift you sent to me."

There was movement in the back of the room, something passing through the wall. *But that's impossible.* Ready with his bow, Tommy waited.

"So . . . as my gift to you, I grant you freedom. Freedom from the hideous life you have here, freedom to enter whatever place your Ellos sends you . . . when—you—die."

Tommy's reflexes jerked at the sight of a tall Gwar emerging the rest of the way from the wall. The young lord released an arrow, but changed his aim at the last second. The arrow passed through where Tommy thought the wall should have been. It stuck solidly in the center of a map that was ten yards farther back than it appeared. The back of the room . . . *it's an illusion!* The Spider King stepped out from a camouflaged anteroom. Tommy felt his heart turn to ice. The Spider King was not alone.

A Hard Choice

THE SPIDER King held Kiri Lee almost directly in front of him like a living shield, but her skin was a ghastly greenish color and her face was blank. Tommy couldn't speak, but his mind whirled. *But Kiri Lee is—*

"Yes, you gave her to me," said the Spider King. "She is full of venom, dying as the poison attacks her vital organs. But just to be sure—" He took out a dagger with a strange serpentine blade more than eight inches long. He rammed it into Kiri Lee's back.

"Only this time, Hamandar," said the Spider King, his voice agitated, rushed, "you will not heal her. For trying to heal the Wisp drained you of some of your power, and now you won't have time or power to heal yourself and her."

Jett screamed out, a wrenching guttural moan, and fell to his knees.

The young lords looked on, thunderstruck. For there was Kiri Lee—the one standing among them—holding the handle of a dagger whose blade had been broken off. The smile on her face was utterly ghoulish when she said, "Jett, your Mr. Wallace perished in much the same manner."

The Spider King let the real Kiri Lee fall to the ground as he raced back through the anteroom. Johnny unleashed a flaring blast of fire on the Wisp Kiri Lee, and it began to burn. The flash of heat snapped the other young lords from their paralysis.

Jimmy ran to Kiri Lee and started to reach for her, but there was already so much blood pooling on the marble. His hands trembling, he looked up to Tommy, anguished, questioning.

Tommy looked away, then stared back at the burning Wisp. Flames licked all around this ghoulish version of Kiri Lee, its burning flesh beginning to dissipate even while it laughed.

"Oh no you won't!" Tommy said, his voice low and menacing. *"Vex lethdoloc vitica anis! Feithrill abysscrahl niy!"* Then he used his sword and plunged it into the Wisp's chest. The grin on its burning face suddenly vanished. Then its head rolled back and the spirit shrieked . . . even as its form dissolved into a red mist.

By this time, Autumn and Kat had helped Jett lie on his unhurt side. Johnny, his hands still smoldering, walked past Jimmy and Kiri Lee, then into the anteroom. "Hey! There's a door back here!" Johnny yelled. "He's getting away!"

"Please help me," Jimmy wailed. "She's dying. . . . Help her."

This can't be! The thought railed against Tommy's mind as he looked upon his stricken friends. He sank to his knees beside Jett. Everything had been going to plan . . . but now? *Learn from history,* the Spider King had said, and Tommy had not. Decision after decision, clue after clue, Tommy had missed it. *And now?*

"What are you waiting for, Tommy?" Jett growled, his words half choked. "All of you, don't let him get away."

Tommy was visibly trembling. "But, Jett, you . . . you're—"

"Get up off your knees, Tommy!" commanded Jett, his expression weakening, but his eyes still fierce. He reached out and grabbed the top rim of Tommy's leather breastplate, pulling his face close. "You are Lord Felheart Silvertree, blood-right ruler of Berinfell, and you have . . . a mission . . . to . . . finish!" Gasping in pain, Jett fell back onto the floor.

Something changed within Tommy in that moment. He knew what he must do . . . what they all must do. *Even the prophecies had said there would be a cost.* Tommy took Jett's hand and looked into his eyes. "Thank you, friend," he said. "For everything." Then realizing what perhaps the others had not yet, he added, "Choose well." Then he stood up. "Kat, Autumn," Tommy said, "we need to go."

"But he's dying," cried Autumn. "And what did you mean, *choose well*? He's dying! Can't you see that?"

Jett nodded at Tommy. His smile and the peace in his eyes told the story. He understood. And then so did Kat. Jett looked up to her. "Take care of them, Kit-Kat. Do what I can't anymore."

"Oh—don't say that—" But she knew it was true, and she covered her mouth, tears welling up in her eyes. "C'mon, Autumn," Kat said. She kissed Jett on the cheek and gently took Autumn by the arm and led her away.

"We need you, Jimmy," Tommy said, walking to his friend and placing his hand on his shoulder.

"No," Jimmy said. "I need to be here. I need to stay with Kiri Lee . . . or she'll die."

Tommy didn't know why he hadn't realized before. But now he saw it. Jimmy had fallen in love with Kiri Lee. And maybe, back in the woods, Kiri Lee wasn't flirting with him . . . maybe she was asking him about Jimmy! *Of course!* "Jimmy," he said. "Kiri Lee would want you to go. We've got to end this horror. Now."

Jimmy let Tommy lift him from his knees. "I should have warned you," Jimmy whimpered. "I should have figured it out."

Tommy took Jimmy by the shoulders and by sheer force of will held his eyes. "That's poison!" Tommy growled. "Don't listen to that! We've got a job to do."

Each of the five lords looked one last time at their friends, and then they went after the Spider King.

Kiri Lee took in a sudden deep breath, eyes snapping wide open. It all rushed back to her: *crash landing the raptor, getting caught by the Cragons, being turned over to the Spider King.* He'd poisoned her by stabbing her with a spider fang. She'd been paralyzed, forced to watch her friends walk into a trap, and then the cold. But she felt warm. Tingling. She turned her head and saw Jett lying beside her. He looked very pale. He had one hand pressed against her side, the other on her arm. "Jett," she cried. "No . . . no . . . what are you doing? No!"

Strength to Rise

HOW HIGH they had come! Tommy blinked, looking through the open archway at the breathless view of the mountainside and down into the courtyards far below. And beyond, the legions of Elves were still flooding the Lightning Fields and pouring over the main wall. Turning away, he continued to climb. Bound only to the cliff face on one side, open to midair on the other, the stairs were narrow and uneven, so the lords had to watch their footing even more. They followed a much wider spiral now, as they circled the mountain, climbing slowly toward the peak of Vesper Crag and the tower of red light.

"Yes, yes, m'lords!" came the Spider King's voice from above. "Come up. Come up if you can!"

Two more turns, and they could see him now, a small figure leaning over a balcony on the tower.

Tommy didn't look down, but he could feel the distance drop away beneath him. It pulled at him, willing him to fall backward.

"Don't think such things," Kat spoke into his mind.

There came a rumbling from above. "Boulders!" Jimmy cried out. "Dodge right!" They moved with no time to spare as a massive oblong stone careened past them to their left, threatening to force them over the rail-less side of the stairs.

"Get low!" Jimmy yelled. "This one will bounce over us."

They obeyed. The stone, a large round spinning thing, hit three steps above the lords, took a wicked hop, and came down behind them. Stone after stone they evaded. "We're still coming!" Tommy bellowed.

"Archers!" yelled Jimmy.

From a ring of black pockets above, Gwar archers appeared. Their crossbows already loaded and wound tight, they fired on the lords. "My turn," yelled Johnny. His hands erupted with a wide spread of white-hot fire. Heat washed down on the other lords.

The enemy's darts were consumed instantly, falling as harmless ash. Tommy was up in a heartbeat and put an arrow into one archer and hastily took out another.

The remaining Gwar fired again, but Johnny's flame took out three. Tommy killed another two. He and Johnny repeated the process, again and again, until the archers were slain.

"Very impressive—even with just five," jeered the Spider King from his balcony. The red light glowed behind him. "Very impressive. Just think if your other friends were still alive."

"I'm taking him out!" Johnny yelled, running up the stairs and launching twin streams of fire up at the tower.

Jimmy yelled, "Wait, Johnny, look out!"

Something moved on the dark stone up ahead, a long, glistening thing. Two bulbous eyes and a nest of clicking mandibles for a mouth. As large as a full-grown Warspider, but in shape more like a wingless Warfly, the creature rose up.

"JOHNNY!" Kat screamed her thoughts into his mind, but he was too focused on the tower.

The creature unleashed an appendage, a mantislike arm that flicked out from the center of its upper chest and slammed into Johnny's left shoulder. A spray of blood, a grunt, and Johnny cartwheeled backward. He hit one step—*hard*—and went airborne.

"Johnny!" Autumn screamed. But he was beyond her reach.

Tommy couldn't watch. The creature was turning toward him, seemingly reloading its appendage. Tommy put one arrow in its left eye. Still the creature approached. He put a shaft deep into the creature's forehead. It collapsed immediately and slid harmlessly onto the steps, then flipped off, careening down the mountainside.

"No!" bellowed the Spider King looking beyond Tommy. "No!"

Tommy spun around and caught his breath. Johnny had not fallen. There in the air, slowly descending, was Kiri Lee . . . with Johnny in her arms.

"KIRI LEE!" Jimmy burst out, tears welling up in his eyes. But then he quickly composed himself and stood back.

"Kiri Lee," Johnny mumbled to her. "I thought you were—"

"Jett," she said.

"How did you do that?" he asked, remembering the last time she attempted such a rescue.

"I caught you," she answered.

"Yeah, but I'm heavy. Remember?"

"Not anymore. You're light," she said. "When I touch you." Her gift had matured.

War horns sounded. The tide of the battle had seemed to turn. The surviving walls of Vesper Crag belonged to the Elves, and they were pushing hard toward the mountain. Johnny, Jimmy, Kiri Lee, Autumn, Kat, and Tommy—they turned as one and gazed at the Spider King.

"You're beaten," yelled Tommy, hoping to keep the Spider King occupied so the others could act against him. "Why don't you give this up?!"

"THIS?" The Spider King momentarily lost his composure. He mastered himself and said, "Arrogant boy. Just what do you think 'this' is?"

Tommy slowly climbed the stairs. He could feel his friends behind him. "This grudge," Tommy exclaimed. "Your hatred of the Elves for enslaving your people . . . let it go."

And then, the Spider King laughed . . . if laughing it could be called. The sound that came from him had not the ring of mirth to it, but rather a compound of anguish, rage, and unassailable confidence. Then he gazed down on the Elves, and it seemed the red light behind him blazed even stronger. "You are mistaken!" He spat the words. "Revenge is but one drop of blood in the cauldron of my mission. There is no giving up."

Confused but undaunted, Tommy continued to climb. "Whatever your reason is," Tommy said firmly, "it will stop today." He saw a flare of orange, and Johnny, his hands alight, was at his side. "Your armies are losing," Tommy continued. The stairs squared off now, aiming right at the Black Balcony. "You have nowhere left to go." They had him.

"One place, I think." And before Johnny could loose a single burst or Tommy a single arrow, the Spider King vanished from the balcony into the red light.

"It's a portal," Tommy said, staring at the face of a radiant blood-red gem that was seven feet tall. "It has to be."

"We've got to follow," said Johnny.

"But we don't know where it goes," said Autumn. Then she looked at Jimmy.

Jimmy closed his eyes and squinted. "Nothing yet."

"It doesn't matter," said Kiri Lee. "We've got to try."

"What about our weapons?" Kat asked.

There was an awkward silence.

"I'll still have my fire," said Johnny. "And Kiri Lee can still air walk—even better now."

"What if the portal throws us back to Earth," Jimmy asked, "in the middle of his other fortress in Canada?"

There was another awkward silence.

"Kat, Autumn, and I will lose our steel," Tommy said. "And we may well be about to leap into a trap. But it can't be helped. Besides, we know Vexbane. *We* are weapons."

One by one, shielding their eyes from the fierce brightness, the young lords stepped into the red light and vanished.

They emerged from the portal without their weapons and wearing only leather armor, tunics, and breeches. It was dark, but a thin band of red light shone down from somewhere high above, creating a blood-red cone made of mist some fifty yards away. The Elves felt a hollow emptiness all around them as if it was some chamber of vast proportions.

"Brave," came the Spider King's voice out of the shadows. "I thought you'd come," he said, stepping into the red light. It almost seemed he spoke with a grudging kind of respect. "And the strong one made the choice to let the air walker live? How strange, given that he was the greater warrior. Your Elf parents had a similar misplaced determination."

Tommy wished, for once, that he had amplified hearing rather than sight because, as the Spider King spoke, it seemed there was another sound. Barely audible . . . a kind of high scraping noise.

"They could have saved us all a great deal of trouble," the Spider King continued. "Had they simply taken you as babes and fled into the hidden passages to Nightwish, we would have learned its location and exterminated the Elves much, much sooner. But no. They gave up their lives . . . so that your race could live on." The Spider King reached to his side and drew a strange dagger from his belt.

The grating sound continued, but Tommy found himself staring at the Spider King's features. He looked familiar somehow. Not the eyes. No, the eyes were very foreign. But there was something in the shape of his face, the high cheekbones and the way they tapered back to the ears. Even the ears were different from the other Gwar he'd seen. His were less like an oak leaf, more compact. More slanted.

"You know, it's fitting that we should duel here," said the Spider King, pressing the point of his strange dagger into the tip of his finger. He laughed quietly as he went on. "When the Drefids showed me how to breed the Warspiders and . . . make them mean . . . my wife and I used to hold tournaments."

Wife? thought Kat.

"We'd watch from that balcony up there," he pointed with the dagger to an opening some fifty or sixty feet up. "Watching as Gwar, spiders, or other things fought to the death. It was quite entertaining."

Half listening, staring full on at the Spider King's face with telescopic magnification, it finally clicked. The thought blasted into Tommy's mind like a freight train smashing into the station house at full speed. He blurted out, "You . . . you're half Elven!"

The Spider King stopped cold, just staring at Tommy. His hands dropped to his sides. "Yes," he said at last, a strange disconnect in his voice. "My . . . father . . . was Elven. What does that do to your categories, young lords . . . your theories about me? About my motives?"

"Don't let him get to you, Tommy," came Kat's thoughts. *"Remember, like Grimwarden said, 'Evil or good, black or white, there's no in between.'"*

"You know," said the Spider King, "I married an Elf maiden. I guess you could say such prejudices run in my family. Would you like to meet her?"

Kat! Tommy thought as loud as he could. *Tell Johnny to ready his flame. When I give the word, I want him to blast the Spider King and everything around him.*

"Got it," Kat said in his mind.

A strange voice came out of the shadows somewhere above and to the left of the Spider King. It was a female voice but raspy, with a subtle buzzing undercurrent. "They speak," she said, "in their minds. They prepare for us . . . a fire."

"That is no concern for us, Navira," said the Spider King. "Come . . . meet our guests."

"NOW!" yelled Tommy. He and the other Elves parted, giving Johnny a clear shot.

Johnny stepped up, braced his feet, and expelled his flames. The darkness of the chamber fled from the inferno, rising as high as the balcony. The walls around them seemed sheer. No way out. No place to hide.

Johnny could not see past the flare of his own hands, but the others could. Through the ten-foot blaze, they saw Johnny's fire cling to something immense, in the shape of a Warspider but with other features. Six legs, not eight . . . a more slender, oval abdomen, rather than the bloated bag common to most arachnids. From the torso rose something humanoid, but the arms were longer and had sharp, pinching claws instead of a hand with fingers. The head was angular and extremely misshapen. It looked like it had long narrow ears that tapered to a point. And where the jaw was supposed to be, a pair of massive curving fangs protruded.

"Your fire avails you not," said the creature with an unnerving hiss. "For I am made from the fire of this realm by the dark arts, far more powerful than those things . . . those spidersssss."

Johnny turned off his flames. His mouth dropped open.

The fire clung to the creature's frame, but bit by bit, it was extinguished. And they all beheld her true form, glistening in the red light from above. She had no skin, but a hard, black, shell-like surface covered her entire body like articulated armor. Whiplike horns protruded from her segmented limbs, up the middle of her torso, and a great many from the back of her head like thick locks of hair. She had two large eyes, slanted ovals . . . dark, shining like black glass . . . and perfectly emotionless. And above these were three smaller eyes. They all seemed to be staring at the Elves. "Your fire tickles," she said.

The Spider King stepped out from behind her and said, "I, too, am unharmed."

"By my protection," Navira said with another hiss.

"Yes," he replied. Then he removed a large ring of keys from his belt. "You will need more freedom to move around this time," he said and he went to work unlocking a great many shackles that bound her long legs and a harness around her abdomen. "Now, kill them."

Navira hesitated a moment. She took one step toward the Elves and said, "I will kill . . . and feed . . . slowly."

The Elves spread out and made ready. But instead she turned on the Spider King, lunged, and sunk her fangs into his neck.

The Spider King pulled himself off of Navira's fangs. "What . . . have you . . . done?" His eyes bulging with shock and rage, he clutched his bleeding neck, stumbled backward out of the red light, and collapsed with a wet thud somewhere in the back of the chamber.

"You . . . you killed him," said Tommy, already rehearsing attack possibilities in his mind. *Go low and evade,* he thought. Johnny's fire was completely ineffective, but if he could use it to hide them, then Autumn could run . . . she might be able to get to the Spider King's body, get that dagger and put out Navira's eyes. Maybe they'd have a chance.

Navira turned and raced with spider swiftness to the Elves. She slammed forelegs down on either side of Tommy, stone splitting underfoot. He was about to try to roll beneath her when she said, "I perceive your thought, Elf. Do not try to escape me."

"Jimmy!"

"I . . . I don't think she's going to kill yu!" he yelled back.

"Don't *think*?" Tommy growled.

"I do not plan to kill you," Navira said. "I was once your kindred."

There was an awkward silence. "Our kindred? I—I don't understand," said Johnny, pointing to where the Spider King had fallen. "Why'd you kill him?"

"That is a long tale," she said, no emotion in her dark eyes, her voice raspy but somehow sweet. "I loved him once, but what began in him as bitterness became something far worse, and he grew to hate even me. I became a prisoner in this land, and everything I knew of him died away. But when he discovered the Drefid clans and their dark arts, he became consumed, experimenting with ancient relics, poisons, and strange elements.

"Each time he created a new potion, he tested it on me. I grew very sick, on the verge of death even. And that was when he inoculated me with venom from creatures that dwell in the deep place of Vesper Crag where volcanic gases replace the air. I became"—she tilted her massive head back and shrieked—"this! He used me to breed his Warspiders . . . and other things. But he was furious with me because my offspring shared only my size, not my power. He put those shackles and chains upon me and tightened them whenever it pleased him to see me in pain. I . . . I murdered for him . . . so many times.

"That," Navira said, "is why I killed him. Those chains have restrained me for nearly a thousand years. When he released them, I had only a moment to act."

"Navira, you mentioned something about your power," Tommy prompted.

"Yes," she replied. "Lords of Berinfell, did you not recognize it? Did you not hear me as I spoke your thoughts? For I am born Navira Hiddenblade." She looked to Kat.

Kat rocked in place and was speechless.

"Does that disturb you?" Navira asked.

"I'm sorry," Kat said. "I did not mean . . . that is, I just wasn't expecting it."

"Remember, I was not always as I am," she said. "I once had beautiful blue skin like yours. I am eighth-generation Hiddenblade. What are you?"

"I, um, don't know," said Kat. "I haven't learned that much about my—*our*—family."

"That is of mixed consequence," said Navira. "Now, young Elven Lords, I am sure there are others in this war who might need your assistance."

"And we need to get Jett," said Kiri Lee. "I had no choice but to leave him."

"How do we get out of here?" asked Jimmy.

"His portal is still active," Navira replied. "It is the only way, unless you can climb sheer rock like I can . . . or fly."

"Some of us can fly, er, sort of," said Tommy. "But we'll take the portal. Our weapons are in the high tower and . . . and we need to get our friend."

They turned to leave, but Johnny hesitated. He looked back at the creature who had once been an Elf maiden. She sat in kind of a crouch and rubbed her leg where a shackle had been for so long. She wasn't so frightening now. In fact, he felt sad for her.

"Navira?" he called back to her. "Where will you go now?"

She looked up. "I—"

"*Rrrrraaaahhhhh!*" The room shook with a deep, rolling roar, and the young lords covered their ears as the horrible sound ended with a high, wailing shriek. Luminous red eyes appeared in the back of the chamber.

Faster than blinking, something massive leaped out of the dark and landed on Navira's back. She hissed and clawed at this sudden intruder. But the creature, larger and heavier than Navira, crushed her to the ground. In one swift, violent motion, it grabbed her head and wrenched it. Her flailing stopped, and she fell limp.

"Nooooo!" Johnny yelled, and he loosed his fire upon the murderous beast.

Laughter rolled out of the inferno . . . familiar laughter. It was the same otherworldly sound that spoke not of joy but of agony and malice . . . the same they had heard near the tower of red light.

"The Spider King," whispered Autumn. "No . . . no, it can't be."

"We need to leave, right now! Follow me!" Jimmy yelled. "He won't fit through." Jimmy stepped into the portal and disappeared.

Roaring, the creature leaped through the fire directly at the Elves.

Johnny shoved Kiri Lee into the portal. Autumn shoved Johnny. Kat shoved Autumn. Tommy shoved Kat, but something struck him hard on the back and he fell through the portal into the tower of red light.

"Tommy, you're bleeding!" yelled Kat.

Rolling his shoulder blades, he stood up. "I'll be fine," he said. "Get your weapons. If there's a way to get here quickly from inside, he'll know it."

"But that's not really him . . . is it?" asked Kiri Lee. "Navira killed him."

"Maybe it was another Wisp," said Jimmy.

"No," said Tommy. "Not a Wisp. And Navira didn't kill him. We all just thought she did. Her venom . . . it must . . . it must have changed him, turned him into that thing."

"Tommy, what do I do?" asked Johnny. "My fire won't work against him. I have no other weapons. Nothing."

"Remember your Vexbane training," said Tommy. "Use your fire for movement, for cover, for distraction. Remember, if we work together, we are far more powerful."

Emboldened, Johnny nodded. "Okay, okay, got it."

Kat strapped on her long fighting knives. "What about the Rainsong?" she asked.

That stopped Tommy cold, and he closed his eyes. While training and reading the book of prophecies back in Whitehall everything had seemed so possible. And after finding the Keystone, Tommy felt sure that everything in the prophecies would come true . . . well, true the way he thought they should. Now what? *We needed all Seven. Jett's gone. What good is the Rainsong, and what good are any of the prophecies?*

"I heard all that, you know," said Kat. "I think we should try it anyway."

Tommy looked at his feet for a second and then turned to Kiri Lee. "Kiri Lee, do you—?"

Kiri Lee sat six steps down from the balcony. She wept quietly into her hands. Tommy went to her and sat down next to her. For once, Kat didn't mind. In fact, she joined him by sitting on Kiri Lee's other side. Jimmy sat down behind her. Johnny and Autumn stood nearby.

"We're going to get through this," Tommy told Kiri Lee. "We will."

"Jett didn't get through it," Kiri Lee cried.

"Jett made a choice," Tommy said. "The right one."

"How can you say that?" She turned and pounded on Tommy's chest. "He was our best warrior, our strongest. He was our healer. All I'm good for is getting away."

"Hey, now," Johnny intervened. "That's no good. If it hadn't been for you, I'd be smeared all over the rocks down there."

"That's right," said Kat. "If it hadn't been for you, we'd have been killed at Dalhousie. Every gift is important, Kiri Lee. Remember what Grimwarden taught us from First Voice? Ellos uses the weak and foolish things of this realm. He gives gifts and prepares good things for us all to do."

Kiri Lee sobbed. "I watched him die," she said. "I told him to let go, but he wouldn't. And I watched the light in his violet eyes fade."

Tommy pulled her to his shoulder. "I'm sorry," he said. "I know it hurts. But we're all glad you're still with us."

"Tommy." Jimmy's voice was tight and clipped. "Tommy, stand up. He's coming."

Tommy was on his feet in an instant, watching the Spider King clamber up the mountain with dreadful speed. He could hear his heart beating in his ears.

"Well, m'lads and lasses," said Jimmy. "This is it."

"What do you mean?" asked Autumn.

"It's quite simple really," Jimmy replied. "He's comin' to get us, so either we figure out a way to kill him, or we all die."

41

Stalemate

AS THE creature traversed the final hundred yards, the young lords saw him clearly for the first time. He was, in general form, very like Navira, only larger. His legs were thicker and had spikes of bone jutting from each joint and segment. His arms, more bulky with muscle, and his clawed fists, heavy and vastly oversized . . . like weighted clubs. His shoulders were peculiarly humped as if an immense tumor had spread across his back, and there was a black socket on either side as if the tumor itself had eyes. But it was the creature's head that was most different, and rather terrifying.

The new Spider King had six eyes, two of them large, deep set, and slanted. The other four were smaller and spread back on his scalp. But they were all red, red as if the normal pigmentation of Gwar eyes had been stoked to a radiant flame by utter malice. Where Navira had had a nest of whiplike strands in place of hair, the Spider King had just three. They curled back over his bare skull, one from each corner of his brow, and the third bisecting his forehead from the bridge of his flat nose.

"Kind of you . . . to wait for me," he said. His voice was deeper and had an odd hiss, and massive fangs jutted from the corners of his misshapen mouth.

"Now for it, lads!" The surprising command came from Jimmy, and he charged down the mountain toward the enemy.

"Everyone, go, now!" Tommy yelled. "All as one! Endurance and Victory!"

Kiri Lee leaped into the air and drew her rychesword. Johnny ran beneath her, pulled fire into his palms, and began to run to his right. His fireballs hit the Spider King across his entire body, and Johnny walked them up, launching four directly at his fanged face. Autumn's axes sang as she darted in and out of the creature's legs. Kat circled around below him to the left, and Tommy stayed at a distance, waiting to take his shot.

Johnny's fire was only an irritant, a blinding cover, but it did no harm. The Spider King swiped with a club hand, missing Johnny but spraying him with volcanic rock. Johnny cut off his flame and covered his head, and that gave the Spider King an opportunity to charge. Johnny wouldn't get up in time. Tommy nocked and fired one arrow at the creature's eye, then another. But the Spider King clubbed them away and kept climbing toward Johnny.

Kiri Lee ran across the air and dropped down toward the monster's head, but he perceived the attack and leaped. His sudden upward thrust caught Kiri Lee off guard. The hump on his back crashed into her like a battering ram from below. Kiri Lee was knocked head over heels fifty yards down slope, but she managed to right herself and slow her descent.

The Spider King leaped again, this time for distance. Autumn sped upslope to the place she thought he would land and, remembering a scene from a favorite movie, tried to position herself so that when he landed, he would impale himself on her sword. But as he plummeted toward her, he drew his six legs to a point aiming right for Autumn. If she didn't move, she'd be killed.

"Run downslope, Autumn!" came Kat's thoughts. Autumn raced out just in time.

"I hear your thoughts," said the Spider King as he landed. "You have no hope."

"You can't fight us all at once!" Tommy yelled as he fired a flurry of arrows.

"Yes," said the Spider King, capturing the arrows with his claws. "Yes . . . I can."

A streak of lightning blasted the rock just fifty yards below where Tommy stood. He gazed down in dismay as he saw a myriad of warriors charging up the mountain far below. Using his telescopic vision, he saw that Gwar, Drefids, and Warspider were racing to the Spider King's aid. But the Elves, and even some Gnomes, were climbing after them, hewing at their heels from behind. Tommy couldn't stare for long, and a warning from Jimmy saved his life. He dove and rolled ten yards before coming to a rough stop in a mixture of ash and broken stone. The Spider King snarled and withdrew the tip of one of his segmented legs from the puncture mark where Tommy had been just a moment before.

Johnny laid down a wall of flame, hiding Tommy from the Spider King's view. Jimmy raced behind it and helped Tommy to his feet. They ran for cover, finding a cleft in the rock where they could hide on the southern side of the peak.

"This is ridiculous," said Jimmy, panting. "We trained to fight Warspiders and Gwar, not some mutant mixture a' both!"

"Don't give up," Tommy implored. "The prophecy said we'd have power unmatched and victory assured. He's got to have a weakness."

"If he does, I'm not seein' it." Jimmy wiped the back of his neck. His hand came back with bits of black rock and a smearing of gray ash and blood. "Wait!" Jimmy straightened his posture. "When he killed Navira—"

Tommy finished the thought, "He got her by the neck."

"*Right*," said Jimmy. "*Bah!* If only Jett were still here. He could leap up on the beast's back and snap his neck."

"We don't have that brute strength anymore," said Tommy. "But maybe we can still cut him there. Come on!"

"Where's, what's . . . huh?"

"Just stay with me, warn me every time I'm about to get clobbered!" Tommy ran out and raced toward Kat.

"Aye," said Jimmy, chasing after him. "I'll try."

While the Spider King was busy with Kiri Lee's air attacks and Autumn's hacking away at his legs, Tommy had given Kat his plan and grabbed

Johnny to circle back twenty yards below the Spider King. Now it was their job to utterly distract the beast. Maybe, just maybe, he would be so engaged in the brazen frontal assault that he wouldn't be able to focus on reading thoughts. If Kat could tell Autumn and Kiri Lee what to do without the Spider King learning, they'd have their best chance, perhaps their only chance, to defeat him.

Better hurry, Tommy thought, glancing down the mountain. The enemy forces were still climbing, fighting the Elves all the way.

"Jimmy, you got our backs?" Tommy yelled.

"AYE!"

Tommy squinted. Waited. Then, "Now, Johnny!"

Johnny split off to the right and opened up the floodgates on his flame. He put his wrists together and sent a dense stream of fire directly into the Spider King's face. The Spider King was not burned, of course, but it did cause him to maneuver. He ducked and bobbed, sliding left and then right, getting dangerously close to Johnny.

Tommy had just a handful of arrows left . . . seven at most. It was time to spend them. He nocked the first and aimed. This was a far cry from the Thurgood Marshall Middle School gym on Falcon Day. And he wasn't shooting at straw-filled targets with a few hundred students looking on.

No, Tommy was lining up to shoot a dangerous, darting, constantly moving target. He glanced down the mountain: the warriors—both enemy and ally—had arrived. And inexplicably only a few of them were still fighting. They stared at the combat above them, the Spider King and the Elven Lords of Berinfell. It was the Battle of Generations, and would be heralded as such for generations to come . . . if any of them survived to recount it. It suddenly seemed that the weight of history pressed down on Tommy. Seven arrows. He'd need to make every shot count.

Tommy fired the first arrow through the fire directly at the spot where the creature's left eye should be. But the Spider King smacked it away.

Another and another Tommy fired, each from a different angle as he changed positions. He loosed all his arrows but one, and still the Spider King blocked.

A good thing, Tommy thought, *. . . means his thoughts are on the inbound arrows, not behind him.*

At that split second there came a freezing, sudden fear. The Spider King hesitated just a moment. Tommy knew what he'd done. He'd just given up the plan in his thoughts. But as the Spider King started to make a move, Tommy fired his last arrow. It flew straight through Johnny's stream of fire and—

"No!" Tommy cried out.

The Spider King had caught the arrow in his claw. But when Tommy looked closer, he saw that the claw held only the back half of his arrow. The creature had reached up a moment too late and clipped the arrow in two. The other half was buried in the Spider King's right eye.

Greenish liquid oozed from the wound, but the Spider King did not seem the least bit troubled by the arrow in his eye. He reached up with his claw and plucked it out without uttering so much as a growl of pain. At that moment, from above and behind the Spider King, Kiri Lee climbed the air—and she was carrying Autumn. In a flash, she dropped Autumn onto the Spider King's humped back. Using her supernatural speed, Autumn used both axes and hacked away at the Spider King's neck. Tommy couldn't see her strokes—they were a blur. She'd have felled a redwood in three seconds with such a flurry. But . . .

There wasn't any blood.

The Spider King shrugged his massive shoulders, propelling Autumn into the air. At the same time, the Spider King clubbed Kiri Lee, not a full-on blow, but enough to send her spinning.

Johnny awkwardly fired himself in the air to grab Autumn. She smacked into him, and as much as he tried to stabilize their fall, they hit the ground, sending up a plume of fresh ash, and rolled toward the surging mass of warriors just below.

Tommy dropped his bow. There were no more arrows. He shook his head in disbelief. *We're supposed to be the saviors of Berinfell . . . of Allyra—foretold by the prophets, trained by the elite, branded as heroes before we'd ever swung a sword.* But it was more than that. The Seven had held powers . . . unimaginable powers! They'd found the Keystone and now possessed the Rainsong. If anything, their powers should be amplified, but they'd tried and now all their powers seemed useless against the Spider King.

Covered in blood and ash, Johnny and Autumn charged back up the mountain. The Spider King turned to their advance and leaned forward. Tommy watched in sick fascination as little white strands appeared around the strange sockets in the creature's humped shoulders. More and more collected there as if a throng of ghosts were trying to escape. The Spider King grunted, and the tiny threads formed into a milky white stream that sprayed out toward Johnny and Autumn. It hit them hard and knocked them backward. But they didn't roll. This liquid webbing adhered them to the mountain. They were stuck fast.

"Help!" Autumn cried out. "Cut us out!"

"It's spreading, going to suffocate u—uh—glguuh—help—h—!"

The Spider King reared up on his hind legs and roared. The Drefids and Gwar on the slope below cheered with shrieks and grunts.

When Tommy and Jimmy got to the place where their friends had been stuck in the web, they found Kat already there. She'd managed to cut the spreading white muck away from their faces. With Tommy and Jimmy's help, they set Johnny and Autumn free.

But what did it matter? Tommy thought as he looked up at the approaching Spider King. They were all sick to their stomachs. They'd taken their best shot. They had nothing left. And death was inevitable.

"What do you know of power?" asked the Spider King. "You are children born of a weak race, raised in an even weaker society."

Thunder rumbled. It seemed to be right on top of the mountain.

"Your elders put too much stock in you . . . no, too much stock in the old ways . . . myths." He held up his claw. "Look, look behind you. See my armies, my fortress, my lands? I KNOW power, real power! Power to create life, power to take it . . . even power to wake the dormant volcano to vomit up FIRE!"

Tommy did look, and at first he saw only what the Spider King told him to see. But then he saw farther out, beyond the reach of the Spider King's six eyes. Tommy saw a train of beings trodding slowly across the Lightning Fields north of the volcano. It was not a precise military march. *Slaves,* Tommy thought. *Grimwarden, Goldarrow, Charlie . . .* they'd succeeded. *Well, if nothing else,* Tommy thought, *we've bought them some time.*

But that was little solace. Time for what? Maybe to get to the Dark Veil. Maybe to the underground rivers. And then what? Another cavern, another Nightwish? All this effort all to go back and hide for another eight hundred years?

"So," said the Spider King. "They have taken the humans . . . how ironic. Elves take generations of Gwar and enslave them. Now they release MY slaves?" His expression contorted. "Hypocrites! LIARS!" He mastered his emotion once more. "What of it? I will kill you, their precious lords, gutting the Elves of their spirit forever. And if it takes hundreds of years to find the remnants and kill them all, what of that? I have new horizons to explore."

"What now?" Jimmy whispered from behind.

Defeat. That was Tommy's first thought. Utter defeat. But no, Tommy wasn't the type to quit.

"Tommy?" came Kat's quiet voice. She wasn't reading his thoughts. Maybe she didn't want to know.

"Come, brave Elves," said the Spider King. "I am waiting."

"We'll fight," Tommy said at last.

"But we'll lose," said Johnny.

"I know," Tommy said.

42

The Rainsong

TOMMY STOOD up, exhaled loudly, and cracked his neck side to side. He turned to his friends and said, "You know how ridiculous this all is?" He was almost laughing. The other lords looked on him with deepening concern but listened nonetheless. "I mean, me . . . the curly-haired nothing, chronically average—the kid known for never having cable TV—and here I am in another world as a warrior, a lord, a prophesied hero. We all are." He looked at each of his friends in turn. "We're a bunch of misfits. A motley assembly of the broken, the lost. And yet . . . here we are. It's kind of a miracle."

A miracle. The Rainsong. Wait, he thought, *maybe it's not a good-luck charm to stick in our pockets or just for information.*

"Where's Kiri Lee?" Tommy asked suddenly.

"He hit her," said Johnny. "I . . . didn't see where she went down." The wind buffeted them as they looked around. Another flash and crack of lightning.

The Spider King was waiting too patiently. "Will you mount one last stand? A final heroic verse to your very sad, sad song?"

"Kat, reach out to Kiri Lee with your thoughts," Tommy commanded. "Tell her to sing the Rainsong."

"But there are only six of us now," said Jimmy.

"Jimmy," Tommy said, "none of this has turned out the way we thought it would. None of us really has a clue what the Rainsong will do, but the prophecies said the Rainsong must be heard over mountain and field. If I'm going down tonight, then I'm going down singing. For us. For Ellos." He laughed. "You remember the words, right?"

"Beneath the burning firmament of heaven," Autumn sang out.

Johnny answered, "Live the Children of the Light."

"Blood of kings, strength of queens," sang Tommy.

Jimmy belted out the last line as loud as he could, "Sons and daughters, each we stand."

"Kiri Lee's not answering," said Kat. "I can't find her mind."

"Okay," Tommy said, "spread out. Sing while you search for Kiri Lee. If she's alive, she'll hear it."

To the Spider King's amusement, the young lords scattered, once more attempting their useless attacks. And now they were going to sing . . . some ancient hymn? "Enough!" he thundered, slamming his claws to the ground.

"Everyone, sing!" Tommy yelled.

But not more than a minute after they started their search, they heard something. Soft at first, but growing in strength, Kiri Lee's exquisite voice. She hovered high overhead and sang with a heart ten times her stature, "Beneath the burning firmament of heaven live the Children of the Light . . ."

Sounds of battle made it hard to hear the words distinctly. Metal and rock, bone and scream. Everything vied for dominance over the small voice that fought to be heard.

"Blood of kings, strength of queens, sons and daughters, each we stand. . . ." Some of the soldiers stopped fighting. Even the Spider King glanced upward.

Kiri Lee's tribe medallion began to glow, a silvery, bluish light that illuminated her weakening face. With every word that poured past her lips, the medallion grew brighter.

"Let every crooked road be straight. Let injustice suffer our wrath. . . ." But she was not alone. The other five lords found their place among the lyrics and began singing with her.

"By the hand of the justice bane, we dispatch the ruthless, wicked, and foul. . . ." Their medallions all began to glow.

Tommy looked to Kat. *Is it working?* he thought.

She nodded; then a wide smile formed on her face. Grimwarden had been right after all. The song was a supernatural weapon to be used against the enemy . . . but how did it work?

The Spider King, moving as only spiders can, raced up on each of the lords, snapping at them with his claws, firing his webbing to trap them. But each time they eluded his blows and eluded capture. Spinning like a dumb beast after its tail, the Spider King grew infuriated, but somehow Kiri Lee's voice rose even above his rants. She dodged globs of webbing, the projectiles arching harmlessly through the air.

Is anything happening? Tommy wondered. He didn't see anything. *Sing faster!* It was all Tommy could think. The song was having no apparent effect on the battle at hand. They must have to finish it first. Tommy ducked a terrible swipe from the Spider King and rolled into a Vexbane crouch, two fingers extended to the ground.

He looked down on the battle between the enemy forces and the flet soldiers. More and more warriors from both sides had come, but they all gave the lords and the Spider King a wide berth.

The last lines couldn't come too soon. Kiri Lee's voice rose like the crescendo of a symphony: "The Lords of Berinfell take up their thrones, and the Mighty of Allyra, their mantel awaits. For Ellos empowers those who draw near, holding hands as one, their destinies intertwined."

And just like that, the melody and the glow of their medallions vanished, swallowed by the sounds of war.

The young lords looked about even as they ran. Nothing had changed. The battle still raged. The Spider King still chased.

Ah, Tommy thought as he ran. *I almost believed something would happen.*

"Me, too," Kat answered, her thoughts going silent while she listened. And then she told Tommy: *"Kiri Lee thinks it's because Jett died. There are only six of us."*

Maybe, thought Tommy.

Laughter. Tommy heard Kat's laughter in his mind. *What?* he asked.

"Jimmy thinks it's because his voice stinks."

Tommy laughed, too, and watched Johnny blasting fireballs at the Spider King, Jimmy directing him so that they wouldn't get caught.

"I'm tired of running," said Kat, a sad finality to her words.

Tommy stopped suddenly. *I am, too.* He drew his rychesword.

Kat was forty yards across from him. She drew her long knives.

Before we do this, Tommy began, *there's something I wanted to say to you. I—*

"Wait!" He thought it but said it out loud as well. *Listen!*

"There's just noise. I don't—"

And then Kat heard it, too. It wasn't very loud at first. Almost a murmur. But present, nonetheless. Kat looked back to the other lords. Mounting wonder painting their expressions, they stopped running. They heard it, too: the Rainsong.

As if their own singing of the ancient verses had summoned a congregation to worship, the song came to life again, only this time with the voices of many. "They're singing," said Kat.

"They're singing," said Tommy.

Each lord in turn said the same, except for Kiri Lee, who did not seem surprised, for she sang, too, lending her dulcet, sweet-sounding voice to the others.

With swords still swinging and bows still firing, the great army of the Elves was actually singing. Word for word, note for note. Louder and louder it grew, spreading across the mountainside, and then down into the Lightning Fields, even up the far side of the battlefield.

Tommy, closed his eyes wondering how they all knew it. Had Grimwarden taught them at Nightwish? Had enough Elves heard Kiri Lee singing it as she walked those long halls? Tommy didn't know. It didn't matter. It was the most beautiful song he'd ever heard. It echoed into every space imaginable, filling the hearts of the noble with hope and the hearts of the wicked with a growing uneasiness. It rang in every turret and tower of Vesper Crag, and surged back into the Thousand-League Forest. But when Tommy opened his eyes, he witnessed a sky unlike any he'd seen before. Dark gray and roiling like a night sea, the clouds churned and seemed to press down on Vesper Crag. Lightning, blue, purple, and white, crawled within the seams and creases, spreading in flashes beneath the clouds but never striking down to the ground.

Even the Spider King stopped his pursuit and stared.

"Come on!" Kat's voice in Tommy's mind.

Kat was quickly on the stairs. The other lords were with her. *"Come on!"*

Tommy ran across and joined his friends.

"It's getting darker," said Johnny. "Something's definitely up."

"Guys, look out there." Autumn pointed to the northwest, past the volcano to the horizon. There was a black wall of cloud moving deceptively fast toward Vesper Crag. It was massive, consuming the sky and lesser clouds as it came.

"There!" pointed Kat. Another such thunderhead rolled in from the northeast. And yet another from due south. The three fronts converged overhead, and the gray was swallowed up in the center. Fingers of lightning began to crawl out of this same central point above the mountain peak.

The thousands of Elves who remained continued to sing. Tommy and the other lords looked about in wonder, then started backing down the mountainside. This was no ordinary song, nor was the God they served a mere religious icon, lifeless and powerless. Ellos was here. With them. The lords could feel him now. In the air. In their hearts.

"We were foolish," said Kiri Lee.

"Foolish?" Tommy felt it but wasn't sure why.

"To think this was just our song," she explained.

Jimmy laughed. "We fancied ourselves as Chosen Ones, we did."

"Well, we are," said Tommy. "But . . . not just us."

"So then the song?" said Johnny.

"It belongs to all of Elvendom," Kiri Lee said. "It should never have been hidden."

"I don't think the Rainsong was hidden," said Tommy, new insights crystallizing in his mind.

"But the Keystone," said Kat. "The Old Ones hid it away in that cistern."

"No," said Tommy. "It was abandoned, while our people chose other songs to sing."

Backsliding

THE YOUNG lords joined in the verses with their kinsfolk, raising their voices and drawing their swords. "Hear now, the song of the Chosen. We lift our voices as one Body, righting ancient evil with our union. Let the captive be set free—The chains of slaves be broken at last."

The medallions glowed again, only this time more fervently. Tommy looked up. The clouds were swirling swiftly now, lowering every second. More and more flashes of electricity came from the deepening hollow overhead. Tommy's fears told him the Spider King was summoning a dark force against them, but his heart believed it was something else. Believed it was Ellos.

There was power here.

"ELFKIND!" Tommy yelled. "Friends! Rally to me!"

"They can't hear you," said Kat.

"Then you tell them," ordered Tommy.

"But—"

"You read my thoughts and project it to them," said Tommy. "All of them."

Kat had never tried to project her thoughts to more than a few at a time, certainly not to thousands. Without another word, she listened in on Tommy's thoughts. Then, taking a deep breath, she focused first on the closest Elves fighting near the tower. She heard such a cacophony of voices but systematically pushed them all away, clearing space for her thoughts to enter. *"Elves and friends of Elves, this battle is won in the name of Ellos the Almighty! Rally to the Lords of Berinfell and flee this place!"*

Again and again she cried out to them, and soon a fair stream of Elves descended toward them, chased by Warspiders and Gwar. The

Drefids remained and their leader, the Spider King, forced to stay to fight the Elves and their allies.

As the flet soldiers approached, Tommy commanded them to leave Vesper Crag, to get outside of the walls as quickly as possible. Tommy knew they had questions . . . he did, too . . . but they couldn't stop, not until they were outside the walls. "Keep telling them!" he urged Kat.

FLASH!

A bolt of lightning blasted down from the inverted whirlpool of black clouds, striking the tower of red light with such force that the structure exploded. Blocks of stone hurled out, crushing those in their path. A massive piece of stone and mortar hurtled into the Spider King, pinning two of his rear legs.

And that was precisely when they all felt the first drops of rain. One splattered on Kiri Lee's forehead. She giggled. Kat held out her hand. Tommy closed his eyes and faced up, letting the drizzle wet his face. As the Elves marched by the lords, the rain increased. It became a shower. Tommy noticed some of the Elves slipping on the stairs. The water mixed with the ash and made a kind of gray slime. The rain came down even harder now and seemed to be increasing in intensity by the heartbeat.

"Kat, tell them now!" he yelled.

"I am!" she fired back.

"Skip all the flowery stuff and just tell them to GET OFF THE MOUNTAIN NOW!"

"Okay, okay!" She closed her eyes and projected.

The area at the top of the mountain was clearing out . . . certainly of Elves who got the message. But even the enemy forces were evacuating. The Spider King struggled still against the weight upon his legs. Five Drefids remained with him, trying to pry the monstrous stone just enough for his legs to come free.

"Uh, I think we need to leave now, too," said Jimmy, spitting out the rain that accumulated instantly when he opened his mouth. "It's about to get really bad."

"Right," said Tommy. "Johnny, Autumn, Kiri Lee—let's go!"

Rain pelted harder than ever, soaking them from head to foot. Every other step was a slip. Many of the Elves slid out of control for great distances until they slammed into enough of their countrymen to stop them.

When the lords reached the last few stairs to the arched window opening, water was running in a stream next to them. Half of it poured into the window, and the rest continued its journey down the mountain. Each of the lords spared more than a glance at that window, but Kiri Lee stopped.

"Kiri Lee!" Tommy called, his words whisked away by gulps of water. "What . . . what are you doing?"

"I'm not leaving Jett here!" she yelled back.

"Wha—no, Kiri Lee, you can't go back in there!" Tommy couldn't say any more from that distance. He grabbed Johnny by the arm. "Can you get any flame going in this?" he asked.

Johnny grinned. He held out his palm, and it instantly pooled with water—which flash boiled to steam and turned to a wild, flickering flame.

"Good," said Tommy hurriedly. "Make yourself a hum—no, an Elven-torch and lead our people to safety!"

"Got it!" Johnny said, and flared the fire in his palm until it shone like a beacon. "Follow me! Follow me!" he yelled.

Kiri Lee had made up her mind, Tommy knew that before he went to her, but he had to try. If she wouldn't budge, then he knew what he had to do.

"Kiri Lee," he said, taking her arm firmly, "if you go down there and this flood keeps up, you'll get washed out like a drowned rat."

"I told you," she said, "I'm not going to leave him here."

"Then I'm going with you," said Tommy, and he put a foot through the window. That was when Kiri Lee shocked him.

She placed both hands around his upper arm and lifted him bodily out of the window. She had air walked and lifted him up as well.

"There," she said, putting him down as if he weighed nothing. "That's just in case you don't think I can carry him by myself."

Tommy blinked and wiped the water out of his eyes. Then he

tenderly put a hand on Kiri Lee's shoulder and softly said, "Bring him back, Kiri Lee. Bring Jett home."

Tears and rain mixed, and Kiri Lee disappeared through the window.

As the streams increased in size and force, the Elves began to slow down.

"KEEP RUNNING!!!" Tommy screamed at the top of his lungs— lungs that burned with every step he took. He caught up to Kat and yelled to her, but the next thing he knew, they were both on their backs, sliding down the mountain. He grabbed her arm and she grabbed his as they hurtled forward. Elves fell one after the other, taken by the torrent and carried away.

Tommy tried to see what was ahead through the pelting sheets. He wished he hadn't. The central turret of Vesper Crag, a monolith of stone some two hundred feet wide, lay directly in their path. "Oh no!"

Kat lifted her head. "Oh no!"

It was too late to do anything.

Using recovered spears and shields, the Drefids managed to lift the stone slab. But the rain was at its most intense, howling and swirling, so heavy it was almost like being underwater.

The Drefids, whose bony hands were not good for much traction, couldn't see to keep the slab up long enough for the Spider King to escape. Time and again, one Drefid would lose his grip, and the stone would fall once more on his segmented legs. Then, with the Spider King roaring and threatening, the Drefids pried the stone up. The Spider King rolled his body to get his legs free. He tried to stand, but two legs were ruined. The third on that side was cracked and oozing green fluid.

That was when the Spider King turned on the Drefids.

"You promised me!" he hissed.

Four of the Drefids began to back away. One stood his ground. "But it was you who broke our agreement! You should never have taken an Elf for a wife!"

The Spider King roared. "Backstabbing liars! If you'd killed them at the sacking of Berinfell—"

"Don't blame us!" the Drefid screamed back. "You should have feared our master above that ignorant curse."

The Spider King lashed out with all the power he had, pushing off with his good legs and slamming into the Drefids. He caught the nearest Drefid by the neck and sheared off its head. The other three he crushed against his body and let them fall away into the coursing streams of gray.

But when the Spider King tried to stand, he found that he'd completely snapped his third leg. And with the pouring, coursing rain, he could not gain any stability at all. His eyes flashed with rage and he pulsed webbing from his shoulder spinnerets, but these sopping threads would not adhere to the slick stone. Using his arms and his good legs, he tried once more, achieving a brief awkward stance. But the force of the wind and rain drove him over onto his back, and he began to slide down the incline . . . and into the main current.

The flood took Tommy and Kat on a hasty loop around the building and over a sudden lip. They felt weightless for a moment, hit a deep pocket of water, and were submerged for a time before bobbing back to the surface. Slowly, they floated out into a shallow lake of incomparable murk. At last Tommy felt the ground under his feet and helped Kat to her feet. Disoriented and exhausted, they looked about for direction.

"Johnny's fire!" Tommy yelled. "Thank Ellos for that light. Come on, Kat!"

Dozens of Elves were climbing up out of the muck, and Tommy yelled to them, "Seek the flame! Follow the light!"

Kat tried to tell them through thoughts as well, but she was so terribly exhausted that she could barely stand. She grabbed Tommy's arm, and he supported her. On and on they pressed, faster and faster. Utter fatigue was setting in, and Tommy was practically dragging Kat through the thigh-deep water. "COME ON, KAT! HANG IN THERE!"

Kat coughed, pulling herself up by his arm. Her legs were just too tired.

When he was sure he couldn't take another step, he noticed the ground pitching upward. *AH!* he thought. *Almost there!* The revelation brought on a final burst of energy, and the young lords strode out of the flood and, before too long, made their way up the flowing face of the western bank. At last they made it to the top of the command hill, and there they were met by a horde of Elves welcoming them to safety.

But Grimwarden broke through them all. "Lord Felheart!" he said. "Thank Ellos you're alive!"

Tommy was about to say he was glad to see Grimwarden when the Guardmaster grabbed him by the shoulder, "I need your eyes!"

He practically dragged Tommy to the highest point on the hill. "Hurry!" he said. "With the storm, we lost sight of the Spider King."

"But this rain," said Tommy. "It was supposed to kill him, right?"

"I hope so," he replied. "But that is the kind of thing we must know for certain. Now look at the top of the hill. Is he there?"

Tommy had a hard time finding an anchor for his vision to pull in. The vague outline of the mountain peak would have to do. His eyes flew through the storm, higher and higher to the peak. "He's not there! Wait . . . wait, I see him! He's caught in the current, sliding. He's out of control, crashing into things. He looks dead."

Tommy watched the Spider King's body rolling and floating until it was about halfway down.

"Ah!" exclaimed Grimwarden. "I see him now!" Together, they watched him careen the rest of the way. He smacked hard into a massive chunk of a fallen tower that teetered on the edge of a waterfall. The body slid off the edge and fell some fifty feet into a waiting pool below. Then the tower, all twenty feet of stone, rolled over the edge and plummeted into the pool.

"That," said Grimwarden, his voice quavering, "is the end of the Spider King."

"Any sign?" Autumn asked Tommy.

"No," he replied.

"She'll make it," said Autumn.

Bloodied and caked with ash, Ethon Beleron appeared and said, "If your Kiri Lee survived that crash near the wall, she can make it back through this deluge."

"She better," whispered Tommy.

Even on high ground, the water flowed past their ankles, speeding toward lower ground. A stiffening chill set in. Johnny hugged Autumn, her teeth chattering. And before Tommy could move, Kat had stepped into his chest, arms tucked up, body trembling. Tommy, slightly startled, felt awkward enveloping her in his arms. But soon he knew she needed him. Maybe for more than just warmth.

The army of Berinfell stood there, motionless, prisoner of the rain that they themselves had called down. Long seconds stretched into minutes, and minutes stretched into an hour. Not once did a Gwar rise up the hill from the field, nor a Warspider to so much as taunt them. The endless clash of metal on metal, or stone on flesh, had ceased. Now all they heard was rain.

Just rain. How long it went on, no one quite knew. But one pervading thought was shared by every Elf who had endured the storm: it was a miracle.

Many rested, some leaning on their spears, some with heads on the shoulders of those beside them. But the cold that set in kept any from falling asleep.

Tommy had drifted into a kind of exhausted trance when a crowd of Elves began to gather nearby. Neither he nor Kat looked up as Kiri Lee stepped down out of the air and placed her friend into the arms of her people.

44

A New Dawn

THE ENTIRE Elven army stood on the west bank as the morning sun broke through the clouds on the eastern horizon. Just the sight of it was life-giving for many of the Elves who had been wounded in battle or nearly drowned in the great flood. For the first time in a long time, the sun shone bright over Vesper Crag, housed in a brilliant blue sky-bowl.

What had been known just hours before as the Lightning Fields was now a flooded basin of destruction. The valley held a putrid brown sea, stretching out to the base of Vesper Crag, as far north as the Dark Veil, and all the way into the southern forest. Boiling sections of the new lake shot steam into the air, lava and water colliding under the surface. But most staggering were the bodies that floated on the surface . . . thousands of them.

For a long while, no one moved. They just took in the scene, staring in stunned silence. Moments before, it seemed, the entire Elven army was fleeing for their lives; the next, they were standing over the corpses of their foes, victorious.

"Thanks to Ellos! ENDURANCE AND VICTORY!!" Tommy hoisted his sword skyward.

He wasn't sure exactly what happened after that, the reality of their conquest swelling in his own heart like a tidal wave. Enraptured, he was caught up in the euphoria of the moment, having just lived a dream. A wild and crazy dream. One that had taken him across time and space, far from home . . . to a new home. He felt his mouth moving and saw the others shouting . . . the Lords . . . Grimwarden . . . Elle . . . Charlie . . . thousands of others screaming down over the bodies of their enemies. *"Endurance and Victory,"* they cried, shouting it for all of Allyra to hear. And hear they did, the thunderous praise ringing through the air, shaking the hollows of Nightwish, the trees of the Thousand-League Forest, even the hidden dens of the Gnomes. The whole world would know: Allyra was free at last. They had endured. And now, together as one, they were victorious.

It took two days to get the army assembled, tend to the wounded, and ready supplies for the trek westward. Five days of travel through the Thousand-League Forest brought them back to Nightwish where their wives, children, and the elderly awaited. Here they were received with a hero's welcome, and Jett's body was borne with honor into the main avenue. There, thunderous applause sustained for almost an hour, wave after wave of adoration and thankfulness exploding from their hearts. And all the while, everyone had to keep reminding themselves that it was over. The war was finally over.

Despite everyone's eagerness to rid themselves of Nightwish forever, they suspected that Berinfell was in great disrepair. It would take weeks, even months for it to be habitable again. And creating adequate shelter aboveground in the forest would simply be a waste of resources and time. No, Nightwish would remain their home for a little longer. But that didn't stop the lords and their generals from heading out on a reconnaissance mission as soon as they were rested.

The journey back to Berinfell did not feel real. No one, not even Grimwarden, had dared venture back to the hallowed halls of their former glory. Not when so many horrific memories covered the stones of their streets with the blood of their people. But no longer. The pain of the memories would fade with each passing generation, but not the significance of their sacrifice.

They headed south, a two-day journey by foot, and arrived at the famed Tree Gate in the north, where Travin had deceived the enemy so many ages ago. It was here that they reentered their prized city for the first time in over eight hundred years.

Whatever damage the Spider King had done was long past. Now

it was the forest that encroached on the space. Miles and miles of vines weaved their way in and out of every stone crevice imaginable; trees bore up through solid rock roads, their leafy canopies now shade for once highly traveled thoroughfares; animals had made burrows in vacant dwellings, and birds nested on ledges and beams alike. And over the entire city deep green grass and weeds burst from every available crack.

Those who had lived here had memories flooding back to them, stretching into their childhood. They touched the stone walls of their homes and kissed the streets with their lips. More than a few of the scouts started to weep. Not of bitterness, but of suffering a long absence. For the Elves were as intertwined with this place as the vines were, wrapped around every stone, every arch, every dried-up fountain, as if their very spirits were connected with the place.

"I feel like . . . like I've been here before," said Kat. Her hand brushed along a hand-carved marble banister that descended along a curving staircase into what seemed to be a lower garden. "But I know that's impossible."

"Impossible?" said Elle, drawing up next to her. "But, Lord Alreenia, don't you remember? We told you . . . you were born here."

Kat held up short. *Here?* She caught her breath. *Berinfell.* It was true. This was her birthplace. More real than California. Stronger than her home overlooking Los Angeles. This was where she took her first breath. And while she had no apparent memory of the city, it was powerfully familiar. Like she was destined for it. Like *it* was destined for *her.*

The small war band spread through the city, uncovering ancient ruins, removing growth from abandoned hallways. On and on they went, deeper and deeper into the city, the flet soldiers among them remembering their last moments here all too well. And all the more when they finally arrived at the Great Hall.

Grimwarden was the first to step in through the wreckage of the main door, the wood long rotted, hinges now rusted blocks of metal. Pale light streamed in through the opening that had once held beautiful glass windows, flooding the musty main hall. The group moved down the corridor, following Grimwarden and Elle along a path the two knew by heart. To the Seven, the castle was extremely foreign . . . yet something about it was endearing. Meaningful.

After weaving down hallways with caved-in walls for more than ten minutes, they finally turned into a large room with a high-domed ceiling.

Autumn caught her breath. "I know this place."

"Excuse me?" said Grimwarden, looking to her.

"Yes," she began nodding. "The book."

"Of course!" said Kat, suddenly realizing.

"*The Chronicles of the Elf Lords and Their Kin*," added Tommy. He had seen it all. In the book. But this was not a story, some fictional movie played out in front of him. This was *real*. He was here. "We saw it all. Eight hundred years ago. This was where—"

Tommy's voice trailed off. He couldn't finish. An emotion he was not expecting swelled in his chest.

"This, m'lords, is where you were taken from," said Elle. "And where you last laid eyes on your noble parents, who would be honored to see you this day."

The young lords moved forward as if treading on sacred ground. Of course, only ruins remained. Yet for all its lackluster appearance, this place shined to them.

The lords moved slowly through the space, Grimwarden and Elle not moving a muscle. To see these young lords back in the place where they had been stolen defied every evil ever pitted against them. They had conquered after all. They were victorious. The lords picked through the rubble, touching even the most mundane rock as if it were pure gold.

Tommy reached the dais, walking slowly up the mossy steps. He knelt down and dug his fingers into a soft pile of decomposing wood. Flipping over a layer of fresh earth, he saw white. The thrones. Just as they had been in his visions of the book. Perhaps his own father had sat in this throne. The feeling was overwhelming and tears filled his eyes.

"It was his."

Tommy rubbed the tears away and looked up at Kat. "What'd you say?"

"You were wondering if it was his throne. And I'm telling you. It was his."

At that, Tommy burst into tears. The father he would never know, had sat right here. His mother had swaddled him right here. He had seen it in the book. Tommy closed his eyes, sobbing. Trying to envision their faces. Trying to remember. Anything.

Kiri Lee felt it all so keenly. Her parents . . . gone before she even knew them. But she felt worse for Jett. His parents on Earth let him go, knowing full well Jett might never return. But . . . somehow, they had to find out. Kiri Lee vowed right then that she would return to Earth one day and tell Mr. and Mrs. Green just what a hero their son had been.

The room filled with meaning now. All of the lords began to experience similar emotions, standing in the very space where all of this had begun so many years ago. On the night of their welcoming, meant for rulership, only to be whisked away at the hands of a wicked foe. They should have been eight hundred years old by now; but they were only thirteen, their maturation slowed by another world's system. But no more.

While they each hoped to return someday to Earth to visit those they loved, they realized where their true home was. The Lords of Berinfell had returned . . . to set things right, to establish a new reign from the thrones of Berinfell. They would usher in a new paradigm of leadership that would restore the glorious position of the Elves and once again bring life to the land.

They were home.

Bloodlines

A HOODED Drefid stood on a cliff outside a cave on the southern-most peak of Vesper Crag. In all his days serving as an assassin in the Sarax Clan, Asp had never seen such destruction.

"Some kind of flood," he muttered, looking at the standing pools of water down in the hollows. But what kind of flood could reach the tow-ers and even the peaks of the mountains, Asp had no idea. Everything from the tower, where the red light once shone, to the main gate had been utterly destroyed.

"Several days past," he said. Judging by the smell of the dead and rotting, perhaps as much as a week.

It had taken Asp several hours just to find a clear entrance into the fortress. But once inside, he'd explored every accessible region. The slave chambers had been blocked by a cave-in. All the maps in the plotting room were shredded, and many of the columns had toppled over. Asp went to the royal chamber last of all and found it had sur-vived with some minor damage. Several of the statues had fallen from their alcoves and shattered. And one of the two white marble thrones, the left-hand seat, had been destroyed. Blackened was a more appro-priate description. Asp knelt and examined the debris more closely. This was not water damage at all. It looked more like fire damage or arc stone residue.

Still thinking about the throne, he walked to the edge of the bal-cony. It was so odd seeing daylight shining down into the chamber where so many enemies and traitors had met their fate in the dark.

Asp leaned forward suddenly. The brilliant rays of sunshine glistened upon something he'd never seen before. Spurning the slow, hidden stairs, he leaped over the side of the balcony and landed lightly on the chamber floor.

As if in a trance, Asp walked to within twenty-one feet of the sunlit wall. There, glittering and sparkling like a vein of precious stones, was a spectacular image. Like a giant blue spider, it seemed, and yet somehow elegant, rimmed with darker blue fading to black. But within its abdomen, there was another figure, seemingly made of delicate glass. An Elf maiden sleeping, holding a small Elf child snug to her chest. The way the sun shone upon it, radiant with a prism of color, she and the child almost looked alive.

Asp had been to this chamber many, many times, but had never seen the image before. How it had gotten there while the Spider King ruled Vesper Crag . . . he had no idea. He turned and looked at the chamber floor leading up to the sunlit wall. There was a blackened trail, quite wide actually, running from the balcony side of the chamber all the way to the image. If he didn't know better, he'd have thought the image of the spider maiden was burned into the wall. Asp laughed. That was ridiculous. To burn crystal into the rock of the mountain would take a source of heat beyond his reckoning.

Asp was furious by the time he'd finished his search of Vesper Crag. He'd found more dead Gwar than he'd ever care to think about, and he'd had to turn them over, dig them out, and sometimes even put them back together to see if one bore a resemblance to the missing Spider King. He'd scrutinized every corpse for his strange hair, slanted eyes, and narrow ears—the marks of a half-breed—but he'd found no such being. There was only one place left to search.

The water.

Asp hated water with a vengeance. But he had to know for sure.

Leaping lithely from cliff to cliff, Asp found several pools where Gwar corpses floated. None of these were the one he was looking for.

But as he prepared to jump to the next cliff, Asp saw something a little farther down. There was a large portion of one of the castle's many turrets smashed on the ledge below. All of the castle's turrets were smashed, but there was something peculiar in the debris near this one.

Fifty feet was nothing for a Drefid, so he leaped down. And there, half-crushed beneath several tons of broken stone, was what at first he took to be a Gwar and a Warspider, seemingly killed at the same time. Asp stared. This was not two creatures but one. *Had she been washed this far out of the stronghold?* Asp wondered. *Would he have even removed her chains, her harness?*

Then he saw something that made his stomach lurch. The creature's head . . . there was the strange hair he had been looking for, the ears, too. Asp reached down and rotated the head, saw that two of the eyes were slanted. *It's him.* Asp could scarcely believe it. So the Spider King had gone back to dabbling in the dark arts, eh? *And then what? You die a miserable death, drowned like a cur.*

Asp would have a lot to report when he returned to his clan and then to Earth. He laid the head down and thought, *I was never convinced you were up for the jo—*

The thing lurched forward, the fangs extended and fell, piercing Asp's thigh.

The Drefid shrieked and kicked the head away. It fell limp beneath the water and bubbled.

Asp held his leg and tried to stand. He lost his balance and fell into the larger pool below. Swimming like a mad thing, he made it to the shore, extended his claws, and scratched his way a few feet away from the water. His body started to spasm; he was wracked with agony, as if things were being ripped out of his body.

Acknowledgments

WTB: *Venom and Song* was an absolutely thrilling book to write. But it was also enormously time consuming. If it weren't for my wife, Mary Lu's, generosity with time and responsibilities, there's no way I'd have ever been able to do my part. Gorgeous, this book is a jewel in your crown. Thank you so much.

I'd also like to thank my kids for understanding why Dad just had to write sometimes. And thank you for being ready to throw the football around, play Ping-Pong and video games, watch movies, or even just talk with me when I stepped away from the computer.

Thank you to my extended family—Mom and Dad, Mom and Pop Dovel, Leslie, Jeff, Brian, Ed, Andy, and Diana—for always asking and always encouraging.

Thank you to my friends for still being there when my deadline is at last met.

Thank you to my incredible readers who are passionate and generous.

Thank you to my students at Folly Quarter Middle School. You inspire me more than you'll ever know.

Thank you to the special venues that have hosted Christopher and me on our various writing excursions: the Banshee and the Radisson in Scranton, DuClaws and O'Lordan's, Panera Bread, and ten or twelve other places we love but cannot remember! LOL!

CH: Without the encouragement of my bride, my rib, I would not have authored any books, let alone this one. Jenny, it is your support, seemingly boundless love, and enthusiasm for my work that has sustained this craft through arduous turning points. Thank you for believing in me and being a woman who prays for her man's success.

To Evangeline, Luik, and Judah, may you know that your daddy lives for another Kingdom, and does everything with passion for his King.

Jason Clement (www.jasonjclement.com) deserves a hearty toast for assisting Wayne and me on our many ventures into web-dom. Without your friendship, generosity, and creativity, we'd be stuck in the throes of birthing HTML and Java, thinking both were new forms of coffee.

I certainly must thank all the online Elves of The Underground for their heartfelt enthusiasm and appreciation for our writing. You have made our work 3-D in that the stories resonate in your actual lives, not just some fictional characters we put together. Thank you for going with us! And to those who completed (or even attempted) the ARG, well done!

About the Authors

 WAYNE THOMAS BATSON is the author of five best-selling novels: *Isle of Swords, Isle of Fire,* and The Door Within Trilogy. His books have earned awards and nominations including Silver Moonbeam, Mom's Choice® Silver, Cybil, Lamplighter, The Clive Staples, and American Christian Fiction Writers Book of the Year. A middle school reading teacher in Maryland for more than nineteen years, Wayne tailors his stories to meet the needs of young people. When last seen, Wayne was tromping around the Westfarthing with his beautiful wife and four adventurous children.

For more on Wayne, go to www.enterthedoorwithin.blogspot.com.

 CHRISTOPHER HOPPER, whose other books include *Rise of the Dibor* and *The Lion Vrie,* has often been called a modern-day renaissance man. Christopher is also a record producer and recording artist with ten CDs, a youth pastor, a painter, president of a Christian discipleship school, an entrepreneur, and a motivational speaker for conferences and schools across the United States and Europe. Christopher has dedicated his life to positively affecting the culture of his generation and longs to see young people inspired to live meaningful and productive lives. He resides with his wife, three children, and three rangesteeds in the mysterious Thousand Islands of northern New York.

For more on Christopher, go to www.christopherhopper.com.